There was great exciteme~~nt~~

one day in August 1982 among th...
cask had been spotted floating d...
ting and weaving, before finally ...
cessible spit in the middle of tha...

GW00402182

The great question ran: Which distillery did it come from?
(There are 27 in the area.)

Notwithstanding the considerable danger, one stalwart braved the depths and current, collected the cask, and lugged it back through the swirling rapids.

An eager crowd, alerted by the news, soon assembled and the cask was broached. 'Anything in it?' 'A drappie.' 'Is it whisky?' "Mebbe.' 'Is it The Macallan?' (the favoured malt on Speyside.) 'No.'

The disappointment hissed over the water. It proved to be, in fact, a pale watery liquor, the dregs of an empty cask.

'I dinna say it wasna sampled,' the hero told us later, 'but it was dreich stuff. We'd go and console our tastebuds after a dram or two of The Malt.'

THE MACALLAN. THE MALT.

The Paris Review

Founded in 1953.

The Paris Review is published quarterly by The Paris Review, Inc. Vol. 41, No. 150, Spring 1999.
Business Office: 45-39 171st Place, Flushing, New York 11358 (ISSN #0031-2037). Paris Office:
Harry Mathews, 67 rue de Grenelle, Paris 75007 France. London Office: Shusha Guppy, 8 Shawfield
St., London, SW3. US distributors: Random House, Inc. 1(800)733-3000. Typeset and printed in
USA by Capital City Press, Montpelier, VT. Price for single issue in USA: $10.00. $14.00 in Canada.
Post-paid subscription for four issues $34.00, lifetime subscription $1000. Postal surcharge of $10.00
per four issues outside USA (excluding life subscriptions). Subscription card is bound within magazine. Please give six weeks notice of change of address using subscription card. *While The Paris
Review welcomes the submission of unsolicited manuscripts, it cannot accept responsibility for
their loss or delay, or engage in related correspondence. Manuscripts will not be returned or
responded to unless accompanied by self-addressed, stamped envelope. Fiction manuscripts
should be submitted to George Plimpton, poetry to Richard Howard, The Paris Review, 541 East
72nd Street, New York, N.Y. 10021.* Charter member of the Council of Literary Magazines and
Presses. This publication is made possible, in part, with public funds from the New York State
Council on the Arts and the National Endowment for the Arts. Periodicals postage paid at
Flushing, New York, and at additional mailing offices. **Postmaster:** Please send address changes
to 45-39 171st Place, Flushing, N.Y. 11358.

Best wishes
Hugh M Hefner

Congratulations to

The Paris Review

on 45 Years of

Literary Brilliance.

From
Time Warner
Trade Publishing

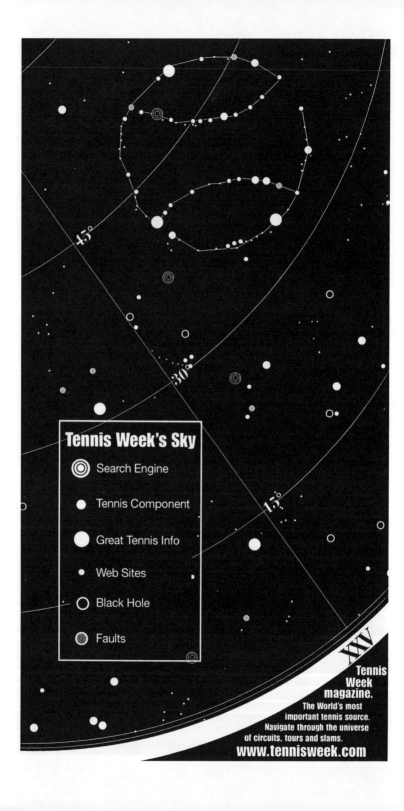

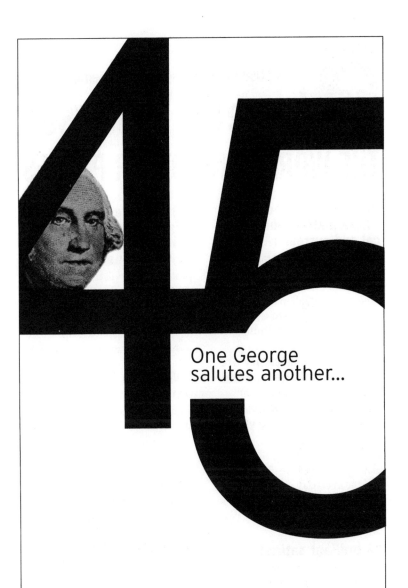

One George
salutes another...

A collection of stories spanning her entire career

Jeanette Winterson

THE WORLD AND OTHER PLACES

"A brilliant collection ...speculative, philosophical and surreal...From 'The 24-hour Dog' on, it will startle. If you don't know her from *Sexing the Cherry* and *Oranges Are Not the Only Fruit*, you will fall in love with this writer."   —JOAN MELLEN, Baltimore Sun

"Excess and intensity are the key words here, admirable both as character traits and as components of a lively literary style ...With its variety of forms and range of imagination, this is a stimulating tour of where 'the visionary and the everyday coincide.'"
—STEVEN MOORE, Washington Post Book World

"A brilliant satirist, Winterson deftly shreds the absurdities of contemporary life. A shrewd observer of love, she records the collisions of emotion and intellect that mark its phases, writing convincingly from a man's point of view and about passion between women. Ultimately, what seems to intrigue Winterson most is the imagination, a realm she navigates with precision and daring."
—DONNA SEAMAN, Booklist

"That Winterson is an original and important writer is surely by now beyond question...What this protean artist will turn her hand to next is impossible to guess, but her work reminds us, often startlingly, that the modes of possible fiction have not yet been used up."
—ANDREW BISWELL, Boston Globe

"Winterson is a grand warrior...She's a modern writer, a modern thinker...Her images are fantastic."
—SUSAN SALTER REYNOLDS, Los Angeles Times

"Exuberant and marvelously varied—like a literary periscope scanning island after island in the sea of Winterson's imagination ...This collection is like Jeanette Winterson's Greatest Hits. All her formidable strengths are here."
—RANDALL CURB, Boston Book Review

Already in its 2nd printing

Knopf

www.aaknopf.com

Photo ©: Jayne Wexler

CONTRARY TO POPULAR BELIEF, THE '21' CLUB TAKES RESERVATIONS. NOT MEMBERSHIPS

Today '21' is New Yorks' most celebrated restaurant ... a place of sophisticated yet comfortable elegance that's always been favored by the city's most glamorous and powerful denizens.

And as part of the Orient-Express Hotels, '21' continues to be a place where the most discriminating diners in this most discriminating of cities can feel right at home. For lunch, dinner, cocktails or a splendid private party, why not make '21' your "home away from home"?

This glowing description from the Zagat Survey: "The landmark restaurant is doing a lot to make newcomers feel welcome.... '21' is back and better than ever."

21 West 52nd Street, New York, N.Y. 10019.
A la Carte Reservations: (212) 582-7200
10 private banquet rooms which accommodate 15 to 400 guests
including our legendary wine cellar for up to 20 guests.
Tel. (212) 582-1400 ext. 512 Fax.(212) 581-7138
www.21club.com

Thirteen·wnet

congratulates

THE PARIS REVIEW

on its 45th Anniversary
and invites
its readers
to watch
a new tv show

a special documentary series

June 4, 1999
10:00pm – GROWING OLD
10:30pm – MAKING IT

If you love THE PARIS REVIEW, you might like CITY LIFE.

Penguin
LIVES

Biographies with a point of view

from Lipper Viking Penguin

Karen Armstrong on Buddha
Roy Blount, Jr. on Robert E. Lee
Patricia Bosworth on Marlon Brando
Marshall Frady on Martin Luther King, Jr.
Peter Gay on Amadeus Mozart
Mary Gordon on Joan of Arc
Elizabeth Hardwick on Herman Melville
John Keegan on Winston Churchill
Wayne Koestenbaum on Andy Warhol
R.W.B. Lewis on Dante Alighieri
Janet Malcolm on Anton Chekhov
Bobbie Ann Mason on Elvis
Larry McMurtry on Crazy Horse
Nigel Nicolson on Virginia Woolf
Sherwin Nuland on Leonardo Da Vinci
Edna O'Brien on James Joyce
George Plimpton on Muhammad Ali
David Quammen on Charles Darwin
Carol Shields on Jane Austen
Jane Smiley on Charles Dickens
Jonathan Spence on Mao Ze Dong
Edmund White on Marcel Proust
Garry Wills on Saint Augustine

From a new literary lifeform to a model of the species.

Cheers to you, Paris Review.

Lipper Publications

Congratulations to

the **PARIS REVIEW**

on its
45th Anniversary

J. Walter Thompson

Congratulations

The
Paris
Review

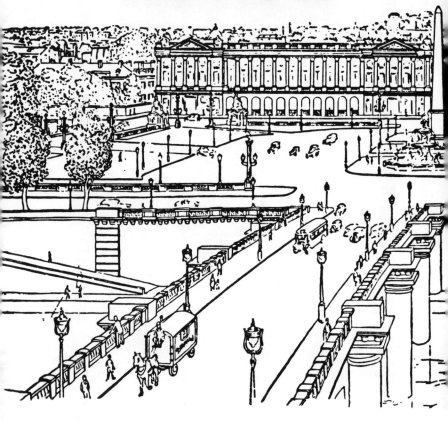

Editorial Office:
541 East 72 Street
New York, New York 10021
HTTP://www.parisreview.com

Business & Circulation:
45-39 171 Place
Flushing, New York 11358

Distributed by Random House
201 East 50 Street
New York, N.Y. 10022
(800) 733-3000

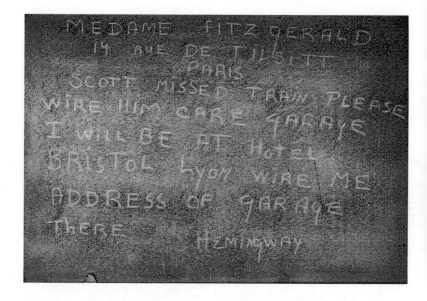

When F. Scott Fitzgerald's daughter Scottie died in 1986, instructions were left that two boxes of books owned by her father were to be sent to her great friend, Professor Matthew J. Bruccoli of the English department at the University of South Carolina. Among the books was a volume by Ernest Boyd entitled *Portraits: Real and Imaginary*. On the front endpaper Fitzgerald had written "Don't bother about first stuff. Read definite portraits"—instructions to someone to whom he was intending to lend or give the book.

Thanks to some fine detective work by Bruccoli's wife Arlyn, we now know who that person is. Noting that the rear endpaper of the book had been torn out, Arlyn observed faint impressions on the preceding page, which suggested someone had written a message in the book before tearing out the page. Applying the familiar method of rubbing the indentations with a soft pencil, she was able to recover the message. It appears above.

From Ernest Hemingway's *A Moveable Feast* we also know the circumstances— Fitzgerald had missed the train the two of them were to take to Lyon together to pick up the Fitzgerald's car and drive it back to Paris. As Hemingway writes: "There was nothing to do but wire Scott from Dijon giving him the address of the hotel where I would wait for him in Lyon . . . "

Hemingway writes of reading a book in his hotel room in Lyon while he waits to hear from Fitzgerald. It is the first volume of *A Sportsman's Sketches* by Turgenev. Who knows whether he ever looked into the Boyd book, except to write in it.

Frontispiece by William Pène du Bois.

Number 150

NOTICE

Two numbers, like converging planets on an astrologist's chart, have cropped up this year that have invited editorial notice here—the fact that this is the 45th year of the magazine's existence and also that this issue is number 150. True, the numbers are not round, like a 100th birthday, or the millenium 2000, or the Dow's 10,000 level, but in our minds they are considered felicitous enough for us to put together a celebratory issue. We have done this sort of thing in the past. The 100th issue (Summer-Fall 1986, a cover by Frank Stella) included among its 416 (!) pages one of Ezra Pound's early short stories, a Mary McCarthy memoir on her early schooling, Gertrude Stein's letters of advice and support to a young writer named Wilcox, poems by forty nine (!) poets, and a missing section of Czeslaw Milosz's *From the Rising of the Sun*. The 40th anniversary (Fall 1993, 392 pages, cover by Larry Rivers) had as its lagniappe a number of interesting documents . . . Ezra Pound's confession to a military officer after his apprehension near Rapallo, Italy in 1945, a letter from Dylan Thomas to Margeurite Caetani, the publisher of the literary magazine *Botteghe Oscure*, explaining why an assignment was late, and excerpts from John Cheever's journals. The 25th anniversary issue with a David Hockney cover (Spring, 1981, 448 pages!!) included Ernest Hemingway's "The Art of the Short Story," Martha Gellhorn's dissertation on writers who beg issue with the truth (including Lillian Hellman, Stephen Spender, Hemingway himself), as well as a brisk oral history of *The Paris Review* itself.

So what have we done for *this* issue? We have put together a portfolio of reminiscences and observations from a large group of writers who lived in Paris at one time or another after World War II . . . from Richard Wilbur and Norman Mailer who were there in the late forties to Rick Bass who visited the city for a couple of hours just last year.

The Art of Fiction series continues with interviews quite appropriate to the celebration—one with Peter Matthiessen, a cofounder of the magazine and the other with William Styron, who wrote a statement of purpose for the first issue in which he proposed that the editorial emphasis should be on publishing creative rather than critical work. Also included is the first interview on the craft of the diarist, conducted with Ned Rorem, who, appropriately enough for this issue, spent the early years of his career in Paris.

Next, perhaps to show how prescient the editors like to feel they have been from the start, Richard Howard, the poetry editor, has asked a number of the poets who contributed to the early numbers of the magazine (1953–1955), young and relatively unknown at the time, to offer new work for this issue—an impressive list: Robert Bly, Richard Wilbur, W.S. Merwin and Donald Hall, of course, who was the poetry editor at the time.

The fiction in the issue is all by newcomers—very much in accord with the magazine's original principles, which were to search out and publish writers of accomplishment who are just getting started.

The cover of this celebratory number suggests an appropriate if perhaps somewhat strained metaphor—that the gentleman with the suitcase, actually the dadaist Tristan Tzara, is in fact a *Paris Review* reader . . . startled by the outpouring of stories, poems, reminiscences emerging from this issue, those white doves rising, which might also be thought of (at least to the undersigned) as filled-out subscription blanks heading our way. After all, the fiftieth year of our existence is not all that far away, and any monetary assistance in getting us to that noble station is certainly to be encouraged.

—G.A.P.

In the Belly of the Cat

Daniel S. Libman

The same day that he canceled all his newspaper and magazine subscriptions, Mr. Christopher deveined a pound of jumbo shrimp by hand. He had never done this before, and used nearly a whole roll of paper towels wiping the snotty black entrails off his fingers one by one. He also grated a package of cheddar cheese with a previously unused grater that he uncovered in his silverware drawer, kneaded a loaf of oatmeal raisin bread, then called the escort service and arranged for a girl. "I want Carlotta; she's a Latina, right?"

He had called *The Tribune* earlier that morning. "Stop my subscription. The relationship is over; deliver it no longer. The advice columns just rehash the same situations—alcoholism, smoking, infidelity—although sometimes those columns are titillating, which I appreciate. The comic strips are contrived, and the punch lines aren't ever that good. That cranky columnist on page three ought to have his head examined; I think he's finally lost it, and your media critic is always biased towards the TV stations you own. But what I object to mostly, the reason I'm canceling, is because it comes too often: once a day, and anyway what good is it? I don't have that much time left and do you know how much I've wasted over the years slogging through, reading and cringing, hands and fingers covered in the ink, hauling paper-bloated garbage bags stuffed with Sports and Food sections, which I never even touch, down three flights of stairs every week?"

Mr. Christopher was hurt by the cavalier way the man at The *Trib* took care of the cancellation. After so much loyal readership he felt that they should have put up some sort of struggle, a little token of respect: "But Mr. Christopher, please think about it; you want to throw away sixty years just like that?" Not that it would have gotten them anywhere. His mind was made up.

He had been a widower now for a year and a half, retired, down to only two-thirds of what he weighed at forty, dentures, a toupee he no longer wore but kept hanging off his hall tree, an artificial hip; and a brother a couple of states to the east whom he didn't like with a mouthy know-it-all wife. This had come to him one evening earlier in the week, a cold-cut sandwich and a pickle on a plate in front of him, eyeing the pile of papers; he had had enough of them.

Mr. Christopher canceled all the magazines too: *The East Coast Arbiter, Harbingers', The New Statesman*, even *The Convenience Store Merchandiser*, a holdover from work that they sent him for free.

He was bundling up the last week of *Trib*s he would ever receive, when his hands landed on a Food section. "Special Dishes to Commemorate Any Event," the headline said. I'll give you an event, he thought, How's finally ending sixty years of crap sound to you, Mr. Tribune.

Mr. Christopher decided to open up the Food section for the first time and cook those commemorative dishes. He mapped out what he needed to do in his head: buy fresh fruit, two pounds of shrimp; he'd need to take a bus to that specialty food store for some of it. . . . He even scanned the tips on what makes a good party: fancy utensils, music and special friends.

He was cubing the honeydew for the fruit slaw when she buzzed. He gave a start and walked to the intercom and thought how odd it sounded. No one had buzzed him for . . . weeks? months? decades? He leaned down to the grill, painted the same off-white as the rest of the apartment, and pressed.

Talk: Yes?

Listen: You call for me?

Talk: Who is it?

Listen: This is Monique. You call for me?

Talk: No. I called for Carlotta.

Listen: I'm Carlotta. Buzz me in.

Talk: Who are you?

Listen: Carlotta. You want me, baby?

He touched *door* and heard the faraway buzzing. She was in the building now; his heart raced. It would take a minute or two to climb the three flights, and then she would have to decide which direction to walk; that would take a few seconds. He was in 3A, towards the front of the building so she would have to look at 3B first, because it was right across from the stairs, and then make a choice, and she might choose right, which would take her to 3C—and in all this time he could back out, decide not to go ahead with this. He slid the security chain across the door.

But he had already gone to so much trouble. He had found the escort service in another part of *The Tribune* never before looked at, the match ads. At the very end were listings for adult services; these included descriptions of women, measurements and height and weight, and he wasn't born yesterday.

Mr. Christopher heard her footsteps and a knock. She had gotten to his door very quickly. Nervously, he touched his front pocket where he had put the money. It was a lot of cash to have at one time, the most he had carried in years. He looked down, considering himself, his paunch and his house slippers; he saw that the end of his belt was loose. He tucked it behind the proper loop in his corduroys, and she was knocking again, harder and faster.

"Yes, yes," he said quickly. "Hello."

"It's me," she answered, as if it might really be someone he knew. He was suddenly grateful that she hadn't said, "The whore you called for," or something equally provocative that might arouse suspicion, and he quickly undid the chain and opened the door.

She was about a foot taller, starchy white, with large fleshy legs that dropped out of a tiny skirt. Her midriff was showing, and her shoulders were bare, too. It was a lot of flesh for Mr. Christopher to mentally process, and he sputtered once before speaking.

"No," he said. "You are not a Carlotta. Not petite and not a coed."

"Carlotta sent me. I'm her friend, Monique."

She pushed past him, Mr. Christopher squinted against her redolent perfume as she breezed confidently into his living room. She had a small purse and tossed it onto his reading chair as if she had been in the apartment many times before.

His apartment building had once been a three-flat, but it had been sectioned off into nine uneasy units. His living room was long, but narrow; a wall had been added to make a bedroom where the other half of the living room had been. Knowing that the other three units on the floor had once been part of his apartment made him curious to know what the other units looked like. On those rare occasions when a neighbor left the door open—like if they were getting ready to go out or trying to get a better breeze in the summer—and Mr. Christopher happened to be walking by, he would linger, just a little bit, craning his neck slightly to get a peek. He always wanted to know how the units fit together, and it vaguely irritated him that two-thirds of his apartment were being lived in by other people.

"Smells good," she said.

"You're smelling the onions and green peppers that I will be using to stuff the pork chops, our main course."

"Having a fancy party?" she asked, turning slowly and

eyeing the elaborately set table for the first time. Although Mr. Christopher usually ate on his couch with his plate and a magazine on the ottoman, tonight he had set out the best plates he had, the good silverware and had even put two candles right in the center.

"No no, it's just us," he said, taking a step to his cassette player.

"I already ate."

"No no. I told the man on the phone this was for dinner and . . . that it would be for dinner as well as the other stuff."

A tinny version of Benny Goodman's clarinet came out of the box.

"No one told me," she said. "I don't have that much time."

"I need you here for at least three hours. I told the man that; I told him. I can't get all the food prepared in an hour, let alone eat it. We're going to have salad and soup and appetizers and bread—the bread's not even completely baked yet."

"You have an hour from when I got out of the car, and that was a couple of minutes ago. If I don't get back to Mickey by then—"

"Who's Mickey?"

"Look out your window. Across the street."

The blinds were shut, but he shuffled between the table and the window and lowered a couple of slats with his hand.

In the no-parking zone, an enormous man sat on the hood of a town car, feet spread-eagle on the pavement, reading a newspaper. Even though it was a large and bulky car, it dipped under the weight of the man's bottom.

"What's he doing?" Mr. Christopher asked.

"Wasting time, now. But I'm telling you, if I don't get down in . . . fifty-three minutes, he'll come tearing up here. You've never seen anything like it. You won't be able to reason with him, you won't be able to stop him. He'll come up those steps, bust down your door, and he'll clean your clock."

Mr. Christopher pulled his hands off the blinds and looked

towards his kitchen. "Okay," he said. "We'll do it first, what you came here for, and that will give time for the bread to rise and also for the sugar—this is part of the dessert—to caramelize so that I can pour it, drizzle it, onto the flan. I need forty-five minutes for dinner. That gives me fifteen minutes for the rest of it. Can we do that in fifteen minutes, not even fifteen, but now it's already just twelve or eleven as you pointed out. Can it be done that fast?"

"Normally I have a routine I do, dancing and a rub down, and tickling on the genitalia to arouse you. If you want to skip all that, go right to it . . . Well, it's your money."

"I wasn't picturing dancing or a rub down, but now that I hear about it, it does sound like fun. This is my first time, Monique, so you'll have to guide me."

"Your first time, a guy of your age?"

"First time with a call girl. Okay, we're wasting time. I need to finish sautéing the onions. We better do this in the kitchen."

The kitchen had once been the hallway that connected Mr. Christopher's third of the apartment to the rest of the building. It was narrow and ended abruptly in a Sheetrock wall. The floor changed from hard wood to linoleum about a foot away from the wall, giving the impression that it might have led to a bathroom or a utility closet at one time. One side of the corridor was a narrow countertop, now covered in fruit peelings, shrimp shells and other food debris. Across the corridor was the sink, mini-refrigerator and a two-burner stove that was already covered with large pots. Another small countertop separated the two appliances.

He found the Food section and brushed some cheese shavings off the page and put his finger on the right passage. He took a sniff of her perfume and knew she was behind him. "Clear and soft . . . I'm going to add the green peppers and the cumin and then cook that . . . Then I have to slice the fat off the chops and carve little pockets—" He put a wooden spoon into his sautéing onions and turned his neck slightly so he could see her bare shoulder.

She reached around him unceremoniously and unbuckled his belt and lowered his pants. His legs were hairy with thick blue veins, but his underwear was shockingly white. When she pulled it down to his knees she reached under and grabbed his limp penis. Her hand was so cold and dry that he jumped, but didn't scream. He reached over to the small counter without moving his feet and began to scoop the melon pieces into a large blue bowl.

"I can't get around you here," she told him from the floor. "Can I open one of these cabinets by your knees, so that I can move my head closer, and I'll be able to reach you while you're working?"

He said, "Hang on a second, I'll be able to turn around in a second. Do you think . . . ," he took a pair of black food scissors and slowly began snipping away at the tips of a large artichoke. "Do you think you could take off some clothing too, maybe just your top. Otherwise I'd feel too self-conscious to enjoy it."

She pulled her tank top over her head, and when he turned around she was kneeling in front of him with her hands folded in her lap. Her shirt was lying next to her, and he allowed himself to stare at her breasts. They were the largest he had ever seen, which made him feel a flash of pride, as if he had gotten a surprisingly good return on a shaky investment. Her nipples were oval, straining to keep their shapes on top of such large breasts.

Monique looked right at him and took his balls in her hand. Uncomfortable at the strangely clinical turn this had taken, he cleared his throat once. "My, eh, testicles . . . They're much larger than they should be for the size of my . . ."

She waved the comment away, which did make him feel better. She surely had seen all sorts of genitalia; and she leaned down and put him in her mouth.

The tail on his kitty-cat clock swung back and forth with each second, matching the absurd ping-pong eyes in the cat's head. The clock, painted into the torso of the cat, showed that he had only six minutes left for this part of the night if he was going to have the minimum amount of time he needed to serve the meal. A burning spit of grease from the onions hit him on the back of the neck.

Concentration was difficult for Mr. Christopher and, without moving from his spot, he picked up the big wooden spoon and pushed his onions around in the oil. When he felt his legs getting wobbly, he put the spoon down and held the countertop.

He was losing time now, it was going by quicker than usual; the kitty-cat's eyes and tail had been sped up by some strange force. But he had to admit that it felt good, what she was doing. His legs shook and he was afraid he might fall. He dug in with the heels of his house slippers and gripped tightly to the countertop, his hips involuntarily moved closer to the heat of her face. He wheezed from the back of his throat and felt her breasts against his legs, and he let himself go.

"Okay," he said. "You can spit that out in the sink."

She waved that comment away too, and put her shirt back on.

"Don't spoil your appetite," he said, as he did the top button on his pants and pulled his belt snug against his waist.

"I told you I ate already."

"Look," he told her. "I've got you for another thirty-three minutes. Go take a seat at the table."

She left, and he turned around and scooped the last melon pieces from the counter and used his hands to mix it all up in the bowl. He felt tired for a second, useless. He steadied himself against the counter and realized he just wanted to sleep—to pull the blanket up to his chest and open a magazine and relax. But the pot on the far burner began to bubble, and he remembered the magazines weren't coming anymore, although he couldn't remember why exactly. Mr. Christopher put the artichoke into the water and watched it simmer for a second before covering it.

She was already sitting when he walked back into the living room. He used a book of matches and lit the candles.

"You're going all out for this dinner, huh?" she asked.

Mr. Christopher wanted to smile, but he felt the pressure from the kitty-cat. The soup was done, and he went back into the kitchen, aware of the pathetic way his hip made him look when he was in a hurry. He ladled out two bowls, making sure each serving had the same number of shrimp and pineapple chunks.

"Lemongrass soup," he said, walking slowly out with the bowls. He placed them on the table and sat across from her.

"What is that smell?" she asked, cocking an eye at him.

"That's the lemongrass," he told her. "It's spicy, and I hope you like it."

"Should we say grace?"

Mr. Christopher had dipped his spoon in and was stirring his portion. "No time," he said, and slurped a loud mouthful. "Mmmm," he said, dabbing his lips with his napkin. "Okay, you keep eating, and I have to finish the fruit."

When he returned three minutes later, carrying four small bowls, he was breathing hard. Beads of sweat glistened on his forehead.

She looked up from her bowl and said excitedly, "You know, this is really good. Much better than it smells."

"I'm glad."

"You know what? The pineapple was even better than the shrimp. Pineapple in soup!" she said, and shook her head.

"This is fruit slaw, and this is a cheese and pea salad." He put both bowls in front of her and took her soup bowl. Her hand clenched momentarily, as if she might yank the soup bowl back and this pleased Mr. Christopher, but he didn't have time to think about it.

"Oh God, the wine," he said. He went towards the kitchen but turned around after a few steps and took the soup bowls with him. On the way, he limped to the cassette player and flipped the tape, which had stopped at some point.

The music was back on, and Mr. Christopher poured two glasses of wine. The song was one that he really liked—one of his favorites—Benny Goodman's "Belly of the Cat," and he suddenly felt self-conscious listening to it while pouring a woman wine. He quickly asked, "So, how do you like the salad?"

"It's okay," she said. "The soup was exotic, and this is sort of everyday type of food, so it's a strange menu."

"The food section said the salad is best served in a glass bowl. That way you can see the layers, the mayonnaise on the bottom, then the peas, then more mayonnaise, then the cheddar cheese, which I shredded myself. It's too bad I don't have a glass bowl."

"Why don't you sit down for a second?" she asked.

He twisted the blinds so he could see out the window. Mickey had put the newspaper away and was leaning against the car now, facing Mr. Christopher's doorway. He was dressed in a bow tie and a sporty tuxedo coat, like a bouncer at a banquet hall or a limo driver on prom night.

"I guess I'll sit down for a second," Mr. Christopher said, lowering himself uneasily into the chair. "And rest. I had planned on a nice conversation with you." He dabbed his forehead with the napkin, but he still felt sweaty. "So," he said, "how many people will you visit tonight?"

"I usually try to get five or six customers a night," she told him. "At least four, but six is a good night. Eight is the most I would do."

"When I worked retail, it was the same. Just like you, get to as many people as possible. So that's something we have in common, me and you," Mr. Christopher nodded once to himself. "But about you, eight times in one night? That's a lot. Good for business, I guess. Right?"

"That would be real good," she said. "Yes. It's not that tough. How many times do you do it a night?"

"Usually, none," he told her.

"But what's the most?"

He made a face.

"Come on, for a conversation. What's the most you've ever done it in a night."

"If I've ever done it twice in a night, then two. But I can't remember. I usually get tired and there isn't enough time in a single night to rest up entirely. So we're different, that's why it's so nice to spend time with someone you don't know, to share different experiences. . . ." These sentences that he had prepared and even rehearsed a few times now sounded stilted and ridiculous in his mouth; although she was nodding in apparent agreement with him. Who was he trying to kid anyway? He looked at his watch to cover his embarrassment. "Okay," he said. "Time for the main course. Let's go, let's go."

He took her bowls away and returned a few minutes later with a platter. "We're going to eat dessert now, but save enough room for the pork chops. They're still a little pink and if we wait for them we might not have time for dessert. So we'll go out of turn."

She put her hand on her bare stomach. "That's fine with me anyway, because I'm not especially hungry. I told you that, that I had eaten already. I don't even know if I could eat another bite."

He brought four helpings of flan, each perfectly shaped like a large quivering eyeball. He had hoped she would want more than one helping, but he knew that wasn't going to happen, so he said, "I think it's time to make a toast."

She picked up her glass of wine, which was still full.

"To a lovely night," he said. "A lovely woman, a lovely meal and a lovely time."

He tipped his glass towards her slightly and she did the same in imitation, and they both drank.

"Okay," he said. "Now dessert."

He looked at his watch for a second and saw that he had nine minutes left. When he checked the window, he was surprised to see Mickey was walking back and forth. His legs and arms and were thick, like sausages. Mickey checked his watch and looked up to the third floor of the building.

"It's time for the pork chops," he mumbled.

"Are you sure there's time? You don't want him—Mickey, coming up here. It's better that I should leave a few minutes early than he get mad—come up those stairs and start banging on your door."

"I have eight more minutes of your time," Mr. Christopher answered icily, and he walked into the kitchen.

When he returned a few minutes later, he was carrying a plate with two sickly pink and gray slabs of meat. Corn and onions had been stuffed into slits along the sides of the chops, but they oozed like puddles of sewage. Mr. Christopher skewered the largest one and tried to get it off the tray, but every time he lifted the fork, the chop slid off. Finally he pushed it with the prongs onto her plate and slid the other one onto his plate. He put the serving platter on the floor.

"Bon appetit, my sweet."

"Are you sure these are done?" She said, poking her chop with a knife. "You've really got to cook meat, pork especially; and I thought I saw these out on your counter, raw, when I was in the kitchen."

"That's right," he told her. He cut off a slice. It was dull pink on the inside and she looked away before he put it in his mouth. "But I turned the oven up as high as it would go and had them in since we began eating. Mmmm. Anyway, I don't have any more time." His lips were glistening and he sliced off another piece and waited for her to begin.

"It smells good," she stood up. "But I ate before I got here, and the custard and the soup, and that's it. I couldn't eat another bite. Thank you for the night. That'll be a hundred and forty bones, and that's not including a tip."

"Take a bite of the dinner. The bread isn't done yet and we'll forget about the liqueur; I haven't even begun to make the garlic butter sauce for the artichoke appetizer. So we'll forget all the rest, but I want you to at least try the pork chop. It's stuffed with corn and sautéed onions. You know, festively."

He wolfed down another bite, swallowing it as quickly as possible to show how good it was.

"My money," she said putting her palm out.

"My time," he said into his plate. "This is all I wanted, for you to come here and have a nice meal and a nice time. It's my special day and this was all I wanted."

"Listen, old man. You didn't cook it long enough; I'm going to retch just from the smell and I'm already nauseous from the spicy soup and the bowl of mayonnaise."

He forced himself to take another piece of the pork chop. When it reached his tongue his stomach lurched, and the meat fell part unnaturally. He put his napkin up to his mouth and spit it up. When he was done gagging and had wiped his lips hard onto the napkin, he said, "The money is in my front pants pocket. Seven twenty-dollar bills." He covered his head with his hands and rested his elbows on the table.

"Give it to me," she said.

"It's too late," he told her. "Check the window."

The door lurched in its frame and then popped open. Monique put her arm around Mr. Christopher's shoulders. "It's okay, Mickey," she yelled. "It's okay, I'm all right."

Mr. Christopher closed his eyes as a hand grabbed his shoulder and pulled him up off the chair. He opened them and saw Mickey's teeth, a row of little rat triangles.

"You see that door, buddy," Mickey snarled. "I suggest you hand over the money right this instant, or that's what's going to happen to your head."

"The money's in my pocket, sir," Mr. Christopher said, dropping back in the chair.

"The money's in my pocket," he repeated. He stood up and took a step back. "Here." He put the wad of folded bills onto the table.

"And hold on you two. Hold on a minute." He put up a finger towards Mickey and Monique and ambled into his kitchen. The pot with the artichoke was boiling over and Mr. Christopher turned off the burners and shut off the stove. A stack of old newspapers were piled under the counter, waiting to be taken to the trash.

"I know your time is valuable," Mr. Christopher called out. "And I know I've wasted some of it. I'm sorry about that . . ." Brightening up, he slipped on an oven-mitt and took the platter of pork chops from the oven. "And six customers is a lot, and I know you've got to be going . . . Believe me, I respect the need for speed. So maybe this will help, with dinner . . ." As he spoke, he wrapped in newspaper three of the juiciest chops he had. He pulled the artichoke out of the water with tongs and put it into a large zip-lock baggie. When that was done, he dumped the rest of the fruit slaw into another baggy, and the cheese and pea salad into a third. "I appreciate you coming over, Monique, and you too Mickey! I appreciate the time you spent with me . . ." Mr. Christopher pulled a brown shopping bag out of the garbage and put the moist newspaper packages and all the baggies into it.

The soup was hot, but he found a square tupperware in a cabinet and poured it in, burped the lid and put it in the brown bag with the rest of it. The flan was more delicate, but Mr. Christopher emptied an egg carton and filled the cups with the lumpy brown custard.

"I remember on Thanksgiving," Mr. Christopher called while skittering around his kitchen, "or any food holiday like that, Christmas and the Fourth of July—barbecues on the Fourth—and at the end the host always would ask what you wanted to . . . take home with you, leftovers . . ."

He had no plastic forks or spoons, but now wasn't the time to worry about his stuff. It would be a long time before he ever had guests over for such an occasion, if ever, so he put his nice silverware into the bag. Two of everything: two salad forks, two regular forks, two sets of each spoon—fruit, dessert, soup—two sets of steak knives and two butter knives. He pulled the bread loaf out of the oven, slapped the bottom of the pan with his mitted fist, and the oatmeal raisin mass fell solidly into the bag.

"That's when you know you've had a good time—didn't waste your time—when you walked out with an armload of food for the next couple of days . . ." He folded the top over twice, put his hand on his hip and walked into the living room.

The room was empty. Mr. Christopher held the warm shopping bag to his chest and looked at his door. It was only attached at the top hinge and looked like it might fall, and he could see past it, into the empty hallway, all the way to his neighbor's closed door.

Paris Review Poets from the Fifties

After forty-five years, as W.S. Merwin says, "the sentence continues." Here are a sheaf of poems from some of the original contributors to *The Paris Review*, which may serve—though many more of the original contributors are still writing poems—to inscribe upon the tablets of memory a certain continuity, a certain faith. Fitzgerald used to say there were no second acts in American lives; how heartening it is, though, to realize that as with this magazine so with the poets—there are subsequences "following after like a dream."

—**Richard Howard**

Two Poems by Ghalib

Some Exaggerations

The world I see looks to me like a game of children.
Strange performances and plays go on night and day.

King Solomon's throne is not a big thing to me.
I hear Jesus performed miracles, but I'm not interested.

The idea that the world exists is not acceptable to me.
Illusion is real, but not the things of the world.

The desert covers its head with sand when I appear with
     my troubles.
The river rubs its forehead in the mud when it sees me.

Don't ask me how I am when I am parted from you.
I notice that your face turns a little pale when you're near me.

People are right to say that I love looking at myself, but sitting
In front of me is a beauty whose face is bright as a mirror.

Just put a wineglass and some wine in front of me;
Words will fall out of my mouth like apple blossoms.

People imagine that I hate, but it's merely jealousy.
That's why I scream: "Don't say her name in my presence!"

Faith pulls me in one direction, but disbelief pulls me in
     another.
The Kaaba stands far behind me, and the Church stands
     next to me.

I am a lover; therefore charming a woman is my work.
When she is near me, Laila makes fun of Majnoon.

The time of reunion brings happiness rather than death.
When reunion came, I remembered the night of parting.

We have a sea of blood now with large waves.
I am content with it; I know worse could happen.

My hands move with difficulty, but at least my eyes are lively.
Just leave the glass and the wine jug standing where they are.

Ghalib is a Muslim also, so we know a lot of each other's
   secrets.
Please don't speak badly of Ghalib when I'm around.

About My Poems

I agree, O heart, that my poetry is not easy to take in.
When they hear my work, experienced poets

Suggest I should write something easier to understand.
I have to write what's difficult, otherwise it is difficult to write.

—Translated from the Urdu by Robert Bly
and Sunil Dutta

Donald Hall

Maison d'aujourd'hui

The night refills itself.
Limestone drops to the sea
that varies blue all day
between capes that curve
like a lover's arms
to cherish tranquil waters.
Here on a stone bench
we can see the darkening
bay, its almost-still
soft skin. This morning
we drove among rock
villages and orchards
to visit Matisse's Chapel
with its carnal blues
and yellows. Underneath
our room an olive's
roots draw virgin oil
from the earth's body,
surging upward to leaves
silvery green and dark.
After siesta we throbbed
with the olive's thrust
and our bodies floated
as buoyant as the sea
that rolls inside us
tonight. Our joyous
flesh sighs, every cell
breathing gaily, alert
to storeys of pastel
stucco with tile roofs
and filigreed balconies,

to the setting sun
that toplights with gold
a Mediterranean cloud.
Last night we wept, knowing
that nothing will remain.
Now we sit idle, content
from breath to breath
in the house of today.
Across from our bench
a woman in a long black
smock closes the shutters
of her pink facade.

Four Poems by John Hollander

To Donald Hall

Gleaming in Monday evening candlelight,
Glass and plate and conversation and good
Fortune then unacknowledged even by
Recognition that it dwelt among us . . .

We were unencumbered then by the likes
Of hope—a childish thing yet put away
Childishly, or standing in some closet
Shadow like a deceased grandfather's crutch—

Or by the likes of an appraiser's eye
Or hand that might take the measure of all
The wealth of fragilities shadowing
Our years of shining moments then, as if

Someone's hard-edged gold had been laundered and
Smelted, sublimated into golden
Soft light reflected in the faces, the
Wide-eyed minds of such a *jeunesse dorée*

—George Kateb Stanley Cavell Geoffrey Bush
Noam Chomsky Ed Wilson Marvin Minsky
Marshall Cohen Burt Dreben Ken Keniston
Paul de Man Jaakko Hintikka George Field

Abe Klein Henry Rosovsky Jaan Puhvel
Cal Watkins Steele Commager Frank Pipkin
Jim Kritzeck—and, giving higher light than
Candles, the peculiar *lux veritas*

Emanates when puzzled at, Renato
Poggioli Harry Levin Crane Brinton
Arthur Darby Nock Van Quine Ed Purcell
Ubi sunt quae ante nos—ubi sumus?

Well, here—wherever that is. And now. Still
Remembering how clueless we were then,
All our tomorrows in the candlelight
hidden (although the hints in rhymed jingle

About how distant thens would reinvent
Our several shining nows lay all about)
We wonder on about the as-we-were
And as-we-are, and who owes what to whom,

And why the matter of indebtedness
Should seem so much to matter here at all.
Garlands—laurel ivy myrtle olive
Cypress—lurked like shadows of promises . . .

Promises unbroken? Never quite made
Or kept, because our eyes were too bright with
Tears of excitement and privilege to
Read aright and understand all its terms

But—and you showed me this—behind us lay,
Hiding beneath his or her malign stretch
Of no longer picturesque landscape, the
Sleeping giant of what will come to be.

Hope

Cast from a simile of Paul of Tarsus
Thence depicted as an anchor (*ancora
Speme*—there's still hope—get it?) and by suchlike
 Renaissance lore a

Person lettered heavily might be versed in;
Then was shown with Nemesis standing by her
—Why?—because false hopes will bring retribution:
   Suffering dire

Pain at being dashed—Hope itself as well as
He or she who foolishly draws upon her,
Blindly and unmindfully thereby doing
   Double dishonor.

Hope I colored blue—for the sky? whose endless
Possibilities . . . well, it seemed that leaving
Room for something not too likely alas to
   Happen was weaving

Gauzy fabric veiling one's gaze from what it
Could not keep from seeing beyond and coping
With. And was I thinking that hope keeps faith with
   Nothing but hoping

Just as blue can only stay true to blue?
Such was not my thinking at six or seven.
Anyway, forget the blue: for the icon-
   Ography maven

Hope is colored green, because she is ever
Vernal, as if "Hope springs eternal" (Rhyming
Alexander Pope), but again, again yet
   Nickel-and-diming

Us if not to death then at least until death
Ends such repetition in casual slaughter—
Hope? Despair? the head and tail of the same old
   Counterfeit quarter.

Some of us—the older folks who had not been
Christian children who would hear *elpis, pistis*

Agape (translated) decreed by Paul still
  Got what the gist is

Anyway: we thought of that last bright figure
Least of three and fluttering up and out of
Frail Pandora's coffer of nastinesses:
  There was no doubt of

Who she was and how she emerged when there was
Nothing else to reach for. In what sad hour
Then does this "electric adjunct" succumb to
  Losses of power,

Now among the wreckage of old conceptions
Faded green and wistfully mothlike, mounted,
Framed—a souvenir whose market value's
  All but discounted;

Dangling anchor, fouled in its chains by some dark
Nameless serpent hissing a string of sigmas,
Coiled below and in its insinuations,
  Knitting enigmas.

En revenant d'auvergne

To sing old songs to little children in
A foreign language made *intime* thereby;
To pose a riddle, putting one more spin
On words to make them twitter as they fly,
To make words be themselves, taking time out
From all the daily work of meaning, to
Make picture puzzles of what they're about
And thereby keep the constancy in *true*;
To feel the quivering figure in the rock
Of fact, to know the thrill of the absurd,

Cutting the key with which you might unlock
The chambers of the heart of any word—
These in their faith and hope remain as much
The works of love as all the plays of touch.

A Mutual Flame

Like the old phoenix which, the more it got
Burnt up, (recycling its own stuff, no doubt,
For it did not burn down) the more it grew—
Although no fire consumes us, we burn with what
Only the fire of doing can put out
As part of me turns into part of you.

Three Poems by Philip Levine

Lies

Belle. As a boy of eight he thought of a bell,
something that rang, like the little crystal bell
on the antique table beside the bed that Mother
rang to summon her imaginary servant months before,
before she went off to get better and Belle
took him in to live and made him sleep with her
even on hot summer nights. In the morning
she'd rise before he did and go off to shower
and return to dry herself where he could see.
"You're watching me," she said. "Is it because
I'm beautiful?" Except for what was missing
she looked like a graceful young man, smooth,
hairless, tall. "Am I as beautiful as she?"
She meant her older sister, his mother, Leah.
How could he answer? How could anyone be
as beautiful as his mother. He had to lie
because he had to.
                              There was a second lake,
a small one, a half mile or so behind their cabin,
and when Belle was napping he'd sneak back through
the thick pine woods to spy on the older boys
who swam there, jumping naked from the rocks,
laughing and crying out with joy or pain—
he couldn't separate the two—sometimes punching
each other on the arms or pretending to grab
at each other's thick cocks. That whole long
summer on Lake Michigan those two lived together
in the little cabin among a stand of birches
far back from the road, though some days he would
waken to hear the big farm trucks on their way
to Benton Harbor or farther south. The town

was close by, and in the late August afternoons
they'd walk together to shop for sweet corn,
bread, hamburger meat, peaches. He'd help
carry the groceries back.
       He could never ignore
the way she looked at the men they passed in town
and the way the men looked back at her. How long,
he wondered, would it be just the two of them.
After dinner he read the same four books
over and over; his favorite was Mark Twain's
The Prince and the Pauper. One evening he asked,
"Am I an orphan?" Belle turned off the radio
and knelt by his chair and began to sob and sob
until he had to take her head in his lap and smooth
her hair down as a form of comfort while the tears
poured down over his bare legs. Her poor eyes
were shut up tight, her whole face balled
like a fist. When at last her breath came back
he recoiled from her first words, savage and simple,
and had to use words of his own, words he barely
understood, soft and deceitful, to calm her down.

Dedication

One boy was hard-of-hearing,
red-haired, freckled, never smiled,
another wore a white bib,
smelled of milk, and wept easily,
a third was taller than I,
taller even than I am now
with long dangling arms, pale hands;
he walked leaning to one side,
his small head pulled down between
narrow shoulders. I'd meet them
just after dawn on Sundays
behind our flat in the cobbled,

glass-strewn alley. Our task was
to break whatever had not
been broken: bottles, light bulbs,
thick, one-sided scratched records
of Caruso and Ponselle
that sailed over back fences
surrendering their music.
Once the cops came with push brooms
and made us sweep the long block
while they smoked and laughed, two large
red-faced uniformed flunkies
who hadn't the least idea
of why the five of us had
chosen this work on Sunday
after Sunday, clawing with
purpose through discards, garbage
cans, used reeking batteries,
black overflowing oil drums.
Of dedication, a child's
need to complete his chosen
role before the snows came down
to hide these treasures, what could
they know, this adult foolish
pair sent this one time by who
knows who to forestall the work
their day of worship required?

Missing Arthur

Eighteen years ago my cousin Arthur
     died alone in a hotel
          in Perugia,

and thus was my contact with the old world gone
     as his ashes scattered
          on the west wind.

I must visit him one more time so we can
   resurrect the past,
      the look of my mother

in a white dress, how she caught my father's dark eyes
   when he came, a stranger, to break
      bread at her house.

We are two old men in the Hotel Violetta
   late at night, each inventing
      a life he can live with.

Always Arthur's litany of regrets: how Federico
   implored him, "Come to Santiago,"
      how Arthur turned

it over in his mind and finally declined.
   "Philip," he says, "I could have
      entered poetry

as a crushed cat, a lost boy, a needle
   singing in the vague forehead
      of a dying bull."

Santiago de Cuba, Federico García Lorca,
   the names themselves music.
      Instead he came home

to grim, depressed Detroit to sell pianos
   to the Grosse Pointe ladies,
      to marry, to father

two stillborn children, only to lose his wife
   before he was even fifty,
      to die in ancient Perugia,

cold and aloof at 4 A.M., silent
   on its promontory overlooking
      the black Umbrian plain.

Someone is missing here: Arthur himself,
   with his crooked teeth, the wide
      welcoming grin,

the deep regard for everything alive.
   What use going back unless
      I can find Arthur

who is slipping away from me as
   I write these words? His eyes,
      were they hazel or gray?

Or did I merely catch the light flashing
   from the thick lenses when
      he turned to address me

in his odd, high voice cracked from use?
   "Philip," he would say, "let's
      pretend I am you and

you are me, together we are one man
   in a hotel in Perugia."
      It *is* his voice I hear

until a tomcat cries out from the street,
   a human cry, a child's
      seized by sudden pain,

and answered by a second human voice
   unrolling in the dark.
      The first light shades

the windows gray, the room takes shape:
  two beds, a long blank mirror,
    an absence of clutter.

The real dawn is grayer still. Then Arthur's
  laughter, his "yick-yick" of joy
    in the new day.

"The Paris Review remains the single most important little magazine this country has produced."

—T. Coraghessan Boyle

THE PARIS REVIEW

Enclosed is my check for:

☐ $34 for 1 year (4 issues)

(All payment must be in U.S. funds. Postal surcharge of $10 per 4 issues outside USA)

☐ $64 for 2 years

Bill this to my Visa/MasterCard:
Sender's full name and address needed for processing credit cards.

_____

Card number   Exp. date

☐ New subscription   ☐ Renewal subscription
☐ New address

Name _____

Address _____

City _____ State _____ Zip code _____

Please send gift subscription to:

Name _____

Address _____

City _____ State _____ Zip code _____

Gift announcement signature _____

call (718)539-7085   Renewal rates expire on 8/1/99.

Please send me the following:

☐ The Paris Review T-Shirt ($15.00)
   Color _____ Size _____ Quantity _____

☐ The following back issues: Nos. _____

   See listing at back of book for availability.

Name _____

Address _____

City _____ State _____ Zip code _____

☐ Enclosed is my check for $ _____

☐ Bill this to my Visa/MasterCard:

_____

Card number   Exp. date

Give The Paris Review!

BUSINESS REPLY MAIL

FIRST-CLASS MAIL PERMIT NO. 3119 FLUSHING, NY

POSTAGE WILL BE PAID BY ADDRESSEE

**THE PARIS REVIEW
45-39 171 PL
FLUSHING NY 11358-9892**

NO POSTAGE
NECESSARY
IF MAILED
IN THE
UNITED STATES

BUSINESS REPLY MAIL

FIRST-CLASS MAIL PERMIT NO. 3119 FLUSHING, NY

POSTAGE WILL BE PAID BY ADDRESSEE

**THE PARIS REVIEW
45-39 171 PL
FLUSHING NY 11358-9892**

NO POSTAGE
NECESSARY
IF MAILED
IN THE
UNITED STATES

Four Poems by W.S. Merwin

The Hollow in the Stone

Not every kind of water will do
to make the pool under the rock face
that afterward will be clear forever

not the loud current of great event
already far downstream in its moment
heavy with the dark waste of cities
not the water of falling
with its voice far away from it
not the water that ran with the days
and runs with them now

only the still water
that we can see through all the way
whatever we remember
the clear water from before
that was there under the reflections
of the leaves in spring and beyond
and under the clouds passing below them

Once in Spring

A sentence continues after thirty years
it wakes in the silence of the same room
the words that come to it after the long comma
existed all that time wandering in space
as points of light travel unseen through ages
of which they alone are the measure and arrive
at last to tell of something that came to pass
before they ever began or meant anything

longer ago than that Pierre let himself in
through the gate under the cherry tree and said
Jacques is dead and his feet rustled the bronze leaves
of the cherry tree the October leaves fallen
before he set out to walk on their curled summer
then as suddenly Pierre was gone without warning
and the others all the others who were announced
after they had gone with what they had of their summer
and the cherry tree was done and went the way of its leaves

as they wake in the sentence the words remember
but each time only a remnant and it may be
that they say little and there is the unspoken
morning late in spring the early light passing
and the cuckoo hiding beyond its voice and once more
the oriole that was silent from age to age
voices heard once only and then long listened for

Daylight

It is said that after he was seventy
Ingres returned to the self-portrait
he had painted at twenty-four and he
went on with it from that distance though
there was no model and in the mirror
only the empty window and gray sky
and the light in which his hand was lifted
a hand which the eyes in the painting would not
have recognized at first raised in a way
they would never see whatever he might
bring to them nor would they ever see him
as he had come to be then watching them
there where he had left them and while he looked
into them from no distance as he thought
holding the brush in the day between them

Before the May Fair

Last night with our minds still in cold April
in the late evening we watched the river
heavy with the hard rains of the recent spring
as it wheeled past wrapped in its lowered note
by the gray walls at the foot of the streets
through the gray twilight of this season
the cars vanished one by one unnoticed
folded away like animals and last
figures walking dogs went in and shutters
closed gray along gray houses leaving
the streets empty under the cries of swifts
turning above the chimneys the trailers
parked under the trees by the river bank
stood as though they were animals asleep
while the animals standing in the trucks
were awake stirring and the animals
waiting in the slaughterhouse were awake
the geese being fattened with their feet nailed
to the boards were awake as the small lights
went out over doorways and the river
slipped through the dark time under the arches
of the stone bridge restored once more after
the last war the bells counted the passing
hours one sparrow all night by a window
kept saying This This This until the streets
were the color of dark clouds and under
the trees in the cold down by the river
the first planks were laid out across trestles
and cold hands piled them for the coming day

Three Poems by Frederick Seidel

Cloclo

The golden person curled up on my doormat,
Using her mink coat as a blanket,
Blondly asleep, a smile on her face, was my houseguest
The Goat who couldn't get her set of keys to work, so blithely
Bedded down to wait in the apartment outside hall.
A natural animal elegance physically
Released a winged ethereal exuberance,
Pulling g's, then weightlessness, the charm of the divine,
Luxuriously asleep in front of the front door like a dog.
Dear polymorphous goddess who past sixty
Could still instantly climb a tree,
But couldn't get the metal key
To turn in any residence
In London or New York or Calabria or Greece or Florence.
Always climbing anything (why
Someone had dubbed her The Goat when she was young),
Climbing everywhere in a conversation,
Up the Nile, up the World Trade Center twin towers,
Upbeat, up late, up at dawn, up for anything,
Up the ladder to the bells.
A goat saint lived ravishingly on a rock,
Surrounded by light, dressed in a simple frock,
The last great puritan esthete
In the Cyclades.
She painted away
Above the Greek blue sea.
She chatted away
Beneath the Greek blue sky.
Every year returned to London.
So European. So Jamesian.
Every year went back

To Florence, her first home.
To the thirty-foot-high stone room in Bellosguardo.
To paint in the pearl light the stone gave off.
Ten generations after Leonardo had painted on the same
    property.
She worked hard as a nun
On her nude landscapes of the south,
With their occasional patio or dovecote and even green bits,
But never people or doves, basking in the sun.
Believed only in art.
Believed in tête-à-têtes.
Believed in walks to the top of the hill.
Knew all the simple people, and was loved.
It comes through the telephone
From Florence when I call that she has died quietly a
    minute ago,
Like a tear falling in a field of snow,
Climbing up the ladder to the bells out of Alzheimer's
    total whiteout,
Heavenly Clotilde Peploe called by us all Cloclo.

St. Louis, Missouri

You wait forever till you can't wait any longer—
And then you're born.
Somebody is pointing something out.
You see what I'm saying, boy!

Can't find a single egg at his debutant
Easter egg hunt and has to be helped.
Jewish wears a little suit with a shirt with an Eton collar.
Blood cakes on the scratch on your little knee.

Excuse me a minute.
The angel is black as a crow.

The nurse comes back in the room.
It shakes the snow from its wings.

The waterfall hangs
Down panting in the humidity.
The roar at the top of the world
Is the icebergs melting in pain.

Don't play on the railroad tracks.
It is so hot.
The tracks click before you hear the train
Which the clicks mean is coming.

British consuls posted to St. Louis in those days
Before air-conditioning had to receive extra pay.
The congressman with a bad limp was bitter.
They had operated on the wrong leg, made it shorter.

My father's coal yards under a wartime heavy snow.
The big blue trucks wearing chains like S/M love.
Blessed are the poor, for they will have heat this Christmas.
The tire chains/sleigh bells go *chink chink*.

The crow at the foot of the bed claws you
Were the Age of Chivalry and gave my family coal.
And when it was hot your ice trucks delivered
To the colored their block of cold.

James Baldwin in Paris

The leopard attacks the trainer it
Loves, over and over, on every
Page, loves and devours the only one it allows to feed
It.

How lonely to be understood
And have to kill, how lovely.
It does make you want to starve. It makes an animal kill
All the caring-and-sharing in the cage.

Start with the trainer who keeps you alive
In another language,
The breasts of milk
That speak non-leopard. Slaughter them.

What lives below
The surface in a leopard will have to live above
In words. I go to sleep
And dream in meat and wake

In wonder,
And find the poems in
The milk
All over the page.

Lute strings of summer thunder, rats hurrying
Away, sunshine behind
Lightning on a shield of
Pain painting out happiness, equals life

That will have to be extinguished
To make way. The sound trucks getting out the vote
Drive the campaign song down every street.
Hitler is coming to Harlem.

*Hitler is coming to Harlem! / There will be ethnic cleansing. /
A muddy river of Brown Shirts / Will march to the Blacks.*
Happiness will start to deface
Pain on the planet.

Richard Wilbur

Elsewhere

The delectable names of harsh places:
Cilicia Aspera, Estremadura.
In that smooth wave of cello-sound, Mojave,
We hear no ill of brittle parch and glare.

So late October's pasture-fringe,
With aster-blur and ferns of toasted gold,
Invites to barrens where the crop to come
Is stone prized upward by the deepening freeze.

Speechless and cold the stars arise
On the small garden where we have dominion.
Yet in three tongues we speak of Taurus' name
And of Aldebaran and the Hyades,

Recalling what at best we know,
That there is beauty bleak and far from ours,
Great reaches where the Lord's delighting mind,
Though not inhuman, ponders other things.

Buom

Phoenix Nguyen

On an invisible star high up in the dark sky a canary yellow butterfly spread its wings, revealing a bodice of intricately woven red and purple. Down this butterfly came in a graceful descent to earth. Its wings, moving like the undulation of the sea, stirred a soft breeze laden with the fragrances of peach and jasmine blossoms. The butterfly entered the room where the district chief and Madame, both naked, lay sleeping inside a white mist of mosquito netting. It alighted atop a bedpost, its wings outspread. Steadily it grew, its bodice swelling, its wings expanding until they were like two fluttering canopies over the bed. Madame felt a chill penetrating her skin and opened her eyes to check the shutters and saw above her the magnificent wings in delicate, hypnotic motion. She gasped, *I have died and am awaiting judgment*. She fumbled onto her knees to kneel at the edge of the bed with her hands tightly clasped before her chest. She turned her face up toward the sky from where she expected God to descend with His staff. In her wide eyes lurked the shadows of uncertain expectation. Suddenly, stormy winds howled as the gentle butterfly underwent a violent mutation that ended in a shattering into purple and gold rain that drenched the bed. Madame shut her eyes. When she opened them, the butterfly was gone, its magnificent and gentle rhythms replaced by ashen shadows creeping across the pale ceiling. Madame shook violently with fear. Meanwhile, the district chief slept on soundly, snoring. The storm winds departed, pulling in their wake an eerie quiet. The temperature began to soar. In no time, the puddles of purple and gold evaporated, forming a thick cloud from which the butterfly reemerged. Madame found herself lifted by rising swirls of purple and gold mist onto a wing whose motion was like a strong water current beneath her body. She inched toward its edge, and struggling to maintain balance on her hands and knees, she stretched her neck and looked down for the district chief. She saw an empty bed; he had disappeared. The butterfly now vanished, too. The bedroom filled suddenly with suffocating incense. Madame floated on a thick cloud of black smoke, unable to see through it to the district chief fighting the fire below.

At breakfast, the district chief said through a mouthful of rice, *Next time, dream of dragons. They're more interesting and, better yet, they can swallow their own fire.* He was tired of Madame's dream. She had talked about nothing else since his return from Vung Tau. Every night found her jerking violently from her sleep, coughing and choking, her hands clawing at the empty air.

Madame rose to her feet. *I prefer butterflies*, she said calmly. She picked the baby up out of a cotton-padded hamper and the woven baskets at her feet, and headed out for her garden, leaving the district chief to finish his breakfast alone.

•

The district chief followed closely behind Madame's heels as she advanced her hoe down a row of white fall lilies. She broke the dirt in quick, sharp bites, bending down every few steps to pick up the weeds and throw them behind her, not caring how often they fell on the district chief's good shoes. He kicked the clumps back over her lilies. He was reminiscing about his Vung Tau vacation, remembering the acrid taste of the fresh oysters he had consumed by the bucket with Fukujiro. Then, every oyster he had swallowed had tightened the longing that knotted his body; the memory of wet, cool flesh on his tongue, of its soft lump gliding down his throat, made him dizzy with desire. More than anything he wanted to take Madame back to the cool privacy of their bedroom, to escape the ridiculously hot sun and make slow, sweet love to her. The district chief hung stubbornly onto Madame's elbow, stumbling behind her. *If you have any compassion, drop that hoe and come inside with me.* He gained nothing from his pleading, except for an occasional blow to the chin from the handle of Madame's hoe, but he was undeterred. He stumbled on behind her, begging, whispering his mouth dry of compliments and seduction, but she had resolved not to forgive him so quickly.

Suddenly, he halted and ordered in the stentorian voice he normally reserved for commanding his troops. *Halt!* She obeyed at once, not from fear, but because the time had come when she felt sorry for him. In the same voice, he commanded, *Turn around and look at me. What kind of game are you playing here?* Madame did not answer right off, taking the time to choose her words carefully. The district chief lost all patience. *Well, what have you to say, woman?! What will it be? Will you come freely? Or will I have to drag you in by your hair?* Madame giggled softly. Now the district chief whined like a spoiled child. *Why won't you come into the house with me?* Madame turned around and eyed him with circumspection. *Go home,* she said. *You are startling the children.*

Under the dense shade of a nearby guava tree, their infant son was happily crawling about on a rush mat covered with a blanket of Madame's own making. Farther off, in the wild field, their six-year-old daughter was chasing butterflies with a net; her head could be seen bobbing up and down in the tall grass.

Torture! the district chief shrieked. He tore off his sweat-drenched shirt, sending loose buttons flying. He wrung it into a tight rope and lashed out at Madame's lilies. A bloom fell, then another and another. Madame stood firm, resting the hoe handle against her chest, calmly watching the spectacle, now and then shaking her head. Once he had felled all the flowers within his range, the district chief slumped to the ground, conceding defeat.

Madame burst out laughing. *My poor husband. Japanese and oysters! An experience you won't soon forget.*

Madame did not like Fukujiro, the district chief's Japanese friend. He reminded her of a soldier from her youth. During the year of the great famine, Japanese troops had come to her village and taken all the rice, leaving the village to starve. The soldiers arrived one day at her house and ordered her parents to empty their rice vats into a truck. Her father begged her to kiss the shoes of the leader, and she did, but the soldier had no mercy. He kicked dirt in her face and took the rice. Her parents died that spring. Every time she set her eyes on Fukujiro, or heard his name mentioned, she was reminded of the great famine that had stolen her mother and father. When, in the spring, the district chief had approached her about vacationing in Vung Tau with Fukujiro, tears immediately flooded her eyes. She shook her head, but said nothing. One night, she awoke from a fitful sleep and found the district chief sitting on his favorite chair by the window with his eyes turned wistfully toward the pale moon. She approached and squatted down at his feet, laying her head on his lap. Like that, they passed the time quietly for a while. Then she rose and settled on his lap, pressing her head to his chest. She said, *Too much synthetic pleasure kills a man. You don't need Vung Tau or the Japanese man. Stay home and take the first crop to market for me.* The warmth of her breath against his chest melted his heart, and he believed then that he would do her bidding, but when the day came for him to go, he kissed Madame on her cheeks and hopping onto his Honda, sped off to Vung Tau to meet Fukujiro. Madame stood by the pomegranate tree, holding on to a gnarly branch, and watched his departure through the thin dust cloud turned up by the motorcycle's wheels.

Go into the house. Madame urged once more, still laughing as she reached out with the hoe handle and gently prodded the district chief's leg. Now he, too, laughed, knowing that the battle was finally over. Madame bent down to kiss him first on the forehead, then the ear, where her lips lingered and her hot tongue thrust into the hollow of his ear. Softly, she purred promises for later that afternoon; but Madame could be unpredictable, and the district chief did not know if she was serious or just aiming to get rid of him. He decided to take her at her word and, smiling, rose to his feet, tied his shirt about his waist, slung a woven basket over his shoulder and followed behind Madame, picking up the weeds she threw behind her.

•

While their daughter chased butterflies and their son napped in his crib, the district chief and Madame locked themselves to one another and rocked their squeaking bed. Madame was panting and moaning, *Snake . . . a snake . . . not a worm, a snake!* when a loud knocking sounded from the front door. The district chief clung to his wife, crushing her breasts beneath his chest. She cried louder, *Snake! Snake!* He cried out, too, trying to drown out the knocking, but it grew louder and more insistent. *I'm going to lay a bullet in whoever that is!* the district chief swore, pulling from his wife. She sighed, closing her eyes and curling her body into a fetal position.

At the villa's front door, a young boy with a terrified expression on his sweat-glistened face folded his arms over his chest and bowed his head respectfully to the district chief, who laid a hand on the boy's head, running his fingers through the messy nest of hair. *You ought to wash it once in a while,* he said.

The boy answered timidly, *I ran all the way here, Sir, as fast as I could.*

You disturbed something very important. It better be good, or you may find that one of the bullets in my pistol has your name stamped on it.

Yes, Sir! A murder, Sir. At the twins' house.

Murder! How?

A gun, Sir. Through the head. Twice.

Who did whom in?

Sir, one of the twins shot the other, but no one knows which did the shooting and which died. Everyone's asking for you, Sir.

With a commanding gesture, the district chief directed the boy into his home and indicated for him to sit in a chair. *Wait here for me while I make myself presentable. You may sample the sweets in that bowl, there, while you wait.* The boy nodded his head, but was too afraid to touch any of the delicacies in the crystal bowl, even after the district chief had left the room.

In the bedroom, the district chief put on a white shirt and dress trousers, which he fastened with a good lizardskin belt. Madame lay supine at the center of the bed, her legs straight, feet pressed together and toes pointing straight up at the ceiling. Her hands were positioned one on top of the other over her abdomen. Her eyes were firmly shut, but she could guess his every movement. Presently, she intuited from the stillness that he was looking intently at her. Indeed, he had been admiring her posture since he returned. Now, bending down to tie the laces of his shoes, he thought, *That's the way I'll bury her one day. Naked and with her hands folded like a saint over her guts.* While combing his hair, he stared into his own eyes in the reflection of the mirror and smiled at himself as he recalled the sweet and frustrating agony he had suffered during their first year together when Madame had refused to make love to him, except in full attire, with her pants pulled down over her thighs. But he had known then what he knew now, time was on his side. Slowly, yet fervently, she had shed her skin and freed a side of herself that she had never imagined existed and for which the district chief had fallen on his knees countless times in admiration.

Madame cracked open her eyes just enough to catch a blurry glimpse of the district chief's reflection in the mirror. She could tell by the manner of his smile the subject of his thoughts, and she exhaled an inaudible sigh remembering the awkwardness of that first year, thinking, *No one who only knows us as we are now could imagine that we were once the way we were.* As the lids came down again like curtains over her eyes, the blurry image of the district chief fluttered, then faded into a gray cloud, so somber that for a minute, Madame held her breath.

Exasperated, the district chief tossed aside the comb. A handful of gel and one hundred strokes through his mop of hair left it looking like a patch of wet animal fur that had been sloppily slapped down on his head. He approached the bed, his eyes fixed on the silky fan of hair that framed Madame's head. *Why was I not born like you?* he asked, bending down to kiss her navel, extending his tongue to run a wet orbit once, twice, three times around it. *Uhm-m-m*, Madame hummed, reaching out, but the district chief had gone, leaving her longing.

•

People swarmed around the twins' house like bees. The district chief parked his aged Honda a distance off under a pomegranate tree and dusted off his clothes. Lao, his most trusted friend, rushed to his side and took his arm, grumbling, *You won't believe it. Even your balls aren't tough enough for this one. Lucky for you, murders are for the province police.* The district chief merely grunted.

Greetings shot out from the crowd as the district chief approached. He waved his hands above his head in response. Near to the door, he stiffened on hearing the wailing of women, and Lao had to push him to get him into the house. Nothing was worse for his composure than women crying. An unbearable itch surfaced on his neck; he loosened his shirt collar and scratched his neck with the desperation of a dog infested with fleas, raising red, burning welts. The relief was short-lived. In no time, the itch resurfaced and spread to the rest of his body, which broke out in a hot sweat.

The front room was crammed wall to wall with grieving, agitated people. The coffin maker had been quick to the scene with one of his crudest boxes into which the corpse had been unceremoniously laid. Someone had nailed a crucifix on the lid. Hundreds of candles were already burning, yet more were being lit and planted down with melted wax on any available surface. A litany of prayers reverberated from one side of the room to other, men chanting one verse, women answering with another. People in conversation almost shouted to be heard, annoying those praying so that they chanted even louder. No one compromised, especially not the children, who shrieked like stock being slaughtered. A dizzying cacophony. The air, dense and humid, reeked oppressively of human sweat intertwined with the unmistakable stench of death.

Lao navigated them across the crowded room, weaving with such deftness between furniture and people that it occurred to the district chief his friend might have staged the ridiculous affair as a prank, and he almost laughed. He bit his tongue, however, when finally they reached the spot where the matron of the house slouched feebly on a wooden chair, gripping the handle of her cane so tightly that the knuckles on her hands shone white. Her cloudy eyes gazed into the far distance as far as they could go from reality. Not a single tear had wet her face. Crying was no longer possible for this ninety-one-year-old woman. The ducts in her eyes had dried and shriveled years ago. The district chief knelt down at her feet, remembering another day from many years back—he had knelt at her feet then, too, to deliver the news about her husband. She had said, *Mr. District Chief, a man kneels to a woman for only two reasons: to propose or to give bad news. Just bring me the body and go.* He had mumbled, *Yes, Madame,* and gestured for his men to bring in the pouch. *An accident with the mines, Madame,* he said, rising. She took the pouch and screamed, *Get out! Everyone, out!* She locked herself in, took out her sharpest needle and sturdiest thread and labored by lamplight through the night to reconstruct the body of the man whom she had vowed before God and men to love forever. The next day, she had refused even the presence of close family. Alone, she had buried her husband in the small cemetery behind her home while the entire village had gathered behind a fence that separated them from her, but not her sorrow, and looked on. The district chief remembered how she had cried then, throwing her body on the mound she had hilled up with her bare hands. *My dear Madame,* the district chief said to her now. She clutched his hand so tightly that the blood stopped flowing to his fingers. *What suffering,* she chanted. *What suffering. Now we have really suffered.*

Say no more. Say no more, came the echoes of two young women squatting to either side of the matron. They were the newest members of the matron's household. The district chief had seen them last on one fine Sunday sitting at the center of a banquet table, white hibiscus in their hair. He recalled now how the sight of them, radiantly beautiful in brocade wedding gowns, had stirred his heart.

The deacon's son brought me your sad news. I am sorry. If I or my wife can be of any service to you, don't hesitate to call on us. His voice cracked. Perhaps he had disappointed them with his simple words, but he saw no eloquence in death and was not about to deceive anyone by speaking false words.

I cannot, but I want you to see, said the matron, taking his hand. She tapped her cane to clear a path for them, leading him to the coffin. *Open it,* she commanded the new brides, who obeyed her at once, removing candles from the lid and prying it open with crowbars. *Look and remember, Mr. District Chief,* the matron implored. His stomach convulsed, but he dared not disobey. He approached the coffin, looked down and gasped, closing his eyes. *Two points of entry. Above the right brow and through the same temple.* Later, when alone with Lao, he would ask, *Why didn't anyone clean up his face?*

No one had the guts to try and take him away from his brother. It was his brother who laid him in the coffin and nailed the lid shut. It was all very creepy, like watching him lay himself down. What a nightmare!

When the district chief returned to the matron's side, she seized his hand and said, *Now you've seen. Everyone is pointing the finger at his brother, but I tell you, he is innocent. They were one and the same. Identical in every way. Same heart. Same mind. For him to shoot his brother is like shooting himself. The province police will come for him, and I will depend on you, Mr. District Chief, to save him.*

He kept a tight lip, careful not to make any promises. He watched with a numbed sense of awe the new brides closing the coffin lid and nailing it shut once more.

You will help us, won't you, Mr. District Chief?

I'm not sure I can do anything in this situation.

You are our district chief. If anyone can help, you can.

I cannot do anything without the benefit of knowing beyond a doubt he is innocent.

Then ask him, she said, raising her cane and bidding the new brides, *Go get him and bring him here.* There was no need. The live twin had come stealthily, like a shadow, to stand by his brother's coffin. No one had noticed his approach, including the district chief, who was startled now to see him standing like the dead man's ghost at the head of the coffin. The district chief patted the matron's shoulder gently. *No need to send them after him,* he told her. *He is here.*

•

A table and two chairs were set up in a corner of the room opposite the coffin. The district chief sat down on one of the chairs. His eyes traced the markings on the table surface while he waited for the live twin to join him. The women left the room. The men crammed themselves around the table, noisily arguing for the best seats and betting on what the district chief would do. At one point, the noise made the district chief so irritable that he slammed his hands down on the table and in his stentorian voice declared, *What is the point of conjecturing when you will soon see what I will do. If you want to set up a betting ring, have the respect to do it outside.* That shut them up, but only for a few minutes, then they carried on as before.

A girl with a charming crooked smile brought the district chief a glass of lemonade. He thanked her, took a modest sip and decided his stomach was not up to the warm, sour drink. Momentarily, Lao approached, dragging along the twin, who came only by force.

Sit down, please, the district chief said, but the twin made no move to comply, and Lao had to push him onto the chair. The twin said, *You are acting outside of your jurisdiction, Mr. District Chief.* The room became so quiet that for the first time since they had left, the women could be heard softly praying in the other room.

Until the province police comes for you, you are my responsibility.

You have no right to question me.

I do not care to play interrogator. I am speaking to you now as a friend for the sake of your grandmother. Can you believe that no one knows your identity? Myself included, I'm sorry to say. Won't you set me straight so that I can call you by name?

The light went out in the twin's eyes. He bowed his head and from then on refused to speak.

I cannot help you if I don't even know who you are, the district chief said.

The twin lifted his head and stared at the district chief. The light returned briefly to his eyes, and the district chief thought that he recognized in that small flash the man's identity, but when the twin dropped his head once more, the district chief felt as uncertain as ever. The maddening itch burned under his skin. He closed his eyes and fantasized of taking his clothes off to roll on the cement floor for relief. After a few minutes, he opened his eyes, turned to the crowd and, throwing up his hands, declared, *I am washing my hands of this matter. I don't even know the identity of the man I am dealing with.*

It's Hoang, a cousin shouted out.

No, it's Hoa, an uncle countered. *I ought to know him. For years, he tended my buffaloes.*

So did his brother, another man grunted.

It's Hoa, I tell you, the uncle insisted.

You don't sound so sure. Maybe we should ask your buffaloes. They probably know better than you.

You shut up!

No! You shut up!

It's Hoang, another man interjected. *Look carefully at the way his right eye twitches, there at the corner. That was the way his mother told him apart from Hoa.*

Someone observed, *Where are his mother and father? Why don't they speak up?*

I am here, the father answered feebly. *My wife is with the women.*

Who do you say he is?

Whoever he is, he is no longer my son.

What are you saying?

I am saying, any man who can shoot and kill his brother cannot be my son.

You are swine to desert your own flesh and blood at a time like this . . .

Thus began the explosive argument among the family. Eyes popped out in fire-red faces; fists shook; spit flew everywhere. Lives were threatened. The fight ended only when the district chief kicked over a chair and ordered in the stentorian voice he normally reserved for commanding troops, *Silence!* The din fell to a buzz and then silence as the men turned to stare at him. He said, *I mean no disrespect, but I haven't come to referee a family brawl.*

He asked Lao to take the twin away, then one by one, he questioned all the men present. Hours later, he looked out the window to see the last traces of the orange dusk fading into the dark of night, and muttered to himself, *Is it possible that no one knows who is whom?*

He stood up and shook his head wearily, saying, *You all assume he is guilty, but how do you know he was the one to pull the trigger? Did anyone see him do it?*

The father answered, *I did not see him pull the trigger, but I see the guilt in his eyes.*

Did *anyone see him pull the trigger?*

They answered him with silence and uncomfortable gazes.

Exasperated, he shouted, *Then why is everyone pointing the finger at him?!*

•

Lac Son had never needed a jail and did not have one. The district chief decided the church was the best place to house the twin until the province police came for him. *He cannot run from God,* he said. The jailer's duty was reluctantly assumed by a scrawny, toad-eyed pastor who felt that giving mass and hearing confessions entitled him to the generosity of the people. *I don't like to get involved in matters of violence,* he complained. The district chief silenced him with this comment, *The truth, Pastor, is you don't like to get involved much in anything that doesn't pour gold into the church's coffers. It's about time you do something to earn your keep around here.*

They locked the twin up in the storeroom located at the back of the rectory. The bolt lock on its door could be opened only from the outside, and its only window was protected by narrowly spaced, solid iron bars for the purpose of keeping out thieves. A cot was brought into this room and set among the many ornate hand-painted dressers and divans whose drawers and cavities housed the priests' silk-embroidered vest-

ments, an assortment of the finest white linen and a most
impressive collection of gold wine chalices and host dishes.
Before leaving, the district chief shouted, *Hoa!* He was disappointed, however, not to get the soldier's automatic response
for which he had hoped. The twin maintained his original
posture: hands dropped between his knees, head hung low.
But as soon as the district chief left, the twin fell onto the
cot and curled up into a fetal position.

•

The district chief's brain felt as if pierced by a thousand
needles, and he had a hard time steering his Honda home.
Madame was swinging on the front porch, nursing their son.
He parked the motorcycle under the pomegranate tree and
went to her, hopping onto the white wicker bench swing.
She gave him a smile. He dusted off his clothes and played
with his son's feet, tickling their rosy bottom sides, pulling
those tiny feet back into his hands whenever the infant
squirmed free. He recounted to Madame the day's news. She
let him talk without interruption, and only when it was clear
that he had finished, did she say, *I heard everything you told
me and more. I heard you squirmed like a nervous dog.*

Who said that?

Our widow neighbor.

Loud mouth boar!

Riled, the district chief dug his nails unmercifully into his
son's feet. The infant writhed in Madame's arms. His hard
gums clamped down on her nipple, making her gasp in pain.
She slapped the district chief's hand and scowled at him.

In a moment, the district chief asked her, *Do you think
he killed his brother?*

Who can tell? This is out of your jurisdiction.

I asked if you think he's innocent.

*I don't care to speculate, and I'm asking you, Please don't
get involved. Leave it for the province police. They will
come tomorrow.*

The district chief was startled. He hadn't expected the

province police would come so soon. *Who told you the province police are coming tomorrow?*

Lao. While you were at the church, he sent a telegram to Da Lat. The Chief Investigator telegrammed back that he will send someone tomorrow.

Why didn't you tell me first thing? Why did you keep me babbling on about things you already know?

She shrugged her shoulders. *You were anxious to talk. I was in the mood to listen.*

The district chief shook his head, thinking, *Impossible woman! She gives you love and understanding, but only if you can live in her house of thin bamboo floors built over a pit of poisonous snakes.*

Madame reached out and pulled him back down on the swing. *Promise me you will not involve yourself in this one. Think of the children.*

The children were not really Madame's concern, but the district chief knew better than to press her for the real reasons. He had a general idea, however, what she really meant, and the thought of it turned his stomach. He walked off into the house without answering. Just as the door was about to shut behind him, she called out sweetly, *I made you a snack and left it on the credenza.*

Later, lying on a hammock strung between two foundation poles in the middle of the house, the district chief chewed absentmindedly on the sugar cubes Madame had set out for him. The sweet juice soothed his stomach and eased his headache a little. The question of the live twin's identity consumed his thoughts. He had worked with both brothers, had commanded them both. When they were not away on assignment for the national army, they served in the local militia under his command. One stormy night about a year past, he'd had an unexpected visit from one of the twins. He returned home from a patrol shift to find the visitor pacing the floor of his living room, lantern in hand. They exchanged greetings, and while his visitor continued to pace the floor, the district chief laid his rifle down, removed the grenade belt from his waist, pulled the string of bullets over his head and went for a glass of water. When he returned, the twin was still pacing. *Sit down!* he ordered. *You're making me nauseated.* The visitor paused for a moment to look at him, then started pacing again. *If you could excuse me just this one time, Sir, I don't think I can sit still.*

It's obvious you have something important to say. Out with it! It's been a long night and I'm tired. I am not home most nights. I like to spend it with my wife when I am.

Of course, Sir. I understand.

Another ten minutes passed and the visitor came no closer to revealing his secret. The district chief finished the water and, casually tossing the glass over his head, remarked, *I am off to bed. You may pace here as long as you like, but take care that you don't spill the kerosene on any of the furniture. It's not good for the lacquer. I've had a rough night. The last thing I want is to wake up in the morning to my wife's screaming about the furniture.* The district chief retired to the other end of the house, slipping under the warm sheets to lie next to Madame; the visitor was left to pace alone well into the morning, when, alarmed by the sun's appearance, he extinguished the lamp's flame and sat down at the writing desk. He hastily scrawled a note, then read it over three times before departing without the lamp, forgetting it at the foot of the writing desk.

It was not the district chief, but Madame who first read the note. She swept it out from between a pot of amaryllis and an ironwood divan where the morning breezes had blown it. She kept the note tucked deep inside her shirtsleeve while she finished the cleaning, humming improvised tunes as she worked. Later, she stood as quiet as a house post by the district chief's side while he read the note. *I can't say I'm surprised, can you?* she asked him.

Nothing surprises you, my dear, once it's happened. Only ideas can surprise you.

Madame forgave him his thoughtless tongue, realizing that the note, and not she, was the source of his frustration. *It doesn't help you that he signed his name. You've never been able to tell which is which.*

The district chief crumpled the note and squeezed it, extending the tight fist with a gentle sweep toward Madame. *He will visit again and set me straight on his identity, won't he?*

I don't know anything until it's happened, she said, wrapping her hands like two halves of a shell around his fist; but seeing how her answer drew a scowl from his face, she opened her hands. His fist dropped onto his lap, where it rested for a moment, then opened, and the note fell to the floor. The district chief dropped his aching head onto his knees. The night visitor had written: *My brother is Vietcong. Do you think he may be responsible for the failure of our mines? Or for the rice disappearing?* What could he do with this information when neither he, nor anyone else, could tell the twins apart? *He means to torment me, my wife.* The district chief sighed. *Why bother to tell me the truth and then swear that he will deny it all if confronted?*

Working alone, the district chief seized advantage of every opportunity to collect evidence against the Vietcong twin. But as Madame sadly predicted, his efforts muddled his mind, so that one fine Sunday morning, she was not at all surprised when, strolling through the guava grove, she happened upon him as he was falling from a weak branch that gave under his weight. She helped him to a sitting position and checked his body for broken bones. She was pleased to find there were none, but still furious with him, she slapped him so hard that the nerves in her palm stung long after the pain was gone from his cheek. *Listen to me,* she said. *In a few days I am going to bear you a son. It's time you stop wandering around like a lost ape. Our son will need a man to mirror himself after.* The district chief looked carefully at Madame for the first time in months and wondered sadly to himself where all the time had gone. Was it not only yesterday that she had grabbed his hands and spun round and round with him, telling him they were going to have a son?

While the district chief's mind was lost in the labyrinth of investigation, one lovely Saturday in May, to the beat of drums and gongs, the twins proceeded under a shower of rose and plumeria petals to church. They were married simultaneously under the dome of St. Joseph. Three days later, when the wedding festivities finally ended, the brothers and their wives moved into the little wood house beyond the sunflower fields where, it was known, they shared in everything except for their brides, for whose benefit they wore on hemp strings around their necks fabric tags embroidered with their names. At the wedding banquet, the district chief had toasted the new couples, *A hundred years of happiness. One thousand blessings.* As he was leaving the table, he turned to Lao, his friend, and said in a voice loud enough for everyone to hear, *If only our beloved Vietnam could be like them: same heart, same mind, no quarrels. Surely then, we would know peace.* He detected, through the corner of his eye, the twin on his right wincing. Taking this as a sign, he later escaped outside on the pretense of wanting to be alone with Madame, but as soon as they were out the door, he asked her to leave him. By the well he waited, impatient. Some time passed before the tingling sensation of being watched pierced the back of his neck and spread like icy water through him. He snapped about just in time to see one of the twins—which one, he could not tell—withdrawing inside.

Once the infant fell asleep, Madame slipped into his room and laid him down. She joined the district chief at the table, where he sat pretending to read a newspaper. She popped a sugarcane cube into her mouth and, sucking on it, followed with her eyes the small movements on his face. The same old thoughts were running through his mind: *My wife is a brazen woman. She dares to sit opposite the table from me like a man, ready to converse with me as only few men ever are. She is nothing like the traditional Vietnamese wife my mother prayed I would marry . . .* Still, he never once regretted obeying his heart. Now he was happy to be sitting across the table from Madame, gazing upon her quiet beauty, knowing she was reading his every thought. Their marriage had driven his heartbroken mother to praying the rosary night and day,

sighing alternately between Hail Marys, *Twice her age . . .
a hundred-year curse.* Once, in a rage of jealousy, he had
stormed about the house waving a rattan rod, shrieking his
dead mother's words. *I married myself a hundred-year curse!*
That incident involving a certain poet's love letters had driven
him into a melancholia so deep, it stole the light from his
eyes and made him obsessed with the thought that he had
grown too old for Madame. To prove himself right, he had
removed his personal things to the guest room, where he
spent night after fitful night pining for Madame to come and
rescue him from his loneliness. Not once did she go to him.
However, she left the door to their bedroom open and every
night, she lit a lantern, placing it at the foot of the bed as
a sign that she would welcome him back whenever he made
up his mind to free himself of jealousy.

You're not thinking of that cold March night, are you?
she asked him now, a smile creeping to her lips.

So what if I am?

If it was the lantern that pleased you, I'll light one tonight.
Madame laughed and, throwing herself across the table, covered the district chief's lips with wet kisses.

Outside, the orange-crimson sunset vanished into a thick
wall of gray. The smell of fertile earth cooling, like that of
aging wood, permeated the air. Crickets began chirping, soon
joined by cicadas, toads, owls, all the creatures of the dark,
in a night symphony. Inside the living room, Madame sat on
the district chief's lap, resting her head on his chest, listening
to the rhythm of his heartbeat and daydreaming of purple
rain.

When it came time for dinner, she lighted an oil lantern
and set it beside a vase of her fall lilies. A rumble disturbed
the peace as their daughter charged into the room, slamming
the door shut behind her. She was named Hue after Madame's
favorite flower, but she was no lily. Her mane of black hair,
in the morning painstakingly combed by Madame—one thousand strokes until smooth and shimmering like finest silk—
was now frizzed and knotted like a crow's nest about her dirt-
smeared face. Cuts and scratches covered her arms and legs.

Madame said, *Go wash for dinner,* but the girl did not hear. She pranced up to the dinner table and slapped her net down on it. Proudly, she raised up above her head a plastic bag filled with the day's catch: grasshoppers, dragonflies, bees and butterflies. *I have something for you, Mama,* she announced proudly, eyes sparkling, lips parting in a toothy smile.

Wash first.

Mama, please.

No argument. Go now before—

Let her show what she has, the district chief interrupted. He was thinking hard about the twin and was annoyed by the disturbance.

The girl skipped over to Madame. Carefully, she parted the mouth of her bag just enough to slip her hand inside and pull from it a canary-yellow butterfly with a blue body. *I chased it all day, Mama. It was the last thing I caught.* The butterfly's wings fell limp and covered the girl's hands. It was still alive but terribly weakened, near death. Madame's eyes widened in disbelief. Sensing that something was wrong, the district chief abandoned his chair by the window and went to his family.

Disappointed, not at all understanding her parents' gloomy reaction, Hue left the butterfly on the table and stomped off, pouting, for the washroom. Madame reached out to touch it, but the district chief snatched it out of her reach. He was at once alarmed by the steady pulses of warmth emanating from its body, a warmth that fired a burning sensation in his hand, frightening him. He was careful not to let his appearance betray his emotions, but Madame read his mind. He cast her a knowing glance, admonishing, *Don't fill your head with silly thoughts.*

It is your head that is filled with silly thoughts, she said. *And your heart with fear.*

•

That night, Madame hovered somewhere between sleep and wakefulness, gurgling indiscernible words deep inside

her throat. Had the district chief been able to understand
her, he would have known that she was calling out for a
landing. The yellow-canary butterfly was flying with her on
its wings through the heart of a storm so dark she could not
see her hands in front of her. She cried, *Land, my butterfly,
land! Your wings were made not for this rain, but for the sun,*
but the butterfly could not hear her over the wind and rain.

Robbed of his sleep, the district chief went to sit in the
padded bamboo chair to look out the window at the pale
moon. A few times, he heard the cries of his son, which in
the night sounded strange and distant. Each time the child
cried, the night nurse could be heard singing him back to
sleep; then the night's ringing quiet would return everywhere
in the house, except for in the master bedroom where Madame's incessant garbles kept the district chief awake well
into the morning.

The cock's crows startled Madame, gasping for air from her
fitful sleep. *God save me! God save me!* Her screams yanked
the district chief from his frail slumber. He flew to her side
and took her in his arms. She was soaked in sweat—glistening
beads of it trickled down her forehead into her eyes. He
carried her to the chair by the window, sitting down with her
in his arms. His hand went under her shirt to her belly. He
moved his fingers in slow circles, gliding them over her moist,
hot flesh, imagining he was spreading rice paper. Gradually,
her cries softened to whimpers as the sound of his voice
whispering sweet-nothings filled her head and made her see
a butterfly skimming golden air under a bright blue sky.

•

At sunrise, the district chief left his house without breakfast
and headed directly for the rectory. Passing by the shrine of
the Virgin, he stopped to venerate and offer up three Hail
Marys. His knocks were answered by the associate pastor, who
then rushed off to throw on vestments for the six-thirty mass.
Silently, the district chief entered the storage room where the
twin lay on the cot, still asleep, his chest gently rising and

falling. The district chief asked himself, *How is it that he can sleep soundly like a dog while my entire family has been restless all night long?* He sat down on the floor at a spot where furniture did not block the wall and leaned his back against it. He concentrated on keeping his breathing regular to calm himself, yet his stomach knotted up and a burning pain crept into his chest. He closed his eyes and mumbled prayers for guidance. He recited litanies automatically from memory, leaving his mind free for fantasies, wispy wishes for a miracle, such as that the twin would expire in his sleep so that he could go home to Madame and tell her she could forget about her dreams. But the twin stirred. His fantasies shattered, the district chief tried in earnest to offer sincere prayers. Soon, the seven o'clock bell rang, and then the seven-thirty, following which, the hushed voices of the pastor and his assistant could be heard coming down the hallway. On the cot, the twin slept on, snoring. The thought of a meeting with the toad-eyed pastor turned the district chief's stomach, and he hastened from the storeroom and slipped out the back door.

●

At Lao's house, the matron answered the district chief's knocks. With exaggerated enthusiasm, she invited him in. She chattered like a bird one minute then fell completely silent the next, always nervous. Lao and his three daughters were seated on a large straw mat in the front room, about to start lunch. The instant they saw him, the three girls jumped to their feet, folded their arms respectfully over their chests and, bowing their heads, chorused, *Hello, Mr. District Chief! How are you?* He answered them, *Very well now that I've had the pleasure of looking at your pretty faces,* as his hand glided from one girl's back to the next, patting each gently. He fished from his shirt pocket three packets of Chiclet mint gum and handed one to each girl. They thanked him lavishly, then skipped away to the kitchen to join their mother.

It's time you had a son, the district chief said, chuckling.

Yes, a son would be very good.

Don't get up. Finish your meal.

It can wait. In fact, it must. When I am home, I eat with my family. You have ruined the appetite of my girls with your candy; and my wife, well, you understand her.

I will leave and come back at a more convenient time.

Now is as convenient as any other time for my good friend. Come, let us go to the table and talk. You look ill. Terrible, in fact. Am I right, you did not sleep last night thinking about the twin?

Yes, you are right. Everyone seems to know my mind.

Ah—your wife. She doesn't want you to get involved.

You are right again. The district chief laughed wryly. *I could have saved myself the precious diesel had I been smart enough to realize you already know everything that has happened with me.*

I agree with your wife. This one is not for you. You don't need to help everybody. I am your friend so I can speak frankly.

The district chief did not come for advice; nor to be told things he already knew. He was in no mood for argument, however, and decided it was best to put on a happy face and be agreeable. *You're right,* he said, *I shouldn't stick my feet where they don't belong. I have no reason to really. Neither of them was ever my friend.*

Now you're talking sense! Come, my wife will set a place for you. Stay for lunch and tell us what you plan to do with yourself before you leave for your next mission.

I'm not sure there'll be another mission for me. The Americans are taking over everything. I'm getting too old for this war, anyway. Let them take over. I wouldn't mind a permanent vacation.

Lao shook his head. *You'll never be too old for the war.*

Thanks for the lunch invitation, but I think I will go back to the rectory and tell Pastor I've washed my hands of the twin's matter. Pastor can hand him over to the province police when he comes.

The matron returned with tea. *How is Madame District Chief and your children?* she asked.

Fine. Fine, he answered, then added out of habitual politeness, *When you have some free time, you must come see her fall lilies.*

Isn't it a little late for fall lilies?

Yes. But they're beautiful just the same.

I would very much like to visit your house and admire your wife's pretty flowers. What do you think of the Pastor's doves, Mr. District Chief?

Doves? I don't think anything of them. This is the first I've heard about doves; I've been away.

If you ask me, Mr. District Chief, they were a huge waste of the parishioners' money. Imagine, Mr. District Chief, the expense for obtaining purebreds all the way from Da Lat. Our pastor promised us that they would come tamed and ready to perch on the church windowsills, but the moment he opened the cage door, every single one of them flew off. If the foxes have not done them in by now, then they're back in Da Lat, perching on someone else's church. Imagine a bunch of wealthy city parishioners enjoying dove-perched windowsills at the expense of poor folks like us! Perhaps the district chief would consider talking with the past—

Lao jumped in, *My dear, I think our district chief has more important matters on his mind this morning.*

Oh, I'm very sorry. I do ramble on sometimes, don't I? It's just the doves cost so much . . . Never mind. I didn't mean to . . . No, never mind. She fell quiet and shuffled off.

She's a funny creature, Lao chuckled. *But how I do love her!*

The district chief took a few sips of tea for the sake of politeness.

Seeing him out, Lao announced, *I am going to Da Lat tomorrow. Do you want something for your wife?*

Bring her green oranges.

•

His motorcycle sped down the dirt road, raising clouds of dust behind him. In no time the district chief was back at the rectory. The pastor received him in the formal room whose ceiling boasted the only electric fan in Lac Son Village.

The pastor repeated one sentence as if logic could be born from redundancy. *You are forcing me to assume duties outside of my experience. I know of no other priest who has ever been forced to be a warden.*

The province police will be coming this afternoon, Pastor.

Still, I do not feel comfortable. A priest must be a priest, not a warden.

Your only responsibility is to unlock the door when the province police come for him.

But if something bad should happen—

Pastor, I hate to resort to unpleasant tactics, but as I don't care to spend all day arguing with you, let me just say, I know, for example, that not only the wood panels in the confessional, but also the wire screen, can be slid aside. I know of women who have willingly parted with as many kisses as it took to gain from you God's pardon.

The matter was immediately settled in the district chief's favor, and he headed home.

•

Coming around the last curve in the snaky dirt road that lead to his villa up on Black Mountain, the district chief caught sight of three figures sitting on his front steps. He recognized the twins' wives, but the man was a stranger. An army jeep was parked under a jackfruit tree. The three waved to him, but he did not wave back. He parked his Honda in the shade of the pomegranate tree and dusted off his clothes. Feeling resentful for the intrusion, he took his time moving toward the visitors so as to force them to come to him.

Dear Mr. District Chief! the women called out, trotting toward him. The stranger lagged behind them. *Mr. District Chief, we have been waiting a long time. We were about to give up, but the chief counselor insisted we wait a bit longer. And here, you've come at last.*

Why have you all waited out here in the sun? It would have been more pleasant inside the house. My wife could have provided you with lemonade to cool your throats.

The stranger stepped forward, extending his hand, which the district chief felt obliged to shake. *We did not want to trouble Madame District Chief and the baby. Besides, the view of the village from up here is breathtaking and worth bearing the sun.*

The view is the same whether you are sweating out in the heat or comfortable inside looking out a window. I'm sorry that I did not return earlier to take you in. Shall we go in now? He felt socially bound to extend the invitation, though he wanted more than anything to be rid of his visitors and go lie down on a hammock for a nap, so he was thankful when the chief counselor declined his invitation.

No, Mr. District Chief. I came to meet you and to let you know that I have been assigned the twin's case. I would refer to him by name, only no one seems able to tell me it. A very interesting case, Mr. District Chief, don't you agree? The district chief shrugged his shoulders. *You look ready for your afternoon nap, Mr. District Chief. I won't trouble you now, but perhaps I may come back in the evening to talk matters over more carefully with you. I would appreciate the benefit of your thoughts.*

I know no more than anybody else why one brother killed another. Surely, Mr. Chief Counselor can burn his diesel making more useful visits, but if he wishes to visit me, my house shall be open to him. Shall we say four o'clock? He chose the hour carefully. It gave him time for a nap and to collect his thoughts, and it was early enough to raise the implicit understanding that he did not wish to invite anyone to dinner.

Yes, dear Mr. District Chief, four o'clock. Good.

They boarded the army Jeep and left him in a cloud of dust, fighting for air and wishing that he had delayed his return from Vung Tau.

•

Thoughts of the chief counselor swam like piranhas in circles inside his head, making sleep impossible. He swung on a hammock strung between two guava trees, munching on the pomegranate seeds and *fromage* Madame had left out for him. He tried thinking of her to clear his head, but rather than calming him, thoughts of her made him feel guilty. He decided that what he needed was not to think of her, but to see her, to touch her.

He found her deep in the guava orchard with a pole, picking fruits. The baby was sprawled sleeping in the shade on a blanket thrown over a soft moss bed. Hue sat on a plank across the nearby pond, fishing and practicing her whistle. He sneaked up behind Madame and, leaning over the basket strapped to her back, placed a kiss at the nape of her neck. He whispered in her ear, *Do you think we could go behind the bushes where we won't be seen?*

She raised her shoulders and giggled. Turning about to face him, she shook a finger at him. *You left home without breakfast this morning. A man cannot worry on an empty stomach. Did you find the snack I left for you?*

I nearly tripped over it coming into the house. She had placed the bowl on the floor a few steps from the door and covered it with a fly dome. *So, how about you take that basket off and we go behind the bushes?*

I can't be myself outside the house.

You scream as loud as you want. I'll put my mouth over yours and swallow all the noise.

He drew close to nibble on an earlobe. She tensed, and he realized that she was not in the mood to make love with him. Pulling away, he said, *We had visitors.* Madame's expression turned gloomy. She lowered her head and turned her face away to hide the tears that soon ran a crooked path down her face, but too late to save the district chief from being struck helpless. She recalled her dreams, which seemed to promise something beautiful but always ended in disaster, and she wondered out loud, *Where has all the time gone, yet we are no closer to paradise?*

What are you saying? Why are you crying? The district chief did not understand the sudden change in Madame's mood, but he felt somehow responsible for her tears.

She shook her head, covering her face with her hands; and the district chief felt helplessness wrapping like an iron bar around him. He became frustrated and angry, guessing Madame's thoughts.

I haven't promised anything, he said defensively.

You will.

You are impossible.

I know you. If you don't want me to speak my mind—

He cut her off. *I never wanted to hurt you.*

I don't want to talk about the past, she said.

Two summers ago, the district chief took in a failed student whose father he owed a favor, first to hide this student from the law, then to bribe the law to turn a blind eye. Madame protested from the very beginning. *You do this, and you are no better than the next man. That boy does not object to the war. He does not object to others killing and being killed. He only objects to the possibility that he himself may be killed if he were forced to accept the responsibility of other men, men like yourself. Let him find another place to hide.* Later Madame complained, her voice coarse with insinuation and hostility, *He looks at me that funny way.* The district chief brushed off the matter. *Every man looks at you that way, but they all know you belong to me. So does the boy. As long as his belt stays on and his zipper stays up, let him look.* In the end, that student cost the district chief things much more precious than all the rice and gold combined: the sparkles in Madame's eyes dimmed. The reasons, however, the district chief never learned; Madame could not bring herself to talk about that afternoon when she had walked under an azure sky over to the west hills to check the progress of the coffee blossoms. A balmy breeze blew and stirred into the air spring's intoxicating perfumes. She was lost in daydreams, humming a song. The failed student jumped her while she was bent over taking in the fragrance of a blossom. He took her from behind, pulling her pants down only as far as her thigh. That night, he disappeared with everything of worth that he had been able to lay his hands on and carry away.

The district chief said, *Speaking not of the past, but of the future then, money isn't everything. A man must act according to conscience.*

Madame could not disagree with such a noble declaration but she pondered what guided his conscience these days. She nodded her head as more tears fell from her eyes.

Prolonged helplessness inevitably made the district chief defensive. *You don't know anything. You lock yourself up in our little paradise and dream your silly dreams. Out in the world, things can be very complicated.*

His outburst unleashed a fresh current of tears from her eyes. A lump bubbled up from the pit of her stomach and lodged itself in her throat, rendering her incapable of answering. She turned away and walked off as if in a dream. The district chief slumped onto the grass, dropping his head between his knees. *You are an impossible woman!* he shouted in frustration. Then he fell quiet, thinking, *Where have all the days gone? Why can we not be young forever?*

Suddenly, a fire lit up inside his heart and spurred him to action. He searched the grove and found Madame leaning into a gnarly trunk, her head pressed to her forearm. He approached and, laying a hand gently on her shoulder, turned her around. While he was searching for her, he had thought up many sugary phrases to whisper in her ear, dressing and undressing them in his mind, but now, looking in at the shadows fluttering in her eyes, he dismissed all those sweet-nothing phrases from his mind. He wiped her wet cheeks with the back of his hand and brought it to his mouth, tasting her bitter tears. Madame pulled away and went back to picking guavas. The district chief headed home, feeling nauseated and disillusioned.

Lying on his hammock, he ate leftovers without tasting the food, mechanically stuffing his mouth until he felt as if he would burst from bloatedness; then he realized it had not been hunger in his stomach, but anxiety. For composure, he tried meditating on the afternoon's pleasant aspects, but neither the balmy breezes, nor the spirited songs of the *chich-*

choe, could soothe his aching heart. Sleep finally rescued him. His consciousness sank quickly to a dark and heavy place, like the bottom of a vast sea, and during those dense, raven moments, he slept peacefully. The empty bowl fell from his relaxed hand; his mouth opened, and drool crept a sticky course down his chin. These blissful moments were brief; and when they were over, his muscles tensed once more and he squirmed in the hammock, fighting a semiconscious battle with the clever monkeys of his dreams, those phantasmal animals of higher intelligence, strutting misty, monkey-crowded streets, flaunting human pets they dragged along on retractable leashes. When the district chief awoke, his body felt weighed down with immeasurable exhaustion. Blotches of white light flashed before his eyes, and he felt startlingly uncertain of his place. During his sleep, the sun had moved steadily west where it shone freely on him, no longer blocked by the guava branches. Crimson diamonds branded his arms and legs where the hammock strings did not cover them. He felt on fire. He flapped his hands furiously, fanning his face. He realized the futility of his effort, but continued to fan just the same. He breathed deeply, but the fresh air did not rejuvenate his fatigued muscles. He checked his watch—nearly two o'clock. Shielding his eyes with one hand, he glimpsed at the sun, wishing that he were on a mission, in action with his men.

•

Rolling on his Honda down the unpaved road, the district chief stuck out his tongue to taste the dust that swirled up from the spinning wheels. It tasted just like his life. He stopped at the variety store and asked the owner for American brand cigarettes. She brought out a pack of Marlboros and laid it on the counter, but did not take her hand off it just yet.

You do not smoke, Mr. District Chief.

We will have a guest today, Madame.

First-time visitor to our village, Mr. District Chief?

Right.

Then please let me make a gift of the cigarettes to welcome our important guest.

The district chief declined her bribe with the same line he had been using on her for nearly fifteen years. *Our crops were good this year, Madame. I can afford to pay for the merchandise.*

The store owner sniggered, lifting her hand off the pack. *Mr. District Chief has never lowered himself to accept a gift from me before. I shouldn't have hoped that he would today.*

Paying, he remarked, *It's hot out there.*

Things are as you say, Mr. District Chief.

•

The Honda came to a complete halt at that juncture where the road forks, one path leading toward the mountains and his house, the other down into the valley and the church. For an excuse to choose the downward path, he told himself he was going to the shrine to light tapers for his mother's soul. After some running around, he found the assistant pastor down in the creek cutting watercress and trying his luck catching minnows barehanded. *Where is our dear pastor?* he called out to the priest, who, startled, lost a minnow and splashed water all over himself.

You might have announced your presence before shouting out like that, the priest grumbled.

You would have preferred that I creep up on you like a Vietcong in the night, Father?

Each man forced a laugh.

I've come to pay a last visit to our prisoner, said the district chief.

Pastor has the key.

And where might I find our dear pastor? In the confessional?

Why would you think that? It's not Saturday.

Never mind. Do you know where I can find him?

The assistant pastor pointed across the stream. *He's praying in the potato field.*

Don't you agree with me, Father, that it would be less intrusive for one priest to interrupt another's prayers?

The priest thought the district chief very strange, but rather than engage him in an argument that might drag on indefinitely and rob himself of the opportunity to resume that afternoon his game with the minnows, he offered to go fetch the key.

•

The district chief found the twin lying supine on the army cot with his hands folded over his guts, and the image of Madame in that very same posture rushed his mind.

I have come to talk with you, he declared, leaning back on one of those dressers that housed chalices cast in pure gold. *The provincial chief counselor has been assigned to your case. It hasn't become clear to me whether he will prosecute or defend you. I am to have a meeting with him this afternoon. A few words from you might help me make up my mind on what to tell him about you.*

The twin did not stir.

What do you want me to tell him?

Nothing.

The district chief closed his eyes and began chewing on the tip of the key. When the smell and taste of rust overpowered his senses, he knew it was time for him to go. As he was about to pull the door shut behind him, he felt a tight grip on his shoulder and he froze.

Tell me, he said.

I am guilty.

The district chief listened intently to the matted sound of the prisoner padding back to the cot.

Your name, urged the district chief. He waited, but when a long time passed and the twin remained quiescent, the

district chief stepped out into the bright corridor and closed
the door behind him.

•

Down in the lowlands, the rice paddies stretched in all
directions. Here and there, a hill, dike or furrow marked the
otherwise uniform landscape whose steadfast extension was
halted only by the invulnerable evergreen mountains. To
reach the Ma shaman's place, the district chief had to cross
the rice paddies from east to west. The dry season was well
underway, and the banks of the dikes were dry, making it
possible for him to cross on his Honda. On reaching the west
side, he searched his surroundings for the rocky hollow he
remembered from previous visits, and finding it, he pushed
the Honda into the bend and covered it with branches he
tore from nearby bushes. He took off his shoes, tied the laces
together and draped the shoes over his shoulder to keep them
dry while he crossed a marshy channel that divided the west
mountains from his docking place. His steps stirred up clouds
of tiny green frogs and water bugs.

The district chief found the Ma shaman squatting on a
rock by the entrance of his hut turning a millstone. *Old
friend!* he shouted, waving. The Ma lifted his face with a
radiant, toothless smile.

They sat under the shade of banyan trees recounting for
each other the things that had come to pass since their last
visit. As always, the district chief did most of the talking as
little happened in those mountains that the Ma cared to
relate. The shaman had often said, as he did now, *You understand, these mountains are for living in, not talking about, but
on the other side, where you are, things are much different.*

*You are right, my friend. Things are much different on
the other side.* Suddenly, the district chief found the heat
and the bugs swarming around his face unbearable. He stood
up and began swatting furiously at the bugs.

The Ma's seemingly permanent smile shriveled as he, too,
stood up. He took the district chief's hand into his own and

looked deep into his eyes. *You are so restless,* the Ma said. *The twin is one thing, but don't forget your wife. Fairies die, too.*

•

Madame didn't know where so many tears came from, nor how to stop them from falling. Her heart felt bruised and swollen, as hearts feel when struck with a hard blow, or rotting from the inside. She had listened to the sound of her husband's forlorn steps dragging him away on the narrow, shadowy path under the guava branches. The fading *thomp-thomp* of the rubber soles on the dirt-pack trail had filled her with sorrow. *Go to him*, she had told herself. *Go with a kiss and a smile.* Her heart and mind had seemed in agreement, yet she held back and shed her tears.

Now she heard the sound of his motorcycle and went to peek out the window to see him parking the Honda under the pomegranate tree, but when he headed for the house, she hurried away from the window and out the back way. She paused for a moment on the brick patio, glancing toward the sun; and then she ran like the wind for the shadowy places in the guava grove.

Madame never used perfume, yet in her wake the air always smelled different, distinctly alkaline as if she had left hidden somewhere petals of her musk roses. When he entered the house, the district chief knew at once that Madame had hurried from the room to avoid him. He felt like tearing his hair out, but instead he proceeded with exaggerated calm to the soft-cushion couch, sat down, put his feet up on the coffee table and began leafing through the pages of *LIFE*. He did not understand a word of English, but he liked the magazine for its pictures. He came across a flower that he thought Madame might like and wondered how he might go about obtaining the seeds. He glanced at his watch often. At twenty after four, he dropped the magazine and began pacing the floor. A few minutes later, his daughter appeared with a vase of Madame's fall lilies for the coffee table.

Very nice, he said.

Thank you, Father, she murmured, ready to dash off.

Come to me, please. The district chief sat down on a straight-back chair and patted his lap. Hue inched forward, lowering her head slightly more with every step. The district chief frightened her in the same way that Jesus of the crucifix did. He seemed to her infinitely important, authoritative and agonizingly sad. Sometimes, he scared her even more than Jesus on the cross because he existed in the flesh. She did not want to go to him, but she felt she had no choice really, not daring to disobey the command of a man more fearsome than God. The district chief picked her up, set her on his lap and began rocking her gently. She kept her head bowed and concentrated on cleaning the dirt from under her fingernails to calm the butterflies flapping inside her stomach. The district chief stroked her hair.

Did your mother fix those?

Yes, Father. She nodded her head for emphasis, still feeling nervous, and tucked her lower lip under her upper teeth. The district chief burst out laughing. How much she looked to him like a bashful newborn duckling, calling to his mind innocence and fresh beginnings. Knocks from the front door abruptly extinguished the district chief's laughter. He lifted his daughter off his lap and stood up, patting down the wrinkles in his trousers. She sped for the back door, her long hair flying behind her.

Hue! he called.

She halted at once and turned to face him. *Yes, Father.*

Tell your mother that your father loves her.

Relieved, the girl sighed, *Yes, Father,* and dashed out the door.

•

The chief counselor had one hand behind his back, the other audaciously fingering the carving in the door frame. *Beautiful design, Mr. District Chief. I have a similar frame on my house. The artist is Indian, I believe.*

This frame was done by a local craftsman, Mr. Chief Counselor. If you have finished admiring it, do come in.

The chief counselor's beady eyes swept a quick circular glance, all he needed to assess the value of the room and its contents. He was impressed, exclaiming, *Beautiful,* repeatedly.

To begin the meeting, the chief counselor exercised a strange ritual: repeatedly adjusting his glasses, smoothing his hair, clicking his tongue, tightening his tie and crackling his knuckles. *He is a peacock,* the district chief thought, *and peacocks, I hate.* He shut his eyes as the chief counselor leaned across the table, speaking in a voluptuously intimate voice like a girl sharing a dirty secret with her best friend. *The province jails are deplorable. If he is a good man, we must do everything to spare him that fate.*

I cannot tell you whether or not he is a good man. I do not know him well.

Then we must talk with those who do.

I do not envy the chief counselor his job. It seems nobody knows anymore than I do. I'd even wager that you may know more than we do. Given your expertise, you can see things we cannot.

The chief counselor sniggered, adjusting his glasses. *Mr. District Chief, this is your place. You are responsible for knowing your people.*

I am only a humble government official, not everybody's father.

The chief counselor sat back, again adjusting his glasses, *His grandmother says he is innocent. She ought to know him, don't you agree, Mr. District Chief?*

So should his parents, and they say he is guilty. They have disowned him, as I'm sure you've learned from your investigation.

The grandmother raised him while his parents were busy working in the fields. So who do you think knows him better?

The chief counselor does not need my opinion. It would be like rain in monsoon April. In the end, the chief counselor will decide what he will decide.

The chief counselor narrowed his eyes and smacked his lips. *The district chief undermines the importance of his viewpoints. I am from far away. I must rely on your knowledge of your people.*

You say they are my people, but the people belong only to themselves. I work for them. I know only what they want me to know, and I've already told the chief counselor I don't know anything that can assist him in his investigation.

The chief counselor stroked his chin, saying, *The district chief speaks cleverly.*

Now came the district chief's turn to lean across the table. *Let me make myself very clear, Chief Counselor. There was a time in my life when I could squander many long hours dancing like a buffoon around an issue. I'm too old for that crap now. Please get to the point.*

The two men locked eyes.

Now that I know the district chief is a man who must be respected, I can speak frankly. I am convinced your man is innocent. I have made up my mind to defend him. As I was saying before, the jails are absolutely horrid . . .

Listening to the chief counselor drone on, the district chief was struck by a powerful sense of déjà vu. Steadily, the peacock reminded him of the dozens of other people who had sat in that very same chair to make their cases for his help. But he had only so much to give. *I don't think I can be of any help to the chief counselor.*

The chief counselor grabbed his hand and squeezed it hard, refusing to let go. *Listen to me, Mr. District Chief, you only need tell me that you, too, believe he is innocent. I have many friends in high places. With your support, I can get him out by the twelfth month in time to enjoy Tet with his family, or at the latest by February so he can still help his wife with the rice planting . . .*

Try to make his stay in jail comfortable, the district chief finally heard himself saying. Puzzled, the chief counselor pressed him for a clarification of his intentions, but his thoughts had moved on to Madame's lilies, and he did not care to respond. The lilies had bloomed very late this year. For weeks, she had complained and sulked, speculating that they would never unfold but shrink drying into themselves and be blown away by the wind. *Damn waste of my land!* he had shouted. This angry declaration had sent her into a rage, in the course of which she ran out into the fields and dug up a clump of dirt, which she carried into the house and hurled at his feet. *Your land! Without me, your land wouldn't even sprout weeds.*

Finally, turning his attention back to the chief counselor, he said, *Excuse me. How rude of me not to have offered you a drink. I've got a bottle of fine French wine. Let me go get it.*

He looked for Madame in the kitchen. He found it empty and eerily quiet. He rummaged the cabinets through Madame's collection of herbal remedies for something to ease the headache that seemed perpetually pounding in his head. He decided on a piece of ginseng root, not realizing that it was not a cure for pains, but a potion for longevity and sexual prowess.

•

The district chief wandered the grounds in search of Madame. He found her with their children at the lotus pond beyond the sugarcane field. He spotted his son sleeping under the shade of a weeping willow. On the wood plank bridging the pond, mother and daughter sat, arms touching, feet dipped between lotus leaves that bobbed around their ankles. Dragonflies and butterflies darted around them as they read deeper into a romantic tale of a prince and princess. How much the district chief desired to settle down beside his son, to be lulled to sleep by the tale and dream of fairylands. But he was keeping the chief counselor waiting with no idea where he had disappeared to. So he shouted *Mother! I need you,* and the tranquility was broken.

In no time, his family was following him home. Madame

was silent, unhappy about the chief counselor's visit. Marching behind her, Hue sang a nonsense song.

•

The chief counselor did not wait alone for long. He was not at all disturbed by the district chief's sudden and prolonged disappearance. In fact, he welcomed the opportunity to collect his thoughts. Shortly before the district chief returned with his family, the chief counselor was joined by the twins' wives and a third woman. The district chief could hardly believe his eyes when he walked into the room. He knew it was rude to stare, but he could not help himself. He fixed his eyes on the woman of copper-colored hair fixed like a mummified beehive. Later, he would find it impossible to recall the features of her face; its plain qualities had failed to create any impression in his eyes, overpowered as they had been, by the mound of hair above, and below, by the curvaceous body wrapped in a lime-green dress that clung impudently, like a second skin, to her figure.

Madame regarded this woman much as she might regard a strange, incomprehensible museum piece. She studied the woman briefly, then losing interest, she turned her eyes away to other things.

Please allow me to introduce Monique, my wife, Mr. and Mrs. District Chief. The chief counselor led the woman by the hand in the fashion of starting a waltz. She curtsied. Impulsively, the district chief thrust out his hands, ready to catch the copper beehive should it fall from her head. The woman uttered an incomprehensible explanation, speaking in Vietnamese, although no one would have realized it if the chief counselor had not revealed the fact. *I'm sorry, we speak French at home,* he began. *She practices her Vietnamese daily for the sake of the servants, but she has never really been able to manage the subtle differences in tone. Anyway, my wife was apologizing, Mr. and Mrs. District Chief for her sudden appearance. We meant to come to Lac Son together, as we had planned to leave from here for a short vacation in*

Nha Trang, but at the last minute, she was detained by family matters and could not accompany me. We won't be able to go to Nha Trang now anyway. The man who was supposed to accompany me here got tied up at the last minute, so it's fallen on me see our twin to Da Lat.

Why don't we all sit down at the table, the district chief offered.

Madame spoke privately with the twins' wives, expressing her sympathy. Then turning to everyone, she said, *Excuse me. I'll prepare a pot of tea, or perhaps some of you would prefer a cool glass of cane juice.* Out of politeness, the guests all chorused, *Not necessary,* but of course, she felt compelled by social dictate to go ahead and fix the drinks, and she left for the kitchen taking the children with her.

At their request, the district chief gave the twins' wives a few minutes in private with him. *Mr. District Chief, we will be forever grateful to you,* one said while the other handed him a burlap sack. Inside were a rabbit and a rooster. He handed them back the sack, telling them, *I have done nothing and probably will not be able to do anything. Your gifts should go to Mr. Chief Counselor,* but they pressed it into his arms and cleverly rushed away to the meeting table. It would have been rude for him argue with them in front of his other guests, so he took the sack to Madame. She refused to look in it.

It's not much. Just a rabbit and a rooster.

Yet you'll pay dearly for them.

He threw her a hostile glance. *I have not promised anyone anything.*

If you can still say that after the evening is over, I'll gladly apologize.

•

The chief counselor again dominated the discussion. He went on at length about the inhumane conditions of the jail, repeating everything he had told the district chief, but here and there, expanding on this or that point with anecdotes.

*Take, for example, the cholera incident that wiped out nearly
all the inmates. The water was filthy* . . . This kind of talk
frightened the twins' wives, but the chief counselor awed
them with his position, and they did not even dare breathe
normally in his presence, much less interrupt him. As for the
district chief, he appeared to be listening but was actually lost
in thoughts of Madame, her lilies and her butterfly dreams.
He snapped to attention, however, when the Frenchwoman
sneezed, spraying his face with her spittle.

Your handkerchief, my dear! Your handkerchief! The chief
counselor prompted, but the Frenchwoman had forgotten to
put one in her purse. The twins' wives each offered her a
handkerchief, but she scowled and shook her head, opting
to wipe away the excretion with her bare fingers. *May I suggest
the bathroom, my dear?* The chief counselor's voice was overly
sweet and tense. The Frenchwoman huffed, rising from her
chair. She teetered off, wobbling for balance in her pointed-
toe shoes with the cigarette-thin heels.

The chief counselor resumed the discussion. *As I was saying,
to save him will not be inexpensive, Mr. District Chief.*

If he is innocent, the truth will save him.

The chief counselor forced a nervous, sarcastic laugh. He
threw up his hands, drawling, *Mr. District Chief, surely you—*

All right! All right. Give me a figure.

I'm sure Mr. District Chief can calculate for himself.

*I don't like guessing, especially when I am under no obli-
gation.*

The chief counselor removed a fountain pen and a small
decorated pad from the inner pocket of his sports coat. He
took his time itemizing all the costs and totalling the amounts,
and reviewing what he had written, before pushing the pad
across the table top to the district chief, who quickly concluded
that separately, the itemized amounts seemed reasonable
enough, but the sum of them was outrageous. He shook his
head, sliding the pad back to the chief counselor. *Impossible.*

Mr. District Chief, it's just one estimate.

Even if I wanted to, I cannot put up that much.

Silent until now, the twins' wives whined in disappointment, each stroking her chest. The district chief glanced at
them and was struck with pangs of guilt; he should not have
accepted their rabbit and rooster. Suddenly, he felt very tired
and hot; his body broke out in sweat and began to itch.
Sensing his distress, his guests became silent, bowing their
heads to avert his eyes. When the Frenchwoman returned tip-
toeing into the room, she, too, was dragged into the silence.

It was the chief counselor who finally broke the spell. *Of
course, Mr. District Chief should not have to carry the entire
burden. We'll all contribute.*

The twins' wives nodded their heads enthusiastically, together chiming, *Yes, of course.*

The district chief glanced at them again, and was again
struck with guilt. He thought resentfully of their rabbit and
rooster, swearing to himself that he would personally kill
those animals, but not partake of their flesh and blood. He
would throw them out with the trash. He was about to make
unequivocally clear that he would not become involved when
a feeble knock sounded from the front door. *Enter!* he
shouted. The door swung slowly open, the foot of a cane
poked through and the grandmother hobbled in. Around
her neck, she wore the red scarf her husband had worn the
day he stepped on the mines. The moment the district chief
saw that scarf, his mind was changed.

•

Madame was bathing the infant in eucalyptus-scented water
when the district chief came to her. She sensed the decision
he had made by the worry that emanated like charged waves
from him. *Do what you want,* she said in a voice that was
choked with sadness. She knew she could not change his
mind. In matters involving other people, he always kept his
promises. She swallowed the lump that was lodged in her
throat and shook her head.

The district chief stood behind Madame, jaws clenched,

arms rod-stiff at his sides, his fists hard and rough as gourds. *Is that all you have to say?!*

She did not answer.

•

Madame hid the family jewelry, gold and money in an ivory box in the secret compartment of the mahogany writing desk in their bedroom. The district chief studied the contents for a few minutes. His heart seemed to be pounding in his ears as he counted out the money. On top of the neat stack, he placed ten gold leaves. He locked the box and pressed his lips to its cold, smooth lid for a minute before returning it to its hiding place.

The room filled with sighs, cheers and compliments when the district chief placed his contribution at the center of the meeting table. Only the grandmother kept quiet. Tears, thick and sallow from having been held back for decades, collected at the corners of her eyes. When the district chief sat down, she reached out under the table and took his hand into her bony hold.

•

It was well beyond dinnertime when the company finally departed, leaving the district chief feeling unsettled and giddy. He looked in the bath adjunct for Madame, but she had left. The hired girl who was tending a bed of coals to keep his dinner warm said Madame had been in the kitchen earlier to feed the children.

How long ago?

About an hour.

Did she tell you where she was going?

No. She just said she was taking the children for a stroll. She does most nights, Mr. District Chief.

He shook a fist, shouting, *Doesn't she know there are mines out there?!* He stormed off, waving his arms, muttering angrily to himself, leaving the girl staring after him, terrified.

Madame returned with the children after nightfall to find
the district chief sitting alone at the meeting table, staring
vacantly. His fingers drummed the tabletop. She sent Hue
to her room and took the infant to his crib. As she walked
about the house, the intensity of her hurt and anger permeated the air, making breathing difficult. The district chief
dared not say a word to her as she set the table for their
dinner. They ate in complete silence.

All night long, she turned and tossed beside him. If he
touched her, no matter how lightly, she thrashed and
groaned. When he could not tolerate another kick to the
shin, knee in the stomach, or flying arms whacking his chest,
his face, the district chief slithered quiet as a snake off the
bed and went to sit by the window. He shifted his gaze
between Madame and the pale, silver moon. How sad and
alone he felt.

When the roosters crowed, Madame jerked awake and
screamed. The district chief flew to her side, took her into
his arms and rocked her back to sleep, whispering, *Rest little
buom, little butterfly. Rest.*

In the adjacent room, the infant cried. The night nurse
sang her song, her voice deep and sad. The district chief
pressed an ear to the wall to better hear her. Like that, he
fell asleep, clutching his wife.

•

At breakfast, the sullen silence destroyed everyone's, but
the infant's, appetite. Madame fed him, then rushed away,
pulling Hue along.

The district chief paced the living room, munching on
fromage, thinking to himself that by now the chief counselor
must be on his way back to Da Lat with the twin. The thought
left a bitter feeling in his gut. He went to lie on the hammock
by the window. After a while, his eyes grew dull. His vision
blurred and he saw a cloud of white light vanishing into a
darkness that then cracked open like an egg and out fell the

wing of a butterfly. Madame's voice called his name, over and over. She was everywhere, yet he could not find her.

He awoke at high noon, feeling more tired than before his nap. Looking out the window, he saw his wife in the lily farm, his son sleeping under guava branches, his daughter chasing butterflies in the grass field. The taste of dust coated the inside of his mouth. Madame was bent over, cutting lilies and arranging them in a vase. While he was watching her, a patch of light swept across her back as the sun moved from behind one cloud to another. His stomach growled. Instinctively, he looked at the dining table and saw that Madame had set out a meal for him. He ate the cassava and salted shrimp and thought he might make another trip to Vung Tau to see Fukujiro before the rainy months. The Americans, not used to living in mud, tired during the rainy season, and there would be a need for him and his men.

Friend, are you in there? Open up!

Lao's shouting broke his thought. He jumped up, dashed to the door, and threw it open. *I'm glad you've come. You're just the person I'm in the mood to see.*

Listen, I can't stay. I wanted to tell you first, but then I must hurry to the twins' house.

You've brought me bad news.

Lao handed the district chief a bag of green oranges. *For your wife.*

Out with your news. Hurry! Don't keep me waiting.

You may want to take this one lying down.

I'll take it as I am.

As you wish. On my way home, I noticed a man lying by the roadside, in the grass. Naturally, I assumed he was a drunkard sleeping off the previous night's binge. I sped right past him without another thought and went on for about four or five kilometers when it struck me that there had been something familiar about him. Perhaps I unconsciously recognized the clothes he wore. In any case, I turned around and went back for a closer look. It was our twin, my friend. His body is in my Jeep if you care to have a look.

Body?
He is dead.
How?
His throat was slashed.
Jesus!
I should really hurry and take his body to his family. It doesn't take long in this heat—
Yes! Of course. You are right. You must not stay with me another moment. Go fast to them, but please don't tell them you've been first to see me.
I wasn't planning to.

The afternoon passed by the window, unnoticed by the district chief who sat like a stone; nothing of him moved, except for his eyes, which alternately widened and narrowed. At one point, Hue appeared with the vase of the lilies Madame had arranged and placed it before him. She came a second time to bring him a glass of lemonade and a bowl of cubed sugarcane. *Where is your mother?* he asked her, his voice hoarse.

We're going to the lotus pond, Father. Mother's going to read me a fairy tale. She said if you ask about her to tell you that you should come read with us.

Hue waited, standing with her arms respectfully folded over her chest. When about five minutes passed and the district chief still had not made any move to follow her, she asked timidly, *May I be excused, Father?*

Go, he said; and she slipped away.

•

The district chief rubbed the petals of the autumn lilies with one hand, and his temples with the other, trying to ease his headache. When the sun sank behind the mountain ridge, painting the horizon in streaks of orange and yellow hues, the district chief went to the lotus pond, but Madame and the children had gone. He wandered through the guava grove, the cane field, the coffee hills and up and down the clear water stream, but he did not find them at any of those places.

The search left him feeling immeasurably tired and a little afraid when the thought entered his mind that he would always arrive at every place a little too late. Finally, returning home, he found Madame swinging on the front porch, nursing their son. On her left, Hue sat with a book of fairy tales opened on her lap. He approached them and sat down on his wife's right to tickle their son's feet.

Lao was here earlier, he said.

Yes, I know, she answered, and her voice was tender, understanding. She took his hand and brought it to her lips, kissing it full of warmth. He sighed, asking her, *Will you light a lantern for me tonight?* She nodded, kissing his hand again. As darkness descended, the first firefly blinked. Then another and another, and soon, a nebula of green flickering light surrounded the district chief and his family. He took a deep breath and rested his head in the crook of Madame's neck and shoulder. In a minute, his ear caught the sound of her pulse, and listening, he thought, *She is the only truth I know.*

Three Poems by Priscilla Becker

Overture of an Hallucination

Six years have gone since I have been loved
by you. All appearances have been more or less
phantom. There is a boy, now, applying for your job.
He does not know this. Nor does he know how narrowly
he fills your ghost.

December and the trees are clinging to their leaves.
Here we are, season #5, fey and fucking
with us like that. Already I can feel myself
wasting this for sure, molding in my overcoats,
curling up my onion-skin

edges like nails from their estranging
beds, dessicating under long johns, hibernating
in my layered look. When I emerge, nobody
looks like me anymore. Most of all you. Or least.
Isn't it strange how either one fits?

You can do that with words, use one
for the other.

My Stint Among the Beloved

Even I can see the flowers are up. I take
like wild vine to my bed. And may I have
a word with the miser measuring out my joys.

A vinyl shade the color of mayonnaise
allowing an inch of the world. I am not
concerned with the people on the street

what they will wear or will not or what
the noises are. I depend on the visitation
of another kind of weather. Comrades, we have come

a long way. From all accounts this is a city.
Sometimes despite myself my body
pulls up artifact—a rock or someone

touching me beneath the stop sign. Over this
I am having it out with God. Fellows,
we have lost the sky. I suppose I do not

need to tell you who is winning. All over
the world after accidents and terrible
estrangements, following surreptitious exits

and deadly protracted silences, we seem to agree upon
regret for being denied the chance to say
goodbye.   Brothers, goodbye.

Preparing for Export

I do not live in Niger, but once
a man begged me to stop living
my life in Long Island City
and come and join him there.
You see my point.
I am a girl of uncommon
inertia. If it weren't for the night,
I'd never leave my bed at all.

You see this life is lived
on the premise that it is worth living it.
Someone said tonight *you can't ignore
the twentieth century*.
Watch me.

Three Poems by Eliza Griswold Allen

Delilah

If I had known I'd reduce you to this,
I would've stopped myself along the way
to see the shape your shoulders took—
surrender's concave face—when I came close,
taking me in, you lovely man, and all
the while I thought you in control: your girth
and laugh made me forget; the tone you'd take
as if the world spun in your palm, turned on
your breath. Sometimes I held my own to catch
the feel of your exhale against my wrist.

You slew a lion with your fists.
Your name became the cleanest word for death,
each letter forged by bees and carrion—
my own name means flirtatious, did you know
this when I pouted, when I wound you tight
with sinews which you'd said would take your strength?
Couldn't you guess, waking bound, that I
meant you all harm? I thought you knew,
and humored me: the insect buzzing by
the lion's mouth until the insect stings.

I sit and watch the courtyard emptying
near dusk, your death tomorrow's fête.
I wonder will the rest of my scant life
depend on being fed by memory—
that meager feast for widows, monks and crooks?
I'll rub the table down with mint, and time
will curl my backbone toward its stooping point—
a human *s* turned in upon myself,
forever looking down for what I've lost:
a strand of fate I snipped and dropped and dread
remembering but cannot leave behind.

Exhibit 1916—a, b, c:

Two drafts of the last letter the Czarina sent to the Czar at the front. Exhibits a and b found among her papers. Exhibit c found among the Czar's correspondence.

a.

Nicholas—

Outside my window, branches are breaking off the trees. The
    sound of glass shattering
fills my afternoons. I tell myself, this is natural for March:
    the frozen rain coating each limb.

The weight, the breaking begins when the sky turns
    plum—we are at tea (the children try
to be so brave for me). They say nothing of the sugar (gone).
    Or that we share one teaspoon

(the others disappeared in a servant's apron). But no one
    comes for tea now anyway.
Our linens smell like metal from lack of change. Alexei's
    sheets are dappled brown:

flecks of blood, I'm afraid. There is no one left to clean his
    terrible spittle. Whom could I ask?
That devil we called friend will not stop his whoring. I fear
    he may turn on the girls with those

ungodly eyes. The trees are breaking, the sound of the sky
    falling against the iron-cold courtyard.
No sugar, spoons gone. Where are you? We hear from the
    soldiers posted at our bedchamber

doors, All is lost. I say come home. How the trees shriek.

b.

Dearest Nikki—

Outside my window, March has frozen the trees to glass. They
    are lovely. The girls lace their hair
with ribbon, admire each other, and pretend they are
    somewhere else—a half-

imagined affair. I tell them stories of ball gowns and
    chocolate, of waltzing on rose petals. Their
eyes grow so wide. And Alexei seems to improve in this cold
    weather. Rasputin remains your loyal

subject. We miss you. How goes all at the front? Some of
    your friends are so thoroughly occupied
with the effort, they are quite too busy for me. We long for
    your return. Sometimes the trees make

strange sounds—   always, A.

c.

My darling N—

Outside my window, winter's a jewel box! The trees turn to
    diamonds—like living in one of your
eggs. The children are off at the birthday of some
    ambassador's child. They're full of stories:

chocolate-creams dipped in gold, pony-rides on marble
    floors—we hear the front goes marvelously
well, and remain your warm and well-fed soldiers, wrapped
    in ermine, stuffed with cakes. Alexei

recovers miraculously: he chases your daughters around the
    palace—no blood on his sheets for weeks. What

would we do without our friend Rasputin? I'd say we pray
    for you, but what would

be the point: you've done so much to keep us alive. I am off
    to Mme. S—'s for one of her endless teas. You
remember the invitations. I'd send you diamonds from the
    window,

but I'm afraid they'd wet the page, and you might think
    them tears.

Your firm little wife,
Alexandra

Midas

I guess like losing anything, I thought
it was coming back at first. And then days
crowded round with nowhere else to go—
I noticed time had passed. One minute
coughed politely, I raised my head to see
the spent hours standing there—that's when I first

felt shame, and not the day I tried to turn
the bird to gold. I gripped her talons in my fist,
and nothing changed. I opened my hand, the hawk
started up—two, three stuttering flaps—
and rose beyond my reach, climbing into
the late afternoon as if light were a solid thing.

She reached the great hall's rafters. Forty heads
tipped up to see her perched on gilded beam.
No one looked me in the face. Maybe a page
showed the audience out. One farmer kept glancing

toward the roof, his honor gone with mine.
Today I'd learn her name. I'd strip her hood,

to stare down failure's glare, to see if God
hid in that face—if God had had enough
of me, my gift, its double curse
of making gold from string, boots, oxen yokes,
but *not* a living thing. It's taken years
to guess at why I lost the touch—years

breathing three sharp beats before she broke
from me. Now, it's parlor tricks—I measure time
by how much heat a stone will hold. My throne
warms as if I still sat in that chair,
before the tiercel tore me from myself,
her moulting feathers proof and consequence.

Two Poems by Rebecca Wolff

Spending the Day on a Sleeping Porch

This is the enclosure my family
has dreamed of, and brought into being
by the sheer collected force of our dreaming:
a fund. Generations of desire for repose, after chatting
away the seamless day in recalling
our forefathers and, separately, their sins: mistresses,
and the oppressions perpetrated on those who were loyal
and lived behind the house. We are
not even midway through yet.

There is something radical about doing this.
Check the action for resonances:
blue planks create a platform;
there is a sense that something will be performed
in this flimsy envelope. "Don't follow me"
is the general cry.
My mom feels that way.
By the close of the reunion day
she is ready to be shorn of all relation.
Uncle Pete is of a
mind: he is ready for his body to hit
the traditional burn-pile; to ash up with paper plates and cups
and blow away in the cool
breeze, much commented-on.

But nothing in the lineage of this house
expresses how I feel about the sleeping porch.
It provides an elegant barrier,
tightly woven of vision: from inside, I can see,
but cannot be seen by, the involuntary squadron

of my genealogy, with their clanking
chains and requisite pedigree.
Never mind the leafy branch of the magnolia tree
which reaches almost all the way now
to the ground. This is the only place
in the house not overrun
by familiars: the family
cat, dog, resemblance . . .
It is outside the house though quite partial to it,
as Aunt Nell was in her day to barbecue.
It offers simulacra to the breeze.

It is a room built for continuity, with one wall
and three veils. Here I have observed that
you must indeed follow children around,
endlessly, or they will kill themselves
at every opportunity.

Portrait

The thing to avoid is in that frame,
the reasoned screen fixing light
and shade in pithy squares of shape.
A man sitting outside in a wood chair,
his shirt is brighter than the page
he squints at. The book has browned,
like skin, with exposure. There is
the indispensable one. If
it is this easy to paint

objects why not call it
portraiture? The hunch
of shoulder, the magnet
of the subject at the center, hedged
around with frets and greenery.

Diminishing and cantilevered
(staying out of my way)
on the gentle slope. Leaving,
when he comes indoors
for respite, a charred spot.

I have changed the wrong thing.
The pang of fixity, a bleached
and empty rocker. If he can burn
so resolutely in a fraction
of the doorway, in the cool hewing
of the garden, then why not call it
martyrdom?

from The King Will Ride

Stephen Clark

ROBERTO IN THE GARDEN

Mrs. Rachelina's property was typical of the crumbling Latin aristocracies. A somewhat jumbled garden, unkempt, but practical—they ate the fruit—to the east of a nineteenth-century house which was large and mostly empty. The hall-ways were airy, long and much too wide, and the rooms made one feel small because of the lack of furniture. The rugs were Persian but worn, the lampshades were different sizes, the fireplace unused. It was a house where the money had run out, leaving its dying scent. Mrs. Rachelina was a reflection of this environment. She was beautiful in a severe way, a woman with her hands in the garden not only on Sundays, but every day and at no particular time, hands in the dirt not as affectation, but for quotidian use. Infamously tight with her checkbook, she was a pernicious bargainer. She ran the house, and if El Señor Rachelina were alive, it'd be the same because she'd always been this way, and if her husband's death had any effect on her whatever (many said it didn't) it was only to reemphasize her characteristics. She became more severe, more beautiful, more tight and so forth. When William Santand's wife died, friends hinted the two might roll around in a little yellow bed once or twice a week, but neither seemed interested. Mrs. Rachelina was not the sort of woman to take on a lover. And remarriage? She likened that to taking on a child and was past the patience: she had no more nurturing disdain to dispense on men. As for William, no one knew much about him. He showed such little sorrow at his wife's death, people questioned whether it was from excess or lack of grief.

Tonight there was more bustle in the house than usual. Mrs. Rachelina on many other occasions hustled in the kitchen before a dinner party, and at times forgot to take off her apron, which she did once while hosting a dinner for the mayor two winters ago upon his reelection. The mayor had laughed in his bombastic way, "My darling, is that culinary garb?" She replied, "If I don't look too awful, you'll let me keep it on." She didn't look awful. The most beautiful woman at the table by far, and her lack of care for her beauty only accentuated it.

Mrs. Rachelina was dressed up, more than usual anyway. She was wearing colors. She'd made an effort. And at the head of the table, which had been polished that day, in front of one long candle, its companion long at the other end, Mrs. Rachelina, alert, heron-like, directed conversation among five guests.

It was an odd group. There was a bald man, Don Juibito, who refused to take off his tricornered hat, which had an enormous pink ostrich feather in the band, one of the few openly homosexual men accepted in society. He was once married to Mrs. Rachelina's best friend's sister, Hulda. Hulda had died from ovarian cancer (maligners said from lack of loving intercourse), and Don Juibito had gone madly *maricón*. No lovers, though (at least none he brought around) and since he was old, the husbands of decent women didn't have to visualize indecorous positions, man-on-man touching and

so forth. Don Juibito was accepted as *eccentric*. Next to him
sat Doña Berta, who was a splendidly fat woman with the
flashy quirk of wearing all her jewels whenever she left her
apartment. A diamond ring on every finger and six broaches
across a black cheongsam, she was the Madame of the redoubt-
able House of Kitty. Mrs. Rachelina's oldest friend. Her father
had lost his fortune in a shipping venture when she was
eighteen. A distant aunt, who'd been educated at Radcliffe
and married a fisherman from the Colombian coast, had
offered to pay her college tuition in the States—Doña Berta
refused, saying all Americans reminded her of cotton candy
and she hadn't a sweet tooth. She went into business for
herself. Attractive at the time, slender almost, she had no
problem finding customers, and within two years she'd begun
her tiny empire of the flesh. When her friends found out,
they all turned their backs, except Mrs. Rachelina. *There's
no difference between the two of us.* And it was mostly for
her that Mrs. Rachelina entertained, a party every two weeks
or so, because Doña Berta wasn't invited anywhere else. Ironically, everyone loved her company (her wicked and foul
mouth), and she was the reason why every few weeks guests
were elated by Mrs. Rachelina's dinner invitation, which was
delivered by hand.

Doña Berta was whispering into Bishop Cavelero's ear, a
patrician gentleman with a long nose, who looked like an
aristocratic walking bird, maybe a stork if it weren't for his
expressions, which were withdrawn and charming—a mixture
of condescending intellect and warmth. It was known that
he kept a mistress, with whom he'd been in love since she
bombarded him with water balloons from an abandoned cam-
panile at age ten. In his twenties, so painful was this variety
of forbidden love that he'd cut his legs at night with a razor "to
bleed her out of him" and now, in his sixties, the mishmash of
longing and ache had eased, and so had he . . . into comfortably spending Tuesdays and Thursdays at her place in torrid
afternoons of lovemaking. The neighbors would look up at the
stomping above and carryings-on, muttering to themselves, *I
suppose the Madame is in confession again. How she loves
to confess!* and then giggle into their sleeves on Sundays,

imagining a puckish glint that the better side of God's nature
had placed in the bishop's sensuous brown eyes.

These were Mrs. Rachelina's favorites. And they sipped
amontillado while waiting for the *cordero*, which Mrs. Rachelina was slicing, her knife-hand's thumb sliding along her
other index finger.

At the south side of the house, past the south side of the
table, a boy was looking through the bottom right window-
pane. In the equatorial darkness of the garden, a flicker of
candlelight shone off one of his eyes, which were bright and
focused not on the bishop, nor William, nor Doña Berta nor
the elegant hostess, but on the woman sitting to the right of
Mrs. Rachelina, and who'd said nothing and around whom
the conversation seemed to revolve. She had perfect posture
(not rigid but firm) and was perhaps small-boned. Roberto
couldn't tell the color of her eyes; he imagined they'd be
always changing as if accompanying a certain music, maybe
a vibrant, gray-green, slow moving but infinitely changing,
drawing deeper into themselves like a well filled with lagoon
water. She was younger than the others at the table though
older than Roberto might guess. He'd have said twenty, but
she was closer to thirty. There was something shy and timid
about her, comfortably shy and timid, that commanded more
attention than the colorful peacocks who surrounded her. She
lent them a salutary hue, and her silence contributed to a
general feeling of well-being and seemed to draw out the
others' essential characteristics. Don Juibito was more flam-
boyant than ever, the bishop was regaled in his own patrician
sensuality, and Doña Berta's diamonds glittered as sharp as
her talk. Roberto rested the top of his forehead against the
coolness of the glass. He longed to hear her voice. Instead
he had to watch, only hearing a kind of compressed laughter
when they all joined in; when they did, he looked to see how
she'd open her mouth.

Leaning back in his chair, Don Juibito fingered the ostrich feather.

"No, it's impossible. It's impossible to care for a life at
all, if you don't see how it ends. It has to end with flair,

panache, something witty. With a ribbon tied. If you die without the ribbon tied, it's a loose life. It comes down to those last few minutes."

Mrs. Rachelina shrugged as if to say, *Latinos can only talk of death.*

"What's wrong with a loose life, *maricón*," Doña Berta said, flashing her teeth at him. "A loose life's a life of angels, and when I go it'll be with one of those waiters from the *Casa Blanca* with all my ribbons untied." She rolled her eyes at him.

"But you've earned that end. You earned it because all your life has been untied, so it'd be the logical conclusion. And no, there'd be nothing wrong with that, a life that begins with laughter should end in laughter," Don Juibito added sententiously and wheezed. "We have to die with strong bones, make the same exit as entrance, so we come full circle, so we exit at the completion of that circle, which is precisely where it began." Don Juibito looked at Doña Berta, "You've lived life from the loins and you'll die from the lions. In fact, I can see all your deaths." He made a sweeping gesture with his hand. "How they'll occur. I see it now. It's easy to see."

Bishop Cavelero said, "I used to play this game when I drank a lot. I'd drunk myself into another place, a kind of shit-faced clarity."

"What *paja*!" Doña Berta said.

"Yes," Don Juibito started excitedly, ignoring Doña Berta, "so if you want to know your deaths—"

"He's dying to tell us," Doña Berta added.

"These moments happen rarely," said Don Juibito.

"Well, then start here," Mrs. Rachelina said, half entertained. "But Don Juibito, you egg, I don't want you insulting my guests."

"You're easy. You're going to die in a forest, there'll be birds in the sky over thick, green trees. Not in this God-forsaken country. Somewhere in the north, maybe northern Europe. You'll die five years after you've found the love of your life. There's only one. You'll die complete, having experienced everything you were meant to. Everything. Three people will mourn you; two of them are seated at this table, the third, you haven't met, and this will be the man with whom you fall in love. Mature love, not necessarily wifely love. You won't marry him. It'll be the love that makes sense and is rational and serene in the other person's, and immaculate and necessary, because under that once-in-a-lifetime spell you realize you're happy while it occurs. You wake up and say 'I feel good' *slowly* to yourself, saying, 'This is it. I'm complete.' You're not anxious whenever he leaves for a night or two. None of 'I hope the car won't crash,' or ' . . . the jet,' or ' . . . if he has a heart thing . . .' I'm digressing. You'll die in a forest on a clear day. Autumn, only beginning to get cold. You'll be walking alone, after breakfast. Your man will be working in the house at a table with a green lamp. Quiet in the woods. You'll sit down and fall asleep. During that sleep, your heart will stop. Later people will say it was a heart attack (uncommon with women) though we'll know, at this table, at least, that it was because you were so content, your heart forgot to beat."

"Ach! . . . Romantics disgust me, even more than faggots," Doña Berta said.

"A woman my age doesn't find love, she escapes it. I've never been one for walking in the woods like a seventeen-year-old virgin," said Mrs. Rachelina.

"Bullshit," Don Juibito said.

Mrs. Rachelina looked around the table.

"Should our tipsy prophet continue . . . ? Who's next? Bishop? How will the bishop die?"

"The bishop, my friends, will die a heretic. The bishop's sixty now. In the next three years he'll have a crisis of faith so large, he'll scorch his soutane . . . he'll pulverize his pallium, chastise his chasuble . . ." Don Juibito breathed dramatically.

"Cremate his cross," Doña berta said.

"Or his crosier," laughed Mrs. Rachelina.

"Lacerate his Lord," Don Juibito continued. "Look at him, you don't think he's a man of upheavals. No. You see a man who probably doesn't even believe in God, a man who is slightly dissipated, a man of lazy faith. He might even secretly roll his eyes at those who talk about God (his own flock!), those who actually do *believe* in Him—yes, he probably even thinks of himself as superior, with his height and all . . . definitely, I'm right, I see it. He thinks he's about to give himself over to a comfortable age of sensuousness, and that *that* is it, that's at least what he expects—not at all! God'll rattle him one more time. How exciting, Bishop! You're not dead yet, old man. You'll have a new chapter. Your final chapter will be almost lewd, you'll swear everything off besides booze and a woman. Until now, you've loved a woman deeply, as we all know, but haven't given anything away for her. Haven't *sacrificed*. And a woman must be sacrificed for, if she's to feel loved. She's been quiet, grateful even, for the time you've allotted her, but now she'll rise, she'll demand more, and you'll be forced to choose. Not since your youth have you been forced to choose anything. You'll choose her at the cost of everything. Some at this table will take umbrage (although not seriously). You'll be complete and happy, you'll revel in it like a child who realizes he's dirty beyond despair and is, like it nor not, going to incur the beating of his life when he gets home, dives teeth first into the mud, that's what he does, he dives *teeth first into the mud*, and that's what you're doing. You ask, 'How's this full circle? I wasn't born in the mud, but by loving parents in a small town.' It's not true, you were born with a black seed in your heart. Lord knows where you received it, but you felt it so heavily, you've been running from it ever since. What'd you do? You became a priest, even worse, a bishop, laughable smock-wearer, and now you're returning. Ha! Ha! You're returning to what you were: a little black seed." Don Juibito stood up abruptly and pointed at the bishop, "Back from whence you came, Bishop Black Seed. Smile with the dirt in your teeth, Captain Dirty Molars! Your mistress will glow. She'll respect you as a man for the first time."

Mrs. Rachelina said, "Get to the death, you old queen. You've been listening to your own eloquence. The death, we only need to hear the death."

"Mrs. Rachelina, death is nothing without the performance before it . . . still if it makes you happy I'll close, or rather tell you *his* close. You, Bishop," and he settled his eyes on him, "will die smothered in grapes." He paused, "You'll die smothered in seedless grapes. It'll be the summer, and you, the night before, will have had your fill of ocean and wine. You'll have swum two miles, and called your woman a 'mermaid' in the night, while asleep. You'll startle her from sleep with that proclamation. You'll say, 'Mermaid, come swim over here.' Your mistress will respond, 'What do you want?' But you'll still be asleep, murmuring, 'Mermaid . . . give me a grape. I'm hungry,' and your mistress will pick one up off the bedside table (they'll be warm and overly ripe from last night) and squash it into your eye, saying, 'Leave me alone.' And you'll not wake up (still reeling dreamily from last night's stupor), you'll say, 'Mermaid, in my mouth, put it in my mouth with your fingers from the sea that don't smell of seaweed, but of coral figurines.' At which point your mistress will say, 'Ach! Shut up.' Then with less anger than fear, she'll say, 'Calvo, wake up, wake up, you're scaring me,' (she'll think you're losing your mind) and you'll say, 'My dear, feed me a grape for all the loves I've had. Feed me twelve grapes.' And she (since she rightfully thought she was your only love until now) in jealousy will stuff twelve grapes in your mouth, and leave slamming the door, whereupon you'll choke in your sleep."

"Why the twelve loves?" the bishop couldn't help asking.

"Maybe, you'll be in the midst of some sybaritic dream . . . How the hell would I know? But you'll die choking on twelve grapes. That's your demise."

"Pathetic," said Mrs. Rachelina. "That won't happen. You're just talking because you're drunk. You're a capital bore."

Don Juibito looked directly at his hostess. "What I've said is true. What you've said is untrue. Therein lies the difference between our sins at this moment."

"Please," said Mrs. Rachelina in a dismissive tone. "Let's have dessert and coffee in the other room." At which point she stood up and left the table, cutting the game short.

Roberto had been watching her the whole time. His feet were cold because he had forgotten his shoes. He had not noticed the bats twittering over his head, crisscrossing above the barbed wire of the fence that separated the large house from *Calle Poniente*. He couldn't understand what was happening. It was a fixation, a necessity, it was breaking open into something he didn't know existed. Now that they'd left the dining room he couldn't see them because the living room was on the second floor. He sat down on the grass, actually a mixture of mud and grass, and imagined himself coming up close to her, holding her hand and turning to her, saying, Don't you see that you know me. *Yeah*, he thought, *I'm young, but she'll know me, I can tell by looking at her that she'll know me.* He sat for another hour or two. He fantasized that she'd look out the window and see him, sitting in the dirt, looking up at the window, and feel sorry for him and say, "What are you doing down there? Come up. Come up right now." Then she'd say, "Let's go for a walk. You and I will go for a long walk and figure out why this is possible." In the middle of the walk, the boy would stoop down to a bush and pick a huge *flor de fuego*, this bright burning orange flower, and say, "I think you should have this . . . you are the most . . ." and then he caught himself. The boy sat there for a long time before he heard a door open, and the guests as they left.

When the boy's father came home, he was singing. *La señorita de ojos marones, la señorita de ojos marones es una canción, una canción.* Roberto listened from his bed. His father had only done this three times before when he was drunk. The man would try to sing in Spanish and would fill the rooms with a slow attempting-rich voice, making up words as he went.

La vida no es un sueño
Es un diamante de un cuello
De los ojos marones
Pobrecita como la quiero
Pobrecita como la pego
Mi señorita tiene ojos marones
la la la la la

Roberto fell asleep while watching the shadows of trees and bats on the dull, red tiles.

My
obvious potential was "sweater girl," and this Mamie
was beyond question. Her complexion was as clear out
as white as a gardenia, and beneath the cashmere she
was all delicious bounce when she skipped up the
walkway next door and sent me a shy, "Hi!" But I
was also shy and for weeks had made up more, playing
a role that was powerfully remote. Her mornings striptease,
as I sourly regarded it, filled me with a lust that was
all the more frustrating because, straining until my
eyes watered, I could scarcely make her out. Then there
was all her hymn singing, no consolation to a man who
had given up God pretty much for good.

I gave up God for good one evening on Saipan
the previous summer, when a small incident
produced a kind of reverse epiphany, following
which God was sucked up into the regions far
above and beyond heaven and simply devinj pooled
And I told my father about this that morning over breakfast.

What I told him, or tried to tell him, had to do with
fear. In the Marines the chief antidote to fear, especially
the inchoate fear of the unknown, of fear in the indeterminate
future — the peril, as I've already implied, of getting your
cock blown off, or having a shrapnel slice in the
bisem turn you into an instant eunuch — was to keep
busy. In the inactivity following that stress you could
ponder all the unspeakable things that might happen
to you if you were to be, as I was probably to be, in the
first wave of the landing on the mainland of Japan.
But the problem on Saipan was a total absence
of busyness. Our training exercises continued —
hardly a day went by without my having my nose in the mud
— but they noticeably slackened off, and we had more and
more time on our hands. In fact, the problem itself was
time. We knew that the invasion of Japan could not take

*A manuscript page from a work in progress tentatively
titled The Way of the Warrior.*

William Styron
The Art of Fiction CLVI

*William Styron was interviewed by this magazine over forty
years ago—actually in its fifth issue. It would seem provident*

enough that he should be interviewed again; his work since that time has placed him in the forefront of contemporary letters. In 1968, he won the Pulitzer Prize for The Confessions of Nat Turner; *in 1980, he won the American Book Award for* Sophie's Choice. *His account of depression,* Darkness Visible, *was an acclaimed best-seller. His awards and decorations are many, including the highest rank* (commandeur) *of the Légion d'honneur from France.*

It is especially timely that the interview appear in this celebratory number since Styron, a friend of the editors, wrote (in the form of a "Letter to an Editor") an outline of the magazine's principles in the first issue, back in the spring of 1953.

This interview took place last year in New York City's Ninety-second Street YMHA. The place, including the balcony, was packed.

INTERVIEWER

When William Styron was interviewed by *The Paris Review* in 1954, he was the only contemporary the editors knew who actually had written a novel. Peter Matthiessen, one of the magazine's cofounders, was working on his first novel, *Race Rock*; Harold Humes, another cofounder, was working on an astonishing novel called *The Underground City*; I was working on a children's book called *The Rabbit's Umbrella*, a classic known only to those few who have read it. Bill had written this remarkable novel, *Lie Down in Darkness*; he was the first of a younger generation of writers to join the pantheon of people interviewed by *The Paris Review*. The interview was done by Peter Matthiessen and myself in a little café called Patrick's—an odd name for a Paris café. I thought it would be interesting to ask him some of the same questions that he was asked way back then, when he was twenty-eight years old. The first question was, "Why do you write?" You said, "I wish I knew. I wanted to express myself, I guess." Do you have anything to add?

WILLIAM STYRON

I think it still applies, but I can't imagine saying anything so dopey!

INTERVIEWER

Then we asked, "Do you enjoy writing?" You said, "I certainly don't."

STYRON

That still applies—in spades. I thought that by now it would be a snap, but it's every bit as hard as it was then, if not harder. It's hard because there are vast baggages and impediments of one's personality that one has dragged through life, which intervene rather than open up one's creative energies: they come between one's desire and one's fulfillment.

INTERVIEWER

What would some of these impediments be?

STYRON

Probably in my case a chronic history of depression, for which I've become, reluctantly, famous.

INTERVIEWER

I've heard you talk about how much music has meant to you. What is your relationship with music?

STYRON

I've said before that I don't think that I would have been able to write a single word had it not been for music as a force in my life. I come from a musical family: my mother had studied voice in Vienna and she played music a lot. We had a primitive phonograph on which she played classical music, baroque music, romantic music; and she often accompanied herself on piano. I was immersed in music from the beginning and I never lost the sense that music is the ultimate inspiration—the wellspring for my creativity. I became enrap-

tured in my early youth by country and western, then called
hillbilly music. I remember how appalled my mother and
father were when they found out that I was in love with
hillbilly music. It disturbed them a little. But for me music has
an eclectic appeal—classical, country, jazz, the swing music of
the forties, some of the rousing Protestant hymns. At their
best all of these modes can transport me.

INTERVIEWER

Would you rather have been a pianist or a guitar player
than a writer? Surely it must have crossed your mind?

STYRON

No, I don't think I have the gift for that, although I can
still play the harmonica, a talent I acquired when I was around
six. Also, my singing voice is reasonably melodious.

INTERVIEWER

What is the connection between music and writing?

STYRON

I think it's the emotion. For many years one of the touch-
stones of my musical experience has been the *Sinfonia Con-
certante* of Mozart for violin and viola. It runs the gamut of
human emotion. It's like opening up windows onto all the
magic in the world. I still play it regularly after all these years,
responding to it as a writer in terms of the inspiration that
it provides me. But there are dozens of compositions—not
all of them classical—that come close to affecting me with
the same power. In the proper mood I have been as deeply
moved by a ballad sung by Emmylou Harris as by the
Missa Solemnis.

INTERVIEWER

In your first interview we asked how you start a novel—with
plot or character—and you said with character. Does that
remain the same?

STYRON

That's a good question, and I'm glad you repeated it because I do think that ultimately character is the sine qua non of fiction. Certainly there are other factors—a captivating prose style, narrative power. But in the end I think that we remember great works of fiction by the characters. For example, I think that Madame Bovary will forever be lodged in my memory because she is the quintessential nineteenth-century French woman who was just dreamed out of Flaubert's mind and slapped down on the page with such authority and passion and reality—she's more alive than most people I've ever met. Flaubert had a magnificent prose style and he had irony and wit, but basically it was the creation of this tragic woman that makes the book immortal. I think that this is true for most works of fiction.

INTERVIEWER

You start with a character in mind. Does that character change as you go along? Take *Sophie's Choice* for example.

STYRON

There's a scene near the beginning of *Sophie's Choice* about Sophie's childhood in Poland, and she begins to talk about her father. I was trying to establish her personality through the memory she had of Poland and her father. As this monologue unspooled and I wrote it down, I began to feel as if I were listening to an actual voice. She tells how her father—a professor at the Jagiellonian University in Cracow—had become a passionate fighter during the war to save Jews from the depredations of the Nazis. Then the most amazing thing happened: I suddenly said to myself, "This woman is lying to me; this fictional character that I'm creating is telling me a lie. This couldn't be!" I knew I had to wait for a long time in the book to reveal it, but I realized that her father was in reality a vicious anti-Semite. This is what I mean about the autonomy of the character: how characters become more real than real. What amazed me was that I discovered this

about this young woman even as I was writing—this revelation
came out of the blue. But I was totally convinced that she
was telling the truth first, and I only realized in my inner
self that she was lying. That to me is a testimony of the ability
for characters in a novel—at least of the kind I was writing—to
take on a life of their own.

INTERVIEWER

Have you had epiphanies of that sort in other books?

STYRON

Nothing quite so striking. But there have been certain
scenes in all my works that came to me with such mysterious
ease—with the sense of being preordained—that I can only
attribute them to the same powerful subconscious process.

INTERVIEWER

We asked if you felt yourself in competition with other
writers.

STYRON

Only with Norman Mailer back then. As a matter of fact,
I wasn't nearly as much in competition with him then as I
later became. By the time I wrote *The Long March* I felt that
there was no need for competition with someone as generous
hearted as Mailer, who was one of the first people to write
me a fan letter about that novel. I think that competition is
foolish. We're all in this game together. There's always a
sense of rivalry, which is hardly unnatural—we want to achieve
on our own—but, ultimately, I think that it's hard enough
to write as it is. It's such a difficult occupation that we should
give support to our fellow writers rather than not—I'm enormously pleased when one of my contemporaries comes out
with a good book because it means, among other things, that
the written word is gaining force. It's good for us to be
throwing these fine novels into the cultural cornucopia.

Are you worried about the future of the written word?

STYRON
Not really. I get moments of alarm. Not long ago I received
in the mail a doctoral thesis entitled: "*Sophie's Choice*: A
Jungian Perspective," which I sat down to read. It was quite
a long document. In the first paragraph it said, "In this thesis
my point of reference throughout will be the Alan J. Pakula
movie of *Sophie's Choice*." There was a footnote, which I
swear to you said, "Where the movie is obscure I will refer
to William Styron's novel for clarification." This idiocy laid
a pall over my life for a dark brief time because it brought
back all these bugaboos we have about the written word. But
in the nineteenth century they said that the railroads were
going to jeopardize the written word; in the 1920s they said
that the appearance of sound movies was guaranteed to drive
novels into purdah; then later, television. All of these means
of communication have existed happily side by side and paral-
lel with writing. I don't think for a minute that literature is
going to perish. Marshall McLuhan's prophecy of forty years
ago simply didn't pan out. Even the internet and the idea
of the electronic book reinforces my belief: they will not
threaten the written word but actually complement writing,
and perhaps even ultimately enhance it.

INTERVIEWER
The last question we asked you in Patrick's café was about
the purpose of the young writer—should he not be as concerned with the storytelling aspects as with the problems of
the contemporary world. You said, "It seems to me that only
a great satirist can tackle the world problems and articulate
them. Most writers would simply write out of some interior
need, and that I think is the answer." You went on to say,
"A great writer, writing out of this need, will give substance
to, and perhaps even explain, all the problems of the world
without even knowing it, until a scholar comes along one

hundred years after he's dead and digs up some symbols. The purpose of the young writer is to write, and he shouldn't drink too much."

I was very cocky in those days. But I do think that my own work has been a demonstration of part of that question. I think that the works I've written since then have been in themselves engagé, which is to say that I have dealt the best I could with some very desperate and pressing issues of the twentieth century. I didn't have an idea in mind of transmitting a message in a propagandistic way. I think that both *The Confessions of Nat Turner* and *Sophie's Choice* are literary works, or works of art even (I would like to think so), that have treated very important issues with some style and some substance.

You must have been profoundly disturbed at the reaction of some black Americans to *Nat Turner*.

I didn't think that I was going to get that kind of reaction because I had written the book with the notion that I could tell people what slavery was like by trying to impersonate a black man, namely Nat Turner, and, through his sufferings and travails and miseries, demonstrate what the horror of the institution of slavery was in this country. I did my best, and for my pains I got really trounced by black critics.

I think they felt it was terribly presumptuous for a white man to try to appropriate the persona of a black person. They had been called *negroes* until a few years before the publication of *Nat Turner*; suddenly they were *blacks*, and blacks wanted to reaffirm their own history and their own identity. Along came a white guy and ran away with the little black boy's marbles once again. It was very tough for them to see a book that tried to interpret their history mount to the top of the best-seller list, get the Pulitzer Prize. In fact, I think most of them must have said, "Why haven't *we* done this?" There was a great deal of resentment for that very reason. I also think it was convenient to use that book as an example of a white man's arrogance and to lambaste it for that very reason. It was a trying time for me, and the black boycott against the book lasted for years. I'm pleased to say, however, that recently I've noticed a distinct shift in opinion among a number of leading black intellectuals—Henry Louis Gates, Jr., and Cornel West among others—who have endorsed the book and I think helped make way for its acceptance in the black community.

INTERVIEWER

What did Jimmy Baldwin think of *Nat Turner*? He lived in your guest house for a while, did he not?

STYRON

Jimmy was my good friend and he was all for the idea. He encouraged me to write from the point of view of a black man because he himself was writing from the point of view of white men and women in *Giovanni's Room*.

INTERVIEWER

How did you plunge into the mind of Nat Turner?

STYRON

I would never have written a book having to do with Harlem or contemporary black experience because I didn't know the idiom—I don't know the idiom now. But I felt that writing about slavery in 1831 in Virginia was to deal with an area of experience in which I was as knowledgeable as a black person because the lifestyle and the manner of speaking—indeed the entire culture—were entirely accessible to me, no more or less than to a black writer. Also, it seemed to me that for a black to deny me the attempt to enter a black skin would be to deny our common humanity.

INTERVIEWER
Did Baldwin look at the text as you wrote it?

STYRON
No. By that time Jimmy had moved on to other living quarters and was traveling around a great deal. He had become an enormously famous figure. He didn't read the text until after the book was published. His remark, to *Newsweek* I think, was quite prophetic: "Bill's going to get it, from blacks *and* whites." He was right.

INTERVIEWER
Who have been your mentors over the years?

STYRON
A great professor at Duke, William Blackburn, and an editor and publisher, Hiram Haydn, who was my guide and mentor for *Lie Down in Darkness*.

INTERVIEWER
What is the relationship between editor and writer, in your case particularly?

STYRON
I think that of a mentor. There was an interesting book published some years ago by a Yale psychologist, *The Seasons of a Man's Life*, the thesis of which was that people who succeed in any aspect of life usually have a mentor who comes along at a propitious moment. He wasn't talking specifically about intellectuals or educated people, either—he was talking about plumbers, streetcar conductors. People—both men and women—who find themselves at a satisfactory level in life usually have a mentor to help them rise to that place.

INTERVIEWER
How much did Haydn, for example, have to do with your work? Would he advise changes in structure or character?

STYRON

Very little. I've always had editors who don't tamper with my work. I've maintained a fierce independence about my own writing and I've had great editors who see that independence. Both Haydn and my present editor, Bob Loomis at Random House, have had the same genius for catching me out in my weakest or most slipshod moments, but never tried to impose their ideas on mine. It's the moral support that's been so valuable.

INTERVIEWER

Could you write at all during your years of depression?

STYRON

No, I was in a shutdown. Clinical depression is the antithesis of creativity: everything in the mind is in deep stagnation. It's like a fog moving in over the intellect. I once wrote that one's intellect blurs into stupidity during a siege of major depression, and so creative work is simply impossible. Unfortunately, too, the chronic aspect of the milder depression I've suffered from has made serious inroads on my productivity. It's a little like having a V-8 engine running on four cylinders, and it has sapped my creative juices during much of my life. How wonderful it's been, however, to make these various breakthroughs and feel the power of creation, which is a great joy indeed.

INTERVIEWER

You've met many people in high places: John F. Kennedy and François Mitterrand and President Clinton. Your friendship with Mitterrand is particularly interesting. The French are very fond of your books. Why do you think this is?

STYRON

I think that one of the reasons I've been so well received in France is that I have been excellently translated. My first works were translated by Maurice Edgar Coindreau, who was

Faulkner's translator and something of a genius. He came across *Set this House on Fire* when he was teaching at Princeton and greatly admired it and wrote to Gaston Gallimard that he must translate it. He did, and it was a huge success in France. Ever since then I've felt very much at home in France.

INTERVIEWER

And Mitterrand read it and invited you around for supper.

STYRON

It wasn't quite as direct as that. During Mitterrand's first campaign for president he spent most of his time reading (in French; he read no English) *Sophie's Choice*, which he liked a lot. I learned that through the grapevine. He invited me and Arthur Miller to his inaugural. We had a fine time, and Mitterrand took time to spend an evening or two with me during those festivities to talk about literature, which was his passion. Politics, he told me, was merely his hobby. It was very invigorating after our having just elected Ronald Reagan. I might add that in a recent memoir about Mitterrand he was quoted as saying that he found Reagan both "a dullard" and "a complete nonentity." Bill Clinton, on the other hand, he greatly admired—among other things for his "animality." I like that word.

INTERVIEWER

You also spent an evening with Reagan, didn't you?

STYRON

It was an evening at Katharine Graham's right during the Libyan crisis, a rather sorry moment. After dinner we lolled around the coffee table, and Reagan sat there for forty-five minutes spinning out tale after tale about Hollywood in the thirties with George Burns and the Warner brothers and the Marx brothers. All of this was good up to a point, but we really wanted to know what the hell was going on in Libya. He didn't; he wanted to talk about George Burns and Gracie

Allen. I was sitting next to Mike Nichols, who looked over at me and mouthed the words: *It's a nightmare!* Can you believe this: there is a Republican congressman who has seriously proposed a bill to have Reagan placed on Mount Rushmore.

INTERVIEWER

And President Clinton? He compares much better—is he a Mitterrand sort?

STYRON

Clinton cares about literature and is extremely well-read. We had a fine lunch at our house in Martha's Vineyard several years ago—he'd passed word along that he would like to meet Gabriel García Márquez, who is a friend of mine, and Carlos Fuentes; they came to the Vineyard and we had a great time. García Márquez and Fuentes wanted to lean on Clinton about the Cuba embargo, but I could see a look of boredom crossing Clinton's eyes. A friend of mine, Bill Luers, a diplomat, sensed what was going on and very cleverly changed the conversation to books. At which point Clinton took fire. We played a game about what's your favorite novel. He wanted to talk about books the whole evening, which is pretty refreshing.

INTERVIEWER

Better than stories about Gracie Allen and George Burns.

STYRON

A bit better, yes.

INTERVIEWER

What was Clinton's favorite novel?

STYRON

He said *The Sound and the Fury*, and within seconds, in an appropriate way, began to quote verbatim some remarkable lines from Faulkner. García Márquez's favorite novel was

The Count of Monte Cristo; Fuentes's was *Don Quixote*; and mine was *Huckleberry Finn*, naturally.

INTERVIEWER

If you had to build a sort of composite writer, what attributes would you give him?

STYRON

I don't know exactly, but first would be a background in reading. A writer must have read an enormous amount by the time he begins to write. I remember when I first wanted to be a writer, at the age of eighteen, just immersing myself in books—marauding forays I made at the Duke University library. I read everything I could get my hands on. I read promiscuously: I read poetry; I read drama; I read novel after novel. I read until I realized I was causing damage to my eyes. It was a kind of runaway lust.

The second thing is that you must love language. You must adore language—cherish it, and play with it and love what it does. You have to have a vocabulary. So many writers who disappoint me don't have a vocabulary—they don't seem to have much feeling for words.

Those are two of the most important things for a writer. The rest is passion and vision; and it's important, I think, to have a theme. Melville said, probably in a grandiose way, "To write a mighty book you must have a mighty theme." I do think there is something to that. You need not have a grandiose theme but you must have an important theme. You must be trying to write about important things, although a truly fine writer will deal with seemingly unimportant matters and make them transcendentally important.

—George Plimpton

The Yearbook

Ron Nyren

Ryan spent an entire afternoon at the medical school searching for what his inventory sheet described as a "stereotaxic with
dog-monkey adapters." Secretaries and doctors kept referring
him to second-floor laboratories, fifth-floor offices, subterra-
nean corridors. At last, in the basement carpentry shop the
carpenters told him that they had just built a platform for
the device, which was on order. The sawdust on the shop
floor reminded Ryan of gerbil cages. Although it was against
department policy, he put his numbered sticker on the platform and bicycled home, clipboard balanced on the handle-
bars, inventory sheets waving in the wind.

This was a Tuesday in June, and here, along the New
England coast, the air was taking on its usual damp summer
feel. Unable to sublet his half of the apartment, he could
not leave until summer's end. He felt he knew precisely what
he wanted to do next with his life: move to Chicago, spend
weekends at blues clubs and the Art Institute, apply to chiropractic school. The spine had always struck him as the body's

core, the tightrope along which happiness flickered, and he wanted to touch and free and ease the fragile filament of it.

When he unlocked his front door, he saw that a blue plastic milk crate, full of books and other items, had appeared on the floor of the empty second bedroom. On top lay a folded white dress shirt, one sleeve trailing over the side, the unbuttoned cuff resting on the dusty wooden floor. "Curtis?" he called, and then went into the living room to lie on the couch. His feet burned, remembering the day's long corridors. When he woke an hour later he knew he was still alone. Solitude always gave the air a certain texture.

No more boxes appeared the next day, or the next. Thursday evening, a woman called and asked for Curtis.

"He's not in," Ryan said.

She told him her name was Johnsia, which she had to spell for him twice.

"That's an unusual name," he said.

"There were dozens of Johnsias in my neighborhood growing up. We got confused with each other all the time." She spoke in such a somber tone that for a moment he nearly believed her. Her voice had the faintest hint of a speech impediment, which took the edge off consonants and made him think of butterscotch. "I've changed my mind," she said, "Don't let him know I called. When do you think he'll be in?"

"I have no idea," Ryan said. "He was supposed to move in last week. I don't know anything else about him. My previous roommate arranged the details."

There was a long pause. "You haven't even met him?"

Ryan felt himself blush. "It all happened at the last minute."

The apartment was on the second floor, on a busy intersection, just above a small breakfast eatery. Each morning Ryan woke hungry, the odor of frying sausage and eggs drifting up through the floorboards and insinuating itself into his bedclothes. Each morning he bicycled to the university inventory department, picked up his clipboard of numbered stickers and went from department to department tracking down

newly purchased equipment. Graduate students let him into
biology labs so he could place stickers on weighing scales
and blood plasma separators; secretaries took him through
underground passages into windowless computer labs. He'd
majored in humanities; he liked seeing a side of the university
that he'd never encountered.

When Johnsia called again a few nights later, he asked her
to describe Curtis.

"We weren't close for a long time," she said. "We were
too close. Too close to get to know each other, does that
make sense?" Although her words expressed doubt, she spoke
without hesitation, as if she felt certain even about uncer-
tainty. "I haven't spoken to him in a long while. I've been
out of town. I don't know why I'm calling for him now. I'm
not sure he'd want me to call."

Ryan sat down in the frayed wicker chair by the phone.

"I tried his old number," she continued. "One of those
electronic voices told me to call here. The kind that over-
enunciates, as if you were a stupid child." She laughed.

"If you give me your phone number," he said, "I'll let
you know when he arrives. I won't tell him anything."

She laughed again. "So, you like complicity." Perhaps it
was an accent that colored her voice—the way she said the
letter *s*, not in a lisp, but with an enlarged sibilance.

He paused. "That's one way to put it. Yes. I've always
liked complicity."

Later, he went into the empty second bedroom. His previous roommate had taken everything, even the cover to the
overhead lamp, so that only a bare bulb hung down. A
dustpan with gray fluff in it remained in the corner near the
closet. He bent over the blue milk crate and lifted the shirt that
covered it. Underneath lay a thesaurus, six worn paperback
thrillers, an alarm clock wrapped in its cord, a box of fluores-
cent crayons, a white silk scarf, a high-school yearbook, a
sweatshirt and a carton of one hundred plain white envelopes
with an automatic pencil sticking out of it. He fingered the
scarf, then put everything back. The shirt he folded neatly

and returned to the top and then, before he stood up fully, he crouched again and pulled out the sleeve so that it spilled down the side of the crate.

The next time she called, he said, "I looked through some of his belongings."

He heard—he thought—the faintest change of breath, even though her voice remained cool.

"He's moved in then?"

"Only one blue milk crate that's been here for several days. Not much in it. Some clothes, some envelopes, his high-school yearbook, crayons."

"I can't tell you how curious I am to see what he looked like in high school. He never showed me any photographs of himself from earlier points in his life."

He was now beginning to detect an ironic tone in the formal shapings of some of her sentences. Perhaps she had grown up, as he had, in a working-class family in a working-class town, had gone to a prestigious university, had adapted without allowing herself to be impressed.

"Would you like to meet somewhere?" he asked. "I could show you the yearbook."

After a delay—he imagined her caught by surprise and having to recalibrate her tone of amusement—she answered. "All right. Let's meet then, and you can show me the yearbook. That sounds dangerous. For you, I mean. He's likely to show up just when you're carrying it out the door."

The next morning, Friday, a light drizzle fell, and he was not assigned to tag any equipment. Instead, he had to type into a computer those items that he and previous inventory clerks had successfully tagged, along with the corresponding numbers. There was a backlog of data to enter. He worked on an ancient terminal, whose monitor displayed skeletal green letters on a black background. The items that the other clerks had tagged sounded much more interesting than the ones he had been assigned: cell disruption bomb, cast acrylic head phantom hole, lesion maker. Deep in the physics, chemistry and biology labs of the university, life had attained a complexity not found in the rest of world, where coffee cups, sneakers, mayonnaise and paper clips had all become so familiar that they faded, hardly existed. He felt that now he understood something about the need for scientific inquiry: it provided reasons for new devices, for new terminology, for throwing out the old. Who could imagine a need to make lesions? Yet a need had been found, an instrument manufactured.

The rain had stopped by the time he left work, leaving the air cooler and less steamy. He dried off his bicycle seat with a Kleenex and rode home. For dinner he made curried potatoes with chutney and eggplant salad, and drank a glass of red wine. It was important, he believed, to treat oneself well, so that one would feel comfortable treating others well. When the time came, he retrieved the yearbook from the empty second bedroom. The blue ink had rubbed off the raised letters on the cover, which was made of a gray leatherlike substance that felt slightly greasy. Only by holding it to the light could he read BELL SPRINGS PUBLIC HIGH SCHOOL.

She was standing just outside the café when he approached. They had not exchanged descriptions, but he recognized her immediately by the intense way she slouched. She was perhaps a few years older than he. She wore denim cutoffs, a lemon-colored T-shirt, and a loose black long-sleeve shirt, unbuttoned down the front. Her short brown hair fell so straight and fine that the tips of her ears poked through. A hollowness to her face suggested either an illness in her recent past or a metabolism in overdrive. When they shook hands, he noticed two black threads protruding from her sleeve like antennae.

He liked her eyes, brown, solemn and, in a certain sense, *fat*, as if in contradiction to the ascetic lines of her body; they did not waver from looking at him.

"Let's have some coffee," she said, and held the door for him.

None of the café's chairs matched, and all seemed to have been bought at garage sales or fished out of junkyards. Johnsia did not order coffee, but rather iced tea, and he followed

suit. When they looked around for a table to sit at, he headed
for one with two huge, overstuffed maroon leather chairs next
to each other. They made him feel cozy.

"What do you do for a living?" he asked. Immediately her
eyes became less interesting; he could see it was the wrong
kind of question to ask.

"I work for the electric company," she said. "I read electric meters."

They did not speak as they sipped their drinks. In the
corner, two middle-aged women played chess. By the windows, a teenager with freshly-trimmed-looking hair sat alone,
slurping from a mug with a guilty air, as if at any minute
someone might require him to show proof he was old enough
to drink coffee. The only sounds were the groans of buses
passing outside, the tinkling of ice cubes in glasses and the
occasional felt-muffled whack of a chessman moving into
battle.

Johnsia slid the yearbook toward her and began leafing
through the pages. He leaned in next to her and they examined the rows of photographs, all polished with a professional
sheen that only highlighted the not-yet-fully-grown faces.
The smiles looked forced, or else naïve. The students with
mustaches had rushed things, and those with perfectly coiffed
hair had only called attention to the immaturity of their
foreheads, their cheekbones. Their eyes gave everything away.
One could tell at a glance who had organized the prom and
who had avoided it. One could tell at a glance who had had
sex and who had not.

Johnsia turned pages idly and then stopped. Curtis faced
the camera with closed eyes. He wore braces, even at seventeen, but grinned as if he didn't care, or perhaps as if—the
heavy eyebrows suggested this—he were flashing weaponry.
Despite the expression, his face was handsome: something in
the line of the jaw, the soft mounds of the eyelids, the simply
combed hair that had the rich coloration of a wheat field.

Johnsia gave an amused snort, riffled the remaining pages
with her thumb and closed the book. She slid it back to him.

"Is that all you wanted to see?" he asked.

She shrugged.

"You're the most nonchalantly obsessed person I've ever seen."

She smiled then and gave him a steady look. "Maybe I'm simply obsessed with appearing nonchalant." She tapped the book with her short, white fingernails. "I don't know, do I seem obsessed with him? I'm not sure I liked him to that great a degree. We were very close for a short while. Not much more than a month. When it's that short a time, when you spend almost every day with someone and then break it off, you feel as if you've missed something. Even if you probably haven't."

He nodded and suggested they go for a walk through the town green. The lamps had come on, even though dusk had hardly fallen, and their white globes made him think, *Too many moons*. The rain earlier in the day had darkened the wooden benches. He talked about his childhood, thinking that perhaps it would be elemental enough to interest her—he told her how, when he was very young, he would stand with his ankles in his grandfather's pond and place a leaf in the shallows; then he stirred up sand with his foot and, when the water cleared, the leaf seemed to have vanished, as if by magic. She told him of the yearly festival in her hometown, in the autumn, devoted to apples, with a parade and booths selling pies and fritters and cider and turnovers, even apple soup; when she was sixteen she had refused the nomination to be the Apple Queen because she had gotten sick of apples. She seemed to relax in his presence. He was not tall; he told her he had been called elfin in the past because of the single black eyebrow that ran across his forehead, and because of the slightly springy way he walked. He could sense that she found him appealing. She touched his arm, and they stopped at a restaurant whose tables were covered with checked tablecloths. They drank red wine. He wanted to get rid of the yearbook, perhaps leave it on the empty chair next to him. She reached across the table and pushed aside the thick black hair along the side of his head; he asked her what she was doing and she said she wanted to check to make sure he did not have pointed ears; he laughed. Wine only made him more aware of her hands, long and thin and prone to folding and unfolding with languid motions. He forgot about the yearbook when they stood up to leave the restaurant. The waiter hurried to hand it to him as they went out the door.

In his apartment they had to wait while he drew all the curtains. The eight tall windows of his bedroom were squeezed together on three walls, with almost no space in between. He had borrowed heavy blue curtains from a friend; they lacked pull cords. He had to stand on a chair and reach with a yardstick to push the drapes together at the top where they hung from the rod. While he worked, she named each item of clothing she was removing. "Now I'm taking off my socks," she said. "Now I'm taking off my brassiere." Slowly the lights of the city were shut out, and the air took on a muffled tone. When at last he turned around and stepped down off the chair, he could not see her in the darkness, but he sensed her, so palpable he felt that he was touching her already, even before his palms brushed her skin.

Through the night, when he woke briefly and only halfway, he thought to himself that what he had been missing most, in however many months it had been, was the smell of another person close to his body. Johnsia's skin had the dark lemony flavor of cumin, the brittle, sweetened-tea aroma of dried oak leaves. He lay there in the dark with his nose near to her shoulder, and the waking and falling asleep he did only seemed to him another kind of breathing, a higher kind, in which sleep was an exhalation, and the awareness of another body an inhalation of something as essential as oxygen.

In the morning he woke to find the other side of the bed empty. For a moment he thought she had gone, but then he heard a faint clacking sound. He swung himself out of bed and walked quietly to stand in the doorway of the second bedroom. Still naked, she sat cross-legged on the floor, looking through the items in the blue milk crate. She held up the sweatshirt for scrutiny, read a page of one of the thrillers, clicked the automatic pencil to discover there was no lead in it. She unwound the alarm clock's cord and got up to plug it in. When she pressed a button, a primitive electronic voice said haltingly, "The time is 12:00 A.M."

"I remember this," she said. "Every morning, the alarm was set to announce 6:34 A.M. If we didn't wake up, it kept repeating the time, more and more loudly."

Ryan leaned his head against the door frame, feeling the hard wood through his hair. He watched her face intently, but could detect no trace of longing, nothing but a detached curiosity that made him feel sadder than longing might have—he couldn't tell if it was sadness for himself, for her or for the absent roommate, who seemed, in some dreamlike way, to have turned into nothing but these few objects, like one of those doomed characters in Greek mythology.

She even looked through the box of plain white envelopes, as if reading letters that had yet to be written. "That's all," she said, putting things back in the crate. She kept out only the green sweatshirt, which she pulled over her head. She came up and rested her forearms on his shoulders. "I wondered where my sweatshirt had gone."

"Was that what you were looking for?" he asked.

"I don't know what I was looking for." She said this with her usual deadpan, but he sensed in her voice a bewilderment he had not heard before. She drew closer and kissed him. "I was curious. You were too. You looked through his things." Kissing him repeatedly, she did not shut her eyes; this close, the brown irises of her eyes resembled live sponges under glass, contracting and expanding minutely with the dilations of the pupils. For a moment he worried, absurdly, that their eyes might touch, that their eyes had thirsty agendas of their own. He moved his hands across her body, underneath her sweatshirt, and drew her to him.

They spent nearly every night that week together. He cooked dinner for her, or she brought take-out food to his apartment, and then they spent the rest of the evening idly, in ways that he could not fully remember the next day—half-finished games of cards, rented movies whose plots lagged and then rushed to tie up loose ends, short walks around the neighborhood. Because most people involved with the university had left for the summer, the city had a certain comfortable emptiness, a roominess like an oversized bathrobe.

He managed to piece together certain facts about her: she had recently dropped out of law school; she shared an apartment with a forty-year-old Polish woman who spoke even less often than she; her mother was a driving school instructor and her father worked in a hardware store; she liked Edward Hopper paintings—she'd read somewhere that all Hopper had really wanted to paint was sunlight on the surface of a building, and she thought it amusing that so many people and dark corners had ended up in his artwork, as if he were helpless to keep them out. But she did not like to discuss her life or tell stories, and he teased her about her reticence.

"I don't have anything to hide," she said. "I just think the only things you can put into words are the dry details, and why bother? The other things, there just aren't words for."

"What other things?" he asked. She gave him a smile, half-amused, half-sad. He had become excessively sensitive to the movements of her face, because they were so small, so rare. Her mouth did not really turn up when she smiled. When she laughed she did not seem to involve her diaphragm, laughing only with her upper body. She was always touching him. In bed she liked to play with his face, moisten her finger and smooth his black eyebrows in the wrong direction, lie on top of him looking down into his eyes and fondling his ears. He had never felt so *handled* before, and he liked it, because he never detected any neediness in her; he felt she liked him without needing him. When pleasure overtook her, her eyelids slipped shut gently and her face took on the serenity of a calm lake, while a faint, drawn-out cry issued from her throat; he had never seen anyone's face *relax* at the crucial moment, it seemed humanly impossible, and it both unnerved and inflamed him.

"Do you think something happened to Curtis?" he asked.

She shrugged. They were sitting on his battered green couch, watching the sun go behind the building across the street. "He's the careless type," she said. "Maybe he's doing some traveling. He's got money from somewhere, he doesn't need it. Maybe he has a girlfriend and he's staying with her."

"What is it that made you try to get back in touch with him?"

"I don't know. I just wondered what it would be like to talk to him after a year had gone by. That's all. Have a kind of perspective. The feeling's passed. Are you jealous?" She bit her thumbnail idly.

"What about me? Do you think you've got any perspective on me?"

She did not seem to know how to answer that. She looked at him, looked away. She kept biting at the nail, examining it casually, biting it again, until he reached out and grasped her hand in his.

One night his older cousin came to town for a conference and took him to dinner. He was a metallurgist by profession, and Ryan could never remember what exactly that involved—his cousin liked to say it involved putting ragweed next to bars of iron to see if the iron sneezed. Ryan liked him, even though he kept his appearance a little too neat, in subtle ways—his fingernails always showed even half-circle slivers of white, the hair on the back of his neck was always trimmed down. Even his blue jeans seemed to have been freshly ironed. After dinner Ryan bought ice cream cones and showed the cousin the university art museum's sculpture garden, whose gates were still unlocked, as they often were, even though night had fallen. There, while they ate ice cream seated in the hollow of a twisted marble cylinder, Ryan told his cousin about Johnsia.

"Sounds like she's just waiting until the other guy shows up, and then she's planning to get back with him."

"I don't think that's it."

"Maybe she killed the guy, maybe that's what's going on. Maybe you're next."

Ryan answered this with only a look.

"She sounds a little on the relentless side, anyway. You have to be careful with women, they—"

"No, I hate that," Ryan said, standing up and almost hitting his head on the top of the cylinder. "I hate blanket generalizations like that. Women this, men that. How do I know, maybe I'm the crazy one here, maybe I'm the relentless one. I call her every day. I think about her all the time, I feel like her face has been engraved in the folds of my brain. I'm not usually like this. All right, maybe I have been a couple of times, a little, but that was when I was a teenager, when you can hardly hear yourself talk because your hormones are fizzing and popping in your ears."

His cousin clamped his hand over his mouth, then opened his fingers just wide enough to say, "I won't say anymore."

"Sorry." Ryan looked at his ice cream cone. Only the tiny point remained, with a milky dot at the bottom. He ate it and wiped his fingers with a paper napkin.

"Let's go for a beer," the cousin said. "Ice cream always makes me think of beer, I don't know why."

Ryan didn't get home until after 11:30. He did not turn on any lights. He went about the apartment pushing all the curtains closed. At the last window, his foot slipped on the chair he used as a step stool, and he fell heavily onto his desk, bruising his knee. The darkness made him feel drunker than he had thought he was. He lay still for fifteen minutes, smelling the pencil shavings on the desktop and the beer on his breath. Almost three weeks had gone by since the blue crate had arrived. All at once it occurred to him that Johnsia and Curtis had gotten in touch with each other weeks ago, that even now they were lying in bed together, laughing at him. His heart shook. He knew it was a stupid notion, but he could not rid himself of the thought. Perhaps his cousin was right, perhaps she was only waiting until Curtis finally arrived. He had not asked her enough questions about herself; he knew nothing about her; he had let her get away with mystery.

He went over to the phone and dialed Johnsia's number. "Hello?"

"He's here," he said.

There was silence. Then, casually, "So he finally showed up."

"Yes." He sat down in the wicker chair, pulled his sneakers off. "I didn't get home until 10:30. I decided I would just go to bed, call you tomorrow. But I couldn't get to sleep. It was too hot. Then I heard something at the door, someone fumbling for keys. I thought it was one of the people who live upstairs. I heard these noises, *plink plink*, like someone trying to get a key into the lock but just hitting the metal around the keyhole." With his toes he unrolled his socks off of each foot, proud of his coordination. "Then I thought, A burglar. But I knew who it must be. I went to my bedroom door and watched the front door swing open. He stood there. I couldn't see his face, just the silhouette of his body. I knew it was him. He kind of swayed there. It was clear he was drunk."

"Drunk," she said. "That would be just like him, to show up the first time drunk."

He smiled and, moving his hand over his chest, felt his heart beating rapidly. "Yes, he kind of stumbled in, and I thought he was going to forget to close the door behind him, but then he remembered. I don't think he saw me. He went over to his room, looked in for a moment. Then he came back out to the living room and started unbuttoning his shirt. It took him a while. I could hear him breathing. He took off his shirt and shoes and the rest of his clothes, everything, and then he threw himself down onto the couch and went to sleep."

"And is he still there?"

"Still there."

"What are you going to do?"

"Do?" He looked at the couch. The windows were open, a soft breeze blowing the curtains into the room fitfully, making light from the street lamp come and go over the couch's nubbly back.

"When he wakes up tomorrow morning. Are you going to kick him out?"

He listened intently to her voice, so intently he almost missed her words. He wasn't sure what he was listening for. He must have woken her up—her words sounded a little thicker than usual, and came like afterthoughts.

"What are you going to do?" she repeated.

"What do you think I should do?"

He heard a rustle and imagined she was leaning back into the pillow with the phone. "Kick him out. Tell him you've rented the room to someone else, he's forfeited it by not showing up."

He closed his eyes. Now he did not know what was true. He could picture Curtis, naked, lying on the couch, the street lamp's light curving along his back. He could picture Curtis next to Johnsia, propped up on an elbow in bed, listening to the conversation and grinning the way he had grinned in the yearbook.

"Okay," he said at last. "I'll do that."

He sat in the chair for a long while after hanging up, the wicker bumps pressing into his shoulder blades. Then he got up, undressed and went to bed.

The next day it rained again. He spent his hours at work entering data into the computer, unable to concentrate. He continually had to correct his typing. The names of tagged items seemed designed to taunt him. Rabbit pump. Forearm plethysmography system. Ethernet sniffer laptop base unit. Male reproductive system. Was that a set of pickled organs floating in a jar, or a plastic model like a child's toy?

He tried to remember the sound of her voice over the phone, whether she had caught her breath when he said Curtis had arrived. I hate this, he told himself. Why am I asking myself these questions?

That evening he ate a quick supper at a sandwich shop on the way home, then called her and asked her to come over. He didn't say anything more. She hesitated before responding, and he knew she wanted to ask questions, but she did not. When she knocked on his door he let her in without a word. She walked to the center of his living room, glanced into the empty second bedroom with its unchanged tableau. She regarded the couch, then sat down on it and studied him where he stood by the front door. He thought he could detect the slightest crease in her forehead.

"So," she said, her words coming slowly, "so, it was all a lie?"

He did not tell her about the drinking; he did not want to blame it on that.

She laughed.

He came closer to her, watching her, her hands still in her pockets, her head back, rolling along the tops of the sofa's cushions, her thin hair spreading out along the fabric. She went on laughing.

"You should be mad at me," he said.

She kicked her leg out and hooked him behind the knee, making him almost fall over. "You bet I'm mad." She kicked again, hitting his legs with the side of her sneaker, not hard, but not stopping until he moved out of reach. "I'm mad," she said, "but that was damned inventive, that little story you told. Where did you come up with that?"

He felt angry that he could not read her face. Even now she revealed so little. She must have learned secrecy at an early age. "I needed to know," he said.

"Needed to know," she repeated.

"I needed to know if it was me you kept coming for, or him."

She removed her hands from her pockets and leaned forward. After a moment, she took one of the long back cushions from the sofa and held it pressed in her lap. Then she stood up and began hitting him with it.

At first he laughed, but her strokes did not let up, and the cushion kept hitting his face, its texture rough against his skin, musty-smelling dust particles assailing his nose, and at times the zipper along the edge struck his skull like a tiny spark. "It was you, goddamn it," she said, "it was you, who

the fuck was I sleeping with? It was you." He could hardly
breathe; he sneezed twice, coughed, buckled to the floor
and found himself taking refuge under his table. The green
cushion beat against him like a wing.

At last the blows stopped. His breath came raspily, and
he sneezed twice more, half-sobbing. The inside of his throat
felt like corduroy. He coughed, and she brought a Kleenex
over and began dabbing at his face. "Jesus," she said
softly. "Jesus."

They rested for a while on the floor, their heads pressed
together at the temples, their arms around each other, their
legs askew. They both radiated heat from their faces and
hands. He could feel her start to shake at times, then stop,
then shake again, and he pressed her tightly to him. When
he felt as if he could stand, he got up, pulling her with him,
and they sat on the sofa for a while, holding each other, and
then they went into his bedroom.

Darkness had fallen, and only the streetlights illuminated
the room. On the street below the trucks were coming out
for the night, coming to wait with their rumble at the intersection, waiting for the light to change. He pulled her T-shirt
off her body but left it hanging around her neck. She removed
one of his shoes but left the other on. Though their gestures
were playful, they did not smile, as if they were actors trying
to amuse a very ill child. They struggled for a while, half-
clothed, giving each other little bites until that seemed too
dangerous, and then they divested themselves entirely.

In the morning he woke to hear her in the shower. It was
a pleasant sound, though reminiscent of the sizzle of bacon
frying, and his stomach growled at the smell of breakfast in
the eatery below. When she came out, toweling her hair, she
held out his hairbrush. "What's this sticker doing here?" she
asked. It had a bar code, and a six digit number, and announced it was the property of the university.

"I had some extras," he said sleepily. "It's time to keep
track of things around here." He dozed off again, and when
he woke, sunlight shone on his head. He threw on some
clothes and went into the living room.

She was sitting on the sofa, dressed in her shorts and shirt from the night before, her hair still wet. She had Curtis's yearbook in her lap and was leafing through the pages.

He must have said something—begun some word—because without looking up she gestured for him to come over. He sat beside her. In the back of the book, where more informal shots of students and faculty had been placed, faces glowered dully in classrooms, young bodies twisted in the air after a basketball, a physics teacher set fire to a sheaf of papers. Across these photographs, students and teachers had scrawled messages: "Curtis—I'm glad I got to know you this year—Rick," "I'm sure you'll succeed, whatever you do—Mrs. Whitlock," "You got a helluva backhand, Curt, but I still beat you on the mat—Ray," "Go Tigers!" (or perhaps—it was hard to tell from the handwriting—"Go, Tiger!").

"See?" she said.

He shook his head.

She thwacked the page with her fingernail. "He's got the same dopey things written in his yearbook as anyone else."

He nodded. "Okay." He tried to take her by the hand. "Let's have breakfast."

"No, wait." She grabbed a pen from the side table. "We can write messages."

"You're crazy."

Pressing deeply into the page, she wrote, *Curt baby—you are the one! Go get'em!*

When she handed him the pen, he hesitated. "I never even knew what to write back when it was legitimate." But he wrote *Curt* in a big looping script and then, after tapping the pen against his teeth for a moment, added, *Wish we could have gotten to know each other better*. He did not sign his name.

Monday he spent in the inventory office. When not entering data, he furtively typed letters to chiropractic colleges requesting informational materials. He knew he would have to take biology and organic chemistry courses on the side to meet the requirements. Perhaps then he would be initiated into the mysteries of equipment. He knocked on the cubicle of his boss. "Do you know what a small rodent ventilator is?" he asked, holding up the sheet. But his boss only shook his head, bemused, and leaned over his desk again.

That evening, when Ryan and Johnsia were drying the supper dishes, a key scraped in the lock and the front door opened. A voice called out, "Hello? Hello?" Both of them froze, Ryan with a cereal bowl in his hands, Johnsia with the spoons. "Hello?" The door closed and footsteps went through the living room. Ryan tried to catch Johnsia's eyes, but she was staring at the side of the refrigerator. The footsteps began to return, then stopped. Quietly, Ryan stepped to the kitchen doorway.

Curtis stood with one foot on the coffee table, the blue milk crate balanced on his knee. He wore a brown rugby shirt buttoned only at the lowest button, dark green shorts, and brand new sneakers with thick red soles. He had let his blond hair grow long—it curled up at the back of his neck, and in front it fell down over his forehead, terminating with a soft edge above the ridge of bone over the eyes. His cheekbones cast the faintest of shadows. His lower lip protruded slightly over the chin. A dried scar left a thin dotted line that ran down the shin of the right leg and disappeared into his ribbed white sock. The laces of the sneakers stood up stiffly in their bows, as if at pains to seem alert. He stood, broad-shouldered and tall, like some kind of furniture.

He was staring at the yearbook. It lay open on the coffee table, where Ryan had left it. Curtis picked it up and shoved it down the side of his crate. Then he looked up and saw Ryan watching him. Johnsia came up behind Ryan, dish towel still in her hands. When Curtis flicked his gaze to her, there was something in his eyes that Ryan could not fully interpret, something troubled and fearful and desiring, something that pulled the muscles of his face back, as if they were retreating. And then his heavy forehead seemed almost to come down like a visor, shutting off all expression. He glanced again at Ryan.

"I don't care," he said, and curled his fingers around his crate. "Why should I care?" He turned and walked out the door. He did not shut it. The key still protruded from the lock.

Ryan's heart beat fast. His scalp itched. He turned to Johnsia, could think of nothing to say. The dish towel was bunched in her hands.

"Why are you looking at me like that?" she asked, but he did not know what it was in his face that made her ask. She went into the kitchen and put away the spoons she'd dried. It seemed to take her a little longer than necessary to arrange them in the silverware drawer. When she came back out, she kissed Ryan's cheek and turned his wrist so she could read his watch. "I promised my roommate I would go with her to the movies. I should probably head out."

Ryan followed her to the door, holding the cereal bowl before his chest with both hands, as if it were a tiny steering wheel. "Call me later?" she asked.

"That inventory number you put on your hairbrush," she said, her voice apologetic, "shouldn't you peel it off?" She backed out of the room, pulling the door with her, studying him as she went. He thought that she seemed less bony than when he'd met her, that his cooking had done her some good, but her eyes were still solemn.

Robert Devlin

Orizaba

I see it like a movie screen:
salty green horizon, cloudy blue water.
You step, a pillar on the deck,
the man who wed Faustus and Helen
in verse; who, in disturbed silence,
recalled his grandmother's dead music.

Swimming: did you taste the salt water?
I find you now, sixty-three years after
you heard about their trial separation.
Your gentle step, a lover's breath,
you curse those vows of constant mist,
and tear-wet kisses below the deck.

We are friends though you are long dead,
two men, young, with lemming blood, hot
and red, roommates by those empty urns,
before noon, with wet, literary tongues.
I see your mother when she heard the news:
New York, white buildings, her outside view,
Moonlight Sonata, soft, perhaps shadowed.

Because you saw morning with broken eyes,
blackened, your cheeks and Peggy: sedated
in her bunk, truant from the morning tea.
She missed your lurch, upwards, the railing,
across the deck your view of sky, seeing
nothing, bruised knuckles on rusted alloy,
your bathrobe aside like an old gentleman.

I see you when I hear that wooden word:
the warm embracing sea, that snuggling
sickle of womankind; you rise on your toes,
perfumed with whiskey and disgrace.
Leaping, dignified, you are the greatest
gymnast who ever died—of love; Peggy
lay below deck in bed, Havana and you a poem
to hide from her husband, the Atlantic kiss;
headfirst into a starless ocean of lament.

Two Poems by Jessica Grant

The Tsar's Daughter in a Forensic Lab

He's made her ordinary, spread her slim
seventeen years across this table,
measured her tight little head,

pieced together seven-hundred bits.
There's a box for her femur and pelvis,
and one more for her ankles and vertebrae.

There's a foot in her jaw, a bayonet
above her ribs, a drill press,
an anvil, a wrench. There's a saw blade

abraded with diamonds like those
in the corset she wore under her dress,
diamonds sewn so close together

she almost survived. And there's her jaw,
its sharp corners moistened
seventy years later in the center of his lab.

She's older than this glossy green room,
air chilled so breath fogs a microscope lens,
colder than bones on top of cabinets,

already boiled free of their flesh.
He loosens his collar, warns us
of bones boiling dry, drains clogging.

He says, *My field is human bones—*
my last case was a massacre,
a tub of children's bones

lit up, it seemed, like many orange flares—
it might have made her smile
before this slow minuet

with too few men, before
that basement slaughter, poised
at once for any photograph.

Of Letters, Miss Millay

I. About Japan

When you wrote about Hotel Ikao to your mother,
eating rice and tea and tea and rice,
you were sitting again where tuners
worked all day on the piano in that "ugly
dining room" you had all to yourself—
commas and dashes and ampersands holding back
the engine of your "tion"s: arm raised
at the auc*tion*, the sta*tion*,
the giant pines moving at their own voli*tion*,

to where the response begins, where old nurse Edna
spoons Mr. Armour's "obscene concoc*tion*"
to patient Edna, absentmindedly asking if
Shelley wrote "as if" while Keats wrote "as though"—
invariably though, you knew, it's time
the bayberry bushes grew. You see, my words are not
another letter, another query of where I shall not be—
offering you a cigarette, just to be playful—
your house, 9 1 / 2 feet narrow, like a sleeve tucked into the hill.

II. About Firewood

These doors are closed. I shall not write another!
Another bathing cap filled with wood, you boasted
to nine Polish dogs you'd find on almost any beach.
What things ought to be a letter? Reminder of a missing
stove in a kitchen where a drake was once found dead—
not quite it: letters ought to chant, *And now I sing: Any food!*
like bedlamites near London, roaming the country to beg
Any food! Any pottage? Any brook to clean? How good
   of you!

It's quite a journey, isn't it, my dear? With the force
of instruction: Let clutter fill the wild raspberry patch!
And the peaches! And the dark berries! Let them reach a chord
above "dark, dark," which is "all I can find for a metaphor"
for the fatigued Mayfair Theatre where they posted
a price for huckleberries—four cents a crate—
and now you'll understand, I've escaped Cassis, too!
And this is really to ask, Will your walls guard
my thickets, too? And will you finally stop that damn chariot?

Two Poems by Cate Marvin

Mortal

How do you find yourself in literature?
All blue-eyed, drinking from green bottles.

Do you think I've done the sky right?
Or was it cloudier than blue? The canoe

is as thin as I can make it: a dry
stick hollowed to make a flute. Could you

think of something more appropriate?
Here, you make some noise with it.

Oh, famous. A tall building swept into
the Mississippi that month of flooding,

roofs like hats floating. Your flat world
then, so green and swaying, wet with muck,

fish too caught in the current to be spawning.
Should I have something about dresses

in the wind, their white skirts waving?
Once you're dry in Kansas, don't think

of thanking me. Don't come to the bar
to find me years later, when I'm bound

to drink's dark spiral, strapped in the same
way to that boat as the still Lady was

when she floated down the river's dim
expanse. Gather, instead, with the rest

of the town at the edge of the harbor.
Or find out about it later in the paper, along

with other reports of torture and death.
This won't be the last the world reads of you.

Stopping for Gas Near Cheat Lake

Trees bent unnatural by wind,
then frozen, looking delicate as jewelry, but unwearable.
Miles of white, palest skin,
and the slash of the road through it. Who named this lake,

who lost? How clear is its water
when not frozen? Do the townspeople refuse to swim in it,
or is it a site for seasonal pleasures?
At the self-serve station, the man insists on filling my tank.

Has everyone in town lost
their money, what can I buy to save them? A cigarette lighter,
a hunter's cap, windshield fluid . . .
some of my blood's origin is here—a family with white gums

and skin blue as this dusk.
Something not right about it—one year they tested vials
over and over. The doctors:
You'll need to come in again; your blood is strangely thin.

What do you know of your heritage?
The houses are red on Fairchance Lane, their windows look
away from the banks of the lake,
tree-shaded places where lovers embraced. I could stop

the car, stand in those shadows,
and try to find my face on the surface of Cheat Lake.
Or I could walk into town, find
my reflection in the eyes of a distant cousin, lead him

to the water's edge, my white face
haunting him. For those who drowned, for those who
    escaped,
I demand an answer. Tell me,
tell me where I can find the bastard who named this lake.

Two Poems by Dabney Stuart

George Herbert

I.

He speaks to me so that my whole
 drift gathers to his verse:
the page like a gravestone, his terse
 stanzas building epitaphs
that draw me to my soul—
 which I believe in even as the drafts
of disbelief shiver its poor tatters.

Though I am a shredding of other matters,
 distracted to smithereens,
he figures it to me: he has a means
 to rise lost to my longing, save
for his tuning of the sinews' tether,
 his windings earthward, his grafts of love.
No other poetry touches me so near

home, that homeless place, my placeless here.
 As graveyards were a school to him—
cursive dust rendering its shapes, a whim
 falling, until it kissed itself, his soul
repaired and flown—so his fit lines appear
 to me, a touchless Braille
I whisper to time turning, our little while.

II.

You sing wherever the exigent will
comes on its own confounding as a stranger
and welcomes him, and they are both undone
by a mercy stranger still—

                    an empty bell
ringing its shadows in the breathless air;
a darkened threshold and a voice inclined
therein; a faint line always forming; time
wound inward and become the body's mind,
a settling troubled by its mean surprise
and tempering echoes—
                    such incarnations
riddle your song with light it could not earn,
is given as it disenchants the peace
also embodied there, the twisted savior's
shading and immanence, your signal prayer.

The Shadow in the Other's Heart

He has none, of course.
Appearing to carry one
in the specious recesses
of his homogeneous cells
is just his way of saying
Look, we're all alike:
we each chew our cow
or our cowslip with the same
raw grin, greet tomorrow
with the same idle threat
of disregard, looking over
our shoulders at our footprints
in the muddle of desire. Like you
I'm normal, tricked out
with darkness seeming to murmur
its undetectable counterpoint
to the beating of my heart,
so perfectly synchronized with yours
you spend the better part

180

of your life walking through me
into your image of yourself.
                              We
do the tricking, just as we
give him words to explain himself,
an image speaking
with our lips, easy to pass
off as the ventriloquist.
But if on a given day
you lay your finger across
his mouth, to still a moment
the voice you suspect might be
tending in your mind, you feel only
cold and motionless reserve,
and you are left with nothing
out there that is you, your finger
in the air, poised, thrusting up
as if making a point
in the long lecture of becoming,
or as if you are counting
the number of people here
whose shadow has been lifted
like a mute veil from the world.

Washerbaum the Crestfallen

Tim Mizelle

"Hats off, gentlemen. Hats off in deference": this was his frantic call, erupting out of the oppressive summer night as though it were heat thunder roiling forth from the past. It drew me from my wife's side beneath our thin, sweaty sheet, to the window, which stood open, helplessly welcoming whatever breeze might come, but never does, from the Garnet River.

"What is it?" my wife asked.

"Washerbaum, I think."

I saw him beneath the streetlight: Captain Washerbaum, the once fisherman, who still held to the docks like a shadow during the day, though his rig had long since been repossessed. No doubt it was him, for no one could mistake his hair, so like the feathers of an osprey, and his unkempt white beard.

"Yes," I whispered, "it's Washerbaum."

"*The Lament*?"

"I think so." Every year, never on the same day, never, perhaps, even in the same month, Captain Washerbaum called a night vigil in honor of his dead wife, Rosina, who had drowned herself in the Garnet River while giving birth. She had been trying for hours, or so rumor has it, to deliver the baby, a baby that the whole of town knew was not Washerbaum's, aboard Washerbaum's rig, *The Giant*. With merely the fisherman there to help her, she tossed herself over the keel when the pain overtook her. Washerbaum, who likewise tossed himself over the keel after her, had managed to save the child, which later died of scarlet fever, but tug as he might on the umbilical cord, he merely pulled in a severed line. Rosina washed ashore the next day: some say she appeared as content in death as any woman could. The evil among town gossips say she had a satisfied smile on her lips.

Over the years, Washerbaum's vigil had become an open joke, *the lament*. But it wasn't a joke to my wife, who now lay on edge, eight months pregnant herself; and it was certainly no joke to Washerbaum.

"Should you go to him?" my wife asked. She reached for the lamp.

I held a hand up to stop her. "No light."

Washerbaum swayed beneath the streetlight, wearing his characteristic hip-waders; his tattered black rain slicker, open and hanging, flowed around him as he issued his proclamation with waving arms: "Hats off, Gentlemen. Hats off in deference."

Lights went on up and down the street, illuminating the gables of the houses opposite the one in which we roomed; I cringed: I had hoped that we had been the only ones stirred. "Go to hell," someone called out to Washerbaum. "It's late you fat bastard. Not even the worms remember your Rosina." Washerbaum did not miss a beat, though, for his mind was on his duty: "Hats off, gentlemen."

I crawled out onto the fire escape, thinking perhaps I could talk him down. He had once been a great friend of my grandfather. They had come to America together after the War, Jewish orphans. I tried to act the part of one uninformed of his misfortune. "What do you mark, Captain Washerbaum?"

"Who speaks?"

"Gillian Hebbel's grandson."

"Hat off, 'Gillian Hebbel, twice removed,' show respect, tonight!"

"Who wears hats anymore?" I asked. "We were dreaming when your voice rudely stirred us."

"Doff a hat, even if you must imagine it lad. A trilby, if you wish for my help, would look grand atop your narrow head . . . It did atop your grandfather's."

There was another call, that of a woman, from an open window directly across the street from our room: "Shut your maw, you old fool! You too, Hebbel, your grandfather was a damned lunatic. You'll do well if you don't end up a lump of muttering fat in the street, yourself, with your beginnings."

This attack brought my wife to the window: "Hard heart, you have, Ingrid Sharps. Don't think your voice is veiled by the night. You, with your epileptic tongue gnashings, should pass judgement on no one! And beginnings . . . You were born in a tub of fish roe, you old carp."

I helped my wife back to the bed, and returned to the window.

I climbed down the ladder of the fire escape. I should not say Washerbaum's cry had summoned me from sleep, for I had been trying to hold onto a dream, although I could feel my fevered body fighting to stir me; in the dream of winter, a small girl in a coat of red and blue wool was dipping up babies, with her mittened hands, from the icy waters of the Garnet River, which, in reality, lay in the darkness, full of stagnant muck, not a hundred yards beyond Washerbaum. "Look," she had said, "when you catch them frozen, they don't flop about so."

"In your nightshirt, you look like your grandfather, Hebbel," Washerbaum said. He reached his hands into his waders, pushed down their bib. "Let me show you something," he said. In his hands, over the edge of the bib, he held his penis, flaccid, but abnormally large. "That's all there is of Captain Washerbaum now, son. Take a long hard look at it." I tried to hide my revulsion. His penis, most likely an object of great pride for him once, was now a sheathed curse. "Lasses paid to see it when I was a boy, can you believe it?" For some reason I could not. "When I was younger, I could swing it like the crank handle of a Model T; do you believe it?" That I could believe. "Now, what with it? My love is gone, Hebbel." I thought of his wife, imagined that she drowned herself to avoid the piston-like proddings of what Washerbaum thought his once grand tool.

"Captain Washerbaum, perhaps you should put it away, now." I patted him on the shoulder; what docs onc do to make a madman unhand his penis? That is not to say he was stroking it; quite the opposite: he held it as though its prepuce burned his fingers. Finally, he pulled his hands from his waders. "Let's remember your wife, Captain Washerbaum. Isn't that why you're out here tonight, rousing the sleeping?"

As though I had reminded him of his purpose, he cried: "Hats off . . ." and the rest, but it was clear to me that his lament concerned his penis alone. His hands went back into his waders; this time, they came forth with a pint of cognac. "Have a drink with me, Hebbel." A cool breeze wafted from the dead waters of the Garnet River. "Let's drink to your grandfather; he was a good man. . . . A bit of a fairy, but who's not, in the end? And let's drink to Rosina . . ." He drew near me and put his arm around me. "She never loved me, Hebbel. You've heard the townspeople cuckold me by remembering her infidelities, I suppose."

"No, Captain Washerbaum," I answered, "I have not."

He eyed me in disbelief. "Well, it's all the same, Hebbel. You're a goodly lad to come out here with me tonight." He nodded his bottle at me, took a swig, offered me a drink, which I accepted. "The child was not mine, Hebbel . . ."

"Surely it was, sir." I returned the bottle to him.

He took another swig, reached for his penis as though he needed it in hand to reassure him of the purpose of this confession. "The child was your grandfather's." He thrust his bottle into my hand. "Enough, Hebbel. You're a good lad, to be sure, but the sight of you sickens my heart, good night."

He made his way back toward the dock, where I supposed he would sleep off his drink. "Hats off . . ." And he disappeared into the shadows.

"Is he all right?" my wife asked, as I climbed in the window.

"I think he will be, in the morning," I answered. I joined her in the bed, turned my back to her to watch the window. She draped an arm over my hip, cupped my inadequate penis in her hand. She gave it a light squeeze to say good night.

A dream: I sat across a table from my grandfather. He opened a salt shaker, poured its contents in a line on the table, then raked his index finger along the salt, forming a trough. "You measure salt in grams, the time of day in minutes, the money in your pocket in dollars. You don't measure love in inches. No one could tell Washerbaum that, the prideful ass. There comes a time, son, when all the pounding mallet in the world won't keep those you love near you."

MASTER SET 2nd PASS

When I came in, my son-in-law lurched to his feet and left without a greeting. "Don't let your customers smell that whiskey!" I shouted after him, intending to be heard in the whole saloon. Being trapped in his booth, Cole did not rise. With a poor smile, he waved me to a seat and asked me how my "cane patch" was progressing. I tried to ignore the sneer in that stupid question, but then, on impulse, to see the shock on that smug face, I told him coolly that I wished to buy his Ford automobile, which I understood he had replaced with that red Reo. I let him believe I had come to town expressly for that purpose.

"What for?" Cole jeered. He also meant *What with?* Cole's nose for money told him who was flat broke busted. But E. J. Watson had built a reputation as a man who made good on his debts, and Cole had no reason to doubt that I would restore my syrup operation in short order, and its profits, too.

"What's your collateral, Ed?" he said, without turning a hair. I thought he was just meeting my bluff, but when he flagged the bartender and paid for two more whiskeys, I realized he was serious, and my heart thudded. I was not going to back down, not with Jim Cole.

"An up-and-coming truck farm in Columbia County. Good credit risk, too."

"Who's on there now?"

"My mother and sister."

"Supposing you forfeit?" He cocked his head to peer at me, grinning again. "You fixin to shoot them ladies, Ed, or just run 'em off there?" I held his gaze, and he covered his nerves with that curly grin. "Where the hell you aim to *drive* the damn thing, Ed? Down to your dock and back?" When I said nothing, he asked for a business reference in town besides Walt Langford. I mentioned my friend Mr. Ben King, who had worked as a mechanic for Mr. Edison before opening this town's first garage. "Go on. Go talk to him. Right now," I said.

Ben King told Cole that Watson paid his debts and also paid his workers, never mind those rumors about "Watson Payday." A lot of those rumors had been spread, Ben told him, by a black man named Dave Smith, a former worker at the Bend. One day while this Dave was still around, little Ruth Ellen had wandered off while her mother was sewing out on the front porch, and got herself trapped in the red mangrove stilts along the riverbank. We found her all huddled up with fright, but otherwise all right. Well, this damn nigger told the Langfords' friend Frank Carson—he worked for Carsons in Fort Myers—that the frightened child wouldn't answer when I hollered, and that I had become so upset and angry that I shouted out, "If she is lost, I am going to kill her mother." Well, if I said that, I was drunk, and this damned nigger knew that but talked anyway. Like everybody white or black in south-

2S
1S
R
1L
2L

A corrected galley from Bone by Bone.

Peter Matthiessen

The Art of Fiction CLVII

Not long after the publication of The Tree Where Man
Was Born, *Peter Matthiessen's classic account of travels in*

*East Africa, I overheard a restaurant conversation between
two well-dressed men on the general topic of midlife. One
said, "My wife and my psychiatrist agree that as a human
being I've atrophied—spiritually. For my fiftieth birthday,
she's arranged a trip to the Serengeti, for God's sake. 'Go
to a place that might change you,' she said." His friend said,
"Well?" and the man answered, "Well, I'd rather read Peter
Matthiessen. I'll enjoy his African trip a great deal more."*

*Peter Matthiessen's writing—fiction and nonfiction—does
not provide approximations. What it does do with inimitable
skill is put a reader at the live heart of life—a powerful rich
sense of immediacy, of being in that moment. Elected to the
American Academy of Arts and Letters in 1974, he has long
been one of our most celebrated writers, best known, perhaps,
for his novels* At Play in the Fields of the Lord *and* Far Tortuga,
his travel journal The Snow Leopard *and his lifelong advocacy
of wilderness and wildlife preservation and social justice.*

*For the past twenty years, Peter Matthiessen has been ob-
sessed by a remarkable trilogy of novels based on the violent
life and death of Edgar Watson, a notorious frontier entrepre-
neur who in 1910 was gunned down by his neighbors in
the Ten Thousand Islands region of the western Everglades.*
Killing Mister Watson, *published in 1990, was followed in
1997 by* Lost Man's River, *and the final volume,* Bone by
Bone, *narrated by Watson himself, appears this spring.*

*This interview forms only a small part of an ongoing conver-
sation between this writer and myself pursued for over a
decade in locations as varied as northern California; Washington, D.C.; Clarksville, Tennessee; Montauk, Long Island; the
Hotel Wales in New York City; and the Hay-on-Wye Festival
in Wales. In all of these discussions, he was, as Conrad put
it, "high up on the top rung of honesty as naturally and
carefully and unashamedly as a man can climb." He is a man
of tough-minded opinion, deeply earned and forthrightly
rendered, with passion and quick humor ringed with what
one writer calls a "useful melancholy."*

*Born in New York City on May 22, 1927, Matthiessen
attended the St. Bernard's School, then Hotchkiss and Yale.
His junior year was spent at the Sorbonne. In 1951 he returned
to Paris, where he became a founder of* The Paris Review *and
finished his first novel,* Race Rock. *In 1953 he moved to the
South Fork of Long Island, New York, where his daughter
Sara Carey was born. For the next three years Matthiessen
worked as a commercial fisherman and as captain of a charter
fishing boat off Montauk, pursuing his writing in bad weather
and in winter. His second novel,* Partisans, *was published in
1955. In 1957, he traveled to the farthest corners of America,
doing research for his classic study* Wildlife in America *(1959).
In 1961 came his third novel,* Raditzer, *and also* The Cloud
Forest, *a naturalist's account of his previous year's travels
through backcountry South America and the first of six books
serialized in* The New Yorker. *The same year he traveled to
Sudan, East Africa, Nepal and Southeast Asia en route to
the Harvard-Peabody Expedition to New Guinea on which
Michael Rockefeller disappeared; his innovative account of a
stone-age culture,* Under the Mountain Wall *(1962), would
influence Truman Capote's conception of his "nonfiction
novel"* In Cold Blood. *In 1965 his novel* At Play in the Fields
of the Lord *was a finalist for the National Book Award. In
1967 came* Sal Si Puedes, *his account of the California grape
strike and the life of Cesar Chavez.*

*That year Matthiessen set out on the turtle-boat voyage
from Grand Cayman Island to the coastal reefs off Nicaragua
that eventually led to the novel* Far Tortuga *(1975), which
Thomas Pynchon called "a masterfully spun yarn, a little
otherworldly, a dreamlike momentum. . . . It's full of music
and strong haunting visuals, and like everything of his, it's
also a deep declaration of love for the planet." In 1973 he
accompanied zoologist George Schaller on a 250-mile trek
across the Himalayas to the Tibetan plateau. His account of
that journey,* The Snow Leopard, *won the National Book
Award in 1979. Since then, Matthiessen's books have included*

In the Spirit of Crazy Horse, *his powerful account of the American Indian Movement and the 1975 shoot-out at Pine Ridge in which two FBI agents and a young Indian were killed (Matthiessen remains at the forefront of international advocacy for the release of* AIM *leader Leonard Peltier);* The Wind Birds; Indian Country; Men's Lives; *and the short-story collection* On the River Styx.

There is, to my mind, no writing life more vital and of greater distinction in the second half of our century. Matthiessen's prodigious and varied works led William Styron to call him "an original and powerful artist . . . who has produced as distinguished a body of work as any writer of our time . . . He has immeasurably enlarged our consciousness."

INTERVIEWER

You are one of the few writers ever nominated for the National Book Award in both fiction and nonfiction. Define yourself.

PETER MATTHIESSEN

I am a writer. A fiction writer who also writes nonfiction on behalf of social and environmental causes, or journals about expeditions to wild places. I have written more books of nonfiction because my fiction is an exploratory process—not laborious, merely long and slow and getting slower. In reverse order, *Far Tortuga* took eight years, *At Play in the Fields of the Lord* perhaps four, and the early novels no doubt longer than they deserved. Anyway, I have been a fiction writer from the start. For many years I wrote nothing but fiction. My first published story appeared in *The Atlantic* the year I graduated from college and won the *Atlantic* firsts prize that year; and on the wings of a second story sale to the same magazine, I acquired a noted literary agent, Bernice Baumgarten, wife of James Gould Cozzens, the author of a best-selling blockbuster called *By Love Possessed*, whose considerable repute went to the grave with him.

INTERVIEWER
And when did you start your first novel?

MATTHIESSEN

Almost at once. It was situated on an island off the New England coast. I had scarcely begun when I realized that what I had here at the very least was the Great American Novel. I sent off the first 150 pages to Bernice and hung around the post office for the next two weeks. At last an answer came. It read as follows: "Dear Peter, James Fenimore Cooper wrote this 150 years ago, only he wrote it better, Yours, Bernice." On a later occasion, when as a courtesy I sent her the commission on a short story sold in England, she responded unforgettably: "Dear Peter, I'm awfully glad you were able to get rid of this story in Europe, as I don't think we'd have had much luck with it here. Yours, Bernice." Both these communications, quoted in their entirety, are burned into my brain forever—doubtless a salutary experience for a brash young writer. I never heard an encouraging word until the day Bernice retired, when she called me in and barked like a Zen master, "I've been tough on you because you're very very good." I wanted to sink down and embrace her knees.

INTERVIEWER
Do you stand by the early novels?

MATTHIESSEN

Well, those first three were a bit green—well-written and well-made, I think, but entirely unremarkable, as were most of the first thirty-odd short stories that are still moldering some place collecting mouse droppings. The third novel, *Raditzer*, was bolder, but I came of age with *At Play in the Fields of the Lord*. I like to think that *At Play* and *Far Tortuga* as well as the collected stories and this present trilogy will endure.

Can you say which writers have influenced your work?

A terrible confession—none. Try as I might to claim some creditable literary lineage, I find no trace that I can recognize in my writing. I don't mean to claim that I am sui generis (though one could argue that all truthful writers are sui generis), nor that I came to work fully formed like a hen's egg or a Buddha. Nor do I seek to be unique or even "different," far less self-consciously "experimental." In *Far Tortuga*, the innovations emerged from the writing process because old familiar novelistic forms simply weren't working.

Many great writers inspired me, of course, but inspiration is not the same as a direct influence. I was often stirred by the beauty of great prose, the passion and startling intensity of hard-won truths, which leapt from that creative fire. I suppose I became a writer to search out my own thoughts (though I was unaware of that for years; I simply wrote). For the writer, therefore the reader, fresh truth is exhilarating, even painful truth, as in Kafka or Céline. Isn't that what good writing finally arrives at? The insights and epigrams of Alexander Pope weren't clichés when he wrote them, any more than those resounding lines in Shakespeare. They only became dog-eared from overuse.

The writers whose perceptions and evocations stirred me most when I first read seriously were probably Conrad and Dostoyevsky. Tolstoy and Gogol, too, of course—I loved all the great Russian writers with a passion, and certain more recent ones, as well, Babel and Akhmatova and Tsvetayevna (though I remain woefully ill-read in poetry, which I regret). And that's just Russia! There are so many fine writers, including too many—a glum realization at my age—whom I haven't got to yet. It is very, very exciting to be a reader!

Are there still exemplary figures whose lives or voices are important to you? Conrad? Which writers do you return to now and then?

MATTHIESSEN

I rarely go back to a book, since I never feel sufficiently caught up in my own work. However, a few years ago, on a stalled expedition, I had an opportunity to reread *The Idiot*, which I've always thought of as "my favorite novel" (if such a thing can be; the great ones are no more comparable than the sun and the sky). I wanted to see if that book held up—if it was as heartbreaking and magnificent as I once thought it, and of course it was. Whereas—well, let's simply say that most modern novels, even the better ones, are pretty dinky in ambition, and certainly unworthy of a second reading when one knows that great ones are still out there unread.

INTERVIEWER

How about contemporaries? Are any of them important to your writing life?

MATTHIESSEN

I admire many of my contemporaries, especially those who risk something or bring some new element to their work. I won't discriminate between my own contemporaries, but among sub-elders, I try to keep up with pretty much everything in the fiction, good and bad (for in very good writers, the intention remains interesting even when a certain work seems less so) of V.S. Naipaul, Don DeLillo, Robert Stone, Louise Erdrich, Alice Munro, Cormac McCarthy and a few others. Of course, there are single novels that are excellent, but what interests me most is the working through from book to book of some recurrent obsession or at least preoccupation, a reverberation from within, which may burst the work wide at any moment, though it often seems half-hidden from the writer. What I'm trying to describe, I guess, is conflagration, a life burning up, as lives do in Dostoyevsky. Obsession that isn't crazed or criminal is always enthralling. I learned a lot about obsession from too much time spent in the mind of Mister Watson.

INTERVIEWER
Obsession or not, you have great faith in this *Lost Man's River* trilogy.

MATTHIESSEN
I do. One has to be mad or have great faith—if these are different—to devote a third of one's writing life to a single project, as to my great horror I discovered I had done, when I came across my early notes not long ago. A twenty-year obsession. I'm just emerging.

INTERVIEWER
Twenty years! I can't think of another project sustained for so long. Do you feel your fiction has been obscured by your nonfiction?

MATTHIESSEN
Let's just say that books such as *The Snow Leopard* made certain less adventurous reviewers imprint on the idea that Matthiessen is essentially a travel writer, trying his hand at the novel, as so many ill-advised nonfiction writers have done—usually just once. Others have me pigeonholed as a nature writer, an anthropological writer, a writer of social advocacy. They're like those blind men who discovered a large elephant and described it on the basis of the part that each first touched. But in fact I had written three novels and at least ten short stories before I tried nonfiction, and even then, I only did it to support a new, young family, eking things out with commercial fishing.

INTERVIEWER
Can you say precisely why you prefer writing fiction?

MATTHIESSEN
Nonfiction at its best is like fashioning a cabinet. It can be elegant and very beautiful but it can never be sculpture. Captive to facts—or predetermined forms—it cannot fly. Excepting those masters who transcend their craft—great medi-

eval and Renaissance artisans, for example, or nameless artisans of traditional cultures as far back as the caves who were also spontaneous unselfconscious artists.

As in fiction, the nonfiction writer is telling a story, and when that story is well-made, the placement of details and events is never random. The parts are not strung out in a line but come around full circle like a necklace to set off the others. They resonate, rekindle one another, stirring the reader with a cumulative effect. A good essay or article can and should have all the attributes of a good short story, including structure and design, pacing and effective placement of its parts—almost all the attributes of fiction except the creative imagination, which can never be permitted to enliven fact. The writer of nonfiction is stuck with objective reality, or should be; how his facts are arranged and presented is where his craft appears, and it can be dazzling when the writer is a good one. The best nonfiction has many, many virtues, among which simple truthfulness is perhaps foremost, yet its fidelity to the known facts is its fatal constraint.

Like anything that one makes well with one's own hands, writing good nonfiction prose can be profoundly satisfying. Yet after a day of arranging my research, my set of facts, I feel stale and drained, whereas I am energized by fiction. Deep in a novel, one scarcely knows what may surface next, let alone where it comes from. In abandoning oneself to the free creation of something never beheld on earth, one feels almost delirious with a strange joy.

INTERVIEWER

It's not unlike what athletes refer to as "being in the zone." How do you reach that state?

MATTHIESSEN

By writing. I learned early that you can't get there drunk or smoking dope or hanging about waiting for your muse. Starting each day is like priming the pump, in my experience; it's plain hard labor, hunting the right way to express that thought that had seemed so penetrating, even beautiful, before you had to reduce it into words. I liken the donkey work of the first draft to the booster apparatus of a rocket—the terrible labor of those energies lifting this reluctant mass against the force of gravity, slowly, slowly, until marvelously—on the better days—the thing achieves its own momentum, and the dead weight of its booster falls away. Effortless, it enters into orbit—in short, "the zone"—sailing free and clear and light and sun-filled, opened wide to the flow of imagination, unobstructed.

Only rarely, in my experience, is nonfiction exhilarating in that same way. I scarcely recall ever entering that zone except in isolated passages. Perhaps that is why, for many years, I discounted my nonfiction books as worthy in their way, yet somehow inferior to my fiction. Finally an insightful friend, a painter, pointed out that my fiction and nonfiction in their various forms were only different facets of a single immense work—the same rage about injustice, the same despair over our lunatic destruction of our own habitat and that of other creatures. An evocation of our splendid earth and an elegy to the land and life that is being lost both lie at the heart of my fiction and nonfiction.

INTERVIEWER

Your travels in remote regions are often perilous—New Guinea and the great white shark, wilderness, rivers and wild peoples in South America and Africa. There were larger literary risks, as well, as in *The Snow Leopard*.

MATTHIESSEN

I dislike risk and I never seek it out, but one can't always anticipate what may occur off the beaten track. The physical risks on that journey across the Himalayas were minor, as things turned out, and as for literary risks, I understood that if that journey was to have any validity, I would have to deal with very personal matters such as my wife's recent death. Being a rather private person, this was sometimes difficult, but I decided to stand by what I had written at high altitude, which tends to air out inhibitions.

INTERVIEWER

In *The Snow Leopard* you write: "In the snow mountains . . . I feel open, clear, childlike once again. I am bathed by feelings." Then: "Simultaneously I am myself, the child I was, the old man I will be." There are these explosions of transcendent feeling.

MATTHIESSEN

Or altered realities, perhaps, induced by altitude and exhaustion. And there were peculiar time shifts as we headed northward, ever higher and farther north toward the Tibetan Plateau, walking out of the present into the past—the Middle Ages, finally. First, time dissolved, then space. It's broad daylight, good visibility, yet mountains move. You perceive that the so-called permanence of the mountains is illusory, and that all phenomena are mere wisps of the cosmos, ever changing. It is its very evanescence that makes life beautiful, isn't that true? If we were doomed to live forever, we would scarcely be aware of the beauty around us. Beauty always has that element of transience that is spoiled when we draw clumsy attention to it. The great haiku poet Bashō wrote, "How blessed is he who sees the cherry blossoms fall and does not say, 'Ah, time is passing.'" He has let go of all such concepts as time passing, in order to enter deeply into this moment. I tried to capture some of that immediacy in *Far Tortuga* and *The Snow Leopard*, too. The first draft of that journal was written in the Himalayas as a Zen practice of close observation, and perhaps that gave it a meditative quality that otherwise it might have lacked.

INTERVIEWER

The relationship between you and the zoologist George Schaller—both of you men who seem to need a lot of space— struck me as not only sharply drawn but humorous and affec-

tionate. For all the abrasions of such a long hard journey, the
friendship turned out to be honest and moving.

MATTHIESSEN

George and I were—and are—content in our own company.
We had no compulsion to be sociable beyond a point. A few
friendly words over coffee and breakfast, then go our way.
Even on the way to the Crystal Mountain—and in the end,
we walked up and down mountains for 250 miles to get where
we were going—we would often be several hundred yards
apart, even a half mile. We rarely talked except at meals,
and even then it wasn't very noisy. Neither of us like to
chatter very much. There's a wonderful Zen story about a
young monk who has had an enlightenment experience. To
celebrate, his teacher takes him up Mount Fuji. All the way
up this snow volcano, this young monk is crying out, "Oh,
Roshi! Do you hear the birds? I've never heard the birds
before! How beautiful!" The teacher scarcely grunts, won't
say a word, just thumps his stave. On and on the fellow goes,
ecstatic. "Oh, the snow, the clouds!" Finally they near the
top of the mountain. "Oh, Roshi," he cries. "Do you see
how the wind blows snow across the cone of the volcano?
How the clouds drift past on the wind? There is no separation
between us and the wind and the great earth!" The roshi
hisses, "Yes! Yes, true! But what a pity to *say* so!"

Schaller and I felt a bit like that old roshi. Both of us had
this lifelong love of animals and remote landscapes. Yes, we
had walked away from civilization through mythic mountains
and ancient villages in clear October light—but what a pity
to *say* that to each other! What I did say was, "If I can't write
an interesting book about an experience like this, I ought to
be taken out and shot."

INTERVIEWER

The Sherpa Tukten still strikes me as one of the more
remarkable characters in your work, fiction or nonfiction.

MATTHIESSEN

I think of him often—that disreputable little catlike man the others were so afraid of. Even George distrusted him. But when I left, he led me down out of those mountains, and I saw how he was treated in every village we passed through— the wary reverence—as if he were some sort of shaman. Over and over again, his actions seemed uncanny, as when he thrust at me a stave he had just cut, only minutes before I was attacked by a horrible mastiff at the outskirts of a village.

After our journey, we were supposed to meet at the great stupa at Bodhinath, east of Kathmandu. He never showed up—what we call a "silent teaching" in the Zen tradition, unless he just got drunk—that's teaching, too. So much for Tukten. We never met again, but I was happy to have traveled with him. I was through with him, but Tukten was not through with me. Perhaps six months after I got home, I had a phone call from a distressed woman in New York who was embarrassed by this intrusion on a perfect stranger. "You see, my story sounds so crazy that it's hard to tell it. I've just come from Nepal. We were at Muktinath when a strange Sherpa came into camp who knew our Sherpas. He had this object wrapped in greasy brown paper. He said, 'You America?' When I said yes, he forced this thing into my hand. 'Give Massin,' he demanded." She gathered that "Massin" must be someone in America, and tried to tell him that America was a big place where not everyone was acquainted with everybody else. He dismissed all this, in fact got cranky, so certain was he that she would find me. "Massin," he insisted forcefully. Finally she accepted the thing and carried it back home, where her daughter said, "Guess what? While you were away, there was a series of articles about Nepal in *The New Yorker* by somebody named Matthiessen." Finally she got up her nerve to call. She asked, "Would such a thing mean anything to you?" I told her to send it, which she did. It was a lama's ceremonial crescent knife with a dorje bell handle used to cut away delusions—just what my teacher Tukten would have sent me.

Sometimes you've regretted having to write a new book
of nonfiction.

Twice. One of those books was *Sand Rivers*, which was only
written because I wanted to reach a very remote and roadless
part of Tanzania, the south Selous. There was no way of
traveling there without mounting a full safari, which is very
expensive. Then some Englishmen turned up, offering to
underwrite such a safari on the condition that the photographer and I do a book about it to defray expenses. The photographer was Hugo van Lawick, who always had longed to go
to the Selous as much as I did. We had to sing for our supper.
Blue Meridian, a book about a diving expedition to film the
great white shark, was also in that category. I wanted to see
the white shark so badly that the book was worth it.

The Indian books and the book about Cesar Chavez were
written for a cause. I don't regret them. So was *Men's Lives*,
a book about the traditional commercial fishermen I used to
work with on the east end of Long Island, though that was
a book I had always known I would do eventually. These men
are being pushed off their own home territory by the tourist
economy, and I wanted *Men's Lives* to be published in a
hurry to help them out. All of these advocacy books contain
good stuff, but I had to work on them especially hard because,
from a literary point of view, they came from the wrong place.
Advocacy can only rarely be great writing.

Let's talk about fictional characters. Where did you get the
missionary characters in *At Play in the Fields of the Lord*,
for instance?

Going to South America in 1958, I traveled with a missionary on a small freighter for forty-one days from New York

throughout the Caribbean and all the way up the Amazon. At the end of that, I had quite a feel for the missionary character. Subsequently, I traveled to mission stations in Brazil and Peru, acquainting myself with missionary activity, which was generally disastrous. A typical tribe contacted by the missions is said to have an average life of approximately fifty years before it vanishes entirely. I'm talking about fundamentalist Protestant missions from the United States, not the Catholic missions, which are—or were—much less intrusive, more respectful of the Indians, adapting their Christian teachings to the Indian culture, not despising it. A few years later, with stone-age people in the highlands of New Guinea, trying to discover the origins of war, our expedition had problems with missionaries, too. Because we had made a difficult contact before they did, they accused us of encouraging these tribal people to go to war, which we did not do. Even had we been capable of that, there was no need. They went to war gladly of their own accord, about once a week.

However, South America seemed a stronger setting for a novel. I knew New Guinea but I *felt* South America—the jungle, the flora and fauna and the Indians, all dimly familiar. I was stirred by the enormous *thickness* and extent of that great forest, the claustrophobia, and the long history of violence by civilized man against wild peoples. Also, a pervasive torpor and brutality in the river settlements, the mindless cruelty to dogs and other creatures. Cruelty and humorlessness pervade the miasmal atmosphere in backcountry South America—perhaps a reverberation of the Spanish conquests and the genocides of the rubber days when the Indians were enslaved. There's a settlement up the Amazon known formerly as *Remate de Males*—Culmination of Evils. And the creatures themselves—the insects, the mosquitoes, the poisonous snakes, like the bushmaster and fer-de-lance, the piranhas and that little sliver of a fish called the *candiru*, which enters every human orifice without exception. The cloud forest and the high Andes above the rivers, the legends of El Dorado, Macchu Picchu and the Inca—all of it has a surreal, fabulous quality, so wonderfully rendered by García Márquez.

How did the character of the half-breed Lewis Moon develop?

Lewis Moon was drawn from at least three people. The first was a young Navaho hitchhiker I picked up in New Mexico when I was traveling the Southwest doing research for *Wildlife in America*. We wandered together across Arizona, and I dropped him off somewhere in the empty desert country of southern Nevada. In all those miles, over two or three days, we spoke scarcely a word. He seemed to have no destination—an enormously alienated, sullen, angry guy. Since then I have spent a lot of time with Indian people, and I realize now that part of his alienation and anger was that he was a traditional from the remote mesas who scarcely spoke English and was ashamed of that. He might have feared I'd think him stupid or backward, which is how some of the acculturated Indians treat these traditionals. Though I'd carried him hundreds of miles and fed him, too, he could not even say thanks when he got out. He just rapped the window, looking straight ahead, and I dropped him off on the road shoulder at this desolate place in the desert buttes without a sign of human habitation. Maybe our culture clash was just too much for him, and he wanted out right then. I only hope he knew where he was going. He was nineteen or twenty, all tied up in anger, as I had been myself at that same age.

I met the second guy in a bar in Belém, at the mouth of the Amazon. He was a French-Canadian ship's carpenter who'd been shunted off a freighter's stern off Trinidad when the deck lumber cargo shifted in high seas. It was night, nobody saw this, and he swam and floated in the ocean for eight hours before he was miraculously spotted. We talked all evening. He told me about the strange places he had been since—a man consumed with wandering. He showed me the small kit that he kept with him, everything he owned in life, pared down almost to nothing—a waterproof packet containing a map, a cut-off razor, a change of underwear and very little else. He said, "It's easier to throw away stuff and replace it. I'm always ready. I don't stay put and I owe nothing, so if a guy tells me he's headed somewhere, and there's a seat, I go." As a merchant seaman, he had made good money and, when he was picked up out of the sea more dead than alive, he understood something about life and death. He had a family in Canada, and he wrote his wife, "I love you, but I won't be home again. I'll send money when I make any. You're welcome to the house." A solitary and indifferent figure, cryptic and memorable.

This man and that young Navaho were joined in Lewis Moon. The third man, inevitably, was me. I brought with me as much as I understood back then about loneliness and anger, which was quite a lot.

INTERVIEWER

In your interview in this magazine about *Far Tortuga*,* form as much as character was on your mind. You felt constrained by the conventional novel form, to put it simply.

MATTHIESSEN

The inception of that book was a nonfiction piece for *The New Yorker* about a Grand Cayman turtle-fishing schooner still under sail off the reefs of Nicaragua. On that voyage, I was struck by the simplicity of those lives, the spareness—the bareness—of their ship and gear. Everything was faded and worn bare. In those heavy trade winds, on unmarked reefs, they had no life jackets and the radio did not work. Somehow this simplicity was very moving, and I knew from the first day at sea that I would do a novel. I also knew that the rich metaphoric prose I'd used in *At Play* would not work here. The prose had to reflect the spareness of those lives. I began by throwing out most of the furniture of novel writing, from

* An interview entitled "The Craft of Fiction in *Far Tortuga*," accompanied by an excerpt from the novel, appeared in *The Paris Review* #60, winter, 1974.

simile and complex sentences right down to the *he said* and the *she said*. I don't mean minimalism, however that's defined. That's not what I was after, nor economy either. I was after spareness, in both prose and feeling. A sense of the spareness and the fleeting quality of our existence.

INTERVIEWER

So there was a lot of experimenting in *Far Tortuga*?

MATTHIESSEN

I suppose so. If I hadn't decided I was overworking it and doing the book harm, I would have spent another eight years gladly. I didn't want to stop. It was the most exhilarating book I've ever written, fun, but also very exciting that other writers seemed to be excited by it. I was fascinated by the problems of how to present that tropical world, the hazed sunlight, the strong trade winds, the old ship, the sea, the almost Chaucerian language of those turtlemen, unchanged for centuries. I wanted to experiment with silences and space—I mean quite literally the extent of white space on the page between incidents, monologues, songs, wind gusts, squabbles, the shudder of the hull in the rough weather, everything. More than anything I've done, perhaps, *Far Tortuga* was influenced by Zen training. The grit and feel of this present moment, moment after moment, opening out into the oceanic wonder of the sea and sky. When you fix each moment in all its astonishing detail, see its miracle in a fresh light, no similes, no images are needed. They become "literary," superfluous. Aesthetic clutter.

INTERVIEWER

Stravinsky said a wonderful thing: "I was for a period of time obssessed with the weight of interval." He meant, of course, the anticipation, even the anxiety, about what's immediately going to follow.

MATTHIESSEN

That's it exactly. Setting up the tension of expectancy.

INTERVIEWER

Did you record those Caribbean voices to inform your dialogue in the novel?

MATTHIESSEN

When I first went to Grand Cayman, I could scarcely understand a thing those men were saying. I couldn't write the book I wanted until I spoke that archaic tongue and heard it truly—until I could think and reason in it—so I made several trips to the Cayman Islands before I sailed south on that turtle voyage. By the time I returned, writing *Far Tortuga* was like speaking directly onto the page—not that I thought I had solved all of its problems. At the same time I had to evoke the reefs and birds and sea and light and the solitude of that doomed schooner and the self-deprecating courage of those turtlemen, who bitched and cursed but went out every day to do a dangerous job and do it well. But I don't think I solved every last problem.

INTERVIEWER

How do you mean?

MATTHIESSEN

I had an instinct, the whisper of an idea that I failed to work through in my head, and by the time I did so, it was too late. All those white spaces—Stravinsky's intervals—were indicated in the manuscript, but of course in the actual printed text, my precious spaces came out truncated, half at the bottom of one page, for example, and half at the top of the next. In the end, the dance of the white spaces was mostly lost.

INTERVIEWER

Let's concentrate on this vast trilogy you have just finished. When did you first hear about the infamous Ed Watson?

MATTHIESSEN

Well, my father loved boats and he loved Florida, especially the fishing. I was a bird and snake fanatic from an early age, so I was enchanted by the Everglades. When I saw my first swallow-tailed kite hawking back and forth over the Tamiami Trail, I almost caused a car wreck. I jumped out, I couldn't stop yelling; they couldn't get me back into the car! When I was sixteen or seventeen, we went north by boat from the Keys up the west coast of Florida to Captiva Island. Off the Ten Thousand Islands of the western Everglades, still a wild region today, my father showed me Chathum River on the chart. He said there was a house a few miles up that river—the only house left in the Everglades that had formerly belonged to a man named Watson, who had killed many people before he was finally shot to pieces by his own neighbors. That solitary house, and a man killed by his neighbors—I was intrigued. Though I did not act on it for thirty years, I never forgot it.

INTERVIEWER

Was Watson a real person? A historical figure?

MATTHIESSEN

Yes and no. There was a real man and also a mythic figure. He was a highly regarded planter, loved by three wives and seven lawful children; he is said to have been friendly with Napolean Broward, who became governor of Florida, and his oldest daughter, Carrie Watson, married the first president of the First National Bank in Fort Myers. But his notoriety was spreading long before his death and it spread far. My daughter-in-law, who was raised in Brooklyn, told me that when she wouldn't go to bed, her mother would warn her, "If you don't get in bed right now, Mister Watson will get you!" She had no idea who this bogeyman was and neither did her mother, but I feel sure it was the same Mister Watson. By the time he reached Brooklyn, he had been transformed into the legendary slayer of fifty people.

INTERVIEWER
So you could have written a biographical account instead?

MATTHIESSEN
No. Ed Watson became what was known as a shadow cousin,
never mentioned even in his own family. Almost all that was
known a half-century later was tall tale, rumor, a few ancient
error-flecked news clips, apocryphal written accounts—old
folks stories, recounted over and over. The only dependable
information still available came from old gravestones, country
records—all the rest was hearsay, which grew even more lurid
with the passing years. To write a biographical account with
such a paucity of fact, one would have to cripple each assertion
with a qualification—"It is said that . . . seemingly . . . it
appears that . . . apparently . . ." and so forth. In fact, it
was the absence of hard evidence that inspired me to reimagine
Watson. By immersing myself in his legend and his times,
and listening for years and years to the old voice on that
southwest coast, I finally would intuit who the real man might
have been.

INTERVIEWER
Why didn't you stop after the first novel?

MATTHIESSEN
Because I already had first drafts of what became two others.
There was no separate first novel, not at the start. I wrote out
the first draft of the entire thing. Only when the smoke
cleared and I got my breath did I realize that my publishers
would balk at the enormity that I had wrought. So I pulled
it into three rough parts as one might separate a loaf of bread,
then went back to the first part and revised and polished.
But those three parts really belong together, so I will have to
reassemble it another day.

INTERVIEWER

The Great American Novel?

MATTHIESSEN

If you like. Perhaps we're *all* writing the Great American Novel, each in our own way.

INTERVIEWER

First we have *Killing Mister Watson*, accounts from neighbors and so forth about Watson.

MATTHIESSEN

I saw *Killing Mister Watson* as the first movement in a kind of symphony, since the whole thing felt symphonic in its rhythms, rising and falling, ever returning to the underlying theme. To establish that, I made kind of a prelude of his enigmatic death, the relating of which would recur in variations throughout the trilogy. The original composition as I envisioned it seemed to demand that Watson's death take place at the start and at the end of all three movements, but later this structure seemed too arbitrary and schematic. However, the death of Mister Watson on that remote shore in the October dusk would remain the ending of all three of the so-called movements.

INTERVIEWER

Wasn't that risky—to give away the plot right off the bat?

MATTHIESSEN

Well, the title already had given it away—that's what I wanted. My British publisher was shocked; others were, too. But I had no interest in the plot; I wanted to get that out of the way and penetrate the underlying mystery. A powerful and respected man is shot to pieces by his neighbors: why? It is the *why* that matters. Was it really self-defense, as claimed by the participants, or was it a planned lynching? How could such a frightening event take place in a peaceful community of fishermen and farmers? And what about the rumor that

the man who fired first and perhaps fatally was the lone
black man in that crowd of whites—an astounding event on
a Florida frontier in Jim Crow days when a black raising a
gun against a white under any circumstances was inconceivable. Who was that man? What was he doing there? In
terms of the American past, and African-American history in
particular, this strange episode had endless reverberations.

Did the separate books stand by themselves when you broke
that first draft into three?

The first book and the third were more or less in place just
as they were, though I was to revise and tighten them over
and over. The middle section, *Lost Man's River*, in which
Watson's son Lucius returns to the islands seeking truth about
his father, worked well enough as a bridge between the other
two but did not stand by itself—it lacked a skeleton, although
it contained much of the brain and heart of the whole creature.
It reminded me, not agreeably, of the long belly of a dachs-
hund, slung woefully between the upright sturdy legs—an
amorphous and unlovely thing when separated from the rest
but critical to the function of the whole. To make it work—to
make it a novel on its own—I was finally obliged to borrow a
powerful and crucial episode, which really belonged elsewhere
had the trilogy been written as a single book as originally
planned.

For a time, that second volume was entitled "The Man
Who Killed Belle Starr." A remarkable book called *Hell on
the Border*, first published in 1898, describes the demise six
years earlier of a woman called Belle Starr, who in that era,
in the opinion of *The New York Times*, was one of the ten
most distinguished women in the United States—no one quite
knows why, since for all her flamboyance, she was a ratty and
disreputable sort of person. At any rate, this book claimed
Belle Starr was murdered on a February day in 1889 by a

man named Watson—a featureless assassin who comes out
of nowhere. According to *Hell on the Border*, this man Watson was sent to the Arkansas penitentiary for horse theft and
was later killed while attempting to escape. That last part was
untrue, of course. He fled to the Everglades frontier.

In *Lost Man's River*, his son, Lucius, is trying to find out
who his father was. He has no cooperation from his family,
which has swept the whole thing under the rug. So Lucius—
this fictional Lucius—does an extraordinary thing. He goes
to live in this backwater community where this dangerous
man was executed by his neighbors. If you happened to be
one of the shooters, what would you think when the son
shows up a few years later? Might this man be on a mission
of revenge? And of course Lucius learns more truth than he
had bargained for.

Lost Man's River is longer and more complex than the other
two, but it is upsetting and sad and also funny, if you enjoy
grim laconic humor. As Naipaul has observed, "You can't
give a dark, tragic view all the time—it must be supported
by this underlying comedy." Just so. I recall thinking that
At Play was hilarious in places, but readers were so overcome
by its tragic story that its humor passed all but unnoticed.
At last a reader wrote to say that he thought it one of the
funniest books he'd ever read—true or not, that came as a
great relief. I wasn't so sick after all, or else somebody out
there was as warped as I was.

INTERVIEWER

And part three—*Bone by Bone*—is Watson's autobiography, as it were.

MATTHIESSEN

In a sense. Its title comes from a beautiful, strange, edgy
poem by Emily Dickinson. This volume takes Watson back
as far as early childhood and young manhood, but like the
other two, it moves remorselessly toward this dire event on
October 24, 1910, when Watson came north from his planta-

tion and, after a short dispute, was massacred. Thirty-three bullets, according to the sheriff, were removed from his body during the autopsy. The reader accompanies him in his head right to that last fatal second, by which time, I hope, one understands this man at last. That's the challenge—to discover the humanity in such a man and even, perhaps, forgive him.

INTERVIEWER

Earlier we spoke of risk in your nonfiction. Risk is present in your fiction, too. I'm thinking of *At Play's* wild drug hallucination scene, and how the novel form was stretched in *Far Tortuga*, and now this twenty-year commitment to a single work. What is important to you about risk? You never seem to write from a place of safety.

MATTHIESSEN

Isn't that the joy of fiction? To probe for fresh experience rather than perpetuate received wisdom? Why turn out endless variations on what we have already done well; what our reviewers, and friends and family, too, assure us we do best; what everyone feels most comfortable with and what might sell. Why not explore new territory and also new means of getting there when that seems necessary? Too few writers these days seem to risk long-term commitment to a project, like that of the great novelists of the nineteenth century, and Proust and Joyce. Not risk painful controversy, as Styron did in *Sophie's Choice* and *Nat Turner*, nor even extend their reach from book to book, as Mailer tries to do, and Don DeLillo. Because these novelists embrace large subjects, they will write long books when necessary, although quite aware that the poor overworked reviewers and the busy readers much prefer slight fictions.

I think serious writers stretch themselves, however subtly, and stretch their good readers, too—otherwise, why do it? There are many too many formulaic novels published already. In paying attention to what publishers or readers may expect

of us, one is no longer an artist but an artisan, however gifted.
To keep that necessary edge, the writer must never feel quite
comfortable, and never satisfied. So many good novels could
have benefited from another draft. I would work all the way
to the printer's, if they let me.

You're not afraid of overworking the material?

Indeed I am. My danger signal in my own endless revisions
is when, next day, I remove more of my corrections than I
keep. The prose dries out with overwork, becomes too literary.

Do you consider this trilogy your magnum opus?

You said that, not me. But certainly it draws together in
one work the themes that have absorbed me all my life—the
pollution of land and air and oceans, the obliteration of
wilderness and the wild creatures, not to mention the more
defenseless members of our own species, in particular the
traditional peoples left stranded by the long-term cruelty and
stupidity of what passes for progress and democracy, especially
among businessmen and politicians.

In the metaphor of the Watson legend, I suppose I am
writing about Uncle Sam, about racism and injustice in our
country and the ongoing destruction of their hopes for Americans living too close to the bone, with no voice in the rapid
changes that gnaw at their beliefs and nothing to confront
their irrelevance with but humor, grit and rage. These concerns are subthemes of these novels. I do my best to keep my
voice down; be ironical rather than strident. I never forget
what Camus said in accepting his Nobel: modern writers can
no longer isolate themselves in the artistic endeavor but must
speak for those who cannot speak for themselves.

INTERVIEWER

What is your review of the reception of the first two volumes of the trilogy?

MATTHIESSEN

Mainly I am grateful that they found a few good readers. The ills of our great republic as seen through the eyes of redneck fugitives, swamp rats and smugglers around the back country, will never be as popular as suburban angst, but losers on the edge are eloquent, with real obstacles to the pursuit of happiness, not mere neurotic ones. In the end, all true novels must finally deal with the human heart, even the heart of an alleged sociopath such as Mister Watson.

INTERVIEWER

Do you see flaws in this long work—problems to look out for?

MATTHIESSEN

Yes. I tend to make my novels too dense at the beginning so that even readers who enjoy them may sometimes find them a bit difficult to enter. This might be because my eye is fixed not on the ending of the book but on the *feeling* of that ending, the distillation of all its foregoing imaginings and intuitions. Philip Roth speaks intelligently somewhere about "the magnet"—that intangible force that draws the author to the subject, the first impulse to pursue and penetrate a certain feeling or idea. It then becomes the navigational aide that keeps the writer on course, therefore the reader, who sooner or later will be made to sense that magnet, too. When the book goes too far astray during the writing, the magnet will guide the author back. If it is lost, the book will wander, perhaps fatally.

I'm wandering right now from my point. The magnet in this trilogy appears to be that lone house on the wild river and/or the enigma of a man slain by his neighbors. I'm not quite sure which is the seed, but in this case it doesn't matter much, since those images fuse into the yearning that drew me in and drew me ineluctably toward the resolution—Watson's end and the book's too, and also in some sense, to the degree that the author grows into the heart of the protagonist, my own. What I sought instinctively but only half-consciously was to prepare myself as the first reader, make sure I was well-oriented in every element I would require to enter and accompany the narrative toward its conclusion. Inevitably the writer has to share this information with the reader—hence these thickety beginnings, which the reader must pierce before being set free into the story.

To orient the reader and to prepare the ground overrules any consideration of easy access. To cite two prominent examples—and I certainly don't mean to invite comparison between these books and my own—*Moby-Dick* and Faulkner's long story "The Bear" are resounding works that prepare their readers by educating them relentlessly for what is coming. We have all heard complaints about *Moby-Dick*—all that "boring and unnecessary" information about whaling. Yet without embarking on that whole hard voyage, with its grit and particulars—the tar smell of hemp, the harpoon rust, the creak of spars and buffet of the canvas, the ocean light—every moment that reminds the crew of its own peril at sea and tightens its accumulating dread of Ahab's obsession—without that knowing, how are we to join these men in the final passages? In the author's grand spectral vision of our death in life?

INTERVIEWER

So now, in *Bone by Bone*, we have Ed Watson's version of events—the final word, since surely he knows better than anyone who he has become and what will now become of him.

MATTHIESSEN

I suppose so, if we trust him. But how well does he really know himself? How wise is he? How honest in his feelings? The reader must be Watson's final judge. And of course, if the thing has been done properly, the reader will ask those same questions of himself.

Anyway, that is the novel's general structure—I say novel because it's really all one work. That's the way it was originally conceived and that will be its final form. As one novel, it will be considerably shorter and tighter, since much of the scaffolding required for setting up three separate books will be dismantled. Not that I can assume it will ever be published in its proper form. It's just that I need to reassemble it before putting it away, if only to know that it exists somewhere in its true nature.

INTERVIEWER

The act of letting go of such a prodigious work—will that be a problem for you? Perhaps you haven't let it go yet.

MATTHIESSEN

I will never let it go. How could I? Such a long work is in my grain, a manifestation of my being, like this carcass that lugs me here and there—I'm stuck with the damn thing, for better or worse. Perhaps their work is what writers become, in the way of people who, in old age, come to resemble their dogs.

—Howard Norman

Bone by Bone

Peter Matthiessen

Old Man William Brown at Half Way Creek, he liked the way I went about my business. He liked my style and saw some future for me so he took a down payment on a worn-out schooner. Young Henry Thompson of Chokoloskee signed on to teach me the sea rudiments, and as soon as we got some stores aboard, we headed south into the Islands, cutting buttonwood for charcoal to sell down at Key West and shooting a few plume birds where we found them. That gloomy boy would show me the great bend of Chatham River which became my home.

In all of the Ten Thousand Islands, Chatham Bend was the largest mound after Chokoloskee, forty acres of rich black soil going back to jungle because the squatter on there with his wife and daughter would not farm it. Like many an inhabitant of the Islands, Will Raymond Esq. was a fugitive and killer, glowering from WANTED posters all the way from Tampa to Key West. The Bend was exactly to his liking because it was surrounded by a million miles of mangrove, giving the lawmen no way to come at him except from the open water of Chatham River.

There was a loose palmetto shack on there, and smoke. We drifted off the shore, keeping our distance. When I hailed, no answer came back over the water, only the soft mullet slap and the whisper of the current, and scratchy wisps of birdsong from the clearing. The boy slid the skiff in under the bank, put me ashore.

Henry Thompson was plain scared to death of this mangy bastard, so I whispered to him to row the skiff offshore beyond gunshot range, but to stay in plain sight to warn Will Raymond that there was a witness. Next, I halloed once or twice before sticking my head over the bank to have a look. Nothing moving, nothing in sight. Set for a backward somersault, I rose slowly, keeping my hands well out to the side, then nervously wasted my best smile on a raggedy young girl who slipped back inside that low rain-rotted shack.

All this while, Will Raymond had me covered. I could feel the iron of his weapon and its hungry muzzle, and my heart felt naked and my chest dead pale, although I wore a shirt. But I was up there in one piece with my revolver up my sleeve, still smiling hard and looking all around to enjoy the view.

What broke a bad silence was a hard and sudden cough, like a choked dog. Then this ugly galoot in a broken hat, hefting a rifle, stepped out from behind a tree. Unshaven, barefoot, in soiled rags, red puffy eyes like sores and a thin split for a mouth, he stunk like a wild boar on that river wind.

All the while I presented my respects to Mr. Raymond, he kept his old coon rifle trained upon my stomach, yellow finger twitching on the trigger. The muzzle of a shooting iron at point blank range looks like a black hole straight into hell, but I did my very best to keep on smiling. This Raymond looked rotted out by drink but also steady as a stump—an uncommon and unpleasant combination, in my experience.

Mr. Raymond, I declared, I am here today with an interesting business proposition. Yes sir, said I, you are looking at a man ready and willing to pay hard cash for the quit-claim to a likely farm on the high ground—this place, for instance. Two hundred dollars, for instance. Henry, who was doing his best to hold that skiff against the current, had told me this was a fair offer for squatter's rights in this cash-poor economy.

Will Raymond wore a kind of a wild unlimbered look, and his manners were not good. He never so much as introduced me to his females, who kept popping their heads out of their hole like nervous prairie dogs back in Oklahoma. In fact he made no response at all to my fine words except to cough and spit in my direction whatever he dredged up from his racked lungs. However, that mention of cold cash had set him thinking, because his squint narrowed. He was considering that boy out in the boat while estimating how much cash might be recovered from my dead body. Will Raymond had reached a place in life where he had very damned little left to lose.

He coughed again, that same hard bark, and then he growled, "If you are looking to farm at the ass end of Hell, seventy mile by sea from the nearest market, and have a likin for the company of nine-foot rattlers and man-eatin miskeeters and river sharks and panthers and crocky-diles and every fuckin kind of creepin varmint the Lord ever thunk up to bedevil his sinners—well then, Mister, this surely is your kind of place."

"My kind of place is right!" I sing out cheerily.

"Nosir, it sure ain't, cause I am on here first. And next time you go to trespissin without my say-so, I will blow your head off. Any questions?"

"Not a one," says I in the same carefree tone, as I signal for my boat. While waiting for Henry, I look around a little more, thinking how much my dear Mandy might like these two huge poincianas with red blossoms. "Yessir, a fine day on the river! Makes a man feel good to be alive!"

"You got maybe ten seconds more to feel alive in, Mister, cause after that you ain't goin to feel nothin."

Under my coat, the .38 lay along my forearm, ready to drop into my hand. To drill this polecat in his tracks would have been a mercy to everyone concerned, especially his poor drag-ass females. But what I needed more that anything right now was a reputation as an upright citizen, so I put aside my motto of "good riddance of bad rubbish" in favor of "every dog must have its day." He was having his day now and mine would come.

Will Raymond's rifle, swinging slow, followed me into the boat and out onto the river. For a long time as we drifted down around the bend, that man stood there as black and still as some old cypress snag out in the swamp, that Confederate long rifle on his shoulder like the scythe of Death. All the same, my heart was set on Chatham Bend, and all the more so when we passed down through the delta and gazed back. That river mouth, all broken up by mangrove islets and oyster bars, would never be seen by any stranger, even from a quarter mile offshore.

That same week, we sailed to Key West with a cordwood cargo, and I had my first look at Lost Man's River, said to be the wild heart of this whole wilderness. From Cape Sable our course led south along the edge of vast pale banks of sand and coral marl, with the blue-black channels and emerald keys of Florida Bay on the port side and the thousand-mile blue sea of the Gulf of Mexico out there to starboard. Henry would point when he heard the puff of tarpon, and here and there one of these mighty silver fishes would leap clear of the surface like the black-winged manta rays farther offshore, crashing down in explosions of white water into the sea.

In late afternoon the spars of an armada of great ships rose slowly from the sunny mists in the southern distance—Cayo Hueso, announced Henry Thompson, who turned out to be an authority on Key West, having been born here. Bone Key, he told me.

On an east wind, we passed the Northwest Light and tacked into the rough water of the channel. Who would have imagined such a roadstead as the Key West Bight, so faraway at

the end of this long archipelago of coral keys? There were so
many masts, so many small craft, so much shout and bustle
of triumphant commerce—New York merchantmen and Havana craft, all mixed together with small schooners from the
Cayman Islands, fetching live green turtle to the water pens
near Schooner Wharf for delivery to the turtle canning factory
down the shore. My mouth must have dropped open at the
spectacle, for my crewman uttered a hiccuping grunt that I
took to be a rare spasm of mirth.

Our modest cargo was unloaded into a horse-drawn cart
backed down into the shallows, and we went ashore. Key
West was a port city, with 18,000 immigrants and refugees
of every color—eighteen times as many human beings as
inhabited the whole southwest coast, all the way north two
hundred miles to Tampa Bay.

While in Key West, I paid a call on the Monroe County
Sheriff, Richard Knight, in regard to a certain notorious fugitive depicted on the WANTED notice in the post office. The
murderer Will Raymond, I advised him, could be found right
up the coast, in Chatham River. The Sheriff knew this very
well and was sorry to be reminded of it. He sighed as he bit
off his cigar. My report would oblige him to send out a posse
when, like most lazy lawmen, enjoying the modest graft of
elected office, he much preferred to "let sleeping dogs lie."

Taking the chair he had not offered, I said I sure hated to
cause trouble for another man, but as a law-abiding citizen,
I knew my duty. Looking up for the first time, Knight said,
sardonic, "That mean you won't be needing the reward?"
Sheriff Knight and I understood each other right from the
first, and our understanding was this: we did not like each
other. We did not even honor and respect each other as fellow
citizens of our great new nation.

A few days later, the Sheriff's posse laid off the river mouth
until three in the morning, as I advised 'em, then drifted
upriver with the tide. They had four men ashore by the time
Will Raymond opened fire, and he never got off a second
round. His executioners removed their hats and paid polite

respects to his loved ones and gave them a nice boat ride to Key West, and Sheriff Richard Knight got all the credit. You'd think that might have won me his affection or at least a benign tolerance. It did not.

On my next visit, I went to the Sheriff's office to offer my congratulations. He winced and slid open a drawer and forked over $250 in hard cash without a word. I never kept a penny of that money. I went straight over to Peg's boarding house on White Street and offered it to the widow as a consolation in her time of bereavement. By this time, she was looking somewhat better or at least cleaner, even kind of perky. She said, "Stranger, this sure is my lucky day and you sure are my savior, bless your heart!" She offered corn spirits and a simple repast, then took me straight to bed, out of pure gratitude and the milk of human kindness.

Buttoning up, I happened to mention the late Mr. Raymond's quit-claim on Chatham Bend, and she implored me to take it over with her compliments, declaring the sincere and fervent hope that she would never set eyes on that accursed place again. Altogether, a very touching story with a happy ending. I strode away to the docks with a lilting heart, confident that my dark path in life had at last made a turning for the better.

Four Poems by Robert Phillips

Imaginary Friends

In first grade I was positive there were
furry creatures called tisathees.
Every morning we intoned, "My country
tisathee, sweet land of liberty . . ."

In Sunday School we were instructed
an angel told Joseph to take Mary
and the child and flee into Egypt.
I asked, "What happened to the flea?"

I crayoned a picture of haloed Joseph,
Mary and Baby Jesus in back of a plane.
In the cockpit was Pontius the Pilot.
I titled it, "The Flight to Egypt."

For a decade I dreamed of a nubile
farm girl, Wendy Moon. Kate Smith
crooned her abundant charms:
"Wendy Moon comes over the mountain . . ."

At Christmastime when we caroled away
I had another friend, a portly monk—
Round John Virgin—as in, "Round
John Virgin, Mother and Child . . ."

South Pacific I thought a musical
about a genial couple, Sam and Janet.
Didn't Ezio Pinza sing, "Sam and Janet
evening, you will find a stranger . . .?"

A hymn became "Gladly, the Cross-Eyed Bear."
Even in high school I attended
graduation ceremonies convinced I was
the class valid Victorian. (I was.)

Where are they now, my imaginary friends?
I miss Sam and Janet, mysterious tisathees,
Victorians, Wendy Moon, the cross-eyed bear,
Pontius the Pilot, and of course the flea.

Say Hello to the Little Woman

She asserts herself at the damnedest times—
when they're working out at the gym, say,
or having a brandy and cigar with the boys.

It's not as if they want her to come out,
and most men manage to keep her down;
but her triumphs are many, from J. Edgar Hoover

to the boy in junior high who swung his bat
just like a girl. And you, my friend—
look how you're holding that wine glass.

In Praise of My Prostate

after St. Anne of Weston, who celebrated her uterus

My internist said you are unnaturally large.
Had I caught gonorrhea from some co-ed?
(In my encyclopedia, you come right between

prosody and *prostitution*, just before
prosthesis. Alphabetization makes
strange bedfellows.) Once chestnut-size,

you've expanded, he said, into a tennis ball.
I told him no score, no love, but I was
urinating with uncommon frequency:

You are like an unruly child—a real pisser.
You are like a porn star—the great climax
a golden shower. Well, not always a shower—

sometimes you just peter out, dribbles
and drabs. It began when I found blood
in my semen, red curled into white

like a viscous Christmas candy-cane.
It whirled down the drain like blood
in Hitchcock's *Psycho*. I told the doctor

I thought you'd given me cancer, Prostate.
(For men of a certain age, Prostate Cancer
is all the rage. I have pals who've had

an orchidectomy—such a flowery name
for such a final and hideous disfigurement,
testicles snipped away like a blossom.

I have a fifty-something friend who,
when asked, "Do you wear Jockey shorts
or Boxers?", grimaced and replied, *"Depends."*)

So I was sure I had the big C. "Does it
burn when you urinate?" "Never." "Do you
have trouble getting it up?" "No, my problem

is getting it down." The doctor lectured,
"Whenever you hear the sound of hooves,
the chances are it's just horses.

"But if you're determined to hear a zebra,
or even a unicorn, go ahead. Be my guest."
So I thought just horses. Until I began

to shit buckets of blood, the toilet bowl
cranberry-sauce red. I was scared witless.
I got a second and a third opinion.

To a man, they all said, "Gastroenteritis."
After weeks of expensive antibiotics,
you became healthy, Prostate. Healthy

as a horse. Still enlarged, but no zebra,
no unicorn. I put away mortality thoughts,
which I'd lugged around like a trunk.

Now men everywhere are chanting their escape,
celebrating their perfect little chestnuts,
their perfect pelvic and spinal lymph nodes.

One throws pizzas over his head on Coney Island.
One gathers discarded tin cans in London.
One occupies an office in the World Trade Center.

One is driving to Enid, Oklahoma, to get married.
One is climbing telephone poles in Germany.
One attempts to teach English to Asians.

One is a hairy sonofabitch on a cement mixer.
One is a perfumed gigolo in Beverly Hills.
One is an Alsatian monk who vowed abstinence.

One implements media-software in Houston.
One is an art student working his way through *collage*.
And one is me. Everywhere we men are chanting,

saying a mantra for you, the Grand Gland.
We shoo away the bluebird of unhappiness.
We'll watch football and baseball games,

eclipses, sniff wildflowers, make love, eat
whatever we want, every meal no longer the last
for the (mistakenly) condemned man on Death Row.

No, we'll not pack our bags yet. The hooves
you guys and I were hearing were just horses.
For now, the zebras and unicorns will wait.

John Dillinger's Dick

Some say it's pickled
(formaldehyde) in the basement
of a funeral parlor in Indiana.
Some say the mortician
had heard of Dillinger's
legendary endowment—
the gangster's gun molls
and cellmates talked.
When the corpse was delivered
by the FBI, the undertaker
couldn't wait for the stiff's
great unveiling. He wasn't
interested in bullet holes
(one in the face was
a matter for makeup).
He undertook to measure
length, circumference:

Even non-tumescent
it was monumental.
Why should such a marvel
be buried? The mortician,
with his wife's boning knife,
carved away his fleshly
trophy. No one would know:
When laid out in his coffin
the gangster wore a suit.
Some nights as his wife
slept he crept down
to the basement, removed
the red velvet cloth
covering the pickle jar,
switched on the lamp—
the jar brilliantly backlit—
and sat admiring.
A few times he invited
cronies from his club
to come view his jar.
They joked, speculated
what woman could accommodate
it all. Some days he wished
he'd taken the balls too.
Against all offers,
the mortician wouldn't part
with Dillinger's private part.
Since 1934 it's floated
and danced in its memorial
waters, lifting its great
purple head, mooning
against the glass. When
will it rise again, source
of so much pleasure
and pain? It was like
Albert Einstein's extracted
brain, dropped by some

doltish technician—
splattered and shattered
on the laboratory floor
before it, too, properly
could be measured. But
no measure in death would do
for such prodigious organs.
Only in life, only in action,
could they reveal all
their awesome capability.

Three Poems by Melanie Rehak

A Pale Ode

Even Atalanta's tongue was turned eventually.
Parting the high raceway grasses
she bent down for that last apple,
its gold a kind of language in the light,
and heard her dialect scatter.

So strains of your argument bear
great darkness and then gleam,
and I do not lose the rhetoric of your approach.
Impossible to refuse, the logic of your arrival
was silent and bright and gaped until
its closure in my throat. I let you leap from there.

Your conclusions, it seems, were wrong
and are lost with the variegated bricks
we used to pass over, that blistering doorjamb.
But I would never have thought to listen to you
for so long; you sound in all crowds.

I do not struggle to remember.
Like a peculiar cadence
you settled in my ear and lilting live.

Apple

An implied corkscrew of peel garners the apple.
For days, wholly curved, the fruit has rested here.
The high lights of various mornings have settled

in its clefted top; around the stem, afternoons
have gathered and dispersed. A dozen apples
would not speak more than this one, shadowless
by the window sash on a rain-blown Sunday,
the week rolling over in foul weather again.
You cannot see the writhing at its core.
Error before the truth, it is there,
it has always been there, like pride,
like desire, clear in its message: I want, I want.

Parallax

There is a kind
of whiteness to the day,
everything pared down,
lucid and still.

I have tried to be
big about it, the way
the landscape is
pressed into itself.
I have tried to move
past this, making
decisions as if the day
was not unnaturally hemmed.

I have tried to fit
everything in as if I knew
this place, as if the sky
was more than a reified
blue thought being portaged
over land by unseen hands.

Three Poems by Vincent Hamilton

Florida, 1521

The ocean climbs the beach in search of salt.
It chases off the piper. It licks away
The driftwood. Mulling over his latest fault,
Cupid hides, see? in the dune-grass?, to waylay
Ponce de León. Mad from the chlorophyll,
And blunted by a native immunity,
He shoots his angel-shot—not meaning to kill.
It bites as loosely as a skeleton key.

Ponce lets fall the armfuls of potassium-
Rich oranges he had sailed for. He cries one word.
He drops—untransformed within the ho-hum
Calx of creation—aged and yet unflowered.

And Love, poor Love! left fishing fruit from the tide
To place (just so) to suggest a homicide.

Darwin in Appalachia

The cattle carry their birds out from under
The tresses of the willow tree, past
The Ancient Ship and into the blooming pond.
With loose-legged balance, egret search the shore.
The cow's legs slowly disappear until
The cows drink with ease. The cows think, if they think,
There isn't enough ship here to build a barn.

Towns above us arch precariously close
To God. Only the Cherubim condescend

This far. Unskilled in lighting and finish work,
Unable to control the circular saw,
They idle on the ridgepole, like seagulls
Upon a beached humpback, forecasting
A rain that has already begun to fall.

Run down from shale-swimming fossils, the rain
Muddies the pond with an ore miners' needles
And oil men's pump jacks refuse imagining;
An ore that, like other ores, once lived. Things change.
The feathers of angels once were scales; no barn,
They'll herd beneath, or flock with egret in
The willow tree. It's true, look at their legs.

Waiting for Grushenka in West Virginia

I

Already, the moon. What wouldn't come with such
A moon? Invisible stars foretell
The precious night. What wouldn't come, as bees
Wear themselves out at the milk-sweet blooms in which
They'll sleep? and in accidents of four and five,
The apple tree releases starving fruit?
(All night, from inside, fruit fall sounds like footfall.)

All Lansing apprehends the moon and feels
The lungworts whisper against each other;
The screen door scraping, scraping the back porch.

II

The sun redeems the night. Almost bloodless,
The moon hangs in the day like a fossil. Bees
Forsake (at last!) the less-melliferous

Flowers, to gorge on colza, refresh the sage,
To stroke red pollen from the mignonette.
What wouldn't come? what monster, while the windfall
Coaxes an extravagance of houseflies?

All Lansing lounges in the moon's disaster,
In lungworts loosening their bluing petals,
And in the labored hum-joy of bees at sage.

A manuscript page of Rorem's setting of Shakespeare's sonnet #30.

Ned Rorem

The Art of the Diary I

"I am a composer," Ned Rorem once said, "who also writes, not a writer who also composes." His music—hundreds of ravishing art songs and instrumental scores, one of which won the 1976 Pulitzer Prize—has brought him fame. But it is his diaries that have brought him celebrity. The first of them, The Paris Diary, *covering his stay abroad from 1951 to 1955, was published in 1966. Its pithy, elegant entries were filled with tricks turned and names dropped (Cocteau, Poulenc, Balthus, Dalí, Paul Bowles, John Cage, Man Ray and James*

*Baldwin, along with the rich and titled, the louche and witty).
Reviewers seemed either shocked or ecstatic; Janet Flanner was
both—she called it "worldly, intelligent, licentious, highly
indiscreet."* The following year Rorem published The New
York Diary, *which took the story up to 1961 and deepened
his self-portrait as an untortured artist and dashing narcissist.
Two hefty further installments subsequently appeared,* The
Later Diaries *in 1974 and* The Nantucket Diary *in 1987, which
carried the account of his nights and days up to 1985. All
along, he had been collecting his essays into other books, and
his memoir,* Knowing When to Stop *(1994), fills us in on
his early life. But the diaries are an incomparable resource,
certainly the fullest version of a composer's daily life we have,
and perhaps the most vivid self-portrait there is of a contemporary creative artist. Work and play, professional and social duties,
the network of lovers and contacts, the underworld of desire
and ambition, the buzz of scandal and rumor, the hangovers,
the pettiness, the glamour, the bright rush of ideas.*

*It wasn't long before Rorem's notorious diaries received
the dubious accolade of parody. In 1975 the poet Howard
Moss, several of whose poems Rorem had set, published in*
The New Yorker *a hilarious send-up called "The Ultimate
Diary." Its little gilded barbs were dipped in a poisonous wit:*

MONDAY

*Drinks here. Picasso, Colette, the inevitable Coc-
teau, Gide, Valéry, Ravel and Larry. Chitchat. God,
how absolutely dull the Great can be! I know at least
a hundred friends who would have given their eyeteeth
just to have had a glimpse of some of them, and there
I was bored, incredible lassitude, stymied. Is it me?
Is it them? Think latter. Happened to glance in mirror
before going to bed. Am more beautiful than ever.*

THURSDAY

*Half the Opéra-Comique seems to have fallen in
love with me. I cannot stand any more importuning.
Will go to Africa. How to break with C? Simone de*

> *Beauvoir, Simone Signoret, Simone Weil and Simone*
> *Simon for drinks. They didn't get it!*

Behind the satire, though, lurk more serious matters. Edgar Allan Poe once wrote that the ambitious man's "road to immortal renown lies straight, open, unencumbered before him. All that he has to do is write and publish a very little book. Its title should be simple—a few plain words—'My Heart Laid Bare.' But—this little book must be true *to its title. No* man *dare write it. No* man *could write it, even if he dared. The paper would shrivel and blaze at every touch of the fiery pen." Yes, there's a strong dose of self-absorption to Rorem's diaries, but there's also an honesty—touched up, as any on-the-spot notation must be, to give it the tone of even more spontaneous ingenuity. Documenting oneself poses as a kind of writing that is both artless and knowing. The intimate journal, as distinct from autobiography, has never especially appealed to American writers, as it has to the French, though both nationalities are high on self-promotion.*

Perhaps it took living for a spell in Paris to help Rorem cultivate the turn of mind that gazes at the world through the narrow lens of a diary. He'd kept one briefly as a child, and again as a young man. Once he moved to Paris in 1951, he resumed a chronicle of his composing called Journal de mes mélodies, *in imitation of Francis Poulenc's. He started it in French, soon reverted to English and began to deal with more mundane matters. In 1959, back in America and staying for the summer at Yaddo, he met the author Robert Phelps who, with his wife, was also a guest at Yaddo. Because Phelps was a Francophile and a "born fan," Rorem read to him from his diary. He may as well have been Scheherazade. Phelps was captivated. He was working then as a reader for the publisher George Braziller, who signed on the book at once. Phelps insisted it would be best if he edited the book, and Rorem, delighted at the prospect of his first publication, agreed. Phelps selected his favorite bits, removed their dates, and rearranged them. Not until* The Later Diaries *was Rorem his own editor.*

"Don't look back," said Cocteau, "or you risk turning into a pillar of salt—that is, a pillar of tears." From the perspective of a half-century later, the events described in Rorem's Paris Diary have the flavor of a novel. In a way, he'd fashioned for himself a miniature Père Lachaise where so many of his friends and acquaintances of those decades lie at rest. In its splendors and miseries, it seems a vanished world. In retrospect he was its Audubon, an American dauphin in disguise, a tender draughtsman taking aim.

I first met Ned Rorem twenty years ago. I even know the precise date: February 13, 1979, at a dinner party given by the novelist Edmund White. I know because I read about it years later in Rorem's diary. (I might have anticipated the entry; after that dinner, while guests were getting their coats, Rorem came over to me and asked, "How exactly do you spell your name?") While this interview was afoot, his friend James Holmes was gravely ill. Rorem had lived with Jim, an organist and choir director, for thirty-one years, and shortly after our interview, Jim died at the age of fifty-nine, on January 7, 1999. In 1974, they had bought a slumping 1919 bungalow on Nantucket, 176 yards (Rorem's reckoning by his daily walk) from the newspaper store that's the town hub. Jim had fixed up the house and put in gardens on the half-acre plot. Rorem doubts that now, without Jim, he'll ever return. Since 1968 he's also lived in a rambling apartment on New York's Upper West Side. Its living room, where we spoke, is dominated by the Steinway at which he works. There are books and recordings everywhere, and they line the walls of nearly every other room as well. His furniture is unstylish, but there are paintings to admire—by Leonid, say, and by his friends Jane Freilicher, Jane Wilson, Gloria Vanderbilt, Robert Dash, Joe Brainard and Nell Blaine. There are several drawings by Cocteau hung near the piano, and at the other end of the room some of the many portraits of himself (I recognize those by Larry Rivers and Maurice Grosser) he owns. At seventy-five, Rorem has the sort of looks men used to try for with injections of animal glands. He's trim, handsome, energetic, voluble. The slight trace of puffiness in his face was probably the result of his insomnia and of his anxiety about Jim Holmes. We spoke on a gray winter afternoon. He had brought in a tray with teapot and cups, and a little plastic carton of tapioca for himself.

INTERVIEWER

Children, it seems to me, have no capacity to distance themselves from their own lives, and so no sense of reflection. All of that starts to well up—in the form of Great Ideas and Deep Feelings—in the teenager. But for the record, did you start keeping a diary as a child?

NED ROREM

Don't be too dismissive of children. While it's true that few children are artists, all artists are children. And insofar as artists adopt the grown-up stance that blinds them to the wide-open perceptions of their childhood, they cease being artists. That said, I'm not much interested in children before they're twenty-one. And yes, their diaries—even Anne Frank's or Daisy Ashford's—are not repositories of Great Ideas. What are Great Ideas anyway, and are mature artists interested in them? Most of my writer-friends gossip when they get together, and reserve their nuance for the page. Deep Feelings were expressed in the college dorm. Not that we don't suffer after fifty, but the suffering is more often about health and death than about Love and Abandonment.

I did keep a diary in 1936, age twelve, for three months when our family went to Europe. Except for frequent references to Debussy and Griffes, it focuses breathlessly on American movies seen in Oslo, or tourists we met on boats. No shred of lust, much less of intellect or guile. Admittedly, words are never put on paper, be it *War and Peace* or a laundry list, without thought of other eyes reading them, even though those eyes might just be one's own at another time. But I didn't think of myself as an author. Ten years later I began a literary diary and kept it up until I went to

France in 1949. It's filled with drunkenness, sex and the talk of my betters, all to the tune of André Gide.

INTERVIEWER

Your Quaker upbringing—did that encourage early habits of introspection?

ROREM

I didn't really have a "Quaker upbringing." My mother's younger brother was killed in the First World War at the age of seventeen. She never got over the trauma. When they were married in 1920 my parents (she a Congregational minister's daughter, he a Methodist) looked around for a group that would work for peace, internationally, and not just in time of war. The Society of Friends was the answer. They weren't concerned with the God part (I'm not sure they ever believed in God), only with the peace part. Thus my older sister, Rosemary, and I were raised as pacifists, to think that there is no alternative to peace. Which I believe. Whether I'm right or wrong, I'm not ashamed of it. . . . So I was not raised piously, much less in silence. We were taken regularly to all the best concerts and plays that came to Chicago. My background was far more structured by the cultured and caring intellect of my parents than by the strictured structure of the stricter Quakers.

INTERVIEWER

What prompted you to start that diary in 1946?

ROREM

Prior to entering Juilliard in the fall of 1945, it was necessary to take some liberal-arts courses to qualify for a degree as distinct from a diploma. So I went to summer school at NYU in Washington Square. During the first class in English literature, our instructor happened to say, "Happiness, then, is an answering after the heart." On the way home I bought a 5" x 9" ruled hardcover notebook and began a diary with the phrase—a phrase that today seems both corny and unclear.

Also, knowing that David Diamond kept a diary was an incentive. Diamond was an example—one I emulated perhaps—of a disciplined composer (who could account for every note) trapped in a self-destructive body. The style of that early diary (my diaries are really journals, since they're hardly daily—although *journal* means daily too, doesn't it?) was often like Diamond's, or like the books he read, *Moby-Dick, The Heart Is a Lonely Hunter*. Probably I took to the form because it was a crazy, open-ended contrast to my rather Spartan music. The entries are all about screwing, drunkenness, suicidal urges . . . the usual. If they ring true at all, it's the truth of the young. I left the book lying around. Once a piece of rough trade stole it and tried to blackmail me. He felt we could make a killing together in royalties! I got the book back, but that's another story.

Incidentally, I kept the diary in longhand for the next twenty years, until I realized it might be published.

INTERVIEWER

You left for France in 1949. That would be incentive enough to continue keeping your diary, but was there a moment when you became more self-conscious about doing so?

ROREM

When I left for France in May of 1949, the visit was to have lasted three months, so I didn't bring my diary. I ultimately remained eight years. On realizing that I'd never come back to America, I wrote Morris Golde and asked him to ship all my previous journals to Hyères, where I was living chez Marie-Laure de Noailles. One morning she came into my room and handed me a pretty little carnet with several hundred empty pages, saying: "Here, write. Even if you feel bad before and after, *while* you're writing your cares are transferred." She kept her own diary every night before bed, faithfully, drunk or sober. It mainly related facts of the day. Mine—which for several months I kept in French, then reverted to English, which was, of course, more *me*—related states of mind as well as of body, and was probably modeled on Julien Green's journal. Green, who had become an intimate friend (the friendship exploded fatally a year later), was as strong a literary influence on me as Paul Goodman had been during my adolescence. And yes, probably I was thinking of other eyes than my own as I penned the pages.

Marie-Laure and Green were the same age (she was born in 1902, he in 1900), but opposites. She: French, half-Jewish, unimaginably rich, Catholic but communist and a nonbeliever, odd-looking but forceful, like George Washington in a Dior gown, vastly cultivated, sophisticated (but like many sophisticated females of the period, more innocent than she pretended about sex), self-consciously bohemian, liking queer men, including her very closeted husband, the Vicomte de Noailles, who was her best friend but whom she seldom saw, and to whom a marriage had been arranged when she was twenty, thus making her noble (the Noailles go back to Louis XIII) and still richer. She was a rather gifted writer and a very gifted painter, but, like many of the rich, undisciplined with pen and paintbrush. She was powerful and famous too, and launched me, sort of. Otherwise I may have returned here sooner. Julien, meanwhile, was American (but raised in France) and the truest bilingual I've ever known. A True Believer, Catholic convert, writer of a strange and passionate passivity, if that makes sense. His force came through a sort of hypnotism. He loved me, and I was infected with the casual cruelty of the young. He felt, probably, that my remarks about God were frivolous, and that I made mockery of his sexual leanings.

He came to Hyères for a one-day visit in 1951, and seeing the two of them together was odd—especially since, exceptionally, the vicomte was also there. They were all so *respectful* of each other, yet their only interest in common (beyond the considerable one of art) was me. This went to my head.

INTERVIEWER

The anecdote that opens *The Paris Diary*—was it meant to be emblematic? It goes this way: "A stranger asks, 'Are you Ned Rorem?' I answer, 'No,' adding, however, that I've

Ned Rorem and Julien Green at the first performance of Rorem's
Second Piano Sonata, *Théâtre des Champs-Elysées, February, 1951.*

heard of and would like to meet him." Was that meant to
point toward some underlying theme of self-discovery, or self-
making? Or worse, some condition that calls for a negation
of the self, or a devotion to the diary as a substitute for the self?

ROREM

Your question ignores this fact: *The Paris Diary* is the only
one of my fourteen books that was edited by someone else.
Being my first book, all suggestions were accepted. Not a

word is changed from the manuscript, but Robert Phelps radically shifted the order of entries. Thus that first remark was originally embedded somewhere in the center. To change place is to change meaning, even when that which is changed remains unchanged, so to speak. Would you have posed your question about that entry if it were elsewhere?

INTERVIEWER

Fair enough. Now, however the entries were rearranged in the end, what first prompted you to record a particular event or idea? The amusing remark? The annals of star-fucking? Or were you, in prose, marking your growth, as with a ruler and pencil on the kitchen wall?

ROREM

Hmm . . . Does the diary, in fact, record events and ideas and amusing remarks? It's a long time since I've reread it. Probably I wrote what I wrote because, although I've always known that nothing in the universe really counts, and that when we're gone we're gone, I still have a terror of being lost, of becoming as anonymous as an Assyrian slave, or even as an Elizabethan poet, whose works, to be sure, are recalled, but not his body—not, say, Marlowe's scalding male flesh. As for star-fucking (your term), I've never practiced that. Of the three thousand people I bedded between 1938 and 1968, only four were famous, and it wasn't my doing. (They're listed in *Knowing When to Stop*.) I can't sleep with the famous, it's an ego clash. But if many of my friends have recognizable names, I know them not for their fame but for what made them famous, their music, or books or pictures. I'd rather have first-rate acquaintances than not. I don't know any baseball players (though they're sexier than, say, dress designers) because we have nothing in common.

INTERVIEWER

Does one have to be a narcissist to keep a diary?

ROREM

Am I really more of a narcissist than other artists? Or do I just admit it more readily? Certainly I'm not hot for myself. I'm not my own type. Nor does the diary use the word *I* more than do most contemporary poets. Jorie Graham, for instance, or Frank O'Hara, or indeed yourself, sprinkle the page with *I*. Marie-Laure used to say that I was more interested in a state of body than a state of mind (*un état de corps, non pas un état d'âme*). But how can I know? We live inside ourselves, by definition, and none of us can see ourselves as others see us. Inasmuch as every work of art, whether vertical or horizontal, has a beginning, middle and end, a diary cannot by its nature qualify, though certainly a good diary hits the mark more convincingly than a dull, but expertly penned, novel. But who makes the definitions?

INTERVIEWER

Speaking of which, Auden defined the narcissist as the hunchback who gazes at his image in the water and says, "On me it looks good." When I asked you about the diarist's narcissism, I didn't just mean the recurrence of *I*, but the self-absorption: whatever happens to the self is deemed of interest to others.

ROREM

Well, yes. Auden was right even when he was wrong. Cocteau said, "*Je suis le mensonge qui dit la vérité.*" All art is a lie, insofar as truth is defined by the Supreme Court. After all, Picasso's goat isn't a goat. Is the artist a liar, or simply one for whom even a fact is not a fact? There is no truth, not even an overall Truth.

INTERVIEWER

Was there something about the French turn of mind and phrase that influenced the way you recorded things then?

ROREM

Yes, but I never said to myself, "I shall now make a French-type entry." I was, after all, living among the French, some of the smartest, and was still young enough to emulate my elders. Also, there is such a thing as writing French in English: Janet Flanner, for instance, or Virgil Thomson. Their English is economical. Illustrative, and terse in the sense of the *mot juste*—yet the *mot* was inevitably Anglo-Saxon. Virgil used to tell fledgling critics on the *Tribune*, "Don't say she had faulty intonation, say she sang out of tune. The best English doesn't use Latinate nouns." German in English? Probably Faulkner, who takes forever to get to the point. Or even, ironically, Proust. Julien Green wrote English in French; at least his subject matter was often about American Protestant misers, described in the tongue of Mallarmé. Very disconcerting.

INTERVIEWER

When it first appeared, *The Paris Diary* was nothing if not a *succès de scandale*, though those were more shockable times. Were you deliberately naughty *pour épater les bourgeois*?

ROREM

I doubt it. When prepublication extracts from *The Paris Diary* first appeared, most notably in this very magazine, I was stunned when people found it outrageous (more for the narcissism than the queerness, although the latter was invariably stressed in straight reviews), because anything we do, when seen in multiple reproduction, is no longer ours. You know how it feels to see your poem in *The New Yorker*? Imagine how it feels to sit in a box and hear your music played. Especially played badly.

INTERVIEWER

Can you recall now an incident you wish you'd recorded and didn't, and one that's included in the published diary but you wish were not?

ROREM

There's nothing recorded that I regret, though I have remorse about certain entries and have lost friends. As for what I didn't record, that can always be remedied in a memoir.

INTERVIEWER

By the end of *The Paris Diary* (or the end that was concocted for it), you sound both satisfied and sated. Or perhaps the word I want is more *American*, in the sense that Gertrude Stein declared Paris is where "Americans can discover what it means to be American." When you return to the States in 1955 and pick up with *The New York Diary*, perhaps you sound a little French—or at least a little out of place. Did that second diary begin with an odd sense of *dépaysement*?

ROREM

You're asking me to ascribe motivations decades after the fact. A diary is, by definition, on-the-spot reporting, even when most introspective. I cannot today be sure that I recall a certain incident purely, rather than what I've *written* about the incident. Thus I cannot know today what made me start the damn book in the first place. I do know that there's less responsibility—less urge to chisel and ply and plot—than when writing a poem or play or novel or, indeed, a song or symphony. Diaries have no beginnings, no endings. They are perpetual middles. But of course I state this only now, with the perception of hindsight, and hindsight is always skewed. Which is why those seminars of Anaïs Nin (Anus Ninny, as Phelps called her) were sheer blather. There are as many shapes to a diary as there are diarists, whereas a sonnet or sonata is always a sonata or sonnet. Oh, maybe not . . . I'm less caught up by our discussion this hour than by concern for the health of my beloved Jim Holmes. He is my diary. You are my sonata. Oi!

INTERVIEWER

The first three diaries have no index, where one could cruise for one's enemies and friends. It's maddening! Was it deliberate?

ROREM

My memory of the reason is clear. Though now that you
ask—not so clear. Joe Adamiak, my boyfriend in 1965 and
a graphic artist, was hired by Braziller to do the layout of
The Paris Diary. He wanted the printed phrases not to be
flush with the margins, but to ramble like handwriting. This
was vetoed by everyone, and nothing remains of those early
plans except his pretty good photo on the cover. For reasons
of naturalism (or was it expense?) we all agreed not to have
an index. Leonard Bernstein said, when *The Paris Diary* appeared, that it needed a list of names, with a plus or minus
sign beside each one. Anyway, the device continued through
The Final Diary (now titled *The Later Diaries*) and everyone,
including me, finds it inconvenient. Or, as you say, maddening.

INTERVIEWER

Music itself is a kind of diary—reflecting the moods and
impulses of the days. I know the differences between the two
activities—the one private, the other commissioned; the one
read, the other performed; et cetera—but what would you
say about the similarities?

ROREM

If the arts could express each other, we'd only need one
art. As one of the few Americans (as distinct from Europeans
who are—or used to be—all general practitioners) who practices two distinct arts professionally, I realize ever more clearly
(though I didn't forty years ago) the evidence of the previous
sentence. When my first book, *The Paris Diary*, was published, and I realized that strangers would be reading about
presumably private thoughts, I immediately acquired a new
sense of responsibility. Perhaps music is also about private
thoughts, but who can prove it? It's not that music's too
vague for words—it's too *precise* for words. Nor does it have
the same audience as prose or pictures or verse. Observe painters: how unembarrassedly they admit to knowing nothing,

and caring less, about classical music. Ditto writers. Not all. But most. It's inconceivable that a composer would admit to knowing nothing about, say, novels, or Matisse. Music is the most abstract of the arts, painting the most concrete. Which is why painters always label a picture *Abstraction Number 7*—because they know that, as with clouds, we'll always find a program there somewhere, while musicians are quick to call their pieces "La Mer" or "Alice in Wonderland," lest the listener lose his way. Anyhow, after that diary came out, my music (I like to think) became rougher, and my prose less scattered.

INTERVIEWER

You've written several books of essays. Have your diaries served as a kind of seedbed or sounding board for ideas later expounded upon in essays?

ROREM

I began writing essays soon after the first diary appeared, and they have nothing of the diaristic about them—and seldom use the pronoun *I*.

When the University at Buffalo invited me in 1959 to present six lectures, each to be followed by a concert of my own devising, I asked myself: What do I know about music that nobody else knows in quite the same way—about the construction of a song, for example—and can this be put into words? Because there's nothing a composer can say, at least about his own music, that the music can't say better, except how it came to be made. These essays, like many reviews that followed, sought to be objective above all.

By today I've probably said, in words, everything I have to say, both about my navel and about other people's. (I hate, by the way, to write negatively about other people's music, and never do so, except for sociological purposes, as when writing of Elliott Carter.) Maybe I've also said everything I have to say, as well, in my musical voice. I'm seventy-five now, and if I died tonight I'd not be ashamed of much of a

rather large catalogue. As for the diary, yes, I still keep it.
But disparately. Once I wrote, "I won't have the courage to
say in these pages what really matters until I'm of an age
when that will seem obscene." Something like that. From
where I now stand, nothing really counts anymore. Did it
ever? The world has no overall meaning, and I have no crying
urge to restate that truism in all sorts of luminous ways.

INTERVIEWER

When you wrote both *The Paris Diary* and *The New York
Diary*—do I have my dates right?—you were a famously heavy
drinker. Did sobriety change your daily sense of things, or
your writing habits?

ROREM

On first dipping my toe into AA in 1959 (it didn't take
for another ten years, though) I realized I'd been subliminally
alcoholic since childhood, and overtly since around age sixteen. Meaning that one drink was too many and twenty
weren't enough. As for the reasons for alcoholism, like those
for homosexuality, who knows? I never felt guilty about being
gay so much as being passive, wanting to be adored, et cetera.
When drunk, I had a good excuse. But beyond that? Anyway,
my earliest unpublished diaries (I do quote from them some
in *Knowing When to Stop*) do wallow a lot in booze, at least
as a subject. But I never wrote either prose or music while
drunk, always segregated good and bad, work and play. My
drunk self is a schizoid other. Thus sobriety never changed
my daily sense of things, or writing habits. But uttering these
phrases today seems somehow trivial. I'm traversing the most
melancholy valley of my life: Jim, my partner of thirty-one
years, is dying. Nothing else seems important, not diaries or
operas, or geophysics, nothing. And though it appears lofty
to say that I've said all I have to say, it's nevertheless true.
Don Bachardy did draw Christopher Isherwood during each
last dying day. I approve. But what can I say that, for example,
Joyce in "The Dead" hasn't said better in those hundred final

words. An hour ago, anticipating your question, I opened the diary to July 7, 1967, *comme si par hasard*: "Is a diary, by its nature, more 'honest' than a novel? Probably not. The undisciplined first-person involuntarily inclines more to disguise than a novelist does. As to whether I know less 'who I am' than, say, Alfred Chester or James Purdy, neither they nor I will ever know, any more than we can perceive the self-awareness of that farmer, that nurse, that dogcatcher." Ah, silly superfluous art. Art.

INTERVIEWER

Tell me about the actual writing. Has it been a daily task? Do you write into a notebook, or type up pages? And do you ever look back over an entry and revise?

ROREM

The first diaries, from 1945 through 1970, were written in notebooks in ballpoint. More recently, typed, since I type everything now. And yes, revised, of course. Because everything is revised merely by being reexamined. Everything is lost instantly (these words here, Jocasta's first view of Oedipus) and can only be retrieved through revision. Yet more literally, I revise in transit. From sentence to sentence, note to note. I do strongly disapprove of authors who, decades later in their collected works, "improve" upon the initial afflatus. Auden. Paul Goodman. They are always wrong, for the early work no longer belongs to them.

All literature is a diary. So indeed is all art, and all organized communication, in the sense of its being a reaction to any aspect of the universe. A diary, no matter how scrupulously revised and edited, is by its nature looser than a fugue or a court report.

INTERVIEWER

When Cocteau's diaries were published in English some years ago, I remember your review of them. You recorded your surprise when discovering that Cocteau had written about an event you too had written up.

ROREM

That was only the second time I'd met Cocteau. The first
time I went to see him as a fan in October of 1950, and we
got along fine. I didn't know Marie-Laure then, but by the
next summer I did, and Cocteau told others—never me—"it's
too bad that Rorem boy is shacked up with Marie-Laure,
because she can only destroy him." Of course she didn't—nor
were we shacking up. I was very anxious to be what I was—
namely, her intimate friend without having to put out. She
much admired industry, and I worked hard, drunk or sober.
What impressed her is that I wasn't a silly gadabout. I worked
several hours a day, every day, in her house, both up in Paris
and down south. She worked hard too.

Ned Rorem and Marie-Laure de Noailles in 1952.

The first time I went down to visit her in the south of
France, we decided that we would go visit her spouse and
mother, who both lived in the town of Grasse in separate,
very comfortable houses. Hyères is a couple of hours away.
She invited Cocteau over. So we all had lunch at Charles's,
her husband the Vicomte, the last great Proustian gentleman.
I don't know what he thought of me. I do remember I stole
a little pair of cuticle scissors from his bathroom. Cocteau

came in Mme. Weissweiler's car. He wore a white leather jacket, which I thought was terribly chic. He sat next to the chauffeur, but had a notebook on his lap. He was never not working. After lunch we took a car over to see Marie-Laure's mother. She had been married to Francis de Croisset, one of Reynaldo Hahn's librettists. Marie-Laure said Croisset used to make passes at her, and she wrote a novel called *La Chambre des écureuils*, about a man who made passes at his stepdaughter. Then *Bonjour Tristesse* came out, also about that sort of thing. She always felt Sagan had got there second but got more credit. Anyway, it was Marie-Laure's idea that I should play my ballet *Mélos* for Cocteau (she had done the scenario). So I played it for him, so they could all see if I had a *sens du théâtre*. We both wrote up the day.

INTERVIEWER

I noticed in your kitchen that little photograph of you with Jean Marais.

ROREM

He just died, you know. Usually when you get to know really big movie stars, they turn out to be nice people. Jean was thoroughly modest. He wrote a not-bad autobiography called *Histoires de ma vie*, in which he's very frank about Cocteau. There was a question of *Dorian Gray* being made into a ballet. Henri Sauguet was asked but didn't want to do it and suggested my name instead. This was for the ballet company of the Opéra-Comique, and the chief dancer was an American named Georges Reich, a husky blond who was Marais's lover. He hardly spoke French and Marais didn't speak English. Reich was to dance Dorian, and Marais was to play the portrait. So Marais came to visit me. I lived in a teeny room on the fourth floor of the Hôtel des Saints-Pères. I still remember the doorman excitedly phoning to say *"M. Marais monte!"* Up came Jean to my humble room. On the sofa were some drawings by Cocteau, and he said, "Oh my God, I certainly feel at home here." It sounds naive to say, but he was just like anybody else. We went carefully through the ballet—this kind of music here, that kind of music there. As things worked out, I had of necessity to see Marais quite often. By the way, the ballet was to be done in Barcelona, in May of 1952. And was. It flopped. After that, we exchanged letters every two or three years until he died, which came as a shock to me. I was pleased to see that he was given a sort of national funeral.

INTERVIEWER

I've read that *The Paris Diary* is credited with helping the emergent gay-liberation movement along. Has that been your sense of things?

ROREM

When the book was reviewed in *The New York Times*, the word *homosexual* appeared in the headline and that gave me a jolt. I didn't think of myself as in any sense political or promotional. In the book, I was merely too lazy to pretend to be something I'm not. I refer in the book to a person named P, and did so grammatically in a way that it could be sexually either/or. Eventually I got tired of that. I was bemused to be taken as a guru, since I never thought of myself that way—as Allen Ginsberg did. But I had to take my name out of the phone directory. There'd been violent threats; and, just as bad, fans ringing the doorbell. I had mentioned in the diary that I'd introduced myself to Benjamin Britten by sending him a photograph of myself half-naked; now people began sending me nude photos of themselves, including women. On the other hand, I met Jim through the diary. He'd read *The New York Diary* and was told by a mutual friend to look me up. But it's not for me to talk here about the effect of my diary; that's for other people to say.

INTERVIEWER

Do you read the diaries of others? I notice Dawn Powell's on your bookshelf.

ROREM

There are certain things I can't get the point of. Bagels,
for instance. Why do people like them? I can't get the point
of Berlioz. I can dislike a composer, while admitting what
others see in him or her. But not Berlioz. Likewise Dawn
Powell.

INTERVIEWER

Well then, are there diarists whom you *do* read with admiration?

ROREM

Not today any longer. But I certainly read Gide, whom I
still think is a marvelous diarist. And Isherwood. Julien
Green's still means a great deal to me.

INTERVIEWER

Did you learn how to write a diary by reading them? What
to include? How to shape an anecdote?

ROREM

I could have. Nobody does anything without being im-
pelled by something already existing. Every note composed,
every brush stroke, everything we're saying here—nothing
comes from nothing. Although I wouldn't have been attracted
to Green's if I hadn't already been writing a diary myself
since 1945.

INTERVIEWER

Do you think the people who know your music know your
diary, and the people who know your diary know your music?

ROREM

No. When the diary appeared I'd been a professional composer for about twenty years—meaning commissions, performances and so forth. But in six months I was far better known
as a prose writer than as a musician. Nine out of ten people

who played my music hadn't the faintest idea I wrote books, and certainly the people reading the diaries didn't know my music. I could tell from the letters I received. Even today, letters about music I get from strangers are all about a possible error, say, in measure thirty-four, whereas the letters about the diaries are invariably much more emotional. But then literary people—or most of them—know little about music. In America, we're getting more philistine by the minute. In France, things may be different.

INTERVIEWER

Do you reread your own diaries?

ROREM

No, never. Well, in anticipation of your visit, I did glance over *The Paris Diary*. It's hard to read because I know it so well, even today. But sometimes I'll come upon sections in any of the diaries and think how good they are—I'd hit the nail of a given situation precisely on the head.

INTERVIEWER

Does the Paris of the late fifties seem increasingly like a fictional world to you now, from the vantage of seedy New York on the brink of the millennium?

ROREM

Two or three years ago the French radio had Elliott Carter, me and a couple of others talk in French on a program about culture. Elliott, being God, did most of the talking. But when he said that after 1951 the musical world really started in France, I had to interrupt to say, "Oh, but that's about when it *stopped*." True, Poulenc still had *The Dialogues of the Carmelites* in him (I could see Elliott flinch), and true, Cocteau still had a play or two left in him, and Gide would die the following year, but the *great* France—and I'm right, of course—was over. The Proustian world still existed up until the mid-fifties—by which I mean literally that people who were friends of Proust or of that rarified milieu were still alive, with their tight-lipped upper-class accent, gleaned largely from their low-class English nannies. I wouldn't know whom to telephone now, if I went to Paris. Oh, James Lord, of course, but who else? Ed White's no longer there. But the older ones, the French writers and musicians—no one's left. The young people in Paris nowadays I don't find especially cute or especially smart, despite their high IQ. Performers are pretty good. Ballet dancers. But except for the movies, what is going on creatively over there? No plays, no fiction. The other writing is still all that bullshit about deconstruction. Paris has had its day.

—J.D. McClatchy

The Infiltrator

Said Shirazi

Subject is a freak. Subject investigates own reflection: Long hair—check. Funky beard—check. Headband—check. Body odor—check. Wardrobe chosen to indicate honest working-class values, disdain for vanity of personal appearance: dungarees and a heavy cloth shirt. Subject is a Natural Man, uninhibited, posture and facial expressions confirm this: merry, even lewd. Subject is Rolling-With-The-Changes, as per specifications. Subject is Carrying, controlled substance in quantity, two fine doobies of Jamaican Red. Subject tokes up to get the day started R-I-G-H-T.

Subject Boogies On Down The Road to rendezvous checkpoint thirteen hundred hours. Individual approaches Subject in transit with radical literature, which betrays allegiance to foreign ideologies. Subject purchases same. Individual: "All Power to the People, man." Subject: "Off the Pigs, brother!"

Subject reads limerick from purchased newspaper, to follow:

> Ho Chi Minh sold the Pope some fine grass,
> which he smoked up before midnight mass.

"Forget Sin," he cried,
"drive one deep inside,"
and thereon displayed his white ass.

Apparent intention to shock bourgeoisie by impugning morals of head of Roman Catholic Church, in perpetration of self-exhibition and intent to commit anal erotism. Also: idealize enemy leader as trickster-hero. Also: attribute supernatural powers of spiritual liberation to the cannabis weed. Also: denigrate white race as risible and ineffective.

Subject is on his way to rendezvous with Affinity Group. Affinity Group, defined: group of five protestors who vandalize in concert. See Weatherman ideology and tactics.

Flashback: Subject had been brought from the San Francisco office, undercover division. Occasion of travel: Republican National Convention, Miami Beach. Trouble expected due to unpopularity among students of current police actions in Southeast Asia, required soldier pool being drawn from same as student.

Subject and partner dropped off at LAX in VW bus. Subject notes with disapproval surprising lack of metal detectors. Passengers frowning, keeping their distance, freaks and those who resemble freaks being unloved by general population. Subject once seated selects attractive stewardess, addresses her.

Subject: "Excuse me, Miss. Federal law requires us to identify ourselves to you on boarding. I'm Special Agent Payne and this is Special Agent Bloom, FBI. Would you please notify the captain we're on board and armed?"

Stewardess (surprised but polite): "Why, yes. May I take your identification up to the captain?"

Subject: "I'm sorry, Miss. Federal law requires us to keep these credentials in sight at all times."

Stewardess returns with Captain.

Captain: "How do I know you're really FBI agents? These pictures don't look anything like you." ID photos depict clean-cut, clean-shaven agents eager and uncertain.

Subject produces badge. Badge issued to all agents, required to be carried on person at all times, rarely used. Conse-

quently public generally unfamiliar with badge. Also: badge
significantly smaller than that of state and local police. Captain unconvinced by badge, expresses same.

Subject displays ticket. Ticket bears designation GTR, Government Travel Request, indicating purchase by government
agency for official use by employees only, abuse punishable
by fine and imprisonment. Captain unconvinced by ticket.
Subject produces FBIRA card, representing membership in
the FBI Recreation Association, SAMBA card, indicating hospi-
talization benefits to be provided by the Special Agents Mutual Benefit Association, library borrower's card, department
store charge card.

Captain relents, recognizes authority of agents, becomes
somewhat apologetic. Captain: "Okay, okay, it's just I've
already been hijacked to Algeria once, and once is enough."

Takeoff is smooth. Flight time six hours, forty-five minutes.
Temperature in Miami is a cool sixty-seven degrees.

End of flashback, narrative continues in natural order. Miami. Flamingo Park unofficially renamed People's Park, in
accordance with opposition to bourgeois institution of private
property, no change in status thereby effected however because 1.) aforementioned name change is unofficial and corre-
sponds to no civic authority vested with powers to effect such
change in status and 2.) park was already public. Park is now
a Liberated Zone, drugs traded and consumed openly.

Inventory of park: SDS, Students for a Democratic Society;
VVAW, Vietnam Veterans Against the War; YSA, Young
Socialist Alliance; PLP, Progressive Labor Party; the Yippies,
familiar name for the Youth International Party; the Zippies,
recent factional offshoot of same. National Coalition of Gay
Organizations, NCGO, subjected to constant harassment by
other organizations. Fringe of fringe includes religious groups,
e.g. Hare Krishnas. Individual: "Hare Hare, Hare Rama,
Rama Rama, Hare Krishna."

Elderly retirees observe these activities with gentle curiosity
until their discovery of the Jews for Jesus. Individual: "You're

no Jew! You have no right to be called a Jew! You don't
know what it means to be a Jew!"

Convention Center. *Mille-neuf-cent soixante-douze*. Center surrounded by new chain-link fence. Riot cops stand shoul-
der-to-shoulder behind the fence. Demonstrators approach-
ing fence are sprayed with Mace. Two days earlier fence was
torn down by demonstrators, who then hesitated before pressing their attack further and so were eventually dispersed.

Scheduled speaker is Nixon, Richard Milhous, thirty-sev-
enth president of the United States, incumbent. Speaker is
nominated by his party as their candidate for the presidency.

Yesterday sky calm over human confusion. Today a rotting
blue carcass swarming with choppers, Huey Cobras, guns do
not appear to be mounted. Blades move at translucent speed
like dragonfly wings. Chopper body floats lazily above the
towers, without clear purpose.

Demonstrator preparations: multiple layers of clothing so
that outer layers can be removed when saturated with gas.
Army surplus field jackets with tight cuffs and high collars.
Jeans tucked into boots. Gloves, goggles, bandannas. Surplus
gas masks. Motorcycle helmets, army surplus helmets, football
helmets. Demonstrators are armed with baseball bats, tire
chains, lengths of pipe. Pockets full of sand to throw in the
eyes of the police when busted.

Now a limousine appears. Limousine tries to force its way
through the crowd, honking and creeping slowly forward.
Demonstrators attack vehicle, kicking and banging on it.
Driver panics, steps on the gas, launches one demonstrator
through the air while others scramble out of the way. Limousine breaks through and speeds away with angry posse in
pursuit. Current of anger sweeps through crowd, yelling,
raised fists.

Six shotgun blasts. Origin: shotguns launching gas canis-
ters. Police have begun to gas the crowd. No prior warning
to disperse issued. Individual: "Incoming!" Crowd scatters in
panic. Elderly retirees oblivious to the danger. Look around

calmly, convinced they are merely observers. Soon they are clutching their chests and dropping. Police in gas masks begin mass arrests.

Subject's bogus affinity group, composed entirely of under-cover agents like himself, disperses in the panic. Meanwhile bonafide Weathermen go into action. Two groups approach each chartered bus carrying delegates to convention. Three women lie down in front of the bus, bringing it to a stop. Two men run to the driver's side and open the engine panel. One rips out the spark plug wires and distributor cap. Two men are on the other side of the bus. One pulls the valve stem out of the tire with pliers. The other snips it off. A fifth man keeps watch as they proceed to disable the other three tires. The bus is fucked. It coughs and sinks to its knees. Interior: no AC, no dispatch radio, no overhead reading lights.

At this point, the delegates make a mistake. They know they are only a few blocks from the convention center. Nixon's acceptance speech, which they have come hundreds and thou-sands of miles for, is going to begin soon. They descend from the bus bravely and attempt to walk. They are screamed at, struck by demonstrators, spit on, stampeded by police, trampled, lost in the mob, gassed. Delegate thinks: This is not really happening. Delegate thinks: Are we still in America? Delegate thinks: But these are our sons and daughters.

Subject waited in an alley and peered out into the street. Coast was clear. Approximate time elapsed in paragraph break: forty-five minutes. Subject proceeded. Subject was in the middle of the road when a police squad rounded the corner and gave pursuit. Subject reversed and ran in the opposite direction. Another squad appeared in front of him.

Subject was in deep shit.

Nixon: As a result of what we have done, America today is a better place and the world is a safer place to live in than was the case four years ago. Subject ran towards first officer, faked left and spun right, getting past him. Farcical nature of scene suitable for banjo soundtrack. Subject ran over the hood of a parked vehicle to evade second officer, turned down alley and poured on the speed. Alley was a dead end.

Subject turned to face third officer behind him. Subject: "I surrender."

Officers gathered around, panting. Officer: "Think you're real smart, huh, puke?" Officer: "Think you're fast on your feet, huh, puke?" Officer frisked subject.

Officer: "This one thinks he's a real bad-ass." Officer: "This one thinks he's hot shit." Officer: "You think you're hot shit, don't you, puke?"

Subject: "That's right, pig!" Subject is uncertain why he said this.

Nixon: That is why one of the goals of our next administration is to reduce the property tax, which is such an unfair and heavy burden on the poor . . . Officers closed in. Officer: "Give me your hands." Subject lowered his hands. Officer struck him with his baton. Officer: "No one told you to lower your hands."

Subject: "Subject was told to lower his hands!" Officer struck him on the right shoulder. Subject: "Subject is not resisting arrest!" Officer cuffed Subject's hands behind his back with plastic handcuffs. Knowledgeable Subject tried to keep his wrists apart so the cuffs would not cut off his circulation. Knowledgeable Officer struck subject again on the right shoulder to prevent same.

Subject: "You guys think you're so fuckin' tough, don't you? You get your kicks beating up a handcuffed prisoner? Look at the big bad pigs! Subject's not afraid of the big bad pigs!"

Nixon: I want the peace officers across America to know that they have the total backing of their president in their fight against crime. Peace Officer pulled Subject's headband down over his eyes. Peace Officers began to beat Subject in the area of the ankles and shins. Peace Officer jabbed his nightstick into Subject's rectum repeatedly, causing tearing and bleeding. Subject tried to ward off the blows. Subject's

mojo was no longer working. Subject gladly would have given
his life to kill them. He would have killed them without a
second thought and never regretted it. He would have given
his life just to find a way to adequately express how badly he
wanted to kill them. Of course the only way to fully express
it was to do it, which he could not.

Subject: "Help! Help!" *Nixon: Standing in this convention
hall four years ago, I pledged to seek an honorable end to
the war in Vietnam. We have made great progress toward
that end.* Individual: "That's enough." Individual raised the
bandanna. Individual was a police sergeant, older, welcome
sight to Subject like you will only ever imagine. Individual:
"I want the arresting officer to come with me and book
this man."

Individual, Subject and Officer proceeded to temporary
arrest processing area. *Nixon: Now it is understandable that
Vietnam has been a major concern in foreign policy.* Subject:
"This is going to cost you your badge. I guarantee it, this
will cost you your badge. You might not think so, but I
guarantee it." Individual: "That's enough."

Subject was photographed with a Polaroid and placed in
a truck with Individual, short, wiry adolescent. Arrest information would be written on the back of the Polaroid. Sergeant
and arresting officer immediately return to duty. Only one
officer remaining to guard the truck. Fat, inferred to be slow.

Subject: "Let's make a break for it."

Individual: "You're crazy, man. After what they did to
you, you want more?"

Arrest not recorded by Officer to avoid possible reprisals for
treatment of Subject. Later identification impossible thanks to
riot masks and prior removal of name tags, hence charges
never brought.

*Nixon: There are those who believe that we can entrust
the security of America to the good will of our adversaries.
Those who hold this view do not know the real world.* Subject's hands were numb. Subject informed Individual he had
a pocketknife in his front pants pocket and asked Individual

to retrieve it and try to cut the plastic handcuffs off. Individual was reluctant. Subject insisted. Individual expressed major concern that Subject's wrists might get all fucked up. Subject pronounced concern understandable, but nevertheless insisted. *Nixon: Let us not turn away from greatness.* Individual moved closer and got on his knees. Subject twisted to the side and held out his wrists. Subject felt cold edge of blade against his skin, biting like an insect. It hurt, it felt good, the pain called up his strength. Subject was in the real world. Subject would not turn away.

Postwar Paris:

Chronicles of Literary Life

The following cast, in order of their appearance, has contributed to this survey of literary expatriates in Paris (and one in Rome) starting in the late 1940s and continuing to the 1990s.

ROBERT LUCID A member of the faculty at the University of Pennsylvania, he taught English there until his retirement in 1996.

NORMAN MAILER The multifaceted author (novels, essays, plays, poetry, criticism, film) is at work completing his series of novels about the CIA.

RICHARD WILBUR An American poet and translator, he was the Poet Laureate of the United States in 1987–1988.

CHRISTOPHER LOGUE The English poet noted for his free-wheeling translation of the *Iliad* entitled *War Music*. The extract published here is from a forthcoming autobiography, *Prince Charming*.

EVAN S. CONNELL A short-story writer, essayist, biographer of George Armstrong Custer (*Son of the Morning Star*), his novels include *Mrs. Bridge*, *Mr. Bridge*, *The Patriot* and *Diary of a Rapist*.

MAX STEELE A contributing editor to *Story*, he ran the creative-writing program at the University of North Carolina, Chapel Hill, for over thirty years. His collection of short stories is entitled *The Hat of My Mother*.

MORDECAI RICHLER A Canadian citizen. Among his most successful novels are *The Apprenticeship of Duddy Kravitz*, *St. Urbain's Horseman*, and *Solomon Gursky Was Here*.

RICHARD SEAVER After many years as an editor at Grove Press, he is now the editor in chief at Arcade Publishing.

MARY LEE SETTLE   Best known for her five-volume series of novels entitled *The Beulah Quintet*, she won the National Book Award in 1978 for *Blood Ties*. She established the PEN/ Faulkner Award in 1981.

ALICE ADAMS   A frequent contributor to *The New Yorker*, her most recent collection of stories is *The Last Lovely City*.

ART BUCHWALD   The well-known syndicated columnist for *The Washington Post*, he won a Pulitzer Prize in 1982 for commentary service. Besides his many collections he has written two memoirs, *Leaving Home* and *I'll Always Have Paris*.

BEN BRADLEE   For many years he was the managing editor of *The Washington Post*. His autobiography is entitled *A Good Life*.

PETER STONE   A playwright with many Broadway hits, among them *1776*, *Will Rogers Follies*, *Grand Hotel*, his latest success is *Titanic*.

PETER MATTHIESSEN   An interview with him, and an excerpt from *Bone by Bone*, the last book of the Watson trilogy, appear elsewhere in this issue.

GEORGE PLIMPTON   His most recent book is an oral biography entitled *Truman Capote*.

JAMES DICKEY   The author of many collections of poetry, including *Into the Stone*, *Buckdancer's Choice*, *Zodiac* and *Puella*, he also wrote a number of novels, the most famous of them *Deliverance*. The letters are from a forthcoming volume of his correspondence.

EUGENE WALTER   The author of a novel (*The Untidy Pilgrim*), poems, children's book, cookbooks, he lived in Mobile, Louisiana, where he hosted a radio program and wrote a local

Sunday column on literary matters until his death last year. The excerpt published here is from an oral biography conducted by Katherine Clark entitled *The Untidy Pilgrimage: A Southerner's Story of Life on this Planet*.

BLAIR FULLER   A San Francisco based writer of fiction and nonfiction, he is the cofounder of the Squaw Valley Community of Writers.

KAYLIE JONES   The author of the novels *As Soon As It Rains* and *Quite the Other Way*, her screenplay *A Soldier's Daughter Never Cries* was filmed by Merchant Ivory Productions.

MATTHEW J. BRUCCOLI   Jeffries Professor of English at the University of South Carolina, he is a leading authority on F. Scott Fitzgerald and the editorial director of *The Dictionary of Literary Biography*.

RICK BASS   A strong advocate of nature conservation, he has written a number of books about the outdoors, including *Oil Notes*, *Winter* and *The Nine Mile Wolves*.

Norman Mailer and Richard Wilbur

Two of the most distinguished American literary artists of their generation—their names as frequently invoked by critics and historians as they are seldom linked—appear here in a conversation that is mostly about being in Paris after the Second World War. The occasion giving rise to this conversation was a late September, 1996, University of Pennsylvania weekend observation of my retirement from the English faculty there. When friends Norman Mailer and Richard Wilbur accepted invitations to attend, I suggested talking about this experience that both had often said was personally important, that neither had ever overtly visited in his works, and that happened to have a particular relevance to the Penn audience in that season.

Penn's entering class in 1996 had been assigned to read Hemingway's A Moveable Feast *before reporting to campus, and so assorted seminars, films and panel discussions were going on concerning the adventures of American artists in Paris following the First World War. It was therefore a sort of useable coincidence that both Mailer and Wilbur had gone there at the very start of their postwar careers. In the fall of 1947 Wilbur's first book of poems,* The Beautiful Changes,

had been published to great praise; and the following May
Mailer's first novel, The Naked and the Dead, *became a*
runaway best-seller. Each writer responded to the pull of Paris
soon after completing his first book, and of course each found
himself encountering a cultural experience there that was
quite significantly different from that of Hemingway and his
fellow expatriates in 1922. So we agreed to carry on an infor-
mal, indeed almost an impromptu, public conversation about
all this, and specifically about their two 1947–1948 pilgrim-
ages to Paris.

—**Robert Lucid**

NORMAN MAILER: I had the idea when I came out of the army
I was going to write a book about the war and show that
damn army up! So when I did come out in May, 1946, I sat
down and wrote *The Naked and the Dead*, which I finished
in late September, 1947. Immediately, my first wife, Beatrice,
and I were on our way to Paris.

I'd dreamed of it all through the war, and I'd dreamed of
it in college. In those days, my idea of heaven was to be an
expatriate in Paris. Indeed, I recall a story from Martin Buber's
Tales of the Hasidim that I think is relevant: there was a
woman in a small ghetto in the center of Russia who could
not become pregnant, and she heard of a famous itinerant
rabbi who was going to be traveling about through part of
the neighboring country, about two hundred miles from her
ghetto. Back in the late eighteenth or early nineteenth century
this was a dangerous trip, but finally she reached the rabbi,
traveling those long two hundred miles on foot from where
she started. He looked at her—he was an immensely holy
man—and he said, "Go home my child, and have no fear.
You will become pregnant once you return," which she did
and immediately became a legend in that village. The next
year another woman who was barren made the same trip over
the same two hundred miles; when she came to him, he said,
"My dear, I can do nothing for you. You have heard the
story." That was what happened to me when I got to Paris:
I was the second woman; I had heard the story.

Norman and Beatrice Mailer, 1947 passport photograph.

I knew everything about what it was to be an expatriate in Paris, so I also knew that we did not fit the description. We were living in a grim little apartment, and I spent my first months in Paris shivering because it was so cold. It was a terrible winter in Paris, equaled only by the awful winter of 1946. I used to walk the streets—my first recollection of my first months in Paris is walking the streets conjugating subjunctive verbs! I'd had three years of high-school French, one year of French in college, and I was hopeless. I couldn't speak a word of French, a terrible thickness would grasp my throat and tongue. I couldn't speak, so I used to conjugate these verbs while walking the streets. I was miserable. But I'll cease for now with the misery of the first months!

RICHARD WILBUR: When I was in the army, I was a signalman in the Thirty-sixth Texas Division. After the Italian business we invaded southern France and came up through France to the Siegfried line. The people in my company were marvelous soldiers, but they were mostly country boys from Texas; they didn't have any French. So my rotten high-school French made me interpreter for the company whenever we needed things—cheese or barbed wire. That really was my first experience of France, which, of course, was no way to learn about the country or the language. In fact, I don't think I can say *barbed wire* in French even now!

After the war I went to graduate school at Harvard on the GI Bill. A couple of friends there, who were refugees from France, turned me on to various French writers about whom they were enthusiastic. They made me start translating—I did a whole novel of Villiers de l'Isle-Adam called *Claire Lenoir*, and they set me to other tasks as well. I soon became a member of the Society of Fellows at Harvard, so I was embarked on being a scholar; I was given three years of the most luxurious and indulged conditions in which to become a scholar. At the same time I had published my first book of poems. From the very beginning of my postwar life I was a hybrid: I was expected to be a scholar; at the same time I

Richard and Mary Wilbur, 1948 passport photograph.

also was authorized to be a poet. (I say *authorized* because
that first book was surprisingly well received.) In the spring
of 1948 it seemed a good notion to ask the Society for some
travel money to go to Paris—I had been hounded into being
a translator of French, and it seemed I ought to go where the
French were and listen to them talking and experience their
tongue as a live language. The argument worked, and my
wife and I went over there in March of that cold year.

I experienced France in two ways. As a poet I ran into
the works of Francis Ponge, a young French poet very much
celebrated at the moment, and I translated a few of his poems;
I met Nathalie Sarraute; there'd be other writers I could name
if my memories were not fading so fast. On the other hand,
my scholarly self went to the Comédie Française and to the
Théâtre Marigny to see Barrault and Madeleine Reynaud play
Hamlet and *Les Fausses Confidences*. That started me off—
although I didn't know it at the time—as a translator of
classic French drama. I too walked along the streets saying
parts of speech to myself and trying to achieve some ease with
the language, which I have never, then or later, been able
to speak with confidence and eloquence.

MAILER: Theoretically, my wife and I were in Paris on the GI
Bill: she'd been a lieutenant in the WAVES—she was a liberated
woman at a very early date, chronologically speaking—and
I'd been a private in the army. To stay one moment with the
army, the great joke in my barracks used to be, "Hey man,
do you salute your wife before you . . . ?" Anyway, we were
on the GI Bill and we took a course at the Sorbonne, *Le
Cours de Civilisation Française*, which the French invented
for us. It was the first time in its thousand-year history that
the Sorbonne had ever gone into the tank. France was desper-
ately in need of dollars at the time, and since the United
States was paying them in that currency for our tuition, they
lowered their very high standards and concocted this special
course, which had about as much to do with French civilization
as an American high-school course in home economics. There

must have been somewhere between five hundred and one thousand GIs taking the course; we all signed up for the year. No ex-GIs who were taking the course were there for any better reason than that they felt the army owed them a year in Paris.

I do remember being influenced by one class that I took with an old French teacher. She was very old, she had a club foot and she wore heavy eyeglasses. She was a remarkable woman—this ugly, crippled woman with a passion for the French language. I had never known anyone comparable to her. She used to speak in a harsh and powerful voice that vibrated with its passion for the language.

The effect was that many years later one of my daughters was trying to enter a small country-day school in the Berkshires and needed French to qualify for admission, so I said, "All right, I'll teach you some French this summer;" I used to drill her, and she began to hate the lessons because I instinctively was imitating this wonderful old teacher. I would say, "*Bonjour, mademoiselle, comment vous portez vous?*" My daughter came to each lesson in fear and trembling. It was incredible. I never could speak French with that good an accent, but my daughter's accent was marvelous. It may have captured the spirit of that old teacher. Well, at any rate, all I ever got was from that course: the remarkable passion of an old woman for French. Other than that course, I never went to classes. As each month went by, I began to enjoy being in Paris a little more; of course, by the end of the year we worried about flunking, which would mean our GI Bill would be lost for the future. So I went up to the dean who controlled the course, and said, "Sir, I have tried very hard all year to learn French. I always went to class." I didn't think it would work, but he just nodded and said, "*Ça va. Ça va. We will give you a special test.*" The test was: "*Vous voulez parler en Français? Respondez: oui ou non.*" Of course, I said *oui*, and I passed.

ROBERT LUCID: Did you discover an expatriate community over there?

WILBUR: Nothing as substantial as that in Hemingway's *Moveable Feast*. If there was such a community, I was tangential to it. Actually, it didn't occur to me to be an expatriate—I was only in Paris for three months. I think I've encountered only two or three true expatriates of the Gertrude Stein kind. One was Stanley Geist, a quite brilliant student at Harvard; he went to Paris after graduation, I think to become another person so as not to be what he had been in America, and certainly so as not to go into the family business. When I knew him in Paris in 1948, he spent part of every day trying to translate Constant's novel *Adolphe*, of which there are about twenty existing translations—undoubtedly, Stanley would have gone them all one better had he finished, but he did not. He gradually became, I suppose by way of conscious choice, a European. He's never come home. I met another person over there, I can't think of his first name, but he was a fellow named Kaplan.

MAILER: Yes, Harold Kaplan.

WILBUR: Right! He wrote a marvelous short story, "The Mohammedans," which was published in *The Partisan Review*—it was about American blacks who had converted to Islam. Everyone waited for a second story from him, but he didn't comply; he went to Paris and became something else—I'm not sure quite what. He was a strikingly intelligent man, although I wasn't sure what he was doing. He was a man of mystery.

In any case, those are two people who really did become expatriates. I think most people don't want to become somebody else to that extent. There are certain classes of people who want to become somebody else: alcoholics want to become somebody else—you can tell that because of the incredible lies they tell about their heroism or their romantic achievements. Actors want to become somebody else—they're not sure who they want to become, so they have to be in play after play looking for it. Then there are linguists, who seek to find another version of themselves by way of another language and culture. Richard Howard once said that the French language afforded him another self: he is another Richard when he starts talking French. Well, at any rate, I didn't become someone else.

I did have encounters with French artists because that was one reason for going to Paris at the time. In the late 1940s it was still the painting capital of the world. It was great to go to a show of Léger and Picabia, and see all of painting Paris there. It was great to meet someone like Jean Hélion, the wonderful painter. He decided to use me as a model, I remember; he thought that it would be nice for me to pose with a guitar so he rented a guitar, which he gave to me to play—I played that guitar during those three months in Paris, not always to everyone's delight. And there was Ferdinand Springer, another fine painter—he whisked us off at a certain point to his house in Grasse, in the Alpes Maritimes. Well, I fear I'm running on. But I'm pleased to be fishing up so many names; it feels as if I'm going back downstream, if that's where the past is.

MAILER: My recollection is that I met no French writer of any importance nor did I ever meet a well-known painter there. The only Americans particularly close to me—our closest friends—were Mark Linenthal, a classmate at Harvard and his wife, Alice Adams, who has since become the writer: we used to go out and eat every night together.

I met Jean Malaquais, who is now my oldest and dearest friend, over there. We didn't get along at all because I was for Henry Wallace and he was considerably to the left of Leon Trotsky—he found Wallace absolutely despicable; he said he was a pawn. In any event, over the years we met again and by now we're great friends.

I met Stanley Geist in Paris. He had an extraordinary critical power: if you liked a book and Stanley didn't like it, you couldn't help yourself—you didn't like the book quite as much as before Stanley had finished rejecting it. That is probably the seat of critical power; very few critics today have that deep authority for me. I remember when he read the manuscript of *The Naked and the Dead*, he said, "You know, it's not bad." I felt ennobled by that!

But for the most part the people I knew were simple French people. There was a French painter who was a sweet charming guy but a terrible painter. Really bad. He had a mistress who was one of the nicest women in the world. My wife Beatrice and I wanted to do something for them but we couldn't buy any paintings directly from him because it would be too obviously an act of charity. My editor, Bill Raney, happened to come to Paris at that point, so we said, "Bill, we'll buy the painting, but you've got to pretend to pay for it." Bill didn't speak any French, and the painter didn't speak any English, so we were the translators. We took Bill over to this little garret on the very top floor of a very old building in the southern depths of the twelfth arrondissement and introduced him as one of the most formidable art critics in New York. Bill would look at each one very solemnly and occasionally I would say, "My friend wants to buy that one." We paid something like seventy-five dollars for two paintings. That was one of the nicer things I did in Paris, although this painter was so bad that it may have been wrong to encourage him.

Who else was there? Mostly we Americans hung out together, and we used to hate the French! We'd go to a party and think, This is a great party; there are no frogs here! (We used a politically incorrect word before the concept even existed.) I don't even know why we disliked them so. They had a confidence that we didn't have as Americans—at the time I felt that it was bad enough being Jewish but now I couldn't even count on being American. But exactly the things I found most difficult about the French manner then, I most admire now: they have a culture and they are proud of it—they won't let go of their native culture.

WILBUR: Norman's mention of Henry Wallace started a train of thought in me in which I shall now spill. Looking into a

A Moveable Feast, I was thinking, Did we—in Paris in the forties—have any of the feelings of alienation from America that Hemingway's crowd did? There's some quotation, not in Hemingway's book but from Gertrude Stein, to the effect that America is a nice place to be a dentist but if you want to practice the arts, do it in France. There was a feeling after World War I that the American publishers were a greedy lot who wouldn't publish good stuff, an attitude which I don't think obtained so much among American writers in Paris after World War II—our arts were now a lot healthier in America.

But there was one thing that made me feel abroad and away from my country for a while, which had to do with Henry Wallace. My wife and I had belonged in the late forties to the Progressive Citizens of America. The PCA met in cells, which was very like the Communists and, therefore, very romantic. We tried to elect local candidates: in 1946, my wife and I were driving a sound truck through all of Cambridge, blaring at the citizens, "Vote for Hughes! Vote for Stokes!"—we were trying to elect two black ministers to local office. Then, of course, as the Progressive Party formed and the Wallace candidacy developed, we worked very hard for that. We were wearing Wallace buttons when we got over to Paris and we were instantly popular with the French—they agreed with our residual Popular Front hopes. In 1948, we hadn't given up the hope that it was possible to join forces with Marxists toward common goals; we thought it could be done. Back in America at that time, of course, the anti-communists, which culminated in the McCarthy business, were building up; and the Marshall Plan was about to be used, not only for the purpose of stimulating the European economy but also for resisting the development of the communist parties in the European countries. Europe resented that for good reason, and we shared that resentment. So for that period we had our feeling of alienation from at least some part of our country. I hasten to say that by the time the election came around I felt that the Progressive Party was altogether too despicably manipulated by the Communists, and I voted for Truman.

LUCID: Norman, were you ever involved in the Progressive Party?

MAILER: I came back from Paris in the summer of 1948 and jumped into the Progressive Party immediately. Looking back on it, I would agree with Dick that various people did manipulate it. The people who were running things at the National Council of the Arts, Sciences and Professions sent me out to Hollywood to see if I could get some movie stars to sign up for Wallace. I asked why they chose me. They said, "Because you're an unknown; you're invaluable. All the old timers have used up their clout." It was one of the most extraordinary times of my life. They sat me next to Hedy Lamarr, whom, of course, I was trying to impress. She asked if I was married, and I said yes, and she asked what my marriage was like. I said, "Oh, marriage is a horrible institution." I was twenty-five years old, you see. She said, "Well, you're a very silly young man." That was the end of my great romance with Hedy Lamarr.

When I got up to speak about Henry Wallace, wondering how to win them over to commit their names to the cause, I started talking about how most artists had an element of corruption in themselves and, therefore, certain basic commitments were needed. I think that I was unintentionally eloquent. Before it was over, some of the people had their hands over their faces because they knew that they weren't going to endorse Wallace. Edward G. Robinson was at the party that night. He got up and said, "See here—who do you think you are, you little punk? You know, I'm known all over the world, I'm world famous, and you're telling me how to vote? I'll keep my vote to myself if you don't mind!" The only two people who signed on, finally, were Shelley Winters and Farley Granger. Shelley said, "Norman, you're asking an awful lot of us. I don't think that I have the guts to sign this because I could lose my career. This is just awful what you're asking." After the party was over she signed her name and went out of the room weeping—weeping for the career she had just destroyed. Of course, I never turned in their names; it really could have ruined them. But we have to find some graceful way to get back to Paris.

One element that Dick brought up with which I agree is that we were not expatriates—in fact, I probably have never been as much of an American as I was in Paris during that year. I became fully aware of all that I liked about my country, and I found myself defending America constantly in conversations with French people. One of the reasons that we Americans hung together and didn't like the French is that they didn't like us.

WILBUR: I remember being supremely snubbed as an American during our visit to Grasse. I was in a bookstore, and the woman behind the counter addressed a man in ecclesiastical garb, pointing at me, "*Delenda est Carthago.*" She had figured out that I didn't have any Latin and that she could make some kind of joke about how America was like Carthage, and cultured France was like Rome, and cultured France had to overcome these base materialists from America. I really did take patriotic offense at that.

AUDIENCE MEMBER: Mr. Mailer, I was wondering if you had any contact with Picasso?

MAILER: No. It's funny, but that year we sort of took Picasso for granted. He lived somewhere in the south of France, but no one ever wanted to meet him. Years later, in 1961, I think I wanted very much to meet him in order to do a book on him. My third wife, Jean Campbell, and I were traveling in France, and she said, "Let's go down and visit John Richardson and Douglas Cooper because they know him and they'll be very happy to introduce us." Well, advice from a Brit is either dead right or dead wrong—in this case, the latter. We visited Richardson and Cooper and had a fine evening. Jean kept bringing up Picasso's name and smiling, and they kept changing the subject. That was the closest I ever came to meeting him—we were maybe five or ten miles away from him.

WILBUR: I didn't encounter him either but I did meet Alberto Giacometti, who was extremely accessible and amiable. Before I knew it we were walking back to his studio. He talked all the way about his aesthetic objectives, and when we got into his studio—which was about the size of a privy and had a solid floor of smashed plaster and a very few narrow-looking figures rising up out of that mess—he stood there and talked about his desire to create in his sculptures figures of perfect anonymity. All the while he was talking about the anonymity and the mereness and the minimal quality of the figures, he kept abusing these already meager figures by hitting them with a beer-can opener and knocking more plaster off them. At one point he picked up a little bust and dug his thumb into its eye socket and knocked its head off.

AUDIENCE MEMBER: I'm reading *A Moveable Feast* and I'm fascinated by what Hemingway says about the process of writing while he's in Paris. How did you write in Paris? Did you write in cafés?

WILBUR: I wrote a lot of the time in my cold room. I never tried to write in a café. I feel a little chicken for not having done that, but I think that it would have made me feel self-conscious. But if you want to be a writer you do keep at it wherever you are.

MAILER: I never wrote in a café either and I used to distrust the fellows who did. But there used to be something so marvelous about them: you knew that whether they were good writers or not, they certainly would look like good writers in the café!

WILBUR: In preparation for this affair, I read over *A Moveable Feast* and I noticed, once again, what riles me about Hemingway's personality: he does want you to know that he is in on everything. He's the guy who talks to the trainers and the jockeys; he's the guy who knows the horses; he's the one who really talks to waiters in the way in which waiters should be talked to; he knows where the good wines are and the good potato salads. After a while, it gets to be a bit much, doesn't it?

MAILER: I think you put your finger on it. This is Hemingway's essential vice: he always had to be the absolute master of whatever was going on. This insistence is one of the things that inhibited him and kept him from writing about any number of topics. The greater part of human experience was, finally, closed off to him.

Christopher Logue

The Hotel Poitou, 32 rue de Seine, belonged to Monsieur
and Madame Claude-Louis Tonture. I agreed to give my friend
Anka the balance of the rent she had paid for one of the
Poitou's smaller rooms. "Monsieur Tonture," she said, "runs
a coal business with his brother, Boniface, in the hotel's back-
yard. Both of them were gassed in the First World War. They
are heavy drinkers. *Never* give him your rent."

As we tiptoed past the Poitou's curtained *loge*, an outburst
of coughing, broken by the phrase *chauffage en plus!* followed
us up the stairs to the first floor.

Anka's room, £3 a month, was ten feet long by four feet
wide with a red tile floor; her bag, packed, was on the two-
foot-wide bed; a hook on the back of the door, a bowl and
ewer, ". . . the tap is on the stairs. One floor up . . . ," a
tin bidet—the first I had seen—and a curtain for the window
forming the room's fourth side, was its furniture.

"Cooking in the rooms is not permitted," Anka said. "The
lights go off at 9:30 P.M. Music of any kind is forbidden.
Madame Tonture is very religious. To her, all music, save
church music, is immoral." She looked anxious, as if I might
say no. When I gave her the money in return for the key,

she said: "I'll leave you my dustpan and brush," took her bag and went. I sat on the bed, incredibly happy.

The Berlitz School of Languages employed foreigners as its method stipulated that pupils be taught by native speakers. Near avenue de l'Opéra, the school consisted of a hall, an office and twenty-five cubicles.

Mr. Watson was the school's inspector. On the wall of his office was a photograph of James Joyce, captioned: One of our ex-teachers. There was a loudspeaker on his table. If Mr. Watson liked the look of you, provided you spoke clear English, after a week's unpaid training in the use of the Berlitz books (*Book One, Lesson One. At the Airport. Pupil: "Where is the check-in?" Teacher: "On your left." Pupil: "Am I overweight?" Teacher: "Let us see."*) you were hired.

The lessons, some communal, mostly one-to-one, were held in the cubicles. Teachers were forbidden to speak any language save their own. On the wall of each cubicle was a boxed microphone allowing Mr. Watson to listen to, and, if necessary, to interrupt, any lesson during which he heard French being spoken.

A lesson took fifty-five minutes, the pupil paying 450 francs, the teacher getting 200—in cash. Thousand franc notes decorated with a portrait of Richelieu were known as *cardinals*; those of a hundred francs, picturing Rimbaud, *rêves*.

Face-to-face teaching is hard work. The bell rang. You went to the cubicle with Book One, say (for which you, like your pupil, paid), at the ready. It was not unknown for a pupil, usually keen, wanting English for business reasons, to enter the cubicle and find their teacher not, as Mr. Watson recommended, "with an alert, welcoming smile on your face . . . " but slumped over the desk, asleep.

Nessie Dunsmuir—the poet W.S. Graham's companion—my fellow teacher at the Paris Berlitz, said that after teaching for five hours in a row she slept through a whole lesson, waking to the time-up bell, and began: "*At the Airport . . .*" to an empty chair.

"Mr. Watson did not sack me," Nessie said. "He never sacked anyone. He was kind. He knew it was inadvisable to let me work that long at a stretch. But he knew I needed the money. Most of his teachers were doing it to get a *carte de séjour.*"

In retrospect I blessed the place. There was a blond girl teacher called Patsy who in our lunch hour used to translate Jacques Prévert's poems as she recited them:

> *Our Father, who are in Heaven,*
> *Stay there . . .*

And I fell in love with one of my pupils, Madame Marguerite Anan. And there was the cash, the flexible hours. And when I came out in the evening, tired though I was, turning into avenue de l'Opéra, my spirits rose. It was so well lit, so busy. Outbursts of hooting from the traffic, the shops full of good things, the effort made to look smart, to be lively. And at once, crossing rue de Rivoli, entering the courtyard of the Louvre, darkness, quietude, the river. Then over it into the Quarter. Where the girls were inventing rough-chic: bitten fingernails, black liner around the eyes, white cheeks, long greasy hair.

At the Poitou the larger room next to mine was occupied by Elmer Hazin, a painter-to-be from St. Louis studying art history on the GI Bill. Elmer's room was full of canvases.

"There are 28,000 artists in Paris," he said. "I am not yet among the two percent who earn enough from their art to eat. There must be many more poets—less outlay. Sugar?"

Madame Tonture allowed her guests to make coffee in their rooms. As the Poitou lacked power points, you bought— usually from someone who was leaving—a cup, a spirit stove, a hand mill and a small saucepan.

"Poets are worse off than painters," Elmer continued. "They have nothing to sell. Look at this," (showing me a painting of a lawn mower), "it's no good. I put black lines around everything like Picasso only my black lines are no good."

Before introducing me to his friend Gaït, we went to the
rue Buci market. I had not dreamt that there could be such
a variety of food. Everyone was buying small portions. Elmer
bought six different portions—three of pâté, three of cheese—
each neatly double-wrapped, sealed with well-designed paper
labels. There were twenty abundant, busy shops.

"People like us survive here because of our numbers," Elmer
said. "What we have we spend with the locals. The trouble
is we dislike each other. Always sleeping with each others'
husbands or wives. You're a homosexual if you don't. That
Elmer Hazin's a fag. I'm not. I masturbate. I have a clean
whore when Uncle Sam's check arrives. When the checks stop
I'll go home, become a dentist like my father, marry a good
Jewish girl, have a couple of kids and thirty years of good
healthy sexual intercourse, then die. Read Céline. You
haven't read Céline? The best French writer since Proust.
He'd have put Proust and me into a gas chamber."

Returned from Berlitz, Madame Tonture handed me a
letter franked *Sûreté Nationale*. "*De la part de la police
secrète*," she said in a mournful voice.

I met Elmer on the stairs. "If they wanted you, they'd
come for you," he said. "It's your *carte*." I must report,
carrying this letter, to the vestibule of the Dépôt de la Préfec-
ture de police, Ile de la Cité.

Early (as usual) I viewed the figures representing Truth,
Law, Eloquence and Clemency decorating the facade of the
correctional court. Then I was led upstairs, along a corridor,
down a circular stairway, over a glassed-in bridge, through
two sets of swing doors, into a lift, out, through a glass door
to a waiting room, bare but for a wooden bench supporting
a young woman, a child on each side of her, looking
straight ahead.

After ten minutes a policeman put his head around the
door and called them in. After an hour the same policeman
called for, then led me into a large office full of men—secret
policemen, I assumed—laughing, talking, smoking, on the

telephone, reading newspapers, looking about, some with their legs up on the desks. Mine, when I had been seated, said:

"*Bonjour, Monsieur Logue.* You work at the Berlitz school?" looking at his papers.

"Yes, Monsieur."

"Why do you want to live in France?"

"I am a writer. France is hospitable to artists. I would like to live where some of the writers I admire have lived."

"And they are?"

"James Joyce, Ezra Pound."

"Hemingway?"

"Less."

"How long are you hoping to remain in France?"

"Five years. I'm not sure."

"Are you a member of a political party."

"No."

"No politics?"

"I'm of the Left."

"Naturally."

"You have French friends?"

I gave M. de Ruyter's name.

"What do you write?"

"Poetry."

"Published?"

At Alex Trocchi's recommendation Princess Caetani, publisher and editrix of the literary magazine *Botteghe Oscure*, had accepted some poems of mine, one of them, "To My Father," my best so far. Published in Rome, *Botteghe* came out in French, German, Italian and English. I had a copy of it—including my work—in my shoulder bag. The police approved.

"*Quatre langues*, eh?" paging through. "*François*"—his neighbor—"*Regarde. Nous avons un poète ici.*" I had realized France was a country where writers counted. The appellation *homme de lettres* carried weight. Sartre, Camus and Company were a force.

The inspector signed my card. For five years I was free to

live in France coming and going as I pleased. Thirty-eight
years expired, I still have my card. One never knows.

There were two English bookshops in the Quarter. Shakespeare & Co., facing Notre Dame, still open, proprietor,
George Whitman, a Bostonian; and just a step from the
Poitou, the English Bookshop, owned by a Frenchwoman,
Gaït Frogé, a quiet, well-read Bretonne speaking elegant English, inclined to reserve, noticing you, not minding if you
don't notice her, a fair judge of character, and, to those who
became the magazine *Merlin*'s crowd, a friend.

Gaït's hair was chestnut colored, her eyes large, brown and
rather mournful. For three years I used her shop as my address.
Sometimes there was no one at the desk. Then the curtain
draped behind it swung aside and Gaït appeared, always
fashionably dressed, handing me my letters, with: "One for
you, and will you be seeing Alex?" (Trocchi, the editor of
Merlin.) "There are two for him—and I would like a word
in his ear later today."

When Elmer and I entered the shop a tall black-haired
man dressed in a brown two-piece suit was reading aloud.
Gaït was encouraging the reader with a smile at the same
time as, without looking at them, she turned the pages of
the book on her desk. The man was reading in Latin. Catullus,
as it turned out:

Flavi, delicias tuas Catullo . . .

Then he hurried out of the shop snapping shut his book as
he went.

Later that week at a program of surrealist films I met the
reader, one Philip Oxman, the son of a wealthy salesman
from Chicago, a medievalist, writing a treatise on Nicholas
of Cusa: "1401 to 1464, anticipated Copernicus's proof of
heliocentricity, wrote a book called *The Idiots*, devoted to
those he disagreed with, and bombed his own reputation—
from our point of view, that is—by predicting the world
would end on the second Thursday of September, 1743."

Philip was a godsend. I was fascinated by things medieval.

Among my books, the essay on falconry by Frederick II (Holy Roman Emperor, King of Sicily and Jerusalem, etcetera), *de arte venandi cum avibus.*

"If I came over to your place, Philip," I said, "would you translate a few pages of *De arte* for me?"

Place, rather than room, for Philip—a scholarship from University of Chicago, an allowance from his father—occupied one of the many apartments into which Raymond Duncan, the brother of Isadora, had divided his *hôtel particulier* a few doors away from The English Bookshop.

Only the rich or those who had bought in the 1890s owned *hôtels particuliers* in central Paris. Duncan's—he must have been in his eighties in 1951—was vast. A pair of shops selling his booklets and the products of his studio flanked the archway leading to its courtyard.

Duncan grew his silver gray hair down to his shoulders, wove and wore smocks of heavy brown wool, fastened by wooden, golf-ball sized bobbles incised with occult signs. Snow or shine he walked the Quarter in homemade sandals, wore no socks ". . . and, I am told," said Gaït, "nothing under his robe." Duncan considered Gaït a rival, an upstart, streaming past her shop with never a glance.

At the back of his courtyard was a large room called the Akademika Duncan, with a stage whereon he performed chants and dances to a tambourine. Pamphlets giving the words and music of the chants, with diagrams of his dance steps, were on sale in the archway shops. After the performance members of the public were offered a bowl of vegetarian soup and a cob of home-baked bread.

Austryn (Wainhouse, an editor at the literary magazine *Merlin*) and I visited the office of Olympia Press. I had submitted to Maurice Girodias a proposal for a dirty book called *The Abominable Circus* featuring a troupe of sexual gold-medalists performing singly, in pairs, trios, quarters or even larger combinations, on horse and/or elephant back, high-wire, trapeze or while being fired from cannons. Their pan-European adventures were to be set in the seventeenth century. Loved by the public, they were pursued from fair to fair by the Pope's secret police. Austryn did not think my outline would appeal to Olympia's proprietor.

Maurice looked pale. He wore a dark gray suit, a blue suit, a dark blue tie. There was a new secondhand sofa in front of his trestle-table desk, a new paraffin heater to his right.

"Please sit down," he said. "You both look so well. How lucky you are to enjoy perfect health. My wife has a cold. I feel a cold coming on. Now, your pages, Austryn." Austryn slid the folder containing his pages across the trestle table, and, while Maurice counted them, we all lit up.

"Lisa," Maurice said, taking a bottle out of his pocket without looking up (Lisa, his secretary, sat at a second trestle table beyond the paraffin heaters), "a glass of warm water, please."

Maurice paid by the page. One thousand francs per page. He liked to receive ten pages every other day. "I must have ten books in print for Christmas rush."

While he read Austryn's pages Maurice unscrewed the bottle cap, rolled a green-black capsule out onto the table, recapped the bottle with one hand (the other, with cigarette, leafing the pages) then slipped the nostrum between his lips plus a tiny sip of water, saying—without looking up: "Very good. A nice touch. Convincing."

Big men carrying plain cartons came and went. Lisa signed. A tense five minutes.

When he finished, Maurice put his hand into his trousers' pocket and took out a sheaf of once-folded banknotes, saying "Let's see what we have here. It was ten pages, Austryn?"

"Twelve pages, Maurice."

"Don't mind my asking. I have the weekend to think of."

The banknotes were held in a flat, unsprung paper clip.

"Well," selecting two of 1,000 francs, one of 10,000 francs "there you are," sliding them across the table, "let's meet again on Tuesday."

As Austryn accepted, Maurice looked at me and said: "I know you have no money at all, Christopher, but this,"—

sliding my proposal towards me—"will never do. You are not writing pornography to amuse yourself. Olympia's customers are men seeking sexual relief in one of the most normal of ways. All mammals, including humans, masturbate. Very few of the latter want to laugh while they do so. Even fewer want to be laughed at for doing so. Did you know—according to yesterday's London *Daily Telegraph*"—Maurice was a *Telegraph* reader—"that Boccaccio is going to be prosecuted in Swindon, Wiltshire? This in 1953. Consult Alex. I want one full encounter of at least five pages for every ten pages of text. I don't mind a joke or two. Nothing snobby."

Alex agreed that *Collection Merlin* would publish my first book of poems, *Wand and Quadrant*, if I could cover half the printing bill by subscriptions. These were going slowly. Of the forms I posted, only my cousin Jimmy Logue, a car dealer—"Three copies but don't bother to send them"—had been returned. The book would cost £150 to print. I had subscriptions worth £50. Then my luck changed.

Jean Crouch, an English friend, and I were sitting on the terrace of Café Monaco, me showing her the manuscript of my book while complaining I was still short of the £100 Alex had insisted on, when a large redheaded girl with an American accent at the next table leaned over and said, "Show me that."

Jean hand it over. The girl began to read. After five minutes, she handed the manuscript back and said, "How much do you need to get this stuff printed?"

"£50," I said.

"How much is that in dollars?"

Bill Boyce, a racing-car driver from Wyoming, was reading *The International Herald Tribune* along the terrace. He gave us the daily rate.

"You've got it," said the redhead. "Give me an address. You get the money in exchange for the manuscript. Okay?"

"You mean he's to leave the manuscript at his address, and when you deliver the money it's yours?" Jean said.

"That's what I mean," said the redhead.

I was so nervous I knocked my glass of wine over the manuscript, saying as I dried it with Jean's tissues, "Never mind, I have another copy."

"This one's mine," said the redhead. "As is. Now I must go."

Jean gave her Gait's address.

"Do you think she means it?" I said.

"Yes," Jean said. "And make sure Gait gets her name and the name of her hotel. Her suit cost more than my entire wardrobe."

My backer from the Café Monaco left the dollars and took the manuscript. I did not get her name or address. Three weeks later the actual printed edition was delivered to Gait's.

Looking at the packages containing *Wand and Quadrant* at Gaït's depressed me. What on earth was I to do with six-hundred books?

"You must sell them, Christopher," Gaït said.

"Well," Austryn's wife, Muffie, said, "Let's look on the bright side. For £150 you have received six-hundred books, worth—minus the subscriber and complimentary copies—at least £1,000."

"I have never sold anything in my life."

"Have you ever bought anything?"

"Don't laugh."

"I mean have you ever bought anything for no particular reason, just because you fancied it, suddenly, out of the blue?"

"A painting of a cat from a girl in Place St.-Michel. To get in with her."

"That's it. You're rich. Become the girl."

The truth was I felt toffee-nosed about selling. One of the copies George Whitman lent out was returned with *drivel* written in a neat hand on the bottom right-hand corner of each page. Another had: "See you in the Royal at 15.30, Jennifer" scrawled across the title page in lipstick.

I was no good as a salesman. Holding a copy, I approached English-speaking visitors at café tables.

"Excuse me. Would you like to buy my book?"

"What's it about?"

"It's a book of poems."

"What are they about?"

Even as it irritated me, I felt that this was a fair question.

"Some are about being in love. Some are about sailing to an unknown country with the help of ancient stars."

"All right, we'll have one. We're in Paris, after all."

As soon as I made, if I made, two sales, I hastened to the Tournon, a left-wing poet concerned with the world's wrongs. I sent Pound a copy. In return, came my one hand-

George Plimpton, William Pène du Bois, Jane Lougee (publisher of Merlin)*, and Christopher Logue at the Café de Tournon.*

written letter from him. It said: "Not bad. I can read quite a bit of it." High praise. Whatever else he was, where verse was concerned Pound was no liar.

A new literary magazine appeared in Paris.

Published from rue Garancière, a prestigious address around the corner from the Tournon, rumor had it as the work of a few wealthy New Yorkers, not serious chaps, a lightweight affair, like its title, *The Paris Review*. Anyway, who on earth were they going to publish? Give it a couple of issues at the most. It was edited by one George Ames Plimpton.

Austryn, who was at school with George, doubted his abilities as an editor, saying: "You will find *The Paris Review*'s editor, his assistant editors and his contributing editors, etcetera, on holiday with the bulls at Pamplona, fishing off the coast of Celebes, drifting from penthouse to penthouse in New York, not in the bookshops and cafés of the Quarter." I saw Alex thinking what I was thinking: Not bad—drifting from one New York penthouse to another.

The rivalry between the magazines did not last, some of us were published in both, their editors became friends.

George was romantic, mad on Hemingway, socially adventurous. "Let's *go* there, let's just *go* there, we'll see what they're like—" from the world's flea-circus chariot-racing championships, to wangling an invitation for drinks at the Duchess of Windsor's.

My first sight of George was him clambering from an open-topped car outside the Tournon draped with a long scarf, hat whacked on the back of his head, a skinny six-foot-fourer managing to get one leg tangled up with the lead of a dog being taken on its daily, re-righting himself, apologizing to the dog's owner and, as he lurched over to our terrace table, dumping a pile of manuscripts under my and Alfred Chester's (that marvelous, undervalued writer) noses before ordering us and himself a drink, asking if we knew the result of the Marciano-Walcott fight.

George concealed his determination. He knew what he wanted from his magazine—that it should last. It was he who proposed its soon to be valued Art of Fiction interviews with celebrated novelists. The *Review*'s 150th issue is just out. *Merlin*'s 7th was its last.

"Why don't you interview me, George?" Alfred said.

"You're not famous," George said. "I am interested in fame."

Alfred had a pink, freckled, ginger owl of a face, and a soft, squeaky voice. He was small, with tiny, delicate hands, though the first thing I and, I suppose, everyone else noticed was his wig, orange brown with an oily sheen sitting unwanted on the top of his head.

"And as far as you, George, are concerned, I'll stay that way," Alfred said. Then to me, "George here—in case he hasn't told you already—has currently rejected a story of mine for his, let's face it, not very distinguished *Paris Review*— couldn't you think of a better, even slightly better, title than that, George?—on the grounds that the main character in my story is *too oozy*. What kind of criticism is that, George? *Too oozy*—it's me you're talking about, not the story. George thinks I am ugly."

"I most certainly do not," said George, embarrassed.

"And the other reason for George's ongoing rejection of my oozy story was that George didn't dare carry my thumbnail biography: 'Alfred Chester is an impenitent, atheistic Jew, a heavy drinker, continually smoking nicotine—with or without marijuana—a pill-popping hairless albino homosexual who cannot keep a lover, and an American citizen of exemplary right-wing views.'

George said: "What about that other story?"

"'Rapunzel, Rapunzel?' You won't like it."

"I might," George said, hurt.

"I can't read it to you here. It's too noisy."

As we walked to Place St.-Sulpice and a quiet café, George said, "Don't be surprised if people cross the road when they see us coming. I bear a strong resemblance to Alger Hiss."

Alfred read "Rapunzel, Rapunzel" very softly, a brilliant reading, his squeakiness working in the story's favor:

> *When Gwendolyn left the house she turned at once in the direction of Market Square; having taken a triple dose of Forgetfulness Drops, she was certain she would get there. Since death's imminence had been announced to her, she rarely went on specific errands, but when she did, if she were not numbed with Forgetfulness Drops she almost never reached her destination, for adventure usually fell to her. Others called it disorderly conduct or, more severely, wickedness. Her favorite adventure was to enter a crowded grocery and insist on immediate service, luring the clerks to her with smiles and promises of money; she would then go round the shop, pointing to random tins and packages.*
>
> *"Four of those," she would say. "And six of these. I want one-hundred thousand of those." And when the clerks frowned she passed several large bills between her hands and smiled. "O never mind. Ten will do."*

© Russ Melcher

Eugene Walter, George Plimpton, Bee Dabney and Alfred Chester at the Café Deux-Magots.

"I'd like to publish that," George said.

It was from Alfred I heard of the house in London where I lived for twenty-eight years. Born in 1928, he died alone, in Jerusalem, in 1971.

Back from the bank Gaït handed me a letter from Alan Pryce-Jones, editor of the *Times Literary Supplement*, saying he accepted my sonnets for publication. My heart leapt. Here was someone who knew about writing, who did not know me from Adam, who was going to print a *whole column* of my work in the best place for new verse to be seen in London. When the *Times* newspaper check for £14 arrived I kept it for days.

Evan S. Connell

Poets, painters, musicians and so forth who loitered about
St.-Germain in the early fifties were, to my knowledge, more
or less impoverished. If any of them did have money, it was
not mentioned. Christopher Logue, I had heard, was highly
impoverished even by poetic standards. I wanted to invite
Christopher to lunch, but there was a chance he might feel

Evan S. Connell in Paris, September 1952.

offended. I asked Max Steele, who knew him pretty well,
what to do. Max suggested that he might criticize a manuscript
in exchange for lunch. That sounded fine. Christopher was
agreeable, so we met at some restaurant. I gave him a five-
page story I had written. I thought he would skim through
it, make a few comments, and we could get on with our
lunch. Ah, no. He took the story apart paragraph by para-

graph, sentence by sentence, phrase by phrase, word by word. I was appalled. It seemed to me that he talked for an hour, pointing out every mistake. Since that day I have, for better or worse, inspected each paragraph, sentence, phrase and word, perhaps fearful that Christopher might be looking over my shoulder. That was almost fifty years ago and I still am not sure if I feel indebted to him. He made things more difficult.

Max Steele

At a *Story* party in Cincinnati, the eight at our table were playing a game of who could drop the biggest name. The winner would be the person who could claim an encounter with the biggest celebrity of our time. While they told of their meetings or friendships, I debated whether to tell of my friendship in Cuernavaca with Lady Mary, a granddaughter of Queen Victoria who, Herself, dropped not names but initials. ("P.E. I learned, after a month or so, was Prince Edward.) But then I decided on Alice B. Toklas.

The last time I had played the game was at a much less grand affair in Café de Tournon where Eugene Walter had easily won by proving he had three of Tallulah Bankhead's pubic hairs. Alexander Trocchi, the contender, had lost by claiming to know himself, but lacked convincing proof.

In Cincinnati, a man was telling about being stuck atop a mesa with Christopher Isherwood, who was so frightened of the height he had insisted on waiting for dark to start down the perilous cliff. My own claim seemed tame in comparison.

"I took Alice B. Toklas to see two plays by Gertrude Stein." So unimpressed was the audience I might as well have said, "I once bought a hammer at Sears."

It really *was* uneventful. A lovely girl, Cam Grey, had asked me to help with steps and taxis to get her friend Alice B. to the plays at the American Club on the boulevard Raspail. Toklas no longer lived at the 27 rue de Fleurus address, but had moved to a small carrefour near the rue de Rennes. I kept the cab at the curb while Cam went up to fetch her quite old friend, who certainly would never have opened the door to me, a large stranger.

Alice B. Toklas descended on time to the dot. She wore a sort of cloche, fashioned entirely of small roses made of voile. One could only think, "A rose is a rose is a rose is a hat." She never looked at me and said only, *"Bonsoir."*

The cab was dark and it was only when we were seated that

Max Steele sitting at the Café de la Mairie du 6th, the café made famous by Djuna Barnes's novel Nightwood.

I could see how dark she was, and how small, a little gnome. I could not determine whether the ugly rumor that she now waxed her mustache was true. (Stein's words came back: "Don't write about what you don't know about, even if you don't know it.") Her upper lip was noticeably dark. But then her whole image was dark: coat, stocking, shoes and drawstring bag, from which she now withdrew a copy of the two plays and a black pen, difficult to unscrew.

She listened with an absolutely total intensity to the second play. Each time an actor misread a line or added or left out a word, Alice B. Toklas marked the error in her copy. By the end of the evening the edition was quite chicken-tracked with her small handwriting.

At the end of the evening it was I who walked her up the stairs to her flat where she said a quiet, *"Merci. Bonsoir, m'sieur."* Three more words to the earlier two, and she had not looked at me the entire three hours.

When I finished the story at the table in Cincinnati it was clear I had been tolerated but not awarded the prize. A young girl next to me said: "I didn't understand your story. Who was the celebrity?"

"Cam Grey," I said. "She was a lovely person."

"Cam Grey?" she asked. "What was she famous for?"

"For being lovely," I explained.

Mordecai Richler

Those of us who surfaced in Paris in the early 1950s, revering, as we did, the cafés and brasseries once favored by Joyce, Hemingway and Fitzgerald, were a second wave, a copycat generation, but this did nothing to diminish the huge pleasures of our sojourn.

A callow, nineteen-year-old college dropout, I arrived one sunny autumn afternoon in 1950, emerging from the metro at St.-Germain-des-Prés exhilarated beyond compare, delighted to have put then picayune Canada behind me, too stupid to grasp that it would eventually prove to be my richest material. Moving into a mice-infested hotel on the rue Cujas, I immediately hurried out to acquire a blue beret. I also considered an ivory cigarette holder, but fortunately good sense prevailed. However, my first night on the Left Bank I did settle into a table on the terrace of the Café de Flore, pulling out my notebook and pen, doing my utmost to appear pensive. Look at me, I'm a writer.

Little magazines published in Paris then included *Points, Id, Janus, Merlin* and *New-Story*. My first embarrassing short story, actually written when I was seventeen, appeared in *Points*, which was edited by Sindbad Vail, who was the son of Peggy Guggenheim and Lawrence Vail. The first issue of *Points* sold extremely well, many readers—according to Sindbad—mistaking it for a knitting magazine, but it soon settled into a circulation of four hundred. Eventually, I fell in with Terry Southern, Mason Hoffenberg and the *New-Story* bunch. *New-Story* was edited by Eric Protter and David Burnett, the latter the son of Whit Burnett and Martha Foley, editors of the original *Story* magazine. *New-Story*, usually one breathless step ahead of bill collectors, was soon surpassed by the moneyed crowd who began to publish the more elegant *Paris Review*: the loping George Plimpton in his snap-brim fedora, Eugene Walter and Peter Matthiessen, who could usually be found at the Café de Tournon, the affable Richard Wright working the pinball machine.

At the time, Terry Southern and Mason Hoffenberg seemed inseparable, but they later fell apart over who had contributed what to *Candy*, which they wrote together. My guess is that Mason was responsible for some of the more outlandish inventions, but that Terry did most of the writing.

The truth is we had come over not so much to absorb French culture as to meet each other, but, all the same, Edith Piaf was big with us, as were Jacques Prévert's *Paroles*, Trenet, and the films of Simone Signoret. In those days, Communist Party members were obliged to peddle *L'Humanité* on the street one day a week, but the fastidious Signoret was reported to have sent out her maid instead.

Anything by Genet, or Samuel Beckett, was passed from hand to hand. I tried to read *La Nausée* in French, but stumbled and gave up, but I did devour Céline, if only in English translation.

It all seems so long ago since we used to gather night after night to shoot the breeze at the Mabillon, the Old Navy, the long-defunct Café Royal St.-Germain or the Select in Montparnasse, never discussing "our stuff," or admitting that we actually labored hard and long in our hotel rooms, real Americans after all, shoulders to the wheel, determined to make our mark. And, alas, there have been so many casualties since those halcyon days and nights, Alexander Trocchi, Alfred Chester, David Burnett, Mason Hoffenberg and Terry Southern no longer among the quick.

Of all the writers I used to know in Paris in those days only Mavis Gallant is still living there, continuing to write splendid short stories.

Richard Seaver

Sitting at the terrace of the Deux-Magots café one early spring day in 1952, sipping a beer, I watched the girls flounce by, provocative and proudly remote, decked out now in bright spring colors, having put away their drab winter coats and heavy scarves at the first real hint of April warmth. My friend Pat Bowles slid into the rattan seat beside me.

"You're ogling," he said following my gaze—which was fixed on a pretty girl in a bright flower print—with an ogle far more obvious than mine.

"Contemplating," I said. "I assure you: contemplating."

"Ogling," he retorted, his face breaking into a broad smile. Patrick had one of the slowest smiles I'd ever seen, but when it broke into full grin it was one of the most luminous and warmest. His speech, like his grin, was long to mature: his poet's brain moved swiftly, but like a film taken at an accelerated rate per second, the words were often slow-motion. A white South African, Pat, like so many of us in those days, had opted to leave, at least momentarily, the oppressive politics of our respective native countries for the heady freedom of Paris.

"Actually," he said, stressing all syllables equally, not an easy linguistic task, "I was looking for you . . ."

The waiter loomed, in full standard uniform.

"What'll you have?" I said. "On me." For some unknown reason I was feeling magnanimous.

"A beer."

"Why were you looking for me?"

"I thought your piece on Hemingway in *Points* was very good," he said.

"Thanks," I said, wondering what Hemingway would think of Paris today.

Points was one of the several mushrooming literary magazines that had recently sprung up in Paris's fertile, postwar soil, emulating their elders of the 1920s and 1930s. Run—which meant funded—by a young man with the improbable

Richard Seaver

name of Sindbad Vail, the son of millionairess Peggy Guggenheim. Sindbad had a French wife and, compared to most of us, a deep pocket, which he was depleting rapidly by printing ten times as many copies of his English-language magazine as he could ever hope to sell.

"Because there's a new magazine just started," he said.

"Another?"

"But this . . . this one is *different*. Very good. *Serious*," he concluded.

"Has it got a name?"

"M-*Merlin*," Pat said. He had a slight stutter when the

synapses were on overload, or too much was trying to emerge too soon.

"Named after the bird or the magician?" I asked.

Pat's brow furrowed. "I don't really know. Anyway, the editor's a Scotsman, brilliant man really, wants to make a new statement. Only important writing. But politically aware, too."

"Who is he?"

"His name is Alex Trocchi."

"That's your *Scotsman*?"

"Half Italian, half Scot," Pat said, almost apologetically, fluttering briefly over the *h*s.

"Money?"

"He doesn't have any, or not much . . ."

"Ah-hh."

"But he has an American girlfriend. Daughter of a banker, I think. From Maine."

"Bangor? A banker from Bangor?" I could feel a limerick forming. As it turned out, the backer-banker was not from Bangor, but from Limerick. With a capital *L*. What would the surrealists say about that?

"Where do they hang out?" I said. "Do they have an office?"

"I'm on my way there now," Pat said. "Why don't you come with me?"

The *Merlin* office turned out to be an hotel room only three blocks away. Under the eaves. A seven-story walk-up. The man who opened the door had to be Trocchi. He loomed large, immediately impressive. Tall, probably six foot two or three: a hawklike nose, piercing blue eyes, a tousled shock of thick brown hair, a ready smile, a warm handshake. And a heavy, lilted Scottish accent.

Pat introduced us, and Alex stepped aside to let us in. The office consisted of a double bed that only looked huge because the room was so small, a bulging armoire whose door would not close, two stiff-backed chairs, and a table that occupied most of one wall, on which sat a couple hundred copies of *Merlin* issue number one.

Perched on the bed like a pert bird, nicely tamed but ready to fly, was a comely lass, dark hair flowing over her shoulders like the running water the room apparently lacked. Miss Maine, I presume. "Jane Lougee." She smiled, extending her hand.

For the next three hours we talked: politics (Joe McCarthy was in full bloom, and two of his petals, Cohn and Schine, were making their way through Europe, sowing fear and disorder, looking in closets and under beds for commie-pinko traitors and other dangerous dissenters); literature old and new; France and its many virtues (virtue number one: you could live—frugally, but *live*—on two dollars a day); renascent Germany and the danger it already seemed to pose; Russia (who was right, Camus or Sartre, in their increasingly heated debate about where the Soviets were headed?) . . .

Night, "having nothing better to do,"—and I quote—had fallen, so we all clambered noisily downstairs and repaired to Chez Raffy, on the rue du Dragon, where you got a steak-frites, salad and your share of a bottle of red wine for roughly a dollar.

"Pat tells me you know the scene here as well as anybody," Trocchi was saying—I had already been in Paris for a couple of years. "Any young writers who are exceptional? American? English? French?"

I reeled off three or four names, younger writers. To my surprise, Trocchi knew them all. "There's one," I said, "who isn't all that young. But he's extraordinary. I've been reading everything he's written . . ."

"In what language?"

"French. But, oddly, he's Irish. His name is Samuel Beckett. Had a close connection with Joyce. I've been told he was Joyce's secretary, but I don't think that's true."

"What have you read of his?" Trocchi's interest was clearly aroused.

"I've just finished a novel called *Molloy*. And an earlier book, *Murphy*."

"Enamored of the letter *m*," Trocchi mused.

"Plus a couple of remarkable short stories."

"Where does he live?" Jane wondered aloud.

"Here. But I have no idea where. He spent the war years in France. Somewhere in the Vaucluse. . . . Anyway, I've never read anybody remotely like him. He's writing on about six levels at once. I'm still working on level three. And he's *very* funny."

"So what are you waiting for, man," Trocchi said. "Write a piece about him," his *man* sounding like *mon*. By now I was getting every second word of his seductive baritone: whenever I had a quizzical look, Jane or Pat would translate. Scottish, I concluded, deep Scottish, *is* another language.

We broke up around midnight. Before I went to sleep that night, I had devoured the contents of *Merlin*'s issue one, and was indeed impressed by its seriousness of purpose. Maybe a tad too serious, but still . . .

Beckett's publisher, Editions de Minuit, was right around the corner, and on a hunch I dropped by a day or so after meeting Trocchi to see if any new Beckett work was in the offing. Yes, I was told, there was a new novel. The title? *Malone Dies*. I got an advance copy and over the next week or so read *Malone* and reread the other novels, finding new nuggets each time. And new puzzles.

It took a good week to produce the promised essay, for the further I dug the more I realized how deep the mine was. A day or two after reworking it for the fourth time I walked the article over to Trocchi. I had no desire to stay while he read it, but he insisted. When he finished he looked up. "Great, man, we'll run it in the next issue," he said. "Have you thought of a title?"

I shrugged. "Something simple," I said. "How about 'Samuel Beckett: An Introduction'?" That modest article, which began: "Anyone interested in today's literature must take into account the work of Samuel Beckett, an Irish writer now living in France and writing in French . . ." was, I believe, the first on the future author of *Waiting for Godot*, who, at age forty-six, was still virtually unknown.

From that day on I became committed to *Merlin*, and for the next two years worked closely with Trocchi and the tight group of English, Canadians and Americans dedicated to it.

When issue number two appeared, I took it around the corner to Jerome Lindon, Beckett's publisher at Les Editions de Minuit, and asked him to send it to Beckett, enclosing a note inquiring about a novel he had apparently written, his last in English, which had never been published, entitled *Watt*. Ultimately, *Merlin* published not only extracts of that novel in the magazine but, a year or so later, when *Merlin* expanded its folly from publishing (sporadically) the magazine to publishing (even more sporadically) books, the novel itself. Every issue of *Merlin* thereafter contained something by the Great Man, so blatantly that when the following year *Merlin* applied for the French equivalent of fourth-class mailing privilege for the magazine, it was turned down by the postal authorities on the grounds that it was judged to be an organ of propaganda for one Samuel Beckett, whoever he might be.

Looking back, it probably was. But if one has to plead guilty to that charge, propagandizing Beckett in those early days was indeed a proud stigma to bear.

Mary Lee Settle

Four years after the Second World War had ended my husband, Douglas Newton, and I went from London to Paris on the Newhaven to Dieppe channel crossing. It took five nervous pitching hours. There was much vomiting, but I didn't: I was too scared. In the harbor at Dieppe the half-submerged wrecks from the Dieppe raid and D day had not yet been moved. The boat dodged around them to dock. On the train to Paris, in Gare St-Lazare, along the streets of Paris we smelled food. We had come from the years of stark rationing in London. It had a name: austerity. We did a lot of thinking about food.

Paris was still dirty, and war-worn. On so many street corners there were small shrines to the people in the FFI, most of them teenagers, who had been shot by retreating Germans during the liberation of Paris. But there seemed to us to be no shortage of food. I ate a month's ration of meat in England in a steak tartare in St-Germain. I was as drunk on protein as a pigmy after an elephant hunt.

Paris is streets, not neighborhoods. So our street that year was the rue St-Louis en-l'Ile, on the Ile St-Louis. We stayed in a hotel called the Normandie. It was four stories high and one room wide. It cost two fifty of the old franc a night, about a dollar. We were on the second floor, up steep narrow stairs. Sometime in the third Empire a drunken paper hanger had put the wallpaper in our room on upside down so that foot-long parrots in a wild Rousseau forest around us stood on their heads. I learned some French reading *Paris Match*, the toilet paper in the hall bathroom. We put our dirty laundry in the tin bidet.

Every morning at five o'clock horses were driven along the narrow street to an abattoir in a broken-down Renaissance *hôtel de ville* with a large courtyard. The clatter of their hooves echoed against the buildings. They sounded like war horses fifteen feet high.

The first floor of the hotel was a café where almost the whole of the front was opened out into the street. In the mornings we shared coffee and bananas and croissants with John Cage who lived on the third floor, and Ellsworth Kelly on the fourth. We never found out who was in the last room at the top of the building.

Across the street was a patisserie where a woman who didn't like anybody made wonderful croissants. She also sold bananas. So each morning we took turns braving her bad temper and asked slowly for *quatre croissants quatre banans s'il vous plait.*

In the evening we walked to the Royale, the café across boulevard St-Germain from the Deux-Magots. It was the meeting arena for artists in Paris on the GI Bill. It had been chosen with great purity by the people who took us there, and we were instructed to look down on the people at the Magots, who we were told were mostly that new breed of American cat, graduate students, and groupies looking for famous people. So the china franc saucers piled high and we talked, talk that, for me, went on wonderfully for six years, every time I went to Paris.

Outside of that one binge on protein, we ate at the prix fixe in the rue Jacob. Our friend Eduardo Paolozzi sat turning a tomato over and over on his fork, sipping Fetish wine, and muttering, "Next stop, the river."

I remember the talk as continuous. I took it back to London to sustain me until the next release into Paris. The café changed, the street, the hotel, during the next six years. But the talk did not. There was little true conversation then in London, not like that, not those easy hours. London "literary" was far too self-conscious and people seemed always to be jockeying for position. In Paris the ones I knew and whom I have been fond of ever since were far too arrogant to give a damn.

Two of the best people I ever met who were of that curious world that outsiders and graduate students call *art*, are John

Cage and Ellsworth Kelly. John spoke in interrogatives, "My name's John Cage? I want to start a group called Capitalists Incorporated so it won't be banned by the Un-American Activities Committee? To be president you have to destroy a mechanical recorder? You can be a vice-president if you destroy a record player? I want everybody to make their own music, even if it's only toilet paper on a comb?" He was a sweet, generous man, and that is why I remember him beyond all the rest on that first time in Paris.

On the morning that he and Merce Cunningham, who lived in a flat on the left side of the island, were leaving for New York, we sat in the café helping Merce wait. Merce was worried, then fidgety, then fit to be tied. John had disappeared and his bags were not packed. The boat train left at noon.

That morning it was raining in Paris. I think it rains harder and with more personal anger in Paris than in any other city in Europe. Ten thirty came and through the rain sloshed John, beatific looking, as if he had been totally emersed like a Baptist. His hair was plastered to his face. His raincoat was soaked and dripping.

Before Merce could say a word, he said, "I've just been listening to the sweetest music this side of heaven? I woke up this morning and realized how welcome I had been at Radiodiffusion and by the musical world of Paris while young French composers had no entrée? So I decided to take an unknown young French composer around and introduce him?" Then he said to us, and to Eduardo, who had joined us, "You are invited to hear his music?"

He gave us the address, and later we climbed those stairs where the dim light went off before you got to the next floor and the next light. In what I remember as a small room with a narrow bed and an upright piano with some of the ivory missing from the keys, the young composer played for us. His name was Pierre Boulez.

John left a record of his own for us, and we went to a

record store in the Rue de Beaux Arts, and asked to play it. When it was over, I went up to the counter to thank the owner. He was talking with a customer. This was the conversation I overheard.

"Qu'est-ce que c'est?"

"C'est le bebop Chinoise."

So this is one of my Parises. There were many.

Alice Adams

In Paris, in the years just after World War II, the neighborhood around the Café de Flore and the Deux-Magots and the church, St-Germain-des-Près, was very much that, a neighborhood. We knew almost everyone we saw on the streets, or at least we knew who they were. I remember standing there on the boulevard one day when someone pointed across to a man coming out of the Brasserie Lipp, saying, "Look, there's Picasso!" and it was, those incredible eyes unmistakable, even at that distance.

By *we* I mean mostly American ex-GIs, now in Paris on the GI Bill. Single men got $90 a month, $120, if married (curious arithmetic, that). My then-husband and I lived on that sum, quite well, on the rue de Seine, in a hotel called Le Welcome. In a large, oddly trapezoidal room, in which on an alcohol burner we made and drank and served to friends an enormous amount of surprisingly good coffee.

I was working on a novel that I called The Impersonators (its title was probably its best feature), which was based on an idea I had at the time that the *real* Americans in Paris were those who came in the twenties; we were merely pale imitations. Luckily for me, I think, this book was never published.

That was what we did in the mornings, usually: Mark the husband went off to the Sorbonne to study, cours de la civilization francaise, and I in the Welcome Hotel worked on my novel. We met somewhere for lunch, any one of the marvelous cheap local student restaurants. No meals ever bad, I thought—though of course I was not many years distant from the Southern cooking on which I had grown up, and I was a very long way from the San Francisco foodie that I was to become.

Afternoons are unclear in my memory; we very likely spent them having coffee with friends somewhere. We did not, as might have been expected, spend much time exploring Paris.

Being tourists. This was an omission that I came to regret very much later on, as I thought of marvels not seen (by this time I was in distinctly not marvelous Palo Alto, California).

Most often we had dinner at Chez Benoît, where we had excellent food, with a carafe of nice red wine, for about a dollar for the two of us. After dinner we sometimes went up the street for a coffee, maybe a *fine*, at the Montana Bar. Everyone went there, especially on those fiercely cold wet nights of a Paris winter. One night Richard Wright was there, still handsome and furiously angry. Almost all of us, the ignorant young, had unquestioningly taken on the politics of the French intellectual left, then more pro-Communist than pro-USA—which enraged Mr. Wright. He would rather live in segregated Mississippi than in the Soviet Union, he said into our shocked silence.

We were almost always together, Mark and I; it was as though we feared that separate activities might lead to trouble, which was very likely true—certainly in my case it was. I was very young, in my early twenties, and restless. Mark was young too, but he seemed to like being married. In Bar Montana there were several couples said to be living together, not married; this seemed to me an interesting and possibly ideal state . . .

Sometimes at night we went to a couple of semi-nightclubs, to the Mephisto, or the Tabu, both right there in the neighborhood. One night one of our friends, Jack L., got into a near fistfight with Liam O'Flaherty, having said just the wrong thing about Ireland. And one night in the Tabu I had a stiff argument with a French friend, Robert, a painter, about a girl across the room whom he said was really beautiful—a dark girl with long bangs and great eyes. I said, No, how could you say that? She's so fat. And yes, I think I did have a minor crush on Robert—who was quite right about the girl, who was Juliette Greco.

As the weather finally softened into spring we spent more time on the terrace of the Flore. One night, with a friend named Booboo Faulkner, from Keene, New Hampshire, for several hours we talked or rather listened to Truman Capote, who was there with Cyril Connolly and his wife. Having sized up Mrs. C. as being rather stupid (accurately, I think) Capote solemnly told an endless and entirely improbable story about a plague of locusts that came down on a farm in Louisiana and ate up the whole family, "even the hired man." (I can still hear his small-boyish Southern voice accenting the multisyllabic *hired*.) "They ate all the flesh and the bones, right down to the *gristle*."

Sometime during that spring Mark got a letter from Wallace Stegner, with whom he had studied at Harvard. Why didn't Mark come out to Stanford for the graduate work? he asked, adding that Palo Alto was almost as nice as Paris (it turned out that Stegner had never been to Paris at that time). And so, ill-advisedly, that is what we did.

But if only (I used to think in California) I could have stayed on in that misshapen Welcome room. Alone, or with some nice man whom I'd met in the Mephisto, or the Tabu. Spending my mornings on a better novel, and my afternoons exploring the city.

Peter Matthiessen, fiction editor; Colette Duhamel, advisory editor;
George Plimpton, editor; Louise Noble, circulation manager;
William Pène du Bois, art editor at the first office of The Paris Review,
on rue Garancière, 1953. Photo by Brassaï.

I Love Paris in the Fifties

In midsummer 1998 a panel discussion entitled "I Love Paris in the Fifties" took place in the Bay Street Theater in Sag Harbor, Long Island. The participants, all of whom were in residence in Paris in the early fifties, included Art Buchwald, the humorist, then writing a column for the Paris Herald Tribune; *Ben Bradlee, then* Newsweek's *Paris correspondent; Peter Stone; Peter Matthiessen, a cofounder of* the Paris Review *and George Plimpton, the ongoing editor of* The Paris Review. *Shana Alexander, the author, acted as moderator. What follows are excerpts from the discussion. Invariably, in transcriptions of this sort* (laughter) *is added after an anecdote or a joke. Rather than guide the readers in this manner, these have been left out. It can be stated simply enough that the Sag Harbor audience was large and appreciative.*

ART BUCHWALD: Every guy on this panel hates me!

BEN BRADLEE: Who told you I hated you?

BUCHWALD: Let me explain. I was in Paris on the GI Bill. I went into the Paris *Herald Tribune*, and I said to the managing editor, "I would like to do a nightclub column and review restaurants for you." The managing editor said, "We don't have such a column, and if we did you wouldn't write it." Some people would consider this a rejection! Two weeks later I came back, and I said to the editor in chief, "The managing editor and I have been talking about me doing a restaurant and nightclub column." Now the reason they hired me is because they knew I didn't know anything about food. George Plimpton said to me, "Where do you have credentials to be the food critic of the *Herald Tribune*?" I said, "I used to be a food taster in the Marine Corps." Anyhow, I signed on at the *Herald Tribune*, and I wrote about restaurants and nightclubs, and then pretty soon I could write about anything I wanted. Then we were all assigned, Benny too, to cover the Princess Grace-Grimaldi wedding in Monte Carlo.

BRADLEE: My name is Ben, not Benny.

BUCHWALD: Huh?

BRADLEE: Just call me Ben, just Ben.

BUCHWALD: Anyhow, on the train down there Ben and I and another guy named Crosby Noyes swore fidelity to each other—we would stick together through the whole wedding. We got off the train, and there was a little car that only had room for two people. Bradlee dropped me! He left me standing there in the street! That was the end of the fidelity! So I was on my own. I said to myself, "How do I get to this wedding?" So I wrote a column back to the paper in which I said, "I know I'm not going to get invited to the wedding because the Grimaldis and the Buchwalds have been feuding for five hundred years!" I listed all the things of the feud. The next day I got an invitation. That night I took notes for my wife on what all the guests were wearing, who was there, and so on. I called her up and said, "Guess what? *She* was wearing this. *He* was wearing that." She was cold to me on the phone. I said, "What's wrong?" She said, "It's my birthday." I said, "I was coming to that!"

PETER STONE: I was part of the CBS team that went to Monaco. There were 1700 reporters at the wedding, more than covered D day! Everybody tried to find a story. The only one I could think of was that, since the wedding took place at the highest point in Monte Carlo, I wondered about the lowest point. There was an American submarine in the harbor. It wasn't submerged, but it went several decks below the surface. So I went down there and interviewed these American sailors who were nineteen and twenty. I asked them, "What do you think of what's going on here?"

BRADLEE: Among other things we were all broke. There was no money in this crowd at all. I really first began to dislike Buchwald when into the *Herald Tribune* walks this guy with a gabardine suit covered with blood, his head swathed in bandages, wearing a silk tie, and he had a two- or three-day growth of beard. He introduced himself as Frank Frigenti. He had served time in Sing Sing Prison for murder, and he was now in Naples. He'd been deported! He hauled out of his pocket what looked like a credit card, except that it read, "Frigenti comma Frank, Sing Sing Prison. Number so-and-so. Charge: murder, mother-in-law." I thought this might be a good, interesting story—a story about deportees. He was broke, so I gave him thirty dollars—just blew the budget! He kept coming back, same suit, same blood, same bandages, the whole thing. Finally I said, "You know, Frank, I've told *Newsweek* about this, and they don't seem to be interested." So I said, "I've got a friend who's a really creative writer. I'm going to send you down to him." So I sent him down to Buchwald, same building, two floors down. I didn't hear from Buchwald for four days and I couldn't figure it out! What he had done was to take a hotel room with Frigenti and milk him for a story, out of which he made a book called *A Gift from the Boys*. It was made into the movie. Buchwald made fifty thousand dollars out of it, which was a goddamn fortune at that time. Frigenti! I never got a nickel.

BUCHWALD: I've always been asked what the highlights of my fourteen years in Paris were. There are two that come to mind. This one: Khrushchev came to Paris to meet with de Gaulle. De Gaulle invited him to the Paris opera; I think it was *Carmen*. I was invited as press. I had on white-tie. I got a little bored in the middle of *Carmen*, so I went outside on the second floor. I noticed a velvet curtain. I opened it and looked out on twenty thousand Communists in the Place de l'Opéra waiting to see Khrushchev. So I went out on the balcony—twenty thousand people cheered! I raised one hand, twenty thousand one-hands went up. Then both hands. For twenty minutes I really knew what it felt like to have power. The next day I called up the State Department and said, "I can make the Communists do anything I want."

The other story: I was with Peter Stone, driving from Paris to Moscow. When we got to Warsaw it was Sunday. We asked the concierge, "What do you do on Sunday?" He said, "Go to the races." So Peter and I went to the races. There were about four thousand people there—all trying to figure out which horse was going to win—and some were betting. Suddenly the bell rings, and everybody goes to the rail and we watch. There's no horses! After three and a half minutes they put up the winners: three, two, one. I said to Peter, "Don't say anything." Second race the same thing! Finally we stopped a man. We said, "Where are the horses?" He says, "They're in Kraków. We have only one string of horses, and one week they run in Kraków and one week in Warsaw." So we said, "Well, we understand that, but why does everyone go to the rail?" He said, "Where else would you go?"

STONE: It was terribly inexpensive for Americans at that time, especially since there was a black market in money. Three hundred fifty francs was the official rate to a dollar, but you could get five hundred francs on the black market. Everybody had his or her own black-market man. Our favorite was a fellow named Pop Landau who lived on the fourth or fifth floor of a building on the Champs Élysées, and you walked up these stairs and knocked on this door. There was a peep-hole—I'd never seen a peephole before. Locks and things. It opened up, and there was an old Polish gentleman in his bathrobe, Pop Landau. Everybody went to him. If you changed a lot of dollars, he would give you pastrami. A dear man, and what was lovely about the whole experience was that some years later when they devalued the franc, and the black market disappeared overnight, we all went and changed our money there anyway! There was no point since you got the same rate from him you did at the bank. But poor old Pop was up there.

A city of delights and of treats. They had buses with balconies on the back where you could smoke. Everybody smoked. Paris was full of displaced people at that time, stateless persons, unattached people, expatriates. My stepfather had a cousin who came out through the Iron Curtain. He got to Paris at a time when as a displaced person you had to have a *carte*, which is good for thirty days or sixty days or whatever. An American with an American passport could stay, but someone coming from the other direction had to get a *carte*. He got one; when it ran out, we called the proper *functionaire*. The cousin said, "I've spent my sixty days. My *carte* has run out." His French was almost nonexistent. He said, "What should I do?" The operator who answered the call said, "*Ne quittez pas*," which everyone knows means "Don't hang up." He took it literally. It was all the French he knew. He said, "Thank you." He took it as permission to stay, you know, "Don't leave." He said, "Thank you," and he hung up. He stayed for eight years!

PETER MATTHIESSEN: I'd gone to Paris for my junior year abroad and I met my first wife there. It was a very romantic place for us as a consequence. So after we graduated from college in 1950—she was at Smith and I was at Yale—we got married the following winter and we went to Paris in the spring of 1951. I was starting my first novel, *Race Rock*. One day I was sitting in the Dôme, a street café in Montparnasse quite close to where we were living, and this guy walked up and said, "I met you in 1948 or 1949. My name is Harold Humes." He said he was starting a new magazine, *The Paris News-Post*, and would I become its fiction editor. I wasn't much interested, less so when I saw it—a Paris *Cue* magazine that listed restaurants, theater, sights to see—but I went along with it. I knew a young writer just starting out, Terry Southern, and I got him to give us a story called "The Sun and the Still-Born Stars," one of his best stories, I think. When I saw it in this dinky little magazine I said to Humes ("Doc," we called him), "Doc, it's great finding new writers, but I don't want to do it for this magazine." He agreed. So he dumped *The Paris News-Post* and we began planning for what was to become *The Paris Review*. Doc was difficult: basically kind-hearted, enormously intelligent, but very erratic in his behavior, a megalomaniac, and he couldn't stop talking. I knew *The Paris Review* wasn't going to come off because no one could work with Doc. So I wrote my old friend George Plimpton, who was at Cambridge University, and asked him, "How would you like to run this magazine?" He said, "Fine," and, as he has said, that one decision ruined his life.

GEORGE PLIMPTON: I remember Peter invited me to his atelier on rue Percival in Montparnasse, absolutely charming place with ivy running over the face of a big studio window, a little balcony looking out over the railroad yards. Humes was there, and Cass Canfield, Jr., who became an editor at Harper Bros., and Humes's girl, who was called Moose. It was Easter time. Someone had produced these cookies with hashish in them. What I particularly remember is that these hashish cookies made us giggle uncontrollably at just about anything that was said. Even someone *starting* to say something would get us laughing helplessly. Suddenly, in the middle of the afternoon, an older couple arrived who were friends of Peter's parents. I think we were too weak from laughing to stand up to shake hands. We sort of stared at them. They'd just been to a service in the Episcopal church, and they would say these innocent things. They would say what a nice service it had been, and we would all go, "Hew, hew, hew, hew, hew, hew, hew, hew!" They would look a little bewildered. The laughter would sort of die away, and they would then say, "We're thinking of going to Notre Dame this afternoon." "Hee, hee, hee, hee, hee"—all very embarrassing. That is how *The Paris Review* began!

Comparisons are made between the Paris of the fifties and of the twenties. The huge difference, of course, was that in the twenties these extraordinary revolutions were going on in all disciplines—Diaghilev in the ballet; Picasso, Matisse, the surrealists in painting; Les Six in music; Joyce and so on in fiction. I mean, that must have been truly an astonishing time—a vast number of eccentrics, a huge turmoil in almost all the arts. In the fifties there wasn't really anything like that at all. I think the only thing in the fifties that seemed to be involved in serious change was film. I remember going to a little film center to see what we were told was an interesting avant-garde film. We all trouped in and sat down. The film started. You suddenly realized as you were watching that it was simply film stock running through the projector. You could see little squiggles from time to time, and we suddenly realized that we were seeing the ultimate nihilist film! There wasn't anything there. At which point it became an absolutely riveting evening because discussions broke out as to whether this was important or not. Chairs were picked up and hurled around, violent arguments, people pushing at each other. But I don't ever remember people sitting around doing that avant-garde sort of thing with any discipline other than film.

STONE: Film hadn't been important until the Italians with realism and Rossellini and De Sica, then the French nouvelle vague. I came to Paris from Hollywood, from a film community, and I went to movies all my life—there was an expression,

"This is where I came in." No one knew when a movie started. The times weren't even posted! You went! Then when you said, "Oh, this is where I came in," you got up and you left. All of America went to movies that way. When I got to Paris and I saw people standing in line outside a theater, I said to myself, "My God, the films are so popular that nobody can get in!" But it wasn't that. They were waiting for the film to start! I'd never seen anything like that. The nouvelle vague—Truffaut and Godard and Malle and all of those really marvelous directors—they affected American film a great deal. *Last Year in Marienbad* was quite an opaque film in many ways, but, as a film writer, my entire vocabulary changed after that film, just the way it had after *Citizen Kane*. Very influential. Vistas were opened. Suddenly even in America, films were taken seriously.

MATTHIESSEN: I think it's important to mention the black writers working in Paris at the time. Jimmy Baldwin was there, Richard Wright, others. Jimmy came for supper one night—a poker evening, I think. Sometime later we pooled our money to help send Baldwin back to New York to finish *Go Tell It on the Mountain*. Jimmy was a very odd fellow. I never could quite locate him, find his center. I was a very good friend of Richard Wright, who had told me before I met Jimmy, "There's a young black guy here in Paris who writes a lot better than I do. He could be doing for black people what I'm doing now, but much better. I'm trying to get him into political writing. But he insists that he's a novelist and that his color doesn't matter and so forth." Well, the curious thing about Jimmy was that up until the time that Richard died, he didn't write any political stuff at all, really. Not a word. He wrote that rather good first novel, *Go Tell It on the Mountain*, and a rather bad book, *Giovanni's Room*. As soon a Richard Wright was buried, Baldwin jumped into the breech and wrote these dazzling essays . . . one was *The Fire Next Time*. He did exactly what Wright had wanted him to do, but I think he had to wait until Richard was dead.

Richard Wright, Peter Matthiessen and Max Steele.

PLIMPTON: Many of the writers made money by writing dirty books—DBs they were called—for Maurice Girodias, who was the head of Olympia Press. As I recall, you got one thousand dollars for every DB. Alex Trocchi, who ran a literary magazine called *Merlin*, which published Samuel Beckett for the first time, wrote a number of these things. Trocchi gave public readings, in the Café Bonaparte. We would all go listen. He would stand on a table, this extraordinary Scotsman with big fawn-like ears, and read this incredible stuff. I tried to write one of these DBs for Girodias. It was turned down. It was based on a Robert Louis Stevenson story called "The Suicide Club," which is about these elderly men who've done everything: shot the tiger, the lion and so forth, thoroughly bored with life. So they decide to play this rather elaborate game of murder to pep things up. They knock themselves off one by one. In my version, the crimes are all hideously sexual. I remember one man had a hook for an arm. It was awful stuff.

MATTHIESSEN: We had lots of people who were writing DBs who were also associated with *The Paris Review*. I don't know why this should be so. One of them was Terry Southern, who wrote *Candy*, the best known of the dirty books. One of the first stories I got was "The Accident," an excerpt from his first novel, *Flash and Filigree*. Terry was a figure to be contended with. He was going through a rather mind-altering substance phase. He lived over near the Sorbonne at that time. In his story was a phrase—a police officer is talking to an angry motorist—"don't get your shit hot." Somebody on the editorial board removed part of the phrase. So the story, quite a long one, was missing a mild and rather minor phrase, but in his sort of excited condition those days he thought that the removal of that word broke the story's back. "I wish to write a letter of protest to the editor." I said, "Fine, we'll publish it, by all means." Well, it finally came in, and it was about fifteen pages long! So I went over and pounded on his door. I said, "Terry, we have to talk shop here. We're very anxious to publish your response, but fifteen pages is about a third of the length of the magazine as it's now constituted, and we simply can't do that!" He said, "You must. You promised you would." He got very one-way about it. Eventually I wrote an erratum notice, which appeared in the second issue: "Terry Southern is most anxious that *The Paris Review* point out the absence of two words from his story "The Accident"; the sentence "Don't get hot" *should* have read "Don't get *your crap* hot; an omission for which we apologize to all concerned." Even then it was sort of bowdlerized.

PLIMPTON: I'm afraid I was responsible for all this. We were scared to death of all four-letter words because in those days we had to worry about the censors in the US who could keep the issues from coming in. I remember Art saying it was the funniest erratum notice he'd ever read, but he couldn't have written about it in the *Herald*.

BUCHWALD: These gentlemen you're talking about were on the Left Bank. I don't know what café you hung out in, but we never saw them on the Right Bank.

BRADLEE: Or any bank . . .

BUCHWALD: Bradlee and I were on the Right Bank. We didn't have any literary connection at all.

MATTHIESSEN: The common denominator for all of us, I guess, was Irwin Shaw. We all hung out with Irwin. After we married in 1951, Patsy and I returned to Paris. Irwin Shaw was on that ship, in first class, naturally, but his baby's nurse, a very nice young Danish woman, was traveling with us down in steerage. She arranged a meeting with the great man upstairs. Irwin and I became friends on that ship and later met in Paris. One night he brought me home as a kind of buffer because he was so late for dinner. Irwin's wife Marian was not pleased to see me, but the friendship lasted, and for a couple of years we had Thanksgiving dinner together. The Shaws are gone now, but their son Adam is still a friend.

BRADLEE: Because Irwin paid. He had money earlier than the rest of us. He had written *The Young Lions*.

BUCHWALD: If you wrote, Swifty Lazar [the agent] informed you he was representing you, but you didn't know it . . .

BRADLEE: I once saw Irwin Shaw pick up Swifty Lazar, who was about five feet tall, at a New Year's Eve celebration in Closters, Switzerland. He put one hand under Swifty's neck and the other under his ankles and sort of turned him around. Shaw was built like a bull! He said, "I've never dropped an agent before," and he dropped Swifty on the table! A terrible crinkling of glass, and nobody dared look for a while. My finest hour!

BUCHWALD: My finest hour was shared with Peter. This happened in 1953, and it's still talked about. It's called "the six-minute Louvre." Peter and I went to the Louvre one day. We knew the only things people wanted to see were the Venus de Milo, the Mona Lisa and the Winged Victory. The rest of the stuff was all junk! So we discussed this: "To see three things and get out in a waiting taxi, how long do you think it would take?"

BRADLEE: It was right after Roger Bannister did the four-minute mile.

BUCHWALD: So we showed up the next week. I stood by the waiting taxi. I said, "Go!" Peter ran into the Louvre. He ran past the Venus de Milo, up past the Winged Victory . . . he said, "I know it'll fly!" . . . then down to the Mona Lisa, . . . and he said, "I know the guy who has the original!". . . stairs again . . . out into the waiting taxi. He did it in five minutes and thirty-three seconds. That record still stands, and I don't think it'll ever be beaten because I.M. Pei built a big glass thing so you can't get through! I told the whole story of the six-minute Louvre at The Kennedy Center with President Carter there, and I said, "Mr. President, we have the man who brought the six-minute Louvre back to America!" Peter stood up, and everybody applauded.

STONE: Like a schmuck, I stood up!

PLIMPTON: I wrote a column for Art about my grandmother. She was staying in the Hotel Continental. Her French was extremely rusty. She wanted a glass of sherry to be delivered to her room, so she said over the phone to the bar or whatever: "*Je voudrai un cheri, s'il vous plait.*" There was consternation at the other end, and a waiter was sent up who was extremely nervous.

STONE: There was an American woman who got into a cab and, with her rusty French, said to the driver, "*Tu est libre?*" He said, "*Oui. Et toi?*"

PLIMPTON: There's always a problem with language. My father told me once that he'd gone to a theater on the Champs Élysées where they were showing a Western. The subtitles were in French. There was a barroom scene in which this black-hatted villain shoots a lot of people, walks up to the bar and says, "Gimme a shot of red-eye!" The translation in the subtitles read, "*Donnez-moi un Dubonnet, s'il vous plait.*"

STONE: There's no better way to learn a language than to sit in the cinemas, hearing it in the language you know and reading the subtitles. They could be tremendously creative. For reasons I never understood, whenever there was a number someone said on the screen, the subtitle always gave a different number. I remember a gangster picture in which this guy says, "Hey, there's something here that's not kosher." The subtitle read, "*Il y a quelque chose qui n'est pas tout a fait Catholique.*" Quite brilliant really! Art had the best attitude toward the foreign languages. He's not a linguist at heart. In France he would speak English to the French people but in a French accent! He would talk to Germans in English but with a German accent. He felt they surely would understand when he talked like that!

BUCHWALD: We used to be asked, all of us, "Do the French dislike Americans?" I discovered when I first got over there that the French didn't like each other, so why should they like us? You had to take the opposite side of whatever side they were on. This was dramatized for me when my hot-water heater broke. We called the plumber. We knew what he was going to say. He got on the line and he said, "Eet is impossible to fix theese hot-water heater. Thees style does not make anymore. Thees boiler is no good! Eet's impossible to fix that hot-water heater!" I said "Of course, it's impossible. No one could fix that hot-water heater." He said, "I could fix that hot-water heater!" In twenty minutes we had a new hot-water heater!

STONE: The electricity used to go out all the time. You'd sit there and wait for it to go back on. My stepfather says, "Let's call the electric company." I say, "Come on, there are a lot of people in the building; somebody's already called." He says, "No, they haven't. Every Frenchman in the building is so delighted their neighbors are in darkness that they don't want to do anything about it!"

PLIMPTON: One of *The Paris Review* crowd was Max Steele, a fine writer, who was in Paris because he was visiting a psychiatrist to get over this love affair. The psychiatrist was apparently helping him. He hated the French and took it out on them in the most extraordinary way. He would go into these cafés. He could barely speak French, but he did have one phrase he'd memorized. He would say, *"Donnez-moi un Coca-Cola chaud, s'il vous plaît!"* There was always surprise on the part of the people behind the zinc bars. But he would insist upon *"un Coca-Cola chaud,"* they would put a glass of Coca-Cola under those espresso machines, and the Coca-Cola would come steaming to his table! I once said, "Max, can you actually drink this hot Coca-Cola?" He would say, "No!" He said, "No, but my great hope is that if I say this in enough restaurants and cafés, the French, who copy anything American, will begin ordering *"Coca-Cola chauds!"*

BUCHWALD: The tragedy for us . . . I speak for myself, and I may speak for the others, is that when you go back there now, there are no buddies—there's nobody! So it's no fun anymore. It's like going to Prague. Back then, you'd sit in the café and six Americans were sitting with you, an American colony within Paris. Most of us were on the GI Bill. We didn't really have to spend much money. The law in France was if you sat at a café you could order one drink and stay there as long as you wanted to! The waiter couldn't do anything about it. When we talk about the fifties and we talk about Paris, we're really talking about a part of American life that was over there then. We had the best years of our lives in a very wonderful place, culturally so different than any other place. The meals were fantastic. Obviously, the wine was. We never went home after dinner. We always went someplace else. It was just a whole way of life that everybody accepted. You didn't have to have a fancy apartment. You didn't have to have fancy clothes. You just were there, and you were accepted. I wouldn't trade those years for any part of my life.

STONE: When I wasn't in Paris I was terribly, terribly homesick for it, and wherever I was I wanted to get back. What was odd, when I got there and I would hear Edith Piaf's songs—and I'm sure the French felt the same way—I was just as homesick for Paris when I was there as I was when I was away. There was a Paris that didn't quite exist on the same level, remarkable in that it permeated everything, so that you were homesick for it even while you were there!

PLIMPTON: I've suddenly remembered a remark I thought was John Ashbery's, though he denies ever having said it, "If you're happy in Paris you can never be happy the same way again, not even in Paris."

BRADLEE: There came a time when I knew I should get out. I've often tried to figure out exactly when it was, but I think it was when a child of mine said, "*Bonjour, Papa.*" Oh, shit, I got to get home!

James Dickey

Letters from France

*Novelist and agrarian Andrew Lytle (*The Velvet Horn*), an
early encourager of James Dickey, was one of the advisory
editors who selected him for the* Sewanee Review *fellowship
that allowed the poet to spend part of 1954 and 1955 in
France. In 1955 Dickey joined Lytle at the University of Florida, where Lytle directed the creative writing program and
Dickey taught freshman composition. When a controversy
resulted from Dickey's reading of his poem "The Father's
Body" to a Tallahassee women's group, Lytle did not support
him, and their close friendship terminated. Dickey abruptly
quit the university to become an advertising copywriter. The
letters below are reprinted without editorial changes.*

—Matthew J. Bruccoli

TO: Andrew Lytle

25 Sept. 1954
Cap d'Antibes

Dear Andrew,

Since I last wrote you, Europe has swallowed us like peas,
and we are only just getting our bearings. Our money was
running out in England, so we went to Paris to see a friend
of ours there. There I got sick again, someone cut the top of
our car open with a knife, we spent more money, and naturally
were very depressed. When our friend left Paris, we stayed
for a few days, and then started south, with no very clear
idea of where we were going, except that prices were supposed
to be less high in the provinces than in Paris. For a week we
shuttled about, becoming more confused and less resilient,
until we struck this vacation-coast down here, just as the

tourists were leaving it. In one or two days the place had quieted so much that we began to look on it as a possible headquarters. Since then we have been searching for a place to live. Yesterday we found just what we need: a big house with a tremendous yard full of red flowers, cactus, lizards, and little birds, with a great yawning silence surrounding it, which I hope to fill with poems. We move in on October 1st; until that time we are staying in an apartment near the villa. Due to the off-season, the rent on the villa is about one-third that during the season, and so we have taken it until June. It would be wonderful if by some alchemical transformation in school administration, you and Edna and the children could be given time to come over, for we have all the room in the world, a little playground for children, and no neighbors or other disturbances at all.

Before I forget: Spender sent the poems back, with some faint talk about "skill" and "daring," though it was pretty clear they were not his dish. I sent them down to Marguerite Caetani at *Botteghe Oscure* in Rome, whom Tate had suggested. She edits a tremendous (physically) review in three languages, and is evidently receptive to new writers, from what I hear.[1]

Now that we have prospects of being settled, I can look back on the trip with some pretense of evaluation. Paris is a great city for writers; that is, for the kind of writers who need other writers around, who need the "literary life," who need to discuss and drink together, and the rest of it. I had a sample of that, but my writing felt too lonely there; I knew none of the latest writers, and had a good deal of trouble understanding what was going on. What money I had to myself, though, I spent on books. There are literally thousands of book-shops in Paris, as you know, and most of them carry good stuff. I've read nothing but French since we've been here, and am gradually getting to understand the written language, though as yet I can't speak it very well. Paris in

---

1. JD's work was not published in *Botteghe Oscure*.

some ways is as great a city as I have always heard it was, but
I missed something there: perhaps it is the lack of personal
discipline everywhere evident. I am not used to so much
personal freedom: in dress, in language, in taste, sex, and so
on. But I have an idea the city will grow in my mind, and
then I will know and like it better.

Provence is the most beautiful place I have ever seen. Everything there: the olive-trees, the vineyards, the red and white
mountains, is in a gentle and sustained state of crumbling,
so that everything you see is soft-edged and half-luminous,
and yet there is strictness of form: the grids of the vineyards
laid subtly up the uneven hills, the poplars lining the roads,
the Rhone leaning furiously on its banks, straight for miles.

The French writers have done me much good. The better
I learn the language, the more sympathetic I feel toward the
work of many of them. I begin to see, I think, what the
imagination is capable of, at its full stretch. I see also that
my own work has got to discover more surely its own laws
and disciplines. I want to study a good deal here. And write.
And write. I want to do some experiments in syntax and
diction, toward developing the sense of immediacy in poetry,
the controlled spontaneity that I am convinced my writing
should have: a form like that of fountain water, wherein the
shape is secured by the substance (poem) falling and arcing
freely, and is maintained thereby. I am tremendously excited
about having so much time to work, and I feel that the proof
shall be delivered at the end of the year, so that you and the
other editors may feel that you have not wasted the *Sewanee's* money.

By the way, there's a poem of mine in the current (Autumn)
Sewanee.[2] At least there should be one, for I read proof,
though I haven't yet seen it.

I have an idea that I will always be a searcher in these
things, for nothing I do satisfies me. But I know now, though
dimly, what I want from poetry: emotional depth: spontane-

---

2. "The Ground of Killing" (October 1954).

ous, immediate: that the poem should strike the reader down through the more obvious levels of his being into the hidden and essential ones, and stay there, giving up its meanings as the reader's life does, not all at once. I want a poetry both human and imaginative: "forcer le plus réel à exister." But there is all that to do yet, of course.

We are all well. I promise to write oftener and oftener, swamping you with details of the projects, and with the projects themselves, as they develop. And may I be forgiven for this delay.

Write soon, and send me what you have done on the Wake, for I have been thinking much of it. My address now is % American Express, Cannes, France.

Yours
Jim Dickey

TO: Andrew Lytle

Vanderbilt
14 Nov. 1954

Dear Andrew,

I got your letter the afternoon of the day I sent the note (and poem) to you. I was very glad to hear from you, needless to say. I knew that you would write, but I was afraid something might have happened to you: that you might be sick, or that your wife or one of the children might be.

It is good to know that you are all right, and are getting ready to tackle your book again. I wouldn't worry about the lay-off. There's more chance, I should think, that the book has been helped by it than otherwise: that the "deep well of unconscious cerebration," as Henry James called it,[3] "has brought out the bones" of the essential.

You ask about our quarters, and the weather. We have a huge house on the only hill of size on the *cap*. We are about

3. In *The American*, James's 1877 novel.

three-quarters of the way up the hill, on the top of which is the *cap* lighthouse. It is very quiet here. Once or twice a week I take my little boy and we make our way up steeply behind the house, on a winding track (very roundabout because of the almost-sheerness of the hill-face), the Mediterranean broadening below us as we climb. At the top, beside the lighthouse, is a sailors' chapel. Sometimes we go in, but usually we stand beside the lighthouse in the wind that is always blowing there, and look down at the whole coast from Cannes to Menton, a huge half-opened wing preparing some hesitant and marvelling flight toward something never to be disclosed, blue with age and hope and inaction. There is nothing so calm, nothing so full of immediate and contemplative beauty.

The house itself, as I said, is big, and consequently rather hard to heat. Now that the weather is colder the sun does not shine every day. There are high thick clouds, overcasts, and often a fine thin rain. I tend the furnace a good deal, and have made some progress in technique (pine-cones are very good to start the fire with). We have coal and wood, and I use them in about equal proportions, and it keeps us warm.

You have only to turn inland to be among mountains, real ones, as wild as any. We go among them as much as we can, and they are fascinating. At one place there is what is left of a slender bridge that at one time spanned one of the gorges. The Germans demolished it before they left. All there is, now, of it, is a tall upright spine of masonry, very fragile, having that wistful and arrogant look of broken objects of use. And it is tall: it comes out of the bottom of a gorge you literally can't see all the way into, and ends at you level in the air, its two halves, where the road went, branching bewilderedly and serenely into the air, and you are left with it.

I have been working slowly, and studying, trying to clarify my intentions. The Spender episode hit, or left, a dead spot in me that is hard to make over. I have had rejections before, plenty of them, but somehow the memory of that professional shrinking violet condescending to me, talking about "com-

pression" and "why don't you read Auden" wrung me about
as disagreeably as anything can. I couldn't believe he read
the poems well. I thought, then, in a rush, that if this was
"literature," if this was the sort your work has to go through
to reach publication, then he and the ones like him can have
it. By the way, he told me that one of the poems (the first
one) that appears next to mine in the *Sewanee* is the best
one he has ever written.[4] And I sit down and look at it and
am dazed. Can such things be? But the proof is there in
print. There is his "best," and a fairly good one of mine,
and I think that the comparison is beyond any doubt in my
favor. And I feel somewhat better. Of course there should
not be comparisons like this, but only the poet and his poem.
But then I was raised, almost from the time I could stand,
in the fiercest strain of competition: on basketball courts, in
boxing rings, on fields, on tracks. Times like this bring all
that back. But Spender is receding in my mind, and I hope
will eventually be out of sight. To hell with him.

The more I read of the European writers, the prouder I am
to be of the same calling. Since the war, which I entered at
seventeen,[5] I have never, until now, profoundly valued life.
Then, it seemed to me that I could see quite clearly that most
of the things I had been told about human life were false:
were constructions, rationalizations only, and would not stand
up under any kind of forceful reality. But then I had not any
of these) and the Spaniard Lorca, and Valery. The better you
understand life, the more you feel *clearly*, the more you begin
to see the value of it (but perhaps it takes it value from this
seeing and feeling more, and in a more pronounced order,
even of spontaneity).

You ask about the people here. For a time we knew no
one, but now we have a good many friends. We met Pablo
Picasso a couple of times. He lives in the little mountain town
of Vallauris, and makes pottery there. He is a small man,

---

4. Spender's "Archaic Head" appeared next to JD's "The Ground of Killing" in
the October 1954 issue of *The Sewanee Review*.
5. JD was nearly twenty years old when he left college for the Army Air Corps.

rather peasant-like, gentle and grave, with many children and relatives, most of the former, I am told, illegitimate. Then there is a retired admiral of the British navy who lives just down the street from us, also with a large family. I play tennis with his wife and daughter. Sometimes he and I sit out in his garden (everyone here has gardens) and talk about naval strategy. He analyzes famous engagements and demonstrates at length what different admirals did in different situations, Nelson included. There is another man I know in Nice, an Englishman named Peter Bent, who has lived in France all his life and speaks with a French accent. Though he is married, the French government won't let him work, being an alien. He and his wife live with his father in a poor section of Nice. Bent is a strange, pale, weakly man who looks as if he is eaten up (but is not apparently, his only passion being bookbinding) by some terrible ambition. A man named Nikos Katzanzakis, a Greek,[6] and twice runner-up for the Nobel Prize in literature, lives here. He is a poet and novelist (I have never read anything by him, though I think he has been published in America). Some people I know here insist that I meet him, and he seems to have been alerted for that purpose also, so we may go by his place some day. My friends tell me that he is receptive to company, and likes to talk poetry.

Before I forget, you mention in your letters someone named Berryman. I once appeared in a magazine next to someone named John Berryman. Is that the same one? Is he a good friend of yours?

Here is another poem I've just finished.[7] It rounds out a kind of design I began with the Maze: to write about the effects of death on people in different familial relationships: in the *Maze* an old man and his wife, in *Father and Sons*,[8]

6. JD reviewed Kazantzakis's *The Odyssey: A Modern Sequel* (1958) in the July-September 1959 issue of *The Sewanee Review*.
7. "The Sprinter's Mother," which appeared in *Shendandoah* (Spring 1955).
8. Drafts for this unpublished poem are at Emory University and at Vanderbilt University.

that, and in this one a boy and his mother: a hard subject. Here, the boy is an unthinking muscle-and-speed american type who has not the emotional equipment to assimilate his mother's death. He tries to go through the proper ritual (putting the flowers on her grave), but it is meaningless. In the desperate quiet of the situation his mind reverts to the most vivid of their relationships: his racing: (the 220 in point of fact: hence the "turn"), and in doing so grasps the fact that "it (the irreparable human situation) is all proved" by the spontaneous and necessary action of his mind to take in the death in its own way, in the only (and now pitiful) categories of his being that have been useful and vivid to him. And at the end, emphasizing the change, the new-life-giving rain comes, at last. I think that the two lines beginning "his legs are sleeping" do what poetry ought to do.[9] But you judge and tell me.

I am working on one now that ought to be far and away the best I have ever written. Its possibilities are so great that I feel like farming them out to Shakespeare or Dante. If I don't muff it, I ought to have it done by the end of next week. Whereupon I'll send it to you. It is all I expect ever to write about the war, and is called, tentatively, "The Confrontation of the Hero."[10]

I sit out on the upstairs porch and write going directly toward the sun, and a lot is coming. Since I have your letter, this is the plenitude.

Excuse the unseemly chaos of this format, but I wanted to send what I had to say as it came.

Write soon.

Yours
Jim

9. "His legs are sleeping among the works / Of the great lock of daylight: it is terrible . . . "
10. "The Confrontation of the Hero (April, 1945)," *Sewanee Review* (July-September 1955); first collected in *The Whole Motion*.

Eugene Walter

T.S. Eliot had come to Rome to receive an honor from the university and was on his honeymoon with that lady who'd been his secretary and such a comfort to him after the first wife, who'd been slightly demented or totally stark raving mad, whichever it was. He was on his way to speak at the university, and there was a mob of students running alongside his car and screaming in the street.

I've just read a piece in *The New Yorker* about Eliot in Rome by a *New Yorker* girl, who's become famous. We published her first short story, "The Statue," in *Botteghe Oscure*. Jewish girl in New York City. Funny name. Ozick. Cynthia Ozick. She says that his car, as he left for the university, was accompanied by these cheering students and what a lift it gave him to feel so acclaimed by the populace.

That wasn't the thing at all. I was there. Fighting off journalists at the Palazzo Caetani. It was one of those sixties student things and they were screaming for the director of the university to resign. There were a lot of younger students who wanted the university reorganized in a certain way and rather more free. They were running along his car, and Eliot thought they were welcoming him. But they were saying, Please don't make the speech, you fool. You know: down with the university.

He was rather hoity-toity. I know that if you live in England and you are of the English language, sooner or later you speak English English. There is no way not to. Because it has something that we just pick up. We can't help it. I would be doing it in ten minutes if I lived there. But he had the snob accent, not just the English accent. The snob, snob accent. It was a kind of artificial snobbishness superimposed on artificial Englishness. After all, he *was* from M'zou. He was born in St. Looey. The hub of the bourgeoisie. Yes, well, the Eliots of Boston. The one *l* one *t* Eliots of Boston. There are laundresses named Elliott with two *t*s and two *l*s. But this was a one *l* one *t* Eliot. You can discard the superfluous at a given moment of greatness. But still, he was born in St. Louis, Missouri. We mustn't forget that. M'zou. Born in M'zou.

I've never understood a kind of sourpuss quality he had. He didn't have the little edge of good humor that is basically American, which all Americans have. It's very rare that an American doesn't have that little "yeah, well, you know" somewhere. Even the crankiest. There is a kind of generosity of spirit that is American. Even with the most closed in or most miserly or whatever. I mean, T.S. Eliot was not my idea of fun.

It's all because he became such a cult figure. Just after World War II, all the Harvard boys—if you said T.S. Eliot, they got to their knees facing England, you know. They forgave him for being born in M'zou. I think he had too much of that adulation.

But his wife was a charmer. So intelligent, so bright, so polite, so humorous, so kind. The princess asked me to go with her chauffeur to take Mr. Eliot and Madame Valerie to the airport when they were leaving Rome. So we were going to go, and he said, "I've never been to the graves of Keats and Shelley." I said, "Yes, we do have time." Now this is another cemetery where nobody is dead—they just ain't dead there. A great place for a picnic, because nobody is dead. Old friends gathered. Keats is there and Shelley is there and a Romanov princess and other grand Russian refugees. There are cats that live in the cemetery—in this little caretaker's cottage, and they sit in front of it. Because they've seen so many people go to the grave first of Shelley and then of Keats, they accompany them like guides. They walk a few steps ahead and look over their shoulders and say "this way" and then they turn at the right corner and turn at the left corner. First we went to Shelley and we were taken by a black cat. At the grave of Shelley, there was a tabby cat waiting. The black cat went back to the caretaker's. The tabby cat took us to Keats, way over in a corner. It says, "Here Lies One Whose Name Was Written in Water." Valerie was busy picking vio-

lets off the grave to take back to her garden in England, and
T.S. Eliot was saying, "I've always thought that inscription
was rather supercilious," and she said, "Dammit, laddered
m'nylons!" It's one of my favorite moments. She was a very
down-to-earth creature with a great sense of humor. She's
cat and monkey. But there was something acid about him
which I just couldn't take.

I had the feeling with him of someone trapped inside
sixteen locked doors. I thought if I could get enough Jim
Beam into him, he would really be great.

Well, the princess did ask me to arrange a party at the
Palazzo Caetani. They were cousins. He was Cousin Tom.
Some distant distant way back when in Boston. That's when
I saw a good side of him. That was my Twenty-third Field
Artillery punch. We brought up from the cellars of Palazzo
Caetani a huge, magnificent old punch bowl that had not
been used since around World War I, I was told. I put a
block of ice in it. And I made a little hole in the block of
ice. I put some sliced oranges and lemon in that hole. Then
I poured two bottles of cognac over that. And then I poured
two bottles of good rum over that. Then I poured two bottles
of very good English gin over that. And then I just filled up
the rest of the bowl with cold champagne.

It tasted like the most delicious orange punch. You would
never guess there was one drop of anything alcoholic in it.
There are millions of punches like that on the Gulf Coast.
For Mardi Gras. You know: "Want a little fruit punch, darling, before we set out for the ball?" It'll make a party go.

The princess had invited all the literary figures of Rome:
Alberto Moravia, Elsa Morante, Natalia Ginzburg. Writers,
writers, writers, writers. She was nervous since there were two
or three famous feuds among the crowd. You know, literary
backbiters are the worst. Italian writers are always feuding
with other Italian writers. Again all kind of lesser Italian
writers begging for Eliot's attention just like the Harvard
boys. We forget that *The Cocktail Party* was written God
knows when, in the 1920s, and only got produced in the

1950s or 1960s in London. That's one of the things that put
him on the map all over again.

I was careful to see that all glasses were kept full. Feuds
were forgotten and toward the end of the evening Mr. Eliot
remembered some football cheers from Midwestern colleges,
which he'd heard in his youth. He had a yellow rose in one
hand and a punch cup in the other, wielded like a pom-pom.
My favorite was:

Rah-rah-rah
Sis-boom-sah!
Go to war
Holy Cross!
Bim 'em, bam 'em,
Skin 'em, scam 'em,
Rip 'em, ram 'em,
Holy Cross!

He was doing that cheer after just two glasses of Twenty-third
Field Artillery punch.

Then those cat poems—I approved of those. Not because
they were cats but just the idea of writing some of that kind
of poetry. Twentieth-century school of fun. The cat poems
took him out of that so-called intellectual in quotes category.
That changed my attitude toward him. I'd always disapproved
of his poetry because I come from a subtropical country. How
could I know melancholy and the bleakness of winter?

Blair Fuller

Headier stuff there could never ever have been!

On a four-month leave I had begun writing a novel while living in the sunshine of Provence with an exquisite woman, memorable in every animate moment, in every touch and Gallic scent. I had found her in Africa where I had been working for Texaco.

Then in September, in New York, Harper gave me an advance on the manuscript; I quit Texaco and decided on Paris, of course, to write the rest of it. *The Paris Review* had published a story of mine in its second issue, an omen. She was there, but would she be when I arrived? She was married to someone else.

I bought an early, two-seater T-Bird, aqua in color with white tires, and we took ship.

French weather had turned. Exquisite had gone back to her husband in Dakar—not quite the end of everything between us, but as good as. And Peter and Patsy Matthiessen, George Plimpton, Max Steele, Evan Connell, Harold Humes, Pati Hill, Terry Southern—people I had briefly seen in Paris that spring—had now all gone home to the US.

The sky lowered. The air of Paris was cool and damp, and the T-Bird got attention that suddenly I didn't want. It was lonely and difficult to sleep.

Of the things remembered from that winter what seem most important are the plays—Ionesco's absurdist one-acts in the tiny Théâtre de la Huchette, and the first production of *Waiting for Godot*, in French in a boulevard theater. The harsh but glimmering depths of *Godot* so stunned me I had to ask myself if my novel was worth anyone's time. Persist I did, however, struggling daily to keep my typing fingers warm, but helped on by a new kind of allegiance to the Review, assisting Paris Editor Bob Silvers in whatever needed doing, and with him interviewing the very young and so self-possessed Françoise Sagan.

I reached *The End of a Far Place* as spring arrived with a blast of heat. The great monuments jumped to their full stature in the sunshine, waving flags. "The girls in their summer dresses," Irwin Shaw's phrase, looked smashing indeed, and he, a new friend, sometimes looked them over with me and they, my newly washed T-Bird.

I interviewed in London for a job teaching at Barnard College. Only after the job had been offered and accepted did it occur to me that I had almost no idea how to perform it.

The T-Bird and I recrossed the Atlantic. *Plus ça change!* But headed toward thrillingly stand-or-fall first book publication and the murky job, it was not the *même chose*, not the same thing at all.

Kaylie Jones

When I was growing up in Paris in the early sixties, my father, James Jones, maintained that he was too preoccupied with his writing to get involved in any protests, although he always quietly gave money to causes—a champion of the underdog. He was supportive of my mother's going on marches, however, and in the early sixties it was the Civil Rights movement. My parents' living room, with its famous bar, an eighteenth-century pulpit from a French village church, which they had bought when they moved into our Ile Saint-Louis apartment after my birth, was the scene of many political discussions. Occasionally, things got so heated that fistfights broke out, candlesticks got thrown and lamps turned over.

In 1963, my mother took me along to the first major American Civil Rights march in Paris, with our friend James Baldwin, the painter Beauford Delaney and other expatriate artists and writers. I was only three, too small to walk far, so Jimmy Baldwin carried me on his shoulders from the gates of the American Embassy all the way up the Champs Élysées. I remember looking out as far as I could see and thinking the sea of people would never end; I remember the joyful, mournful sound of people of all races singing American spirituals. From then on until the end of his life, every time we met, James Baldwin would remind me of that day.

In May of 1968, when the Sorbonne students revolted and took to the streets, schools and businesses closed down for almost a month, and every night there was street fighting in the Latin Quarter, just across the river from our apartment. It was party time at the Joneses: our apartment became a kind of open salon and, once again, heated discussions took place around the pulpit bar as the sky across the river turned a hazy red from the fires and tear gas. Friends who couldn't get home camped out in the living room. My father stacked

James and Gloria Jones at the pulpit bar.

canned goods, batteries and candles to the ceiling of the
storage closet. He had this excited, wild-eyed look, clearly
enjoying himself, the tension the emergency situation created
much like a real war, but one where nobody got killed. He
loved to take us out during the day to tour the Latin Quarter
and assess the damage. Burned-out skeletons of overturned
cars and barricades made of ancient cobblestones blocked the
streets. The students, my father explained, built these to
protect them from the CRS, the French riot police. My father
liked to visit the Sorbonne, which was occupied by the revolu-
tionary students, and talk to them about the situation. If
asked whose side he was on, he would say the students'—the
underdogs against the stodgy and staid de Gaulle administration. But of course, he did not want a real revolution, just
as he did not really want Robert E. Lee to win the Civil War,
although he greatly favored him over Ulysses S. Grant.

Georges Pompidou, the prime minister, lived only a block
down from us on the quai de Béthune, and CRS trucks stood
night and day on the corner of our quai. One afternoon,
bored with our forced vacation, my brother and I and a little
group of classmates decided to dress up like revolutionaries
(leather jackets, hair in our eyes, bandanas across our faces)
and make flags and banners out of old sheets and towels (black
for the fascists and red for the communists). We marched into
the living room where the grownups were as usual gathered
around the pulpit bar and made for the tall French windows
that overlooked the quai and the Seine. We screamed down
at the CRS policemen, "CRS—SS! CRS—SS!" which we'd
heard the students shouting on the evening news, although
we had no idea what it meant. It took a minute before the
adults realized what was going on and ran over and dragged
us back in and slammed the windows.

A few years later, my mother marched against the Vietnam
War, my father still supporting her quietly from the sidelines.
He was against the war, but not against the soldiers who
fought it, who in his mind were not the mercenary madmen
portrayed by the media but rather poor, ignorant grunts who

William Styron, Irwin Shaw and James Jones in Paris, circa 1970.

had no idea what they'd gotten themselves into, just as he had been when he enlisted in the army in 1940. My parents, who had a reputation as being big liberals, were invited to attend a reception at the North Vietnamese Embassy in Paris in honor of NVA General Giap. Bemused and more than a little curious, my father decided to put his writing aside for an afternoon.

Scraggly looking young men with lost expressions had been showing up at our door, the sons of friends back in America, looking for comfort and perhaps a few francs or a place to stay. They were draft evaders who had chosen to live in Europe rather than fight in Vietnam. My father was always kind to them and he was just as kind to the Vietnam veterans he met. He told my brother and me that we could be against

the war, but we were never, under any circumstance, to spit
at the soldiers as he'd seen other kids do, to his great dismay
and horror.

General Giap stood up and announced that he was going
to bury the US Army in Vietnam, rekindling some wild,
dormant patriotic love my father felt for the army. He went
completely wild, standing up and shouting in a booming
voice that if we really wanted to we'd damn well kick their
sorry gook asses. He was roughly escorted out by a group
of guards and thrown into the street, my mother following
sheepishly behind.

Matthew J. Bruccoli

In the summer of 1973 the *Fitzgerald/Hemingway Annual* sponsored a Paris reunion of twenties expatriate figures. The official purpose of the endeavor was to commemorate the fiftieth anniversary of the first meeting of F. Scott Fitzgerald and Ernest Hemingway at the Dingo in April 1925. The celebration was two years premature, but I was concerned that the old Paris hands were dying off.

James Jones was invited to participate in the panel discussion. I had never met him, but it was worth a try. When Frazer Clark—the coeditor of the *Fitzgerald/Hemingway Annual*—and I checked into the Hôtel d'Angleterre, there was a note from Jones setting up a meeting at Lipp's.

He arrived bearing a shoulder bag packed with cigars, a complicated knife, and other necessities. I expected to meet Prewitt, but Jim was soft-spoken, polite, well-read and funny. He proposed that we have a drink in every extant Left Bank café mentioned in *The Sun Also Rises* and *A Moveable Feast*. After we used up Hemingway, Jim conducted us to other noteworthy resorts, such as the Falstaff. By restricting ourselves to red wine and walking from shrine to shrine, we fulfilled Jim's plan. The conversation was mostly Fitzgerald and Hemingway, about which he qualified as a scholar. Yet he resisted my attempts to start him on his relations with the House of Scribner.

Later that night we three ended up at Jim's flat on the Ile de la Cité overlooking the Seine. When one of the *bateau-mouche* tour boats came by, Jim ran to the window and shouted, "Hey, Harry, your wife is looking for you." In response to my inquiring look he explained: "I do that whenever I can. Some night there will be a guy named Harry on board with a woman, and it will worry the hell out of him when he hears me."

Rick Bass

Coming back from the book festival in Aix, I was scheduled to stay overnight in Paris; I would be there less than twenty hours. Christian, my publisher, had to get back to work and prepare for another festival—this one in England—but his son Mathieu kindly offered to show me around the city that day. We had coffee at some famous place where Hemingway and other great writers and artists used to drink coffee—the coffee was good but the café was crowded—and then we walked for a while and Mathieu showed me this beautiful church, a massive stone cathedral that dwarfed the other buildings around it. There were two golden ornamental structures atop it, at either end—one ornate, one simple, but both of them majestic—and Mathieu told me that back in the 1700s the church, or maybe the government—or maybe they were the same back then—had commissioned the two greatest sculptors of that time to submit separate designs. I don't think it was a competition, not in the way that we normally think of such things, for there was no winner: they built one artist's ornament atop the south end of the church, and the other artist's design atop the north end.

We stood there on the crowded sidewalk—people walking in all directions—a walker's city, they call it, though there were plenty of trucks and cars driving it too—and we admired the shining gold monuments—each of them seemed to shout the word *glory*, seemed to radiate that notion—and Mathieu grew somber and explained to me that one of the artists, when seeing how beautiful the work of the other artist was, committed suicide, believing that he had failed: but it pleased me that, staring up at the church, we couldn't be quite sure which one that would have been.

We went to lunch and had a fine meal, a sandwich with eggs and ham and cheese on it: next to wild game, my favorite food. My grandfather loved ham, bacon and sausage, and used to say, "Yessir, I never see a pig that I don't tip my

hat." He liked wine and cigarettes and vodka too, and lived
to be eighty-seven existing pretty much on those four basic
food groups. He might have liked Paris.

Mathieu showed me around some of the restaurants that
had Jim Harrison's picture in them, the way a diner or café
in the States might have on its walls the pictures of, say,
Michael Jordan or Cindy Crawford, and I wasn't sure if they
had Jim's pictures up to celebrate his writing or his cooking
or perhaps even simply his great joy of eating.

We walked some more. The midday light was harsh and
it was hard to ignore the smell of automobiles and so many
people—I was really looking forward to getting home to Montana—but it was an old, pretty city, and a big one, and I
could see why they were proud of it. It felt good to be walking.
A lot of the back streets were nice quiet shady narrow alleys,
and I was enjoying looking not so much at all the buildings
but at the individual stones themselves—the lithologies and
textures of them, the color and weathering and shape of them.

Consulates, ambassadors and generals lived with their families and staff and assistants behind all those square stones,
but I wasn't interested in any of that: the stones themselves
were what were so amazing. Granites, marbles, limestones,
even brown and red sandstones.

We were heading to a little city park, where Mathieu in-
tended to take some pictures of me. He said that whenever
a newspaper ran a review of one of my books, they would
always call Christian asking for a picture to run with it. They
wanted a new picture each time, however—they were complaining that it was always just the one same old picture that
Christian sent them (the only one he had; the only one I
had)—and that furthermore, each newspaper wanted to use
a picture that no other newspaper had used. So Mathieu
wanted to take a bunch of pictures.

"I'll bet you don't like to have your picture taken, do
you?" he said.

"No, I don't," I told him.

"Me neither," he said. "I'm glad it's me with the camera,
and not you."

I might as well get it out of the way right here: all my life I had heard that the French people were not nice or kind to tourists; that they scorned those who did not speak their language, and were even more contemptuous of those who attempted to learn it, or who had an accent, or who were not born from French soil.

To me, those rumors had the sound to them of the awful stereotype, and it was quite easy to disbelieve them, all the way up until it was time for me to go over there, at which point I began calling my liberal friends—some of whom had lived in France for a while—asking them to discredit this rumor, but none of them could do that for me, and so I went over there with apprehension and interest, eager to find out on my own for better or worse whether it was yet another vicious xenophobic American stereotype, or whether, in fact, the French were every bit as bad as we are. While over there, I walked as carefully as if on ice, not wanting to contaminate the experiment on account of my own at-times rampant moodiness and strangely chemical societal declivities.

Like all awful stereotypes, this one was spectacularly easy in which to find holes. While in France, I found that numerous people were exceedingly kind to me, but that even better, most of them didn't treat me one way or the other, and instead went about their business as if—get this!—they had their own lives to lead, and other concerns on their mind. So it was quite a nice feeling to be invisible-in-the-world, and able to stroll the sidewalks touching the stonework of the old buildings—tapping them, rapping my wedding ring against them and *stroking* them—without feeling like an infidel.

Except for the police.

Everywhere we went, it seemed, they were standing there watching us. Sometimes they followed us for a short distance, until they encountered another of their profession, at which point they would stop and talk, presumably about us, or, more specifically, about my stone-handling. The *gendarmes*.

Mathieu was already jumpy, explaining to me that it was

going to be hard to find a place to take a picture and that
we were going to have to move fast once we did, because the
French government would swoop in almost immediately and
begin demanding taxes and permissions fees if they found
out he was a professional photographer. If anything belonging
to the city of Paris or the country of France appeared in the
photo—a blade of grass, a cloud, a bird flying overhead—he
would have to pay.

So me, with my shining pale Americanness, stone-tapping,
and Mathieu, furtive and nervous, with his big black attaché
case of camera gear, had almost a dozen of them following
us by the time we ducked into the little city park, which was
surrounded by a beautiful stone wall and daunting black iron
spikes, so that it felt a little like being trapped, or in a zoo.

In the little park—about the size of a large suburban yard—
there were only two police, a man and a woman, and there
was that sinking feeling I got when they looked at us that
told me instantly they were bored and had been waiting for
someone like us.

There was a fountain. Mathieu held no fondness for the
park; he used to bring his little sister here to play, but back
when Christian had published Salman Rushdie, and had to
have bodyguards around his home and office, the parents of
other children asked that Christian's children be banned from
the park for safety concerns, and of course the police com-
plied. . . .

Mathieu started snapping away. The park police watched
with focused interest, not wanting the game to be over too
quickly. But they couldn't help themselves: they had no
restraint, no discipline. They began walking toward us.

There were only five other people in the park: a young
sweetheart couple picnicking on the grass, and a woman over
by the fountain with her two children. Pigeons were cooing.
I could hear the sounds of the city alternately rushing and
murmuring on the other side of the high stone wall. I missed
Montana already and was eager to be home.

The police engaged Mathieu in conversation. He looked

exasperated; it was clear from his manner that he was thinking they had no intelligence; that they could never fathom the intricacies of the situation. This is never a good way to appear, in my experience, before the police in any country. The police talked to Mathieu some more, then looked at me, clearly trying to figure out why in the hell he was taking my picture.

Mathieu began feeding them some line of bull—it's amazing what you can glean from the air, even when you don't know the language—and I could tell by the way their restrained curiosity turned to scorn that he had identified me as a tourist.

Because of my back injury, I had been sitting on one of the wooden park benches, but had been sitting atop it, with my feet resting on the part of the bench where you usually sit. The bench seat was a little butt-scalloped, and I didn't want to lower myself down into it and then twist or strain when standing back up. It felt better to sit up high on it.

The police didn't like this one bit. They told Mathieu to tell me to get down and sit right. Mathieu rolled his eyes and motioned to me to come on, that we'd go over to another corner of the park.

The picnicking couple were rolling on the grass, kissing, as we passed them. The man had his hand inside the woman's blouse. Birds were singing. I asked Mathieu what all that was about, and he sighed and said that the police said I was setting a bad example for the children. I blushed with shame, and anger.

The young couple was off their blanket by that time, writhing in the grass. The young lady had her hand in his pants and appeared to be applying manual administration to his love pump, but the police did not interfere. They ignored the thrashings with the casual indifference of two farmers whose cattle are breeding out in a pasture.

We took a few more photos. Then the police came toward us again and told us we'd have to leave. Mathieu argued, exasperated again—he let them get to him, which caused

Rick Bass and friend in Paris, 1999.

them immense delight; you could see the laughter behind their eyes. I was relieved, however—I didn't *want* to have my picture taken—and I wished I knew the language well enough to be able to tell them that.

We visited bookstores—most of them French, but one American bookstore, with books in English, good books, run by a nice woman with a nice name, Odile. I browsed the books, reading their titles and authors as if taking a meal, homesick already and further, and then we went walking some more. The light was slanting softer now—it was a fuller, denser light, loaded with deep yellows, and allowing all the other colors to assume a previously masked resonance, as well—and Mathieu told me a funny story another writer whom Christian publishes, Thomas McGuane.

McGuane and his family had been in Paris not for two

days, but two *weeks*—a television crew was following them
around everywhere, filming a documentary on him—and
McGuane, an experienced horseman, kept peering into the
camera and speaking the only sentence he knew in French,
with perfect enunciation: "I love to smell the legs of little
horses." But even that fun faded after a couple of weeks, and
finally he had to bail out and head home the night before
some conference or reading series began—the very reason
he'd come over there in the first place. Mathieu told me that
near the end, all he kept saying was, "I miss my dog. I miss
my pony. I miss my house. I miss the *dirt*," and he was gone.

And already, I felt the same way. What a joy it is to live
in a place that you think is more beautiful than any other.
What strange folly, to willingly separate oneself from such a
place, given the extreme brevity of a life, when measured
against the scale of that beauty.

•

Mathieu was still upset about the police. Only someone
who loves his country deeply has the true authority to criticize
it, and the police's behavior had triggered in him a list of
other grievances: taxes were outrageously high, the cost of
living was too high, and nobody knew how to work any more:
the whole country took turns going on strike. The way he
described it, it sounded like a wave or pulse that was forever
rolling across the country, various factions and services stopping and starting, so that the economy could never build up
any momentum. It sounded like it had its own rhythm, a
thing totally beyond the control or even influence of any
individual, and I imagined that for him, here in Paris, as he
awakened each morning to read the paper to see who would
be on strike that day, and what alternate or substitute steps
he would need to take as a result, it was for me as it was in
Montana, watching for clues to the next day's, or the next
morning's, weather: a thing also beyond control or influence,
but with some larger rhythm, whether discernable or not.

•

Supper. Time to eat again, after a brief nap back at the hotel. Mathieu had wanted to go to some knockout-fancy place, but then realized I had not brought my suit and tie with me, and rather than insist that I borrow one of his, was gracious and kind enough to realize that the reason I didn't bring one was that I didn't care to wear one.

Instead, we went to a restaurant in the Louvre, which was fancy enough. Mathieu's girlfriend, Shelagh, went with us. They were both all dressed up, and I dressed as nicely as I could. Another great meal, of which all I can remember is, again, strangely, the bread and wine, while we looked out at the Louvre, all lit up and glittering, and almost as majestic as a mountain. Then we walked some more, walked all over the city, beneath streetlamps and under the intersecting light rays cast by all those lit-up old buildings, and it was like being in some fairy-tale place or submerged in some new land. When we stood right above the Seine and looked out across the spread of the illuminated city and at the river itself—not dirty-seeming, as it had been in the daytime, but black and iridescent, as if it had come to life, and flecked shiny with the reflections of all those lights—it was disorienting, as if rather than being above the river, we were in some lighted world beneath its darkness overhead—the river the only dark thing in the city at night—and that we were looking up at it from the bottom, and that the lights reflecting on the black-slick river were really stars above us. I tightened my grip to keep from tumbling over the edge, as the rest of the world around me revolved, almost cartwheeled. It seems strange to me that we think of the world as having a northern hemisphere and a southern hemisphere, but not an eastern or western. I understand that the seasons dictate, or scribe, the difference between north and south, while the earth's daily rotation tends to cancel out or scramble any notion of east and west— what was light and east at noon becomes dark and west at midnight—and perhaps, tired from traveling and more receptive, less resistant to the earth's tremblings, that was all

I was feeling. But it was beautiful, and I think I must have kept marveling out loud at all the beauty, because finally Mathieu nodded and said, "That's why they call it the City of Light."

It was like a little epiphany for me. It lit up simultaneously some understanding of the external world before me as well as my own interiors.

I had heard somewhere earlier that Paris was called the City of Light: but my first and lasting impression had been that it was so named for the quality of its sunlight—that same light I'd seen late in the afternoon of the first day, thick as chalk dust, or like something smudged from a palette. Something almost tangible, almost elemental, like stone or wood. Never in a thousand years would it have occurred to me that a city would pride itself on its ability to provide a gaslit or electrical display.

It loosened me up a little bit. It's not that I particularly hate humanity or society, as much as I simply have such respect and admiration, love and a physical tactile hunger—for more elemental things.

It was good for me, I think, to be so awed by a city.

I went to sleep excited, drifting, floating—happy.

•

In the morning, that same wonderful light was there again—the thick sunlight—only coming from the opposite direction. It made you feel younger and it made you feel like an artist—or like trying harder, working harder, with whatever you were already doing.

I walked by myself, waiting for Mathieu to come and pick me up and take me to the airport. I didn't have much time, and didn't want to spend it sitting down eating. I knew how to order coffee—*un café, s'il vous plaît*—and I walked around the block twice before getting up the nerve to go into a little bakery and point and say *croissant, s'il vous plaît*. I walked some more, wading through that beautiful light as if crossing a stream. If I stayed longer I was sure I would learn new words. All the storefront windows were clean, and decorated with watercolor paintings that advertised the day's specials: not just the words of it—*fleurs*—but the paintings of those things: roses, lilies, irises, daffodils. There were a lot of bakeries and a lot of flower shops and in that slow thick beautiful light you could smell the croissants and the lilies with extraordinary clarity. People moved slowly, also—comfortably—for such a big city.

I thought about those watercolor paintings—painted fresh daily—on all the storefront windows. Art seemed to be coming up from between the cracks in the sidewalk. Why? How?

I thought about what little I knew of the language. *Romancier* was a novelist—a little much, perhaps—but *poésie* was poetry: just right, just perfect.

Those little shopping-cart carriages you rent in the airport to haul your bags were called *chariots*. Someone had mentioned that my wife and I have two young daughters, *deux filles*—again, just right, and real nice.

I was anxious to see *deux filles*, and to get back to the *vallée lointaine*.

I'm not conceding anything. I love American art—I respect and admire the best of it beyond, I would hope, the boundaries of any parochialism. And one of the things I think that can be strongest about American art—capable of giving it a fierce vitality—can be a stony kind of elementalism, a weaving of and careful attention to the natural forces that have sculpted us, and of which we are still a part. There's nothing worse than art filled with air—an excess of art, and a self-conscious art.

But even though it was all over the place, over there—art in the bakery windows, art in the Louvre—art in the sunlight, art in the dirty river, art in the ancient buildings—a continuum of it, so that it was almost like bedrock—it still didn't seem like too much: I mean, they didn't go around talking about it all the time. They just lived comfortably within it.

I don't know if I'd say France has too much art. Certainly I think our own country doesn't have enough—nor do the prospects seem evident of it becoming foundational, bedrock to our own culture at some point in the future—though who can say, for sure?

I wonder what Paris will look like in another hundred years. Probably the same. I wonder what my remote valley will look like in a hundred years.

I guess the sunlight in the two places will be the same as it is now. I suspect the hearts of humans will be pretty much the same.

It's interesting to think about and consider what art lies out there waiting to be released—not yet written, not yet painted—but enmeshed in a culture's foundation, as if within the soil, awaiting its release.

NOTES ON CONTRIBUTORS

FICTION

Stephen Clark is an associate editor of *The Paris Review*. The excerpt in this issue is from a recently completed novel. It is his first published fiction.

Daniel S. Libman is a graduate of the Johns Hopkins Writing Seminars. His work has appeared in *The Baffler* and *The Chicago Reader*.

Peter Matthiessen's interview on the art of fiction appears elsewhere in this issue.

Tim Mizelle lives in Chapel Hill. He teaches creative writing at the University of North Carolina, where he was a Morehead Scholar.

Phoenix Nguyen was born in 1966 in Lac Son, a strategic hamlet in South Vietnam. The daughter of a fisherman who was elected district chief, she fled the country with her family in a small fishing boat when North Vietnamese troops marched into Saigon on April 20, 1975. This story, which is the basis for her forthcoming novel from Dial Press, is her first published work of fiction.

Ron Nyren is a Wallace Stegner Fellow. This story received a Hopwood Award at University of Michigan, where he completed an MFA. His fiction most recently appeared in *The Missouri Review*.

Said Shirazi lives in New York City. His stories have appeared in *Columbia* and *Fiction International*.

PORTFOLIO

Notes on contributors to Postwar Paris: Chronicles of Literary Life *can be found on page 267.*

POETRY

Eliza Griswold Allen is an associate editor of *The Paris Review*. Her poems have appeared in *The New Republic*, *The Antioch Review* and *Western Humanities Review*.

Priscilla Becker is a graduate poetry fellow at Columbia University. Her work has appeared in *Western Humanities Review*.

Robert Devlin attends the Iowa Writer's Workshop.

Ghalib (1797–1869) wrote 235 ghazals in Urdu, three of which are translated here. Born in Agra, he spent most of his life in Delhi. **Robert Bly**'s work first appeared in the debut issue of *The Paris Review*. He is the author of *Morning Poems* and a forthcoming book of Ghalib translations written with his cotranslator, **Sunil Dutta**, a scholar of classical Indian music and poetry. Born in Jaipur, he lives in Santa Monica.

Jessica Grant is a doctoral candidate in creative writing and English at the University of Houston.

Donald Hall was the first poetry editor of *The Paris Review*. His most recent collection of poems is *Without*. His work appeared in the debut issue of *The Paris Review*.

John Hollander's first published poetry appeared in the eleventh issue of *The Paris Review*. His first book of poems, *A Crackling of Thorns*, won the Yale Series of Younger Poets award in 1958; his most recent book is *Figurehead*. He is Sterling Professor of English at Yale.

Vincent Hamilton lives and works in New York City.

Philip Levine received the National Book Award in 1991 for his collection of poems *What Work Is*, and the Pulitzer Prize in 1995 for *The Simple Truth*. His work first appeared in the sixteenth issue of *The Paris Review*.

Cate Marvin's poems have appeared in *The Georgia Review*, *The New England Review*, *Western Humanities Review* and *The Antioch Review*.

W.S. Merwin is the author of thirty-nine books, most recently *The River Sound*. His work first appeared in the eleventh issue of *The Paris Review*. He is the recipient of the Pulitzer Prize, the Tanning Prize, a Lila Acheson Wallace Reader's Digest Award and the Ruth Lilly Poetry Prize.

Robert Phillips's sixth book of poems, *Spinach Days*, will be published next spring, as will his *New Selected Poems by Marya Zaturenska*. He is a John and Rebecca Moores Scholar at the University of Houston and a special consultant to *The Paris Review*.

Melanie Rehak's work has appeared in *The New Republic*, *Partisan Review*, *Salmagundi* and *Western Humanities Review*.

Frederick Seidel's books of poems include *Final Solutions; Sunrise; These Days; Poems, 1959–1979*; and *My Tokyo*. His most recent collection is *Going Fast*. His work first appeared in the twenty-sixth issue of *The Paris Review*.

Dabney Stuart is the author of fifteen books, including *Long Gone*, *The Way to Cobbs Creek* and the forthcoming *Settlers*. He is a former Guggenheim and NEA fellow.

Richard Wilbur's work appeared in the second issue of *The Paris Review*.

Rebecca Wolff lives in New York City. Her poems have appeared in *Grand Street*, *The Iowa Review*, *Exquisite Corpse* and *Open City*.

INTERVIEWS

J.D. McClatchy (Ned Rorem), the editor of *The Yale Review*, is the author of *Ten Commandments*, a book of poems, and *Twenty Questions*, a collection of essays.

Howard Norman (Peter Matthiessen) most recently published *The Museum Guard*. His two previous novels, *The Bird Artist* and *The Northern Lights* were finalists for the National Book Award.

George Plimpton (William Styron) is the editor of *The Paris Review*. His most recent book is *Truman Capote*.

ART

Guy Peellaert lives in Paris. The art that appears on the cover is from *20th-Century Dreams*, coauthored with Nick Cohn.

Congratulations are due

The Paris Review

On an Extraordinary Achievement

45 Years

The Leading Literary Quarterly in the World

Sam F. Adrignola

Lawrence J. Christensen

John M. Kaheny

J. Milton Keller

Frank McGrath

William T. Mitrovich

Daniel S. Mitrovich

George S. Mitrovich

Alfred E. O'Brien

Patrick F. O'Connor

Frank P. O'Dwyer

Wade R. Sanders

Richard A. Scherer

The Kensington Group

Celebrating the Gift of Friendship

San Diego, California

National League Champion

San Diego Padres

Congratulate

The Champion of Literary Quarterlies

The Paris Review

&

The Man Who is Out of Everyone's League

George Plimpton

On a Remarkable Achievement

45 Years

Providing the Best in Poetry, Fiction and
Incomparable Insights into the Writer's Mind

SeaWorld California
one of the
Anheuser-Busch Adventure Parks

Salutes

The Paris Review

and editor

George Plimpton

on 45 years of

literary excellence

SeaWorld.
ADVENTURE PARK
California

Congratulations are due

The Paris Review

&

George Plimpton

On an Achievement of Great Distinction

45 Years

The World's Finest Literary Quarterly

From:

The City Club of San Diego
One of America's Great Public Forums

The San Diego Public Library

&

Friends of the San Diego Public Library
National Leaders in Library Services

Sponsors of:

The Great American
Writers Series

the modern writer as witness

W|I|T|N|E|S|S

Special Issue
American Families

Volume XII   Number 2 $7   1998

Contributors
Marcia Aldrich
Pete Fromm
Dan Gerber
Jean Ross Justice
Julia Kasdorf
Anna Keesey
Maxine Kumin
Thomas Lynch
Joseph McElroy
Roland Merullo
Kent Nelson
Linda Pastan
Maureen Seaton
Floyd Skloot
Paul West

"*From its inception, the vision that
distinguishes* Witness *has been consistent:
it is a magazine situated at the intersection
of ideas and passions, a magazine energized
by the intellect, yet one in which thought
is never presented as abstraction, but rather
as life blood. Each issue is beautifully
produced and eminently readable.*"
Stuart Dybek

Call for Manuscripts:

Witness invites submission of
memoirs, essays, fiction, poetry and
artwork for a special 1999 issue on
Love in America.
Deadline: July 15, 1999.

Writings from *Witness* have been selected for inclusion in *Best American Essays, Best
American Poetry, Prize Stories: The O. Henry Awards,* and *The Pushcart Prizes.*

W|I|T|N|E|S|S

Oakland Community College
Orchard Ridge Campus
27055 Orchard Lake Road
Farmington Hills, MI 48334

Individuals
1 year / 2 issues $15
2 years / 4 issues $28

Institutions
1 year / 2 issues $22
2 years / 4 issues $38

THE PARIS REVIEW BOOKSELLERS ADVISORY BOARD

THE PARIS REVIEW BOOKSELLERS ADVISORY BOARD is a group of owners and managers of independent bookstores from around the world who have agreed to share with us their knowledge and expertise.

The magazine for urban style & substance

MANHATTAN FILE
SALUTES THE PARIS REVIEW
ON THEIR 45TH ANNIVERSARY

Congratulations to an American Original

George Plimpton

&

The Paris Review

On an Amazing Achievement

45 Years

America's Finest Literary Quarterly

From:

Point Loma Nazarene University

San Diego's Liberal Arts Leader

Sponsors of

The Finest Literary Gathering in the West

The Writers Symposium By the Sea

Honoring in 2000

George Plimpton

With Our America Literature Award